unborn

MELODY

Books by Leah Lindeman

<u>Canadian Reminiscence Series</u>

Redeemed From the Ashes

Ghost of My Heart

Wisps of Gold

Scathed Bones

unborn **MELODY**

LEAH LINDEMAN

LINDEMAN PUBLISHING HOUSE

*May you all love and be loved
unconditionally.*

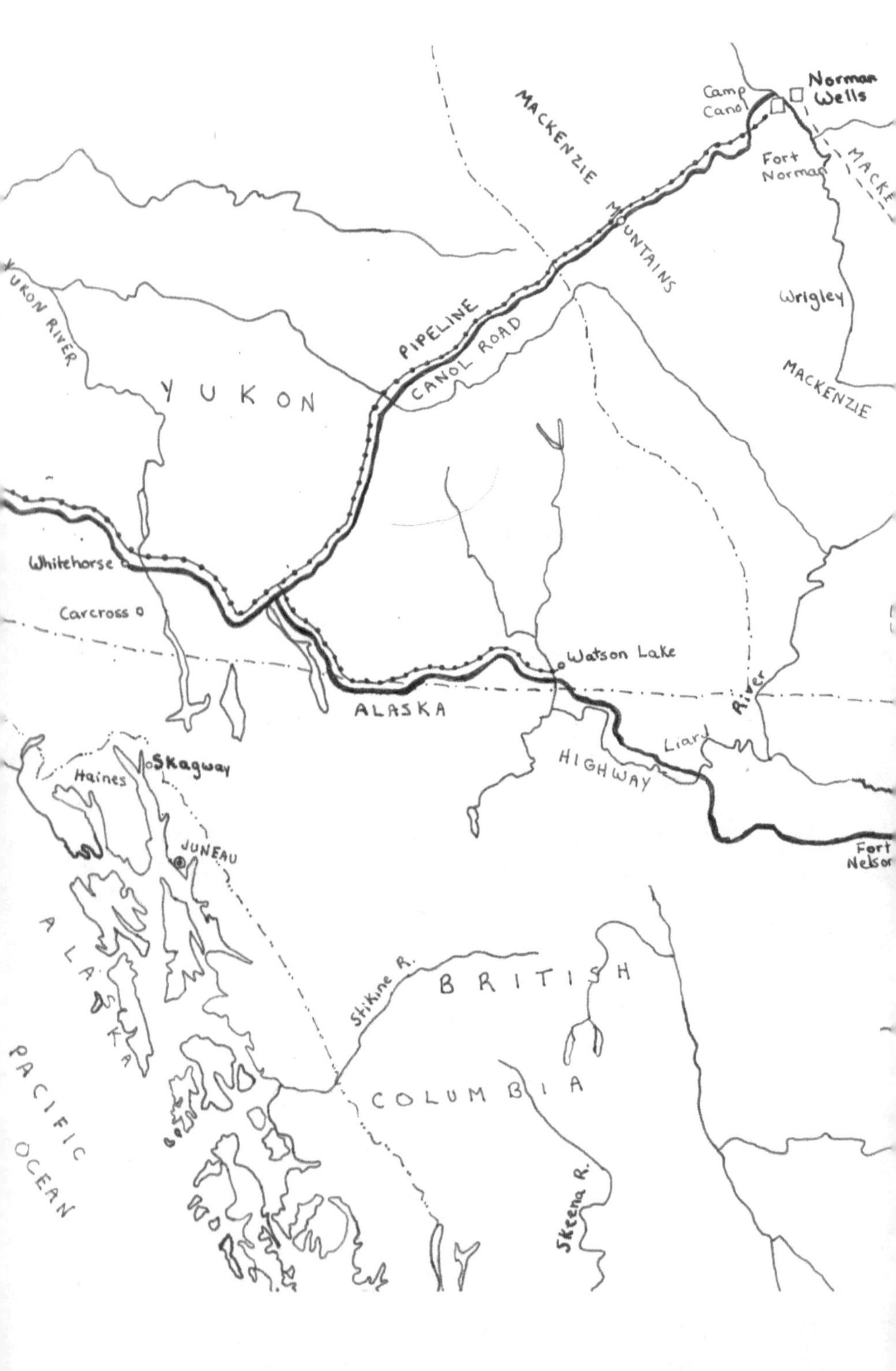

MACKENZIE
Camp
Canol
Norman
Wells
Fort
Norman
MACKE
Wrigley
MACKENZIE
YUKON RIVER
Y U K O N
PIPELINE
CANOL ROAD
MOUNTAINS
Whitehorse
Carcross
Watson Lake
River
Liard
ALASKA
HIGHWAY
Haines
Skagway
JUNEAU
Fort
Nelson
A L A S K A
PACIFIC
OCEAN
Stikine R.
B R I T I S H
C O L U M B I A
Skeena R.

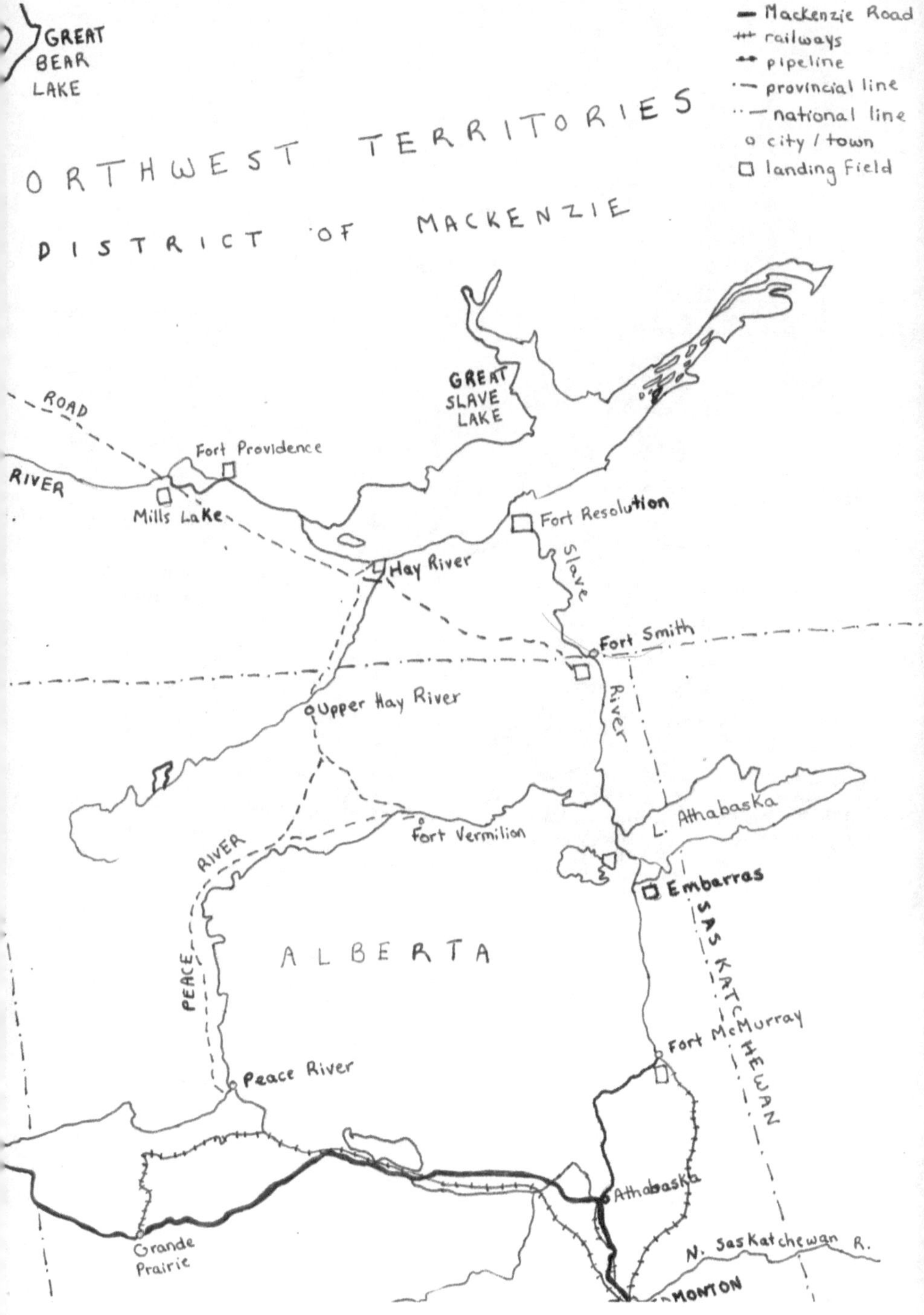

Mackenzie Road
railways
pipeline
provincial line
national line
city / town
landing field
GREAT BEAR LAKE
ORTHWEST TERRITORIES
DISTRICT OF MACKENZIE
GREAT SLAVE LAKE
ROAD
RIVER
Fort Providence
Mills Lake
Hay River
Fort Resolution
Slave
Fort Smith
River
Upper Hay River
L. Athabaska
Fort Vermilion
RIVER
Embarras
ALBERTA
SASKATCHEWAN
PEACE
Fort McMurray
Peace River
Athabaska
N. Saskatchewan R.
Grande Prairie
EDMONTON

CANOL PROJECT

NORMAN WELLS

&

CANOL CAMP

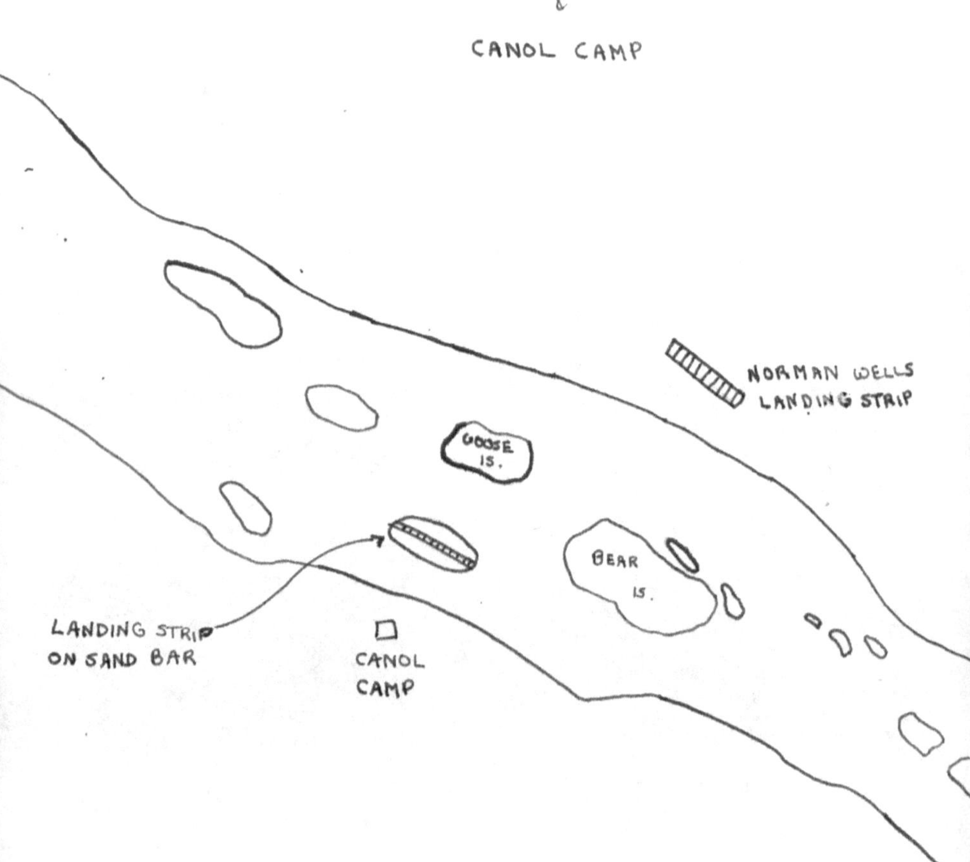

ELEANOR

PART I

The Fall

Chapter 1

Late May 1943

"Mike, what am I supposed to do? I can't make more than seventy here at home in Edmonton. Can't you help out?" Eleanor growled her frustration at her brother while attempting to keep her voice from reaching the ears of her woebegone mother in the other room.

"El, you know I can't. With my bum leg, finding a job to sustain my own family is hard enough. Lily is going to have the baby next month, and we've got to move out of the slum hole we're in. It's not a proper place for raising a family. I've got to keep whatever is left over for us for a new home."

She could hear his great exhale like someone drowning finally breaking to the surface—an act of survival.

Eleanor slammed her hand against the wall and sighed. "I don't mean to be insensitive. I just don't know what to do. We're behind on the rent by a few months. All of daddy's friends are long gone. There's no one else to help."

"Don't give up, El. Keep thinking! I'm sure you'll think of a way. You always do."

She bit her lip and rolled her eyes. His praise for her ingenuity was flattering. It faded quickly when she saw his praise for what it truly was, a tool to pass off his responsibility. Yes, his leg was a great hindrance, yet even before his accident he never had the drive to push himself as far as he could go. She wondered where the lines blurred between dealing with his injury and his slacking off because it was easier.

"Bye, Mike." She slammed the phone on the receiver and marched out of the house.

Ever since the dull unexciting tones of Edmonton switched, almost overnight at the start of the war, to a constant, industrial thrum, Eleanor was enticed to go on more walks. She couldn't walk a single block without seeing a pack of American GIs and soldiers, mechanics, and construction workers from all across the Commonwealth: Australia, New Zealand, and Great Britain that were stationed in Edmonton or travelled regularly to the city.

Many of her neighbours turned their homes into boarding houses for the great influx of newcomers. The year before the war, Edmonton's population was around 88,000. It had now boomed to around 105,000.

All these scenes were a constant reminder of her family's change in luck. Her father was too old and sick to go to war. Her brother Mike had injured his leg in a horse race many years ago, therefore not fit to fight.

Despite having endured so much heartache in the past years, they were now in a time of reprieve when most other families were grieving the loss of sons, fathers, and even daughters, who had gone to the front as ambulance drivers, nurses, doctors, and translators. She had even heard rare stories of women fighting on the frontlines.

When the Navy, Air Force, and Army recruitment centres had sprung up, it seemed as if every young man she knew had enlisted.

Many of her female peers worked at the Aircraft Repair Centre or had taken on civil jobs that the men had traditionally held such as mechanics, streetcar conductors, and postal van drivers.

She had found work as a typist.

As she was passing by an American recruitment office, she saw a poster about a job posting for typists needed on the Canol project in the Northwest Territories. It was exhibited beside another poster titled "This Is No Picnic." The second promised new recruits to the Canol project danger from the extreme work conditions and the elements: freezing temperatures, bugs, and swamps.

She entered the office and wondered why an Uncle Sam recruitment poster was nailed to a wall. She approached the moustached middle-aged officer and asked, "Hello. Why is the American Army recruiting for this Canol project? I'm interested in applying as a typist in the Northwest Territories."

As he reached for the proper enlistment forms, he answered, "We have an understanding with the Canadian government that allows us to build a highway from Dawson Creek, BC, to Fairbanks, Alaska, and an oil pipeline from Norman Wells to the refinery in Whitehorse, Yukon so we can fuel our Allied forces in Alaska in defence of our Pacific borders against an invasion from the Japanese."

"Oh," Eleanor responded. "Why is it that I've never read of it in the newspapers?"

He handed her the forms to fill out. "Only a small number of army personnel and civilians know about it. It's even debatable how much the Canadian government knows of the project's intricacies."

Her plucky outlook morphed the sure danger of living and working in the North into adventure, advancement, independence —the three voices chanted in perfect unity starting as delicious whispers which crescendoed to glorious song and instilled hope into her burgeoning heart. And the pay—well, they would all be set. She filled out the forms and signed her signature on the dotted line.

A brisk wind blew through the door as Eleanor let herself back into the modest sized living room where their upright grand piano stood against the dark panelled wall. She averted her eyes from the piano as she always did. She unwrapped her navy scarf and unpinned her hat to hang upon its hook. "Mother, I'm home."

A faint sobbing wended its way to Eleanor's ears. She looked up the stairs. She peeked into the bedroom directly off the entrance to the left. The curtains were closed. Her father's slumbering form filled the three quarter bed.

She closed her father's bedroom door, shook off her coat, and searched for her mother upstairs.

Her mother was kneeling on the hardwood floors of the old bedroom she had shared with Eleanor's father before he had become a cripple. Eleanor's mother's hands were raised and clasped in supplication to a God that Eleanor had, for so long, forsaken.

After she heard her mother whisper, "Amen," Eleanor spoke up, "Mom?"

Her mother slowly turned her bleary eyes to view her daughter. She bit her lip, and fresh tears flowed.

Hesitatingly, she approached her mother and awkwardly hung her arms upon her mother's wiry frame. Her mother was a phantom compared to the last time she had embraced her. How much time had passed since the last time?

"I feel like I'm drowning. I don't know what to do, and I'm —my hips are in so much pain. At times, I can barely lift your father to bathe him, clothe him. I hardly am able to or have the time to walk outside and enjoy the sun." She took a few deep breaths. "I truly appreciate your working as a typist but—oh, I don't want to sound ungrateful."

"Don't. What can I do?"

"The $70 a month just isn't enough." A moan reverberated through Eleanor's mother's frame.

Eleanor knew enlisting for the position up North had been the right thing to do; for she would never be able to earn more than she already was in Edmonton. Up North she could earn almost double. After soothing her mother by rubbing circles on her back and helping her up, she moved to the phone and dialled Mike. "Mike? I figured it out, and I have a place for you to stay."

Early June 1943

"Will you wait for me? I can barely catch my breath!" Eleanor's mother's hand pressed upon her chest. Another hand clutched her right hip.

Eleanor took the opportunity to light a cigarette while she waited for her mother to catch up. "I'm sorry, Momma. You need to go for more walks, especially when I'm gone. Who will push you out the door?"

"What did I tell you about those death sticks?"

Even though smoking was a popular pastime among all classes and trades, her mother firmly believed it was poison to the body.

Eleanor retorted, "Please, Momma, only you think they're bad! Now about those walks."

Her mother frowned. "I can't, not with your father.... "

"Yes, you can! Mike is here now, and his wife is more than capable of helping out."

"You mean Lily."

"Yes, of course."

"Why won't you say her name?"

Eleanor shook her shoulders. "She's always going on about how wonderful it is to be a housewife. I swear she looks down on me for making my decision to work outside the home, go North. She's almost as bad as…. " She swallowed the last word in shame.

Her mother touched her hand. Eleanor stopped in her tracks. She dared to peek over her shoulder.

Despite the abundant traffic navigating the streets and all the noise of conversation, vehicles motoring, and GIs catcalling, she could hear her mother whisper, "You were going to say 'you,' weren't you?"

Eleanor's mouth gaped open, grasping for words. There was a part of herself that believed her mother was less of a woman than she was for not having dared to reach for her dreams despite what the times had told her.

Her mother explained, "I may not have had the chances you have now to have made something of myself when I was growing up. There was mostly one set course I could follow. It doesn't mean it was bad. Even if I had all the opportunities of today, I would still choose to be home with you and your brother, to be a wife to your father. It is a noble pursuit. Whatever you're chasing, whatever you're so sure can't be found here—I just hope one day you can find peace and purpose."

Tears pricked at the corner of Eleanor's eyes. To hide them from her mother, she drew into a gentle hug.

It was time to go North. She whispered in her father's ears that she would return as soon as she was able, as soon as she had made enough money to provide the extra care he needed, the care that had fallen on her mother's shoulders for too long.

The lie that she would return soon tasted bitter on her tongue. What he didn't know wouldn't kill him. There were a myriad of excuses she could make to prolong her future in the North. Why, there was no end in sight for the war. The army or civilian contractors would need secretaries until the end.

The next couple of years would be filled with men, adventure, and lack of parental supervision. Ever since she was twelve, over the past nine years, she had been sequestered from society, except from her two closest friends Anthony and Mary, and, as a result, any kind of adventure, not only because her parents wanted to keep her safe but mostly because their friends, neighbours, and community had turned their backs on her and her family for having spoken the truth, a truth she wished she could erase. The North offered a new beginning in which she could exercise her independence and freedom.

Arm in arm, mother and daughter walked to the streetcar in silence. Even though her excitement for a new life was strong, she couldn't trust herself not to shed tears over leaving her family. They arrived at the streetcar stop. She wrapped her arms around her mother's neck and squeezed hard.

An infectious smile graced her features. She picked up her suitcase and hopped onto the streetcar that would lead her to Blatchford Field, the airfield destined to bring her to Norman Wells, the oilfield where she had been posted. Once she found an empty seat, she waved to her mother until only a sea of faces could be seen.

Mid-July 1943

The mournful cry of the loon was a rude awakening in the twilight hours of the early morn, a morn in which the sun had never set. Instead, it had kissed the horizon and held it in its embrace.

Eleanor's eyes cracked open. She lay on her side on a woollen blanket, laid out on a flat patch of forest floor sprinkled with fragrant evergreen needles. She stretched out her arms from her chest and turned onto her back. Dusty rose pink and burning orange painted the backdrop of the forest canopy.

She barely slept a wink after being with a man since the one time many years ago. After they had made love, Major Burns had dozed off while spooning her. She lightly massaged her upper pelvis. She had hoped she would feel mended for choosing to take part in this momentous rite. She had controlled who, when, and how. Then why did a dull ache still reside in her soul?

She expected her lips to widen in a satisfied smile as they had after the man whom she had secretly pined for over a month finally asked her to dance the night before. His bright blue eyes and thick wavy blond hair had cast a spell upon her the second she had laid eyes on him a month ago when she first arrived.

The landscape of his broad, well-defined shoulders, the hard planes of his chest, his chiselled jawline, and enigmatic eyes lended to Major Burns being the most handsome man at Norman Wells, perhaps even all of the Northwest Territories. He was the man Eleanor had always dreamed of being loved by.

All the girls working as typists, waitresses, cleaners, and all other jobs, upon which the whole of Norman Wells camp life functioned, tittered at how Major Burns was the prize stud.

He had chosen her, and she was willing to give him everything except her heart; for she knew that giving her heart would make her vulnerable. Vulnerability was the last emotional state she could afford to endure if she were to stake her independence and architect a life for herself.

The sun's continuous muted strength throughout the early morning hours was disorienting. She couldn't tell if it was two or four in the morning. In order to slip into her bunk unnoticed, the detail in time was important to how quickly and stealthily she should slink back to camp.

The hinges of the door to the pre-fabricated steel structure (made from a half-cylindrical surface of corrugated iron, a Nissen hut) which was used for the personnel living quarters, creaked. She grimaced as she turned to close the door. The fog horn snore of the head matron continued undisturbed. Eleanor tiptoed past eight slumbering women, a row of four beds parallel to another row of four beds, to her bed at the other end of the hut and exchanged her clothing for her nightgown and woollen socks.

Though her given bed was no downy haven, she placed herself in the sweet spot she had found when she had first arrived, the spot (which was missing its original spring) between two springs. She was thin enough that she fit perfectly. It felt as if she had slumped into a cocoon, a bearable one. The other girls hadn't been as fortunate with their assigned beds.

Tired after the night's activities and her 2 km trek back to Norman Wells, she was thankful her bed was furthest from the two small windows on either side of the door. Even though they didn't let in much light and ratty laughable curtains covered them, she needed complete darkness to get a good sleep. She turned her back on the door and shut her eyes.

A calloused hand fiercely shook Eleanor's shoulder. The head matron Miss Dansk's voice bellowed in her ear, chasing away what precious sleep had visited her. "Eleanor Mackenzie, get up this instant! All the other girls are dressed and off to work for the day. The Major won't be happy to hear his secretary is slacking off and sleeping in."

Eleanor scrunched her face in exasperation and rolled her eyes under closed lids. If only Miss Dansk knew that the Major might be indisposed himself. He was just as much to blame for her tardiness as she was.

Miss Dansk harrumphed out of the Women's Quarters and said over her shoulder, "I'll be outside. Hurry up!" She closed the door.

Eleanor shimmied out of her nightgown and socks and donned her one pair of jeans (for which she had saved up many years after she had seen them in a Levi Strauss & Co advertisement in 1934) and pink collared shirt she had prepared the night before. She combed through her short wheat blonde locks, splashed a little water on her face, and grabbed her navy cardigan.

As soon as she opened the door, Miss Dansk declared, "I'll be accompanying you to your post."

Determined not to be bullied into submissive shame, Eleanor jutted out her chin and suppressed several yawns threatening to crack her imperturbable demeanour down the short gravel walkway, no more than fifty feet, to the one storey white wooden office building.

Miss Dansk bellowed, "You young, foolish people will reap the consequences of what you sow. How will you be a bastion of self-discipline and hard work for future generations when you're so dishevelled half the time in looks and temperament?"

Eleanor, who was walking a few paces ahead of Miss Dansk, rolled her eyes and retorted in her own mind, "I'm not thinking about future generations! What a bore! The here and now is what's important to me."

They entered the office, a fourteen by fifteen single room. The officer's desks were furthest from the door, and Eleanor's desk, along with the other typists' desks, were closest to the door.

To Eleanor's surprise, Major Burns was seated at his desk, his hair coiffed, his uniform crisp, and his features lacking a single line of fatigue.

She breathed, "Major—"

Miss Dansk interjected, "Major Burns, here is your secretary. I assume you will deal with her directly for her tardiness."

Major Burns' eyes steeled over, a sharp cold lacing his voice, "I assure you I will, Miss Dansk."

Eleanor swallowed. Her nervousness shifted to a piqued flame of anger. He wouldn't, would he?

Miss Dansk nodded, her smug lips puckered as she stalked out the door. "Young women these days! Their heads are filled with…. " Her words were carried by the morning's brisk breeze.

Eleanor's defiant look melted as the Major waggled his eyebrows and stood next to her, his shoulder kissing hers. His head snapped to her. In his hands were a couple of folders he plopped onto her desk. Then he lowered his voice and said, "What do you think your punishment should be, Miss Mackenzie?"

She smirked and held his gaze, "Why do I deserve one?"

He moved a hand's breadth closer. "You left me to wake on my own. I would've thought after our marathon you would've slept in my arms until we would wake up to repeat it again."

Her cheeks flooded with heat. An entering officer

slammed the building's door causing her to jump away from the major.

He whispered, "Eleanor, call me Paul from now on." His eyes twinkled as he leaned away casually and walked to his desk.

Chapter 2

A new week brought a new crop of several female typists who had travelled a 1500 km distance, travelling over ten airfields from Edmonton to Norman Wells, via the U.S. Army transport. Eleanor had done the very same trip when she had arrived a month ago.

Many of the girls looked worn and uncomfortable from their harsh travels. One of them kicked off her heels as soon as she disembarked so she could stretch the soles of her stockinged feet on the dirt.

"Ew, Jen! How could you get your stockings dirty?" one exclaimed.

The one who had kicked off her heels, Jen, blew a stray piece of her strawberry blonde hair from her face and exhaled deeply. "I don't care a bit. I just need them off." She craned her neck back and stretched it from side to side.

"Well, if you won't take care—ugh, here, at least put your feet up on this piece of luggage."

Jen peeked her eyes open and fought a smile. "No, thank you. I need to feel the ground beneath my feet."

"Oof! Don't expect me or anyone else to do your laundry."

Jen's went wide. "There are washing machines, aren't there?"

"We're in the middle of nowhere. We shouldn't expect any decent appliances here."

Jen slowly moved her feet onto the luggage.

Another girl couldn't hold one standing or sitting position for long without switching to her other bum cheek or leaning the opposite hip against a pile of crates.

Eleanor, who had been waiting ten feet from the base of the airplane stairs tucked in her chin to hide her amusement, said, "Welcome to Norman Wells, ladies. Cheer up! There's plenty of adventure and men to go around."

The red haired girl who was looking toward the Mackenzie Mountains turned her freckled face toward Evelyn and smiled shyly. She put out her hand to shake Evelyn's and said, "I think I'm going to like it here. My name is Julia. On the way in, we saw another camp across the river. Is that Camp Canol?"

Eleanor replied, "It is. The Mackenzie River only spans about 6 to 7 km between the Norman Wells oilfields and camp and Camp Canol. The two islands in the river are Goose Island and Bear Island."

Julia asked, "Will we be meeting everyone at Camp Canol at some point?"

Eleanor nodded. "I've met many of them already. There's a few tugboats like the *Mary T* and *Distributor* that travel between both camps regularly."

Julia also asked, "How did Norman Wells get its name?"

Miss Dansk answered, "It comes from the Slavey language. It means 'where there is oil.'"

A tan-skinned girl who sported the highest heels and a fiery red lipstick cradled a lit cigarette in her fingers and eyed the approaching group of GI's as if she were choosing the best cut at the butchers. She snorted, "I'll have my pick of men by the end of the week, you'll see. The name's Leticia."

The other girls around her rolled their eyes. Jen groaned, "We know! If you're always the way you were on the ride here, you'll have all the men falling to their knees and worshipping the ground you step on." She looked directly at Eleanor, "I promise you we're not all sex-crazed."

Eleanor asked Leticia, "You from Mexico?"

"My mother is. My father's from Montreal."

A group of GIs arrived and grabbed the girls' suitcases to bring to the Women's Quarters. Leticia grabbed the lapels of the GI who grabbed her bag, licked her lips seductively, and kissed him, leaving the mark of her lips on his.

The GI breathed a "wow" and tried to form words. "Uh—af—after you. I could give you a tour, that is, if you want…. "

The GI and Leticia's conversation faded as they walked toward the women's hut.

Julia said to Eleanor, "You get used to Leticia real fast."

Eleanor chewed on the inside of her lip as she wondered whether Leticia would turn Major Burns' head with her voluptuous curves and forward manners.

Eleanor waved over the girls in the direction of the living quarters, mess hall, and office buildings, which bordered the Mackenzie River and was situated south of the oil tanks and rigs. "Come on, I'll show you where you'll be staying."

Jen began to put on her shoes and then baulked. "No! I can't wear them a second longer, washing machine or not." She lifted her suitcase and picked up her pair of shoes. "Lead the way."

The other girls followed suit. Julia sidled next to Eleanor and said, "Thank you for welcoming us."

Eleanor replied, "You're very welcome. Although it's Miss Dansk's job to orient the new recruits, I join her whenever I can. Her welcome can make a girl think she's landed in a frozen hell."

"I can believe it. She's barely said one word to us. She's uptight, a cold fish."

"You are very polite." Eleanor chuckled.

One girl pointed at a patch of muskeg swamp east of Norman Wells where there were row upon row of tractors, jeeps, and heavy equipment. "What is that?"

Eleanor replied, "Those are the vehicles that made the long journey from Peace River in Alberta to Great Slave Lake and all the way up here. They just died out from being overworked and from the elements."

The girl shuddered, "Creepy. I hope we don't end up like that."

Eleanor's step faltered for a second. She shook her head and kept moving. How strange that one person could view this place as a second chance at life and another view it as a potential grave.

That evening after supper in the mess hall, the festivities hub at Norman wells spanning a width of thirty-five feet and a length of a hundred, some of the new girls sang "Goodnight Sweetheart" for the soldiers and civilians. Tables seating eight on benches stuck out from each wall from one end of the mess hall to the other.

Julia played the piano remarkably well. The men were enraptured even though during some moments the girls' harmonies wobbled and toppled. As the girls held out their last note, the men leapt to their feet, their clapping crescendoing to a triumphant note. Some whistled and others made a beeline to the girl they wished to impress.

Leticia set her eyes on Major Burns immediately. Eleanor expected it. Without argument, he was the most handsome man in the room.

Eleanor watched as Leticia's red lips parted seductively. Her curly black locks fell over her shoulder as she brushed her fingers up the major's arm. Leticia closed the gap between herself and the major by standing on her tiptoes and whispering in his ear. He leaned in and chuckled. Eleanor couldn't hear his reply. He put his hand on Leticia's arm and gave it a warm squeeze. He excused himself and walked toward Eleanor.

Eleanor looked over his shoulder and saw Leticia send her a wicked wink. What response had Leticia received that she could act so cocky? Eleanor rolled her shoulders back and snapped her eyes on Major Burns. He grabbed her hand and led her to the drinks counter off to the side where the kitchen adjoined the hall.

Miss Dansk's stare, like a pair of daggers, followed her to the drinks. Let her complain about her loose morals. Miss Dansk was strung tight enough by her moral code for the lot of women in Norman Wells.

Seeing Major Burns occupied with Eleanor's company, many of the girls pouted, their heavy red stained lips a field of angry posies. Nonetheless, a few of them sauntered over to the Major while he had his arm around Eleanor's waist, flirting shamelessly and, to their ignorance, badly. At first, Eleanor rolled her eyes and was annoyed at their hopeless attempts to sway his attention away from her.

Julia sidled next to her and whispered, "Doesn't their flirting bother you?"

Eleanor responded, "Maybe a little, but then again, why should I be? I'm all about modern women going for what they want. In a way, I salute their efforts." She raised her cup filled with moonshine. "Ah, the perks of being twenty-one."

Julia pouted, "I'm a year shy. They won't give me a liquor permit."

"Lucky for you, I like to share." Eleanor poured some of her moonshine into Julia's empty cup.

After a few rounds of playing craps, Major Burns sneaked Eleanor out through the kitchen when Miss Dansk wasn't looking. He and Eleanor caroused all the way to the forest floor where they made love the night before.

Their lips latched onto the other's and explored the soft ridges of collarbones and jawlines.

He plunged his hand into his pocket. "D—mn it!"

Eleanor jumped, "What's wrong?"

"Ah! Never mind. It's in this pocket." He held out the small cardboard box that held his rubbers. He opened it and cursed. "Empty."

"Didn't you have a couple left from last night?"

"I thought I did. Someone must have swiped mine."

Determined to slake her sexual thirst, her hands and lips conducted their dance of seduction, causing Paul's conviction of using rubbers to crumble.

The next day at lunch, Julia asked Leticia, "Which man fell under your spell last night?"

"Who said there was just one?" She winked.

Most of the girls leaned in, waiting for her to reveal a name.

Leticia whipped her head toward Eleanor, "Did you enjoy a saucy evening with Paul?"

Rankled Leticia was already on a first name basis with Paul, Eleanor quipped, "I'm not the kind of girl who kisses and tells."

Leticia tutted, "Of course, you're not. There's not much to tell, is there?"

"I'll have you know…. "

Eleanor was distracted from finishing her sentence by a troupe of drenched whisker-faced men flooding inside the mess hall and stomping their muddy boots at the entrance. The ajar door gave her a glimpse of the battering storm pummelling the ground into mulch. At least she had the foresight to wear her rubber boots.

Out of the corner of her eye, she saw Lieutenant Smith exit the hall at the opposite end and arrive moments later with Paul.

Her eyes gleamed as he passed her table. He gave no notice of her as he usually did, even in passing. His focus was on the group of strange men.

The man who had entered first was gruff and hairy as a bear. Though his appearance was summed by everything dirty, smelly, and uncultured, his eyes were sharp.

Paul shook the man's hand and nodded toward the men behind him. After a few words, Paul led the bear-man to the back. The rest of the men grabbed plates of food and found a table to sit at.

Puzzled by the exchange between Paul and the bear-man, Eleanor shuffled outside and ran to the Women's Quarters. A few of the girls who had finished their lunches were in their beds whispering amongst themselves. The girl whose bed was stationed next to one of the windows gazed forlornly outside. Another girl was reading.

Eleanor neared Miss Dansk who was knitting yet another scarf (she had knit twenty in total the last month alone) for the many G.Is who had put in orders for themselves so that they could be warm during the winter. "Miss Dansk, do you have any idea who that group of men was? They just arrived at the mess hall."

"I haven't been out there for the last half hour or so. I don't have a clue as to whom you're talking about."

"They were gruff-looking, about a dozen of them. Looked to be from out of camp. Major Burns singled out their leader to discuss, I don't know, things."

Miss Dansk replied, "From what I've been told, that's the new crew of civilian engineers. The man you saw towing behind Major Burns was probably the new head engineer for Norman Wells."

The victory of knowing one less impure couple would pollute the camp was stamped upon Miss Dansk's features. It gutted Eleanor, bile threatening to rise. "Why would the camp need a new crew of engineers, let alone another head engineer when we have Major Burns and his crew of men?"

Miss Dansk's fingers slowed and stopped. "Did you really think they'd be here forever? There's a war to be fought in Europe, and that's where they'll be heading, very soon."

Eleanor's nostrils flared, and she sharply jutted her chin.

Miss Dansk smirked as she cocked her head.

Eleanor breathed in deeply to help her mask her rising chaotic emotions with a cool reserve, a nonchalance.

Miss Dansk continued, "Once the soldiers are at their new posts, they'll find other tramps to warm their beds."

Eleanor's fists balled tightly, aching to give a socking. Her nails bit into the tender flesh of her palm. She retorted with a pasted smile, "Of course they will! That's the way of the world after all."

"Glad you know what you're in for."

For the remainder of the day, Eleanor typed out numbers; numbers of caterpillars, bulldozers, rigs, and many more equipment coming through camp to build the Canol road; numbers of screws, nuts, and bolts down to the smallest of tools; numbers of personnel, flights in and out—all typed on six sheets of different coloured tissue paper, red, yellow, white, blue, and green.

Though her fingers were preoccupied with the typewriter, her mind was infected with disappointment in herself. The discovery that she had broken the rule she had set for herself—the rule that she could find freedom for her body without being chained by expectations from her heart—clouded her mind. What had she expected from Paul? Flirtation had led to fulfilling, regular sex which had led to this, the unknown. Isn't that what she had craved, living in the moment? Yet, the thought of his leaving her, of his lavishing attention vanishing, to be given to another a world away left her with a bitter taste in her mouth. Would she find some other to fulfil her newfound wants? There was none like him. The group of civilian troupe of engineers flashed through her mind. Heaven forbid she would lower her standards to such a degree.

With the major and his company of men leaving, did it mean that the girls would be deprived of all men in uniform? The dashing entourage (even though not all had the most handsome faces) was the source of all the girls' elations since they had walked off the cramped and cushion-less plane.

A few minutes after the minute hand had ticked past the end of the work day, Julia, who worked in the adjoining office, popped her head into Eleanor's building.

Eleanor greeted her. "Hey, Julia, done for the day?"

Julia replied, "Yes! My fingers are so stiff right now. Means there's going to be a crazy north storm whipping up soon. The women in my family are notorious for weather-induced arthritis in our fingers."

"That's really a thing?"

"Another unbeliever," she ticked off her finger. "Want to walk by the river before it hits us? I'd really like to get to know you. I had a good feeling about you when we first met. "

"Sounds swell. I'd like to get to know you too. Give me a second." Eleanor put aside the last folder of notes. "I'll just add this to my workload tomorrow. Can you believe we're making $120 a month compared to the $70 back in Edmonton?"

Julia snaked her arm through Eleanor's. "Me? I came here for the soldiers." She winked. "I didn't have the stomach to leave Canada and go to the war front. But I also couldn't stay home and do nothing except grow victory gardens, knit, and slowly starve from the increasing food rations and starve in another way, the decreasing sight of men."

Eleanor sighed, "I'm sorry to disappoint. I think most of the soldiers are heaving off soon for the front."

"What?!" Julia cried. "Now I just might have to follow them to Europe."

Eleanor added, "Who knows, you may like the civilian engineers just as much. I sure won't."

She screeched in delight. "Why not? Tell me all."

"Didn't you see them?"

"I had a splitting headache during lunch and was trying to sleep it off before work."

Eleanor sighed. "There's not much to tell, and they're not much to look at. They looked like a pack of bears that bumbled into the wrong space."

"Aw, we might just need to give them a good shave in all the right places." Julia winked. "Say, you'll be sad to see the Major go, won't you? I assume you're together. He only had eyes for you even after Leticia tried to wrap him around her finger."

Eleanor looked straight ahead. "Why do you think I'll be sad?"

"It's no secret you two are galavanting off into the forest to give and take a little something regularly. That's what all the girls are telling me. Why, last week, Susan said she heard your party of two. She listened for a few minutes before heading back closer to camp."

Eleanor cheeks reddened. "She did?" Though she enjoyed exploring this new side of herself, she wasn't willing to share her explorations with others through others overhearing.

Julia nodded. "You keeping a close eye on your cycle?"

"Yes, there's some days when I forget. So I'll write it down the next day. It's the first time in my life that I can enjoy men this way. You?"

"I religiously write it down in my booklet. My first time was a while ago."

"At least you won't end up like poor Nelly. Did you hear?"

"No, what happened?"

"One night of drinking and fondling was enough for her to lose her virginity. Poor girl, she has no clue how these things work. She told me she comes from a very conservative family. End of the story, she told me they're shipping her out tomorrow because she's pregnant." Eleanor laughed.

Julia giggled in response, "At least that won't be us."

The girls ambled out of the copse of buildings and toward the docks, where a group of singers were practising some musical numbers on shore. Behind them, coloured soldiers plodded on with their work of emptying barges carrying loads of pipes. Beyond the workers, the mighty Mackenzie Mountains stood sentinel against the coming invasion of bulldozers blazing a trail where no white man had ever walked. The birch, spruce, pine, and balsam were to be mown down in order to pave the way for the Canol pipeline, the pipeline in which Norman Wells oil would flow to Whitehorse, Yukon and then to Fairbanks, Alaska, all in the name of Allied defence.

Eleanor and Julia walked the shoreline, a row of oil tanks and other structures belonging to Imperial Oil, the company drilling the oil, to the east looming over the bluffs.

Julia prodded her shoulder with her own. "Are you in love with him? Would you marry him?"

Eleanor chewed on her bottom lip before answering Julia's question. "I might be in love with him. When he's around, I want to be nuzzled against his side. I can smell him as soon as he enters the room. I look for him everywhere, in every face. But what do I know? I thought I was in love a long time ago with my childhood friend Anthony, but it became very clear we weren't willing to change for each other."

Eleanor continued. "He wanted to get married and start a family, and I didn't. One day, Anthony took me out on a picnic. He was fidgety which was very odd considering he was the calmest person I knew. I kept asking him what was wrong. Then he just bent down on one knee and asked if I would make him the happiest man alive."

"What did you do?"

"I was ecstatic at first because I dared not believe he'd ever ask me after…. " Eleanor's eyes became unfocused.

"After what?"

"Oh! After, uh, after my family lost their fortune in the Depression."

"Did he care a lot about the money?"

"No, it was just a silly notion I had at the time."

Eleanor glanced at her ring finger and rubbed an invisible stain. "Anyway, he put his mother's ring on my finger and said he had already put a downpayment on a home with all the money he'd saved from working for his father. According to him, it wasn't much to look at. He was hoping we'd fix it up together. Then he wanted kids."

"Let me guess, you didn't."

"My goal isn't to be a housewife. I definitely don't want kids now. I feel like my life is just starting. Maybe I'll never want kids."

As if she were wishing upon a wishing star, Eleanor clasped her hands and looked into Julia's eyes with her own gleaming ones. "I want to travel the world. It's changing so quickly, and I want to change along with it. I'm a modern woman or at least I want to be. I didn't want what he was promising."

Eleanor smiled bitterly. "The stupid smile I was wearing was wiped clean off when he said that's all he was offering. I told him it was never going to work. I wouldn't change for any man. What self-respecting woman would?"

"Holy mackerel. What did he say?"

"He asked what self-respecting woman just wants to have fun and not seriously think about her future? Then he pried the ring off my finger and started packing up our picnic. I asked if we could still be friends. He emphatically said no and walked off. Surprise, surprise, Anthony and another good friend of mine, Mary, married three months later."

"No!"

"As I said, I thought I was in love. Attracted? Yes! He was muscular, and he had a kind face and curly blond hair. All the girls were throwing their caps at him."

Julia sighed, "What do you think true love looks like?"

"I think true love is selfless. My parents would do anything for each other, go through everything with each other. If ever one of them would have to sacrifice something for the other, they wouldn't keep score. They've been through the happiest and worst of times, and still they want each other."

Eleanor huffed. "Just why is it always the women who have to sacrifice? Why do we always have to become the perfect little housewives with a brood of children running around and with perfectly cooked roasts in the oven?"

"Not always perfectly cooked roasts. Ha! My mother can't cook for the world."

Eleanor looked sideways at Julia and waggled her eyebrows. "You know what I mean."

Julia asked, "Did your mother choose the housewife life? Or did she sacrifice any ambitions for your father?"

Eleanor answered, "She never said. From what she's told me, the life she has is the life she wanted. Maybe marriage is more about two people's visions for the future lining up."

"So Paul…. ?"

Eleanor shrugged her shoulders. "I'm far from ready to commit to a relationship. If Paul is more than willing to be my active duty gentleman, I'll keep him close for as long as he's here. When he leaves, I'll be perfectly fine. I don't need anyone else to be happy. And you? Did you find anyone you fancy?"

"Now that they're all shipping out, I'll have to give them a quick comb over so I can say I've been with one American GI in the North. Wouldn't that be a killer diller story? Unlike back home in Edmonton, you can find packs of them on every muddy street corner."

Eleanor sighed, "Perhaps the men shipping out was a cruel rumour after all. Miss Dansk is the one who told me. I think she's just jealous that we're young and beautiful and have lovers. She's old and such a prude. Who would want an old fart?"

"I hope we never end up like that."

"Ugh! If we ever do, we'll have to be sure we never snore the way she does." Both girls laughed all the way to their quarters.

That evening, all the girls dabbed on their blush, pink-hued powder shaken from makeup brushes, and plopped open their lipstick caps to smear the colour onto their chapped lips. Lips, hands, feet—every area of their skin had cried out for body cream as soon as the day of their arrival.

The girls vied for the single mirror's attention. The mirror decorated with lipstick kisses hung upon a nail hammered into the sloped wall. There was barely time for a girl to pin her curls before she was firmly shoved to the side to make way for another girl.

Eleanor decided to sit on her bed and wait out the gaggle of girls. She combed her fingers through her hair. Even though she could coax some curls to form and stay, the rain outside would flatten them. She fished underneath her bed and pulled out her navy cloche hat.

Leticia's hard smile and toss of her hair crowded Eleanor's vision. "Earth to Eleanor! Are you really going to join us tonight looking like that? If you want to keep your man, you're going to have to put in some effort. Who knows which one of us his eyes will wander to next?"

Eleanor matched Leticia's chagrin, "Oh, Leticia, it's so sad marking yourself as the camp whore. If you want Paul to be another check mark on your list, go ahead. It won't give you any credit."

Out of the corner of her eye, Eleanor could see Leticia's fists clenching, readying to slap Eleanor's cheek.

"Excuse me." Eleanor bent down to grab her bag of makeup and made her way to the mirror, leaving a seething Leticia in her wake.

The merry tune belting from the piano in the corner of the hall and the singing of the sopranos and altos fanned out in a semi circle in front of the instrument tickled Eleanor's attention as she shook the droplets from her coat.

The singers were more on key than usual. Having seen them singing together in a huddle on the dock at the tail end of the lunch hour the day before explained their improvement.

The GIs and officers were interspersed throughout the mess hall, some with girls already on their arms. The new engineer and his team were chatting with the army medics near the table with spirits.

Most of the newcomers looked slightly more presentable. They had shaved off most of their scruff and had combed through their unruly hair. Some of them had even had the chance to make their way to Corporal Lightfoot who had been a barber before the war had begun. Perhaps they could land a girl, a companion, a comfort after all.

Major Paul Burns turned from his companion, the new head engineer, and strode toward her.

As she looked over Paul's shoulder, the man who had come to take his job gave her a nod. A lock of his dark brown hair swept across his broad forehead settling just above his deep set eyes. His thin lips framed by his slightly trimmed beard gave her a small smile before returning to his men.

"There you are!" Paul wrapped his arm around her shoulder and kissed her hard on the cheek. His eyes buzzed bright, and his breath, warming the hollow behind her ear, was tinged with alcohol. His hand gripped her waist. "Won't you come and sing? I'm sure you have the voice of an angel."

She guffawed, "Where did you get your intelligence from? Don't put me up there with the other girls. I'll croak, and you'll never want to be seen with me again. I'll sing quietly beside you and enjoy the music."

Paul led her to a table where some of the men were playing poker. He sat in an empty chair and pulled her close to his side. His hand tightened on her hip. "You'll be my good luck charm, won't you?"

She smiled shyly. "Sure, but I don't know anything about poker."

"You don't have to. I'll win a hand and share my good fortune with you."

She kissed him on the cheek and said, "Sounds good."

As the dealer was dealing the deck, Paul shot out his hand and hailed the new head engineer, "Seth! Come play a round."

Seth looked over his shoulder and gave a rueful smile. "You know I don't touch gambling, Paul. You can keep fishing, but you won't make the catch."

Smirking, Paul picked up his cards and looked at his hand. "One day I will. I always eventually do."

Eleanor looked back at Seth, his straight, broad back holding firm against Paul's prodding.

Though Paul drank heavily throughout the game, it didn't hinder his ability to amass his winnings.

As soon as Paul had raked in his bills, a thick 32 millimetre rope was thrown at his feet. He turned around and faced a grinning Seth.

Seth said, "How about a friendly competition?"

Paul shoved himself away from the table and shook Seth's open hand. "It's on."

Seth gripped Paul's shoulder. "You sure you didn't have too much to drink?"

Paul swiped his drink from his table and chugged to the last drop. "Of course not."

Seth and some men from his company picked up their side of the thirty-five metre rope while Paul and some of his men picked up the other side.

With a damp dish towel draped over her shoulder, Blade, the head cook of Norman Wells camp, left her place in the kitchen to join the gathering crowd and throw in her bet along with many others.

Eager men and women, elbows touching, whispers shared between close huddled heads, hollering from frenzied spectators —the commotion came to a halt as Corporal Tranter placed himself in between both teams after placing a mark on the floor and around the middle of the rope with black tape.

He raised his arm, readying to give the signal.

A pin could be dropped, and all would hear.

He yelled, "Go!"

Paul and his men yanked hard in quick succession.

One of Seth's men fell to his knees yet kept holding his portion of rope.

A sheen appeared on Paul's forehead as he began to lose momentum.

Seth whistled sharply. Every three seconds in perfect unison, he and his men regained their ground and began to drag Paul and his staggering men over to the impending line.

Desperate, shocked, Paul and his men heaved backward haphazardly, granting Seth and his men the victory.

Shouts of hurrah, claps on the back resounded in the hall. The winnings from the bet were being distributed.

Seth gave Paul his hand and hauled him up. "You almost had us."

Paul shook his head and smiled with grim determination. "Next time we will." He staggered toward Eleanor. Before he could reach her, his men draped his arms around their shoulders and dragged him back to his quarters.

Eleanor fingered her jacket absentmindedly. A restlessness rushed through her body,. A dizzying pulse pounded in her head.

"You going to bed or what?"

Eleanor snapped her attention toward Blade. Though Blade's easy smile and twinkling eyes hinted she had an amiable personality, her quick bite and dexterity with a chef's knife had earned her the nickname Blade. Greasy, sweat-soaked strands of hair had escaped Blade's hair net.

Eleanor leaned in to get a closer look. "How'd you manage to get a nylon snood? I haven't been able to get my hands on nylon for so long."

"Well, our boys are needing it for parachutes, airplane cords, and such. A small price for us to pay for their service." She touched her snood. "Mine's homemade. Made it from my cousin's chopped black hair before she went overseas to serve at the hospitals."

Blade swung her head toward the door. "So, bed?"

Eleanor answered, "I…I don't think so. Not yet. Need any help?"

Blade gave a goofy grin. "Well, aren't you an eager beaver! I can use your help anytime you're not being scuttled off by the Major for some romp."

Miss Dansk plodded toward the pair and said, "I have to round up the girls to the Women's Quarters and sleep away this nasty headache. It must have been Anne's warbles. Why did the girls have to pick a song with such high notes? Goodnight."

Blade elbowed Eleanor. "Good luck on her rounding up the girls. How many does she usually find alone? Maybe a couple?"

Eleanor replied, "Sometimes none at all."

Blade cackled. "Come. Grab the broom. I'll wipe the tables down."

It wasn't the appeal of doing dishes or wiping tables that made her stay later than usual. There was a chord in her heart that needed tending, that only in facing the ghost of her past could heal. She waited until not a soul was left in the mess hall, waited until the doors were shut and only she remained.

The ochre glow of the sun kissing the horizon at midnight dotted the room in small shafts where the windows allowed except for the corner where the piano stood. It was untouched by the sun's weak light. She tentatively walked to its cover and lifted it. The standup grand's ivory and ebony keys welcomed her with its toothy grin. Far away from the origin of her excruciating memories, she could try to play again. The corners of her mouth lifted, its nostalgic magic enticing her to play its chords. Her index finger swiped a key. A low timbre resounded within the room.

Her finger let go as if the sound had scalded it. She turned her eyes to the door leading outside, beckoning her to leave the past behind her. That's why she was in the North after all, to reinvent a new woman, free of constraints and the places and people that had shaped her.

Yet the sudden memories of her father's hand atop hers as he moved her fingers to song were too strong to deny, too crippling to overcome....

Her father, his almond eyes sparkling with excitement, beckoned her to sit by his side. Eager to play the instrument that had always perked her ears into submission, she skipped to it. He nudged her arm with his. She returned the gesture.

"Go on, play a few notes," he said.

Despite her intense anticipation to do so, she could not turn away from the love in his eyes. She breathed in deep, and delicately settled her fingers on top of the keys. She swept them down and gasped in delight. Each note equaled a word, an expression that she felt in her soul. She could build a language all her own.

The first time she had sat down at the piano, she learned by ear the little sonata she always heard the local piano teacher on her street teach his students. Every Thursday after school, she would sit beneath Mr. Benson's open window as she heard the students play through and eventually master the sonata.

She would play the song in her mind and find the necessary notes to recreate it. Of course, she couldn't tell if she were placing her fingers in the correct positions. Perhaps she could find a job and make just enough to pay for lessons.

After so many years, she could finally stay seated at the bench and caress the keys as if they were dear old friends she had not seen in many years.

Her first strokes were stilted, their voices straining to push past the dam she had so desperately constructed back in Edmonton. The agility of her joints and movements grew until, at last, the song which had been building within her broke free. Her fingers roamed each note, each soar, desperate to unify them, crash them, all in a glorious state of wild abandon. Her song de-crescendoed slowly until her fingers wobbled off the keys, trembling in the song they had produced.

Eleanor's deep exhale almost masked the creak of a door. She looked over her shoulder and saw the outside door graze the frame as it closed. She grabbed the piano's cover, and banged it down. The echo of her sudden anger plunged her into a familiar revolt for the instrument, no, the memories she'd rather not relive.

Someone had entered her safe space and breached the security she had built around her most vulnerable self in the middle of the night! Like a coward, they had left before she could turn and confront them.

She slid off the bench and scurried away into the night.

Chapter 3

"Every civilization has been built on the principle that women do the work of the home while men call the shots!" Corporal Tranter jeered, his egotism bleeding into the atmosphere of the mess hall during dinner.

Eleanor bristled at the condescending stationing of her sex. She opened her mouth to retort, but he yammered on.

"Even Betsune Yeneca, the Athabaskan-Dene Caribou god our local Indians worship, believed it. Have you heard the legend? One night he came back to his grandmother covered in ice. Well, she thought it was ice. Instead, it was the foam from the mouths of the deer he had just killed. In his coat, he was hiding the tips of the deer's tongues he had killed. The next morning he brought his grandmother to where he had killed the deer. Listen to what he told her." The corporal held up his index finger. "He said, 'You must pound and dry the first deer you see, gather the grease, but don't eat it.'"

Blade, holding the baked beans tray with a dripping ladle in hand, slopped the last scoop into the corporal's plate and said,

"Sounds about right! I slave away all day to feed your sorry arses. I always eat last, and I hardly get a thank you." She shook her head.

Tranter jumped out of his seat and laid his arm over the cook's retreating shoulders. He squeezed her tightly, kissed her on the cheek, and said, "Thank God for you Blade! Not only do I need you to do the cooking and dishes but also remind me of my manners. My nana would be ashamed of me."

Blade shook off his insincere embrace and poured the residue baked beans sauce in the ladle over his head. His dinner mate sputtered through his lips as he attempted to hold in his laughter. The man's face turned beet red as he opened his mouth and chortled. More uproar ensued as the sauce dripped down Tranter's face, and Blade returned to the kitchen, throwing her head back in laughter.

Tranter scowled, his jaw clenching.

Eleanor was one of the first to laugh. She bent her head against Julia's, and the pair snickered.

Tranter turned to face Eleanor who sat at the table behind him, and he smiled slyly. "Want to take a lick? I hear Major Burns is heading out of town and won't be around to taste."

A man shouted, "Good thing Paul isn't here to hear you move in on his girl."

Eleanor slowly crossed her arms, smirked, picked up her glass of water, and strolled over, swaying her hips seductively. "You would like that, wouldn't you?" She leaned her back against his table facing him.

Tranter's eyes were bright, and his breath ratcheted a notch. "I've got an opening tonight. You game?"

Eleanor leaned in, closing her eyes, puckering her lips near his cheek. As he positioned his lips, closing the distance, she lifted her arm and dumped her water over his head. "Did you really think I would stoop so low? No wonder your nights are lonely."

She caught some of the girls' eyes widening like saucers as she spun on her heel toward the door. Tranter's mates slapped his back to comfort his bruised ego. Fervent whispering broke out among the men. When Tranter rounded on them, they pressed their lips together and furtively gauged his reaction.

He bit his lips, blood leaking from chapped broken skin. He blinked rapidly and swiped a few runny beans from his forehead, sloughing it a few paces away. He grabbed a handful of napkins off the buffet table and dabbed away at the shameful mess.

Eleanor sneaked out to grab a cigarette from Jen's sack under her bed and scampered outside behind the Women's Quarters. She decided to indulge in a smoke for the first time since she arrived. She lit the death stick her mother had warned her of countless times and inhaled the sweet poison. A prickly sensation snaked its way up her throat as she coughed out her first exhale. All the noise she had made masked the snap of twigs behind her.

A man cleared his throat.

She jumped and swirled, ready to defend her use of the smoke.

Seth Brooks held out his hand to relieve her anxiety. "Sorry, didn't mean to scare you."

"You didn't." Her lips puttered as she lifted the cigarette to her mouth.

He didn't say anything but only stared for an awkward amount of time.

"What?" she asked.

"You shouldn't have done that."

How did he know she stole the cigarette?

He added, "You shouldn't have made him look like a fool."

A small relief washed over her before she scoffed, patted the embers of her burning cigarette, and stamped it out. "What kind of man are you? You'd rather stand up for a pig than for a woman's dignity?"

"You shamed him, and now he'll come after you."

Her smoke-veiled eyes challenged his direct gaze. She asked, "Is that a threat?"

"It's a fact. Just take care of yourself." He lifted his hand toward her shoulder. He paused and let it drop. He dipped his chin in farewell and strode into the woods.

"I can take care of myself just fine," Eleanor muttered. She rolled her eyes. Whatever words he had spoken, she chose to disregard them. She diminished the cigarette she had been smoking into a pyre of regret for stealing something that hadn't helped her whirling emotions at all.

Soon after her smoke, many girls trickled into their quarters to settle for bed. Miss Dansk cleared her throat. "Girls, I have an announcement to make.

The girls turned their heads halfway nonchalantly, their bleary eyes unfocused and half closed.

"I regret to inform you," she said with a satisfied smile, "that Major Burns will be shipping out in two mornings along with the rest of the army on base. Time to say goodbye to your lovers. Goodnight."

The languid atmosphere of the room erupted into frenetic exclamations of horror. One girl bawled. Jen, declared, "Thank God! I'm sick and tired of the one that keeps pawing me."

A girl retorted, "You mean Corporal Tranter? I wish he had pawed at me!"

Jen growled, "Have at him, why don't you?" She stuck her head under her pillow.

Eleanor turned on her side facing the back of the hut and closed her eyes, the girls' reactions fading to dampened noise. Her thoughts scrambled to come up with a way to keep him close to her for longer. With each flailing lunge, the scenario of him staying slipped further and further away. She slept restlessly.

In the morning, Eleanor woke with bleary eyes and a headache. Not having much of an appetite, she skipped breakfast and typed out all the documents Paul had put in her pile. He attempted to catch her eye many times, and sometimes he did. When he was successful, her heart grew heavy in the ocean blue of his eyes. Too many times she was sinking without a way to come up for air. She refused to drown. So she kept her eyes trained on her fingers typing on the keys.

Her persistence to resist him didn't pay off. That same evening after supper, she couldn't deny her yearning. She went to his hut and knocked. No one answered. She tapped the toe of her shoe and wondered where he could be.

The scent of burning firewood piqued her attention. She followed it around to the back of the hut. Sitting on two chairs in a laid back fashion were Paul and Seth. She considered leaving the way she came, but Paul's voice arrested her exit.

"Thank you for taking this job. There's no one else I'd rather see take my place. Don't mess it up now."

"I promise you I won't. Thank you for always looking out for me. You and your parents have given me opportunities I would never have been able to get on my own. I enjoyed gaining engineering experience building Sunoco's lubricating oil and grease storage plant in Toronto. This is the perfect next step. Nana's glad I'm home. Where are you being placed next?"

"I'm going to Washington for a quick trip. Edmonton's supposed to be next. I'm gunning for Washington permanently. I've got to keep climbing the ladder. My parents have certain expectations they want met." He fell silent and stared at the fire.

Eleanor couldn't leave until they started talking again. Her steps would draw attention her eavesdropping.

Paul said, "Listen, I need you to do something for me." The rest of his words were too quiet for Eleanor to hear. She daintily made her way to the front of his hut and walked back to hers.

At the end of the next day, which was Paul's last, he nudged a note on her desk toward her trembling fingers. She opened it when he left the office.

Tonight. Same time and place.

Her breath stopped for two reasons. She hated that his words were short. Cheap. She also hated that they wouldn't deter her from a last fervent rendezvous. Wasn't he using her just as she had used him?

Even though the day dawned bright, a chill blanketed her skin, gooseflesh pimpling in its wake. The fresh pungent scent of pine filled her senses. Small notes of the cologne she had become acquainted with over the last several weeks lingered. Her eyes opened to see an empty spot on the bed of moss beside her. Not a trace of his effects were left. He hadn't even left his blanket wrapped around her. The usual ache after giving herself to him was a cold reminder that what they had was finite, an unfaithful anchor in the storm of life.

She scooped up her jeans and white cotton blouse and shimmied them on. She plucked her sweater off a branch and plodded toward work. Even the thought of work dredged a numbness that quickly shackled her soul into oblivion.

Just as she rounded the Women's Quarters, she spied Paul gripping Seth's hand and giving it a firm shake. They both tipped their heads in deference toward the other. Paul jogged toward the air strip and onward to his military duties.

She hoped that he would look backward to catch one last glimpse of the girl he had kept warm on many a night, the girl who had dished out a heavy dose of flirtation when he had initiated, the girl who now ached for his presence. Of course, he didn't. He didn't know she was awake. He could have woken her up and kissed her with a romantic drawn out goodbye.

No, his eyes were fixed on the future.

Would he dream of her as she would dream of him?

Her eyes flitted to Seth Brooks. He shifted his gaze from Paul and spied her watching Paul's leave. Was that a softening of his face? Pity?

She didn't need any pity, and she didn't need a single man. There were plenty of other men to choose from, and there were plenty of men who, judging by the way they looked at her, would be more than happy to take Paul's place of forest lover.

Two weeks later, after breakfast, she sat at her desk, eager to attack the fresh stack of papers. Two lines of keystrokes in, she could feel a rising in her stomach. Air seemed to evade her. She felt lightheaded. As she inhaled, a stroke of power shoved from her stomach upward, her meagre breakfast of hot gruel threatening to be released.

Eleanor straggled out of her chair and launched outside. She ran toward a nearby copse of trees. Her breakfast made good on its promise and fought its way out.

After she lost the battle, she fished out her handkerchief and dabbed around her mouth. A crack of twigs signalled an unwanted visitor.

"Eleanor, here I've got a glass of water for you." Julia's soothing voice calmed Eleanor's racing heart.

Eleanor planted her palms on her squatting thighs and turned her head toward her friend. "Oh, thank you, you're a doll. How did you get here so quickly?"

"I saw you running out of the office looking as if you were about to hurl. Then I ran to the mess hall and grabbed some water."

"I think—I think I may have eaten something bad this morning. Did the gruel taste funny to you?"

Julia smiled gently and laid a hand on Eleanor's arm. "I don't think it was the gruel. That's how I knew to bring out a glass of water. When I was living with my eldest sister for a season, I saw her do that same escape from her room every morning when she was pregnant."

Eleanor's smile faltered. Pregnant? Absurd! "I'm not pregnant! I just, eh, I'm—I must be sick."

Julia held the inside of her wrist to Eleanor's forehead. "You don't have a fever. Listen, were you and Major Burns always careful?"

"Yes, every time, except…. " There was that one time a couple weeks ago when he had forgotten his protection. She had wanted him without thinking of any consequences.

"When was the last time you bled?" Julia asked.

Eleanor put her hand on her forehead, unable to think clearly. "It was—I can't remember."

"Did you write it down in your booklet?"

"I did. I need to go look."

Julia held out her hand. "Come, I'll walk with you."

"What about your work?"

"I already told Mr. Brooks you would need a few minutes. He granted me leave to help you."

"Okay, let's go."

The two women scurried toward their quarters and knelt next to Eleanor's bed.

Hands shaking, Eleanor reached underneath and pulled out the aforementioned notebook. Her fingers slipped as she attempted to turn the page to her last notation. She hoped to see that it had been only three weeks since her last cycle so that the growing tightness in her throat would ease. Oh, how she needed another glass of water! Moonshine would be even better.

Six weeks! How did she not notice before today? The excitement of a new life and a new lover had taken centre stage these last few weeks. What she had been meticulous about before today had been undone by the foolishness of her heart. Now she might pay with a baby.

She heard Julia's sharp intake of air. "Why don't you wait another week or two? Maybe your cycle is reshuffling. Maybe it's stress. I know you said you didn't care that Major Burns was leaving but maybe that's what's affecting the change."

"You're right." Eleanor attempted to smile courageously. "I can't possibly be pregnant. I must be stressed. I should check with the doctor. They'd be able to tell me for sure, no?"

"I think it would be too early for them to tell. Usually, the woman can tell at first by the signs. And you shouldn't go to the medics."

"You're right. They'll ship me out just like they did with Nelly. If they get a whiff of me being pregnant, I'll be gone. That can't happen."

Over the next couple weeks, Eleanor ritually threw up her breakfast and felt nauseated. There was no doubt in her mind—she was pregnant. How would she provide for her family in Edmonton now?

Eleanor walked over the office threshold.

"You won't find your new boss in there." Leticia's suave voice cascaded over her with the softness of velvet.

Eleanor plastered a smile as she averted her eyes from the lipstick sticking to Leticia's front tooth. "Where is he?" She pointed her thumb toward his desk.

"Hard to say. He's barely ever in his office, haven't you noticed? Sometimes I see him helping out the coloured soldiers with the unloading of piping and all that."

"Thanks, I'll find him when I need him."

Eleanor finished the papers Mr. Brooks had set upon her desk to be done for the day. She waited all day for him to show up. Five o'clock rolled by and no boss.

Groups of sweaty men came from the direction of the docks. Their arms were around each other's shoulders laughing and soaking in the sunshine of the fading light. All to soon the North's bounteous smile of light and warmth would warp to a crackling cruel grin, the face of its winter. Or so she heard from the men who had welcomed her to Norman Wells when she had first arrived a couple of months ago.

She scanned the men's faces, most of them dusted from their exertion. The last two men, one of them Mr. Brooks, hefted a four inch twenty-two foot long steel pipe over their shoulders. They relieved their burden into a pile of pipes which had been stacked near the opening of the dock. Mr. Brooks waved the other man away and perused the pile with his fists on his hips.

As his lips widened in the largest smile she had ever seen him give, his hand wiped the sheen of sweat off his forehead. He craned his neck back and stretched it from side to side, drinking in the simple pleasure of the sun shining down on him.

He turned and found her staring at him. His fist swung into his palm. Shrugging his shoulders, he asked, "How can I help you, Miss MacKenzie?"

Her cheeks coloured as she realised that she had been staring, with no apparent reason for her lack of words. "I need a doctor."

He took a step forward, his brows furrowed in confusion. "You look all right."

His statement, indicating he knew better, snapped her out of her reverie.

She scoffed, "Just because I'm not doubled over in pain, doesn't mean I don't need a doctor."

He looked down. "You're right. I'm sorry. I can point the way to the U.S. Army medics."

"No!"

"I don't understand. I thought you wanted to see a doctor."

"Yes, just not the medics, please."

He put his hand on his chin. "I'll see what I can do. I'll talk to Frank, our bush pilot, to see if he can fly us to Fort Norman tonight instead of tomorrow morning. There's a Doctor Barnes with a practice there."

"Us?" She cringed inwardly. "Why do you need to come along?"

"Some business I need to attend to. I promise I won't pry, and I won't make any unnecessary conversation."

"Fine. I'll be in the mess hall." She turned on her heel and didn't look back.

Eleanor sat on a table with a pair of girls. All three flirtatiously glanced at the three civilian crewmen standing in front of them. The boys sidled closer to ask whether the girls could join them at their table for dinner.

Eleanor wrapped her arms around her middle. She politely declined saying she had plans to fly out.

Julia strode in and led Eleanor away from the goggling group. "So, any luck with Mr. Brooks giving you permission?"

"He gave me permission all right. He's coming too!"

"To see the doctor?" An edge of scandal coated her voice.

Eleanor growled, "He says he's got his own business to take care of."

"Aren't you being a little hard on him?"

"At least he promised not to talk to me," Eleanor mumbled.

"He said that?"

"Well, I made it obvious I didn't want him around." Eleanor shrugged her shoulders sheepishly.

"Gosh, poor man. What did he ever do to you?"
"He replaced Paul."

Chapter 4

Mid-August 1943

While Frank did his checks to make sure the Fairchild 71 plane was ready, Eleanor hauled herself into the seating area which was sandwiched between the top and bottom pair of wings and sloping downward behind the pilot's cockpit. Seth hoisted himself into the seat beside her.

A "V" settled between her brows as she asked Seth, "Why aren't you sitting up front with Frank?"

He replied, "I thought I should be back here in case—"

"In case what?" she interrupted.

"Well, you said you needed a doctor. In case something happens."

She mumbled, "It's nothing like that."

Frank asked them if they were strapped in and asked Eleanor if she had ever flown in a bush pilot plane before.

"No, I haven't," Eleanor replied. "Must be just like the army transport plane, right?"

Frank held in his laughter as he looked at Mr. Brooks and winked.

Eleanor asked Seth nervously, "Why did he just do that?"

The only answer she received was the whirring of its engine. Frank maneuvered the plane toward the takeoff strip. Its metallic frame buzzed. The plane arrived at the starting position. Frank thrust the throttle forward, and the plane began its acceleration, which mildly jolted her before increasing with such a force that her eyes squeezed shut and her hands looked for purchase on any object near her. Only she didn't find an object. She could only find a hand, Mr. Brook's hand. In desperation, she gripped it all the while hating the fact she was doing so in the first place.

Just when she thought she could take the experience no longer, her stomach somersaulted as the plane lifted, inducing a fresh wave of nausea. Hoping the nausea would be relieved, she closed her eyes and breathed small breaths in through her nose and out through her mouth. It seemed like forever before the insufferable malady abated to a point that she felt she could open her eyes.

The feel of his hand in hers piqued her immediate attention. She recoiled her hand to her chest and glared at his hand. Their eyes met. He turned his away first, and he removed his hand from the armrest. True to his word, he refrained from speaking to her.

She peered out the window and gasped at the breathtaking view.

The Mackenzie River which Norman Wells and Camp Canol bordered on either side rushed toward the Beaufort Sea. The whitecaps frothed, resembling the manes of wild horses streaming at a gallop. The balsam, poplars, and black spruce blanketed the entire landscape interrupted only by summits and lakes. Every shimmer of sunlight kissing the current, every rock face adorning Franklin's summit produced a longing within her to root herself to this place, to feel its ancient call and answer with her prolonged presence.

Before she had come, she had thought she would have to fight the wilderness daily. Yet, the American army's station and all the equipment on which it was run had tamed the wild enough to feel safe. Perhaps, that would all change when winter came, making the North a formidable foe. Only she couldn't imagine it now.

Soon after they sighted Fort Norman, the plane descended onto the single air strip. Mr. Brooks opened her door and held out his hand to aid her in descent.

"No, thank you." She waved his hand away and stepped onto the wing before leaping down about five feet to the ground. She put out her hand against the plane to regain her balance.

He shrugged his shoulders, placed his hands in his pockets and started walking toward the first set of log buildings. She followed him.

"I assume you're bringing me to the doctor?"

"Hmm, mm."

"Not much bigger than Norman Wells, is it?"

"It's a small town. You can walk from one end to the other in about ten minutes. There's the post office, and that's the general store. Keep going down, you've got the seamstress, the saloon, and the Anglican church."

They continued to walk down toward the private residential area. Eleanor's brows lowered as she looked from side to side then back toward the air strip. "Where are you taking me?"

Mr. Brooks didn't deign to answer. It seemed he had as little interest in her as she had in him.

They came to one of the last homes in the row. He turned down the little path before the door. A sign hung in the window saying "Out now. So sorry."

Mr. Brooks sighed gruffly, "Looks like doc's out of town."

Eleanor said, "I can read. For how long?! I need—"

Seth interrupted, "Let's ask." He quickened down the steps and headed to the neighbour's door. With pinched lips and narrowed eyes, Eleanor followed. She cocked her head to the side as she passed a variety of rocks displayed along the path. Each rock had a different hue. Eleanor noted the display's resemblance to a rainbow.

Just as Eleanor was about to trail up the steps after Seth, a townsperson passed by and said, "You two look new in town."

Seth turned toward the new voice. "We are," he said with a friendly smile.

The townsperson looked both ways and took a few steps closer to the house. "Just a friendly notice, you may not want to knock on that door."

Seth replied, "Why's that?"

The townsperson said, "The resident mad woman lives there."

"Really?" Seth scratched his beard.

"Don't say I didn't warn you." The townsperson hurried off.

Eleanor touched Seth's elbow. "Maybe we should listen and ask someone else."

He replied as he knocked on the door, "She can't be all that bad."

A sallow face, lined with years of toil and grumbling, came to the door. The old woman's eyes squinted in the glaring sun. The sun's touch stripped away the dark interior and highlighted the dust motes swirling quickly as if they were racing to escape the sun's rays.

The grimy doormat, handwoven with saskatoon branches, cracked underneath the woman's bare feet.

She asked, "Whaddya want?"

Mr. Brooks asked, "Good day, Mrs…?"

She licked her lips nervously. Her rodent-like teeth peeped out as she attempted an awkward smile, as if she hadn't smiled in a decade. "Call me Charlotte."

He put his hand to his heart and placated her in low soothing tones, "I'm Seth Brooks. This is Miss Eleanor MacKenzie. Could you tell us when Dr. Barnes will return?"

"How'd you know doc told me where he was going?"

"I thought you might know since you're his neighbour."

"I do, I do. He can always count on me for being reliable about sharing his comings and goings. He only tells me. That way people have to talk to me. Even still, no one comes to my door ever." As she hugged herself and stroked her arms in comfort, her lips turned down. "When I go into town, they barely look at me."

Seth said, "I'm sorry to hear that, Charlotte. I'm glad I could meet you."

Charlotte flapped her hand as if to cool herself. "Pshaw! You know how to make a woman blush." Her hand shot out and gripped his wrist. "Could ya—I mean will ya help me? An important shelf of mine fell down from my wall. I need it up right away else my friends won't be too happy. Doc didn't have time to do it before he left. Could ya?"

Tired of faking kindness to a woman whose mind wasn't all there, Eleanor rolled her eyes and said, "Well, we can't—"

Mr. Brooks interjected, "What she means to say is we can't leave without helping you. Lead the way."

Charlotte blessed him with a toothy grin. Her smile turned to an unforgiving scowl when she looked at Eleanor before leading the way inside.

Eleanor had expected Mr. Brooks to pass by Charlotte as every other sane person in this town did (Charlotte had said as much). She would have done so if she had been alone. Eleanor grimaced as they followed Charlotte into a dingy kitchen. The smell of mildew and old cheese stung her nostrils. There was a single window, and a ratty, thin sheet hung over it. She walked over to it and lifted the sheet only to see that the window was nailed shut. A creeping fear slithered around her heart as she wondered just what kind of person lived in such a hovel.

Charlotte handed Mr. Brooks a hammer, nails and the shelf. He cartwheeled the hammer in his hand and placed the two nails in his teeth.

Charlotte's hand flitted upward. "There—there—that's it. No, wait, that's all wrong. How did they say they wanted it again?" She scratched her head, her unkempt hair loosening from its tie.

Mr. Brooks patiently moved the shelf around the wall until Charlotte settled on the spot she believed *they* wanted.

Eleanor examined all the rocks littering the dining room table. These rocks weren't colourful like the ones outside. These rocks were covered by carpets of lichen, and upon the lichen was little stick furniture. On one wide flat rock there stood a little shelter made up of tiny twigs. In front of the shelter was a chair, the twigs held together by twine—no, human hair.

Suddenly, someone yanked her away from the rocks.

Charlotte pointed her finger at her face and hissed, "Don't be poking your nose into my friends' belongings."

Mr. Brooks spun around and surveyed the exchange with grim anxiety and announced, "There, your shelf is up."

Charlotte threw her hands into the air and beamed. "You, dear man, thank you."

Shocked at Charlotte's eccentric behaviour and impatient to be in the sunlight, Eleanor announced, "I'll be waiting outside, Mr. Brooks."

Eleanor couldn't exit the house fast enough. Not even past the four by six porch, she bent at the waist, hands planted on her knees and inhaled deeply. The need to vomit abated.

Mr. Brooks came out minutes later. There was no way he could step around her bent over form so he tentatively laid his hand upon her back. "You all right?"

Eleanor swiped his hand away and growled, "I'm fine. What did she say about the doctor?"

"Doc's gone until tomorrow."

"But I need him now."

"We can return tomorrow."

"You'd do that for me?" Her voice was tinged with disbelief.

"It's a medical need, isn't it?"

"Yes!"

"Then that's all I need to know." He glanced at her and seemed to take note of her wrapping her arms around her torso.

Eleanor asked a few beats later, "How could you stand to be around Charlotte? She's loopy, dirty, odd to say the very least—"

Mr. Brooks put up his hand to interrupt her. "Put yourself in her shoes. Everyone talks behind your back, makes fun of you, doesn't want to be around you—how would you like to be treated?"

She snorted, "No one treats me that way. I'm—"

He interrupted, "Young and beautiful?" Eleanor was surprised at his compliment, but her pride was quickly slapped into submission when he continued, "Even the young and beautiful grow old and wrinkly one day. Where will the young and beautiful be to help you then?"

Eleanor walked past him, fuming at the condescension in his voice. He promised he wouldn't talk to her. He had kept his promise until it was time to rap her knuckles. Couldn't he just pretend to agree about Charlotte? None of this unpleasantness would have happened if it weren't for him.

Next day in the afternoon, Mr. Brooks drummed his fingers on her desk and said, "Let's go." They walked in silence to the plane. As Mr. Brooks opened the passenger door to the plane, Eleanor sullenly ignored his civil gesture. Instead of settling into the seat beside her as he had done the day before, he sat up front beside Frank. She narrowed her eyes and imagined she could burn a hole through his seat, through the back of his head.

As they taxied into the air, she bit her lip and jiggled her leg. She had foregone breakfast because she knew her stomach would flip flop, yet threatening bile rose. She breathed in deeply through her nose and out through her mouth. It barely kept the overwhelming force of vomiting away the entire flight.

When they touched down, Eleanor hoped this visit would prove successful. She didn't know how many more bush plane flights she could take.

The roads were muddy after a recent local rain. She regretted not changing into her rubber boots before leaving Norman Wells. As they walked to Doctor Barnes's office, her brown leather pumps sank into the mud so deep that mud seeped and squelched among her toes.

Eleanor's fingers bunched the fabric of her dress as she and Mr. Brooks waited for the doctor to answer the door. She attempted to smooth down her dress when the door opened.

"Good morning, I'm Doctor Barnes. What can I do for you?" He looked between Mr. Brooks and herself.

Eleanor said, "Yes, I can see that you are." She pointed to his brass name plate beside his front door.

Doctor Barnes laughed heartily. "Ah, yes, of course, habit, my dear."

Eleanor announced, "I'm here for a diagnosis."

Dr. Barnes flashed a full smile of white teeth despite being in his sixties. His black framed glasses perched upon his bulbous nose. His jovial laugh caught Eleanor unawares. He said, "Yes, I suppose you are. And you, sir? Brother? Husband?"

She yelped, "Gosh, no! Mr. Brooks, if you please?" She gave him a pointed stare in the direction of the airfield.

Mr. Brooks extended his hand to shake the doctor's and replied, "I'm Seth Brooks, the new head area engineer at Norman Wells. I'm going to check on Charlotte and see if there's anything I can help her with."

Dr. Barnes laid his hand over his heart and said, "Thank you for treating her with such kindness. She's not used to it."

Mr. Brooks said, "My pleasure." He gave a little wave as he retreated.

Dr. Barnes glanced at Eleanor. "Now, dear, let's see what we can do for you." Her caked shoes caught his attention. "Ah, er, perhaps, leave your shoes at the door. I'll get a towel for your feet."

After wiping her feet, she walked inside and wondered if Dr. Barnes would look down on her for her possible condition.

I'm not ashamed of my behaviour. I'm a free woman. I don't care what he thinks.

He guided her toward the first room to the left. There stood a bed wrapped with a fresh white linen in the centre. The wall to her right was lined with three pine bookshelves housing medical, chemistry, and botany titles. Along the parallel wall was an oak roll top desk. It was open showcasing a neat pile of letters, a typewriter, and a few strewn notes.

A worn picture in a black frame caught her attention. It was a younger Dr. Barnes with his arm around a petite woman around his height with curly blond hair and a broad smile. In front of them stood a ruddy child of about ten. This was a family who appeared to have the secret to a happy life.

As far as she could tell, there were no sounds in the house that indicated someone else living there. Was his wife simply napping? Or had some tragedy befallen her?

Before she had time to inspect the table holding glass tubes, a microscope and other medical instruments, Dr. Barnes patted the bed and said, "Hop on! What ails you today?"

Eleanor sat on the bed and tented her fingers. "I think I'm pregnant."

"Ah."

"Well, isn't there a test to know for sure?"

He took a step toward the bed. "Yes, there is. It's called the Bufo test. I would take a sample of urine and send it to a laboratory where they would inject it into a toad. By the end of twenty-four hours, if the toad has laid eggs, that would mean you're pregnant. Of course, putting that all into effect takes time and is an unnecessary cost. Listen to your body and the signs."

She groaned, "Would throwing up my breakfast be a sign?"

"Yes, along with sore breasts and fatigue as the main ones."

She was done for. All her dreams of getting out and making a life for herself were dashed. She was a plane whose propellers got knocked out by a pair of geese and was now nose diving into the ground, all to be burned in an explosion of definite destruction. Her dreams were snuffed out.

He asked, "Are you experiencing any other symptoms, the ones I mentioned?"

"Yes."

"Since you're not in any apparent danger and it's an unnecessary expense at this point, then no need for the test. You're pregnant. Time will make it quite clear."

Eleanor muttered to herself. "I don't have time."

Dr. Barnes added, "I never got your name, miss…?"

She ground out, "It's Eleanor."

"You have to forgive me for keeping to some of the formalities in address."

"Sure, if you'll excuse me—"

Dr. Barnes halted her. "Hold on, Eleanor. If there's anything I can do—"

She whirled on her toe and shouted, "Can you show me how to travel back in time and undo the one time he didn't have his rubber good on hand? Can you prevent me from being fired and sent packing to Edmonton now that I'm pregnant? I need this gone!"

He blanched. A trembling hand flew to his downturned brow. "I hope you're not suggesting—"

"Well, maybe I am!" Blazing heat furled in her cheeks. So great was the pressure in her head that she felt as if her top would blow. She left the perch of her tiptoes and wallowed in the satisfaction of his eyebrows drawn like a high top tent over skittish eyes.

Her feet planted and fists balled, she rocked back on her heels and blew out a shuddering breath. "I'll do this on my own." She fished out some money. "Is this enough to cover my visit?"

"I—yes, just about." His fingers touched his bent forehead.

Her vision was blurry as she walked, no, ran back to the airstrip. Their pilot Frank was missing. She guessed he hadn't finished his own errands in town. Who knew how long Mr. Brooks would help the snivelling shell of Charlotte! How she hated the threads which held this tempestuous moment together!

She stood facing the plane and crossed her arms.

She thought that by coming to the North she was taking a match to the ready kindling of her old life for a grand bonfire she could dance around. It seemed as if one bonfire wasn't enough. She dumped the concentrated fuel of her anger onto the already raging inferno and was ready to burn with it.

The squishing of heavy set boots upon the soft earth unbridled any restraint she had left.

She swirled to face Mr. Brooks.

He neared her warily.

She raised her voice. "Did Doctor Barnes share the reason for my visit?"

"Of course, he didn't." He averted his eyes.

"I don't believe you." She marched right up to him until there was only a hand's breadth between them. She tilted her chin up to seek out the truth in his eyes.

Mr. Brooks's hand slowly, gently lay on her shoulder. "I promise you he didn't."

His firm hand was a brand she couldn't withstand. Her torrential flood of anger swooshed from her head to her hands. She beat his chest with a single stroke.

He said firmly, "Enough, Eleanor."

She could see in his eyes he knew, and he was lying to her. He was never supposed to know or not until she could deal with the problem. She hated being stuck in a corner. She hated him for knowing her secret. Her fists rained down upon his broad, unmoving chest.

He threw his arms upward in between her fists and broke her attack. Though her mad frenzy was stunted, she aimed one last feeble punch which he easily grabbed. His iron-like grip didn't inflict pain, only a ceasing of her hostility. He levelled his eyes with hers and breathed, "Enough."

She gripped the fabric of his shirt, wavering between tearing it to shreds or holding onto it as a lifeline. His arms tentatively wrapped around her. Tears pricked the corners of her eyes. She furiously blinked them away. The hot red that seared behind her eyes wavered to a bristling warm orange which faded to a dull yellow. As her reason returned, she stumbled backward a few steps, her hands unclenched and fingers trembling.

She had no voice or power left when Mr. Brooks turned her toward the plane, his arm placed around her shoulders, and helped her in. He grabbed the buckle and placed it in her hands so she could buckle herself in. She nodded feebly.

Surely, he would send her packing not for the obvious reason that would show in a few months but for her lack of temper and respect. She could have worked a few more months before she would have to return home and look for a new job. What had she done?

As soon as she exited the plane when they returned to the Norman Wells airstrip, Mr. Brooks said as he looked down, "Take tomorrow off. Rest. Come to work fresh in two days. Have a good evening."

She watched him walk away and bit her nail. "Ugh!" She withdrew her hand behind her back and squeezed it with the other. It was an old habit that had started after—and she never wanted to go back.

The next morning after all the other girls had gone to work, Eleanor sat upon her bed with her head in her hands trying to find a way out of her mess. The door banged open, and she gripped the edges of her bed.

Julia asked, "What's happened?"

"Oh, it's you."

"Yes, it's me. Well? How come you're not at work today? I asked Mr. Brooks and—"

"What did he say?"

"Not much. He hedged around the answer, only saying you needed some rest."

"I'm afraid I'll be out of here by tomorrow morning. He's just pitying me."

"Why? Does he know about the baby? Is there a baby?"

"Yes! I don't know! The d—n doctor wouldn't do a test!"

"Why not?"

"Because there's no great cause. I'm not in any danger. He doesn't find it a necessary expense. There are ways of feeling the body's changes. That's the thing, I don't want to find out the slow way."

Julia sidled beside Eleanor, and clasped her hand.

Pinching her nose, Eleanor sighed. "Deep down, I know I'm pregnant. Even before I threw up, my breasts were sore. My mood swings…. " She chuckled deprecatingly. "Well, because of them, I won't be here tomorrow. I messed up. After I walked out on the doctor, I—I hit him, Mr. Brooks, when he approached me minutes later at the plane. The last time I lost my temper like that, well, my neighbours thought I was mad."

"What happened back home?"

"I'm not ready to talk about it. Besides, you wouldn't want to be my friend anymore."

"You haven't had many friends have you?"

"Sure, I have!"

Julia chided. "Admirers and friends aren't the same."

"I know that!"

"Do you? It seems you don't know that friends, or at least real friends, are with you through thick and thin. Girlfriends are the glue of life. At least that's what my mama told me. Even though she went through a nasty divorce with my father, her girlfriends were her rock. Always have been, always will be."

Eleanor moped. "As I said, I won't be around past tomorrow morning."

"Maybe it's not as bad as all that."

"Oh, it is! What man would let a woman show him such disrespect and let her get away with it? I know times are changing, but I *know* I went too far."

Eleanor slept only a couple of hours. She didn't try too hard to snatch a wink of peace knowing full well she didn't deserve it, yet she somehow managed to sleep in. Miss Dansk filled the entrance to the Women's Quarters. "You had an hour of grace. Your boss would like to see you now."

Eleanor moaned and shoved her head underneath her pillow. In a flash, the covers were stripped from her body making her curl into a fetal position. Despite the balmy summer weather in August, some of the nights and early mornings were kissed with a frozen glaze. The biting air indicated this was such a morning.

"All right!" Eleanor threw out a hand in protest and poked out her head slowly as if she were a turtle coming out of its shell. "Please leave so I can get dressed."

"I'll be just outside."

"There's no need," Eleanor groaned.

"I think there is. You're an hour late to work. I told Mr. Brooks I would personally escort you to make sure you go straight to work. What a hoot! I have to bring the secretary to her work again."

"Good grief," Eleanor mumbled. She hastily dressed and switched to some warm woollen socks instead of the cotton ones she had been wearing recently. She didn't put much stock this morning into styling her hair or applying light makeup. She gave a few quick tugs of her brush, shoved her hair behind her ears, and left her quarters.

She followed Miss Dansk to the office. The indelible feeling of being branded a tramp, loveless, a failure—the entire walk to the office made her believe that all eyes were on her, disgusted with her.

As Miss Dansk opened the office door, Eleanor broke into a sweat.

Miss Dansk proclaimed, "Mr. Brooks, here's your secretary Miss MacKenzie."

Mr. Brooks' back was toward them as he was leafing through some documents. "Thank you, Miss Dansk, please leave."

Miss Dansk turned to exit, a grin splitting her fleshy face.

Eleanor stood still. The office was empty except for the two of them.

He turned to face her and said, "Please sit."

She did as she was told.

His appearance was greatly altered. The heavy beard he had sported was gone. In its place was clean shaven skin.

"Mr. Brooks?" she blurted out. She first spotted the cleft in his chin. Her eyes followed his strong jawline up to his soft cheekbones and centred on his calm grey blue eyes.

She inhaled sharply and looked away.

"Uh, yes, I thought I might be more approachable if I didn't have…. " His fingers waved around his non-existent beard.

She lifted her chin. "It would've been better if you had left it."

"Huh, too late now. Anyways, about yesterday—"

She clasped her hands together. "Please, I'm begging you, don't send me away."

"No apology first?"

She looked down at her fingers and intertwined them tighter. "I don't know what came over me. I'm sorry."

He nodded and waited a moment before saying, "I know what came over you."

"Excuse me?"

"You're pregnant, aren't you?"

Chapter 5

Eleanor bit the inside of her cheek until it drew blood. The taste of iron spurred her anger to rise. She looked sideways before gritting out, "Dr. Barnes told you, didn't he? I knew that —"

"No, he didn't. I wasn't lying."

She stole a look his way. She expected to see a corner of his lips upturned in a grin, a competitive twinkle in his eyes as he readied to tell her how he had come to know. All those were absent. A shaky businesslike clearing of the throat and schooling of features greeted her peruse instead.

"I took a look at your file and the details of where you've come from and why you took this job. Of course, you were asked these questions during your interview because of where the job is geographically and the dangers that come with the territory. You send money to your aging parents to help with the expenses of your father's condition, money you can't possibly make as a secretary back in Edmonton."

She snarled. "So what? You know what everybody else knows."

He held up his hand and continued as he sat down across from her. "I have three sisters, two married with children of their own. Before the war, we all lived close to each other, within two miles. I've been a witness to a couple of their pregnancies and the telltale signs each of them showed. Your inability to hold down your breakfasts, your irritability—"

"How do you know it's not because of you?" she shot back.

"Are you always like this?" His question was like a slap across the face. All the things she had endured before coming here, losing Paul, now this baby—how dare he ask her as if he were entitled to know her deeply.

He rubbed his hands down his face. "I'm sorry, that was out of line. It seems as if you've had a rough go here."

She gave a feral grin. "Hardly! I was having a wonderful time until you came along and took Major Burns's job."

He sighed. "He's the father, isn't he? I don't go looking for gossip here, but it's easy to overhear people's conversations."

She shrugged her shoulders. "If that's how you want to console yourself."

"Listen, it wasn't my fault that he left to take another post. I was offered the job."

"Doesn't matter anyway. I don't need him, and I don't need you."

He muttered, "Maybe you do."

"Excuse me?"

"Just answer the question. Are you pregnant or not?"

There was no use trying to hide whatever feeble attempts at lying she could make. By the hard set of his jaw and his arms crossed over his chest, he was already sure. She would look like a fool for trying to pull the wool over his eyes. They both already knew.

She reluctantly said, "Yes, I am. You know the reason why I'm begging. Please."

His arms slackened at his sides and his ocean patterned eyes softened. "I wish—I can't. I'm sorry."

Hot tears began to flow down Eleanor's cheeks. "Is there any other job I can take?"

"It's not my decision to make. It's the army's protocol. It can't be broken, not for just one case."

Eleanor rested her chin upon her collarbone. The memory of giggling with Julia when they found out Nelly was being shipped back home because of a pregnancy stung.

Who was laughing now? Her stomach convulsed at the thought of her "friends" snickering about her once she was sacked.

Mr. Brooks said, "Listen. Continue to—"

Shutting out whatever words of his came next, she heaved herself out of her chair and trembled as she walked out the door.

Mr. Brooks's calling her name fell on deaf ears as she stumbled toward the forest grove Paul and her shared.

How could she have been so stupid? She should have had the self control that one time to say no to what her body had been thirsty to experience. She had been desperate, and Paul had been like an oasis in a desert.

At Dr. Barnes' office she intimated that she could make this problem go away. She couldn't allow this baby to take away the one chance she had of a future of her own making, a future in which she could be happy. This baby was against her, and she was against it. It had to be removed. She would find a way to make it happen.

Eleanor was sitting on Julia's bed when her friend returned from shift. A hard mask shuttered Eleanor's features. Her white knuckles unclenched, but she was still biting her lip. Eleanor couldn't find the words to speak.

"Ellie!" Julia threw her hands into the air. "You running off not only left me with my boss's share of the work but also Mr. Brooks's. At least he didn't give me his whole pile of papers to type—but still!" She calmed momentarily. "I know you're dealing with a lot. Believe me, I'm not totally unfeeling. You just…. " She strode a couple steps closer. "You've got to do your job!"

"I don't have a job any more."

"Did Mr. Brooks explicitly say you were fired?"

"He knows."

"You work until he says you're on a plane ride home."

"Do you know why I came North?

"Why, Ellie?"

"It was finally a way to live my life, a way to make my own decisions without anyone else needing to have their say. It was the perfect opportunity to be independent of my parents' expectations while providing them with more money."

Julia added, "This war sure has paved the way for us to work out of the home."

"Yes! I'm just not sure if our freedom is a reality or an illusion. Now I'm at the mercy of what I ran from." Eleanor rubbed the tops of her knuckles with her fingers over and over. Julia stilled her harsh movement.

Eleanor said, "I'm not keeping it."

Julia kneeled in front of Eleanor and held her face between her hands. Their eyes met. Eleanor hoped there would be no judgement in the eyes of her only ally. "I'm here for you, whatever your decision." Julia dropped her hands. "How? Do you know what to do?"

Hot tears ran down Eleanor's cheeks. "I don't know anything about it. If I tell anyone, I'm gone. If I get caught, two years in prison. How will I be able to help my parents? Have a life?"

Julia grabbed Eleanor's hands. "Let me see what I can find out. Until then, go back to Mr. Brook's office and do your work. I can't take more of your pile." She flicked Eleanor's nose and rose. "I want to change for the gathering tonight. Put something pretty on. You're young and beautiful, and we'll have a grand old time."

"Good morning," Eleanor said as she entered the office the next morning.

Mr. Brooks blinked rapidly and paused. He laid down the notes to be typed out for the day in front of her.

She coolly accepted the papers without meeting his gaze. The too familiar colour of his eyes had her internally screaming d—nation against them.

Day in and day out, she could feel Mr. Brooks watching her for moments at a time from across the room as she typed. She was tired of being watched as if she were an oddity. The next opportunity the office was empty of everyone except the two of them, she gritted out just loud enough for him to hear her, "Stop watching me." She glared, attempting to appear as menacing as she could.

He didn't shrink but continued to look at her as if she were a problem to be solved. A beat later he looked down at his work, pushed away from his desk, and walked out.

She resented having to hold her tongue so she could keep her job even though it was only for a little longer. Any little bit she could earn to save for herself and send back home would help.

She felt as if he had pulled her into a dance she would never have said yes to unless he was her boss, which he unfortunately was. Would his hand create pressure that would make her wince? Or would he twirl her out and let her crash? There was only way she could leave the dance unscathed. With bated breath, she waited for Julia to investigate how she could restore her happiness.

Who could she ask? Of course, the men were a complete write off. Dr. Barnes wouldn't dare utter a word on his conscience. The other girls—who was to be trusted?

One night, as Eleanor dropped onto her bed after a long day of typing, and the other girls were readying for bed, Leticia shouted, "Girls, we're on our own tonight! The men are off on a hunting trip. Who's going to join me for a gin and tonic?" Eleanor looked up, curious at the offer.

With a gleam in her eye, Leticia leaned backward against the door and planted her hand on her pumping hip. She continued to shout, "You hoo! Anyone coming?" Eleanor bet Leticia was already drunk, her gay fumbling and annoyingly high-pitched tone grated her ears. Though she wouldn't enjoy the company, she needed a night to drink away her woes.

Eleanor replied, "I'm ready to get down and drunk!"

Leticia hopped on her toes and stretched out her hand toward Eleanor. "Yes, who needs Major Burns when we've got each other and the spirits!"

Eleanor asked, "Who else is joining?"

"Constance and her smug gang, of course. Julia is also waiting for us. You two are close, aren't ya?" Leticia threw her arm around Eleanor's shoulders and steered her out of the Women's Quarters toward the men's.

She continued. "We've got to be very quiet. We're meeting in a place we shouldn't," she winked and put a finger to her lips.

"Ah," Eleanor whispered, "we're invading the enemy's territory."

"More like lover's territory. Gosh, Eleanor, not all of them leave. Find yourself another man and have fun. Ah, here we are."

The creak of the door did little to muffle their giggles. They traipsed over to the group of already present girls.

Leticia announced, "Girls, our last initiate. Where's the moonshine?"

Constance handed out two paper cups filled with the night's tongue loosener. As Eleanor went to grab her cup, Constance spilled half of the cup's contents all over her hand and uttered a high-pitched fake "Whoops!" smirking as she turned to set the moonshine down.

Eleanor said, "Can't hold your liquor?"

Constance glared.

Leticia stepped in between them. "Girls, let's play a game of truth or dare. Me first! Eleanor, why don't you grab a shirt from any man's bed and smell it in front of us."

Eleanor said, "You didn't let me pick!"

"Can't do a simple dare?" Leticia winked.

"No, of course, I can, easy." She spied a ukulele which she saw a man named Dick use at times to serenade any girl who would give him a minute's worth. She plucked a shirt from a pile of folded ones and brought it back to the girls. She held it up, and the girls giggled. She inhaled deeply. Hints of lavender soap mixed with musty tones tickled her nose.

The girls held their breaths in anticipation of what Eleanor would divulge.

Eleanor said, "Well, a little underwhelming, as I'm sure he is in other areas." At this saucy punch, the girls roared with laughter.

Leticia said, "Shhh! We don't want Miss Dansk catching us in here and giving us an earful. She's probably wandering around camp trying to find us."

"I don't think his mama taught him how to wash his clothes very well." Eleanor sniffed more. "It's still a little damp."

The girls played deep into the night. Many fell asleep over the beds, huddled over each other in drunken revelry. Two girls snored, another whimpered like a kicked dog, and the rest attempted to keep their eyes from fluttering closed.

The game had officially ended less than an hour ago, yet three still had their wits about them to continue.

Leticia whispered and inclined her head toward Constance, "I dare you to pick your nose and eat it."

Eleanor asked, "How old are you again?"

Leticia snorted, "Old enough to think this is funny."

Intoxicated Constance began to move her finger upward. However, it went past her nose and nicked her eye instead. She huffed, "This is dangerous! Leticia, I'm going to get back at you now."

Leticia waved her hand back and forth over her head as she lay on her back on the floor. "Fine, I'll go with truth."

Constance yawned, and, before she could ask, fell asleep.

Eleanor asked softly, "Have you ever had a baby?"

Leticia's hand motion stilled. She lay her hand on her forehead.

Eleanor could barely hear her whisper.

"Yes, I have," Leticia answered in a halting breath.

Eleanor hoped this next question wouldn't scare her off. "What happened to it?"

Leticia was silent for a minute and seemed to have closed the subject. Then she answered, "I got rid of it."

"How did you do it?"

"I went to a local midwife and told her about it. I didn't know who to turn to. She told me under no circumstances could I ever tell anyone else that she helped abort babies in cases like mine. She knew I couldn't take more pain and heartache and that I had my whole life ahead of me. It wasn't my fault after all, was it?"

Eleanor asked, "Were you taken advantage of?"

Leticia's silence was her affirmation.

"I'm so sorry."

She waved away Eleanor's sympathy.

Leticia continued, "She gave me some pennyroyal extract and told me to put a teaspoonful in my tea. The next day it was gone."

"Do you regret it?"

She turned over on her side and looked into Eleanor's eyes. "To this day, I can't answer that question. Most of the time, I'm happy to be living my life without having to worry about someone else's well being. It's hard enough to care about myself. Then there's those other times—I feel haunted—I'm convinced that I ended a life that wasn't mine to end. But I had the power to do it. So I took it. You know there's always a flip side to the coin. I see women with their babies; they look like they're full of joy. What about the times their babies are crying and they can't stop them? Or the times when they don't know if they can feed themselves properly let alone their babies? Put it all on the scale. When does the joy outweigh the bad and vice versa? Maybe it comes down to what I can live with? The answer is always out of reach, for me anyway."

There was an obvious struggle etched upon Leticia's face. Would Eleanor look the same after making the same decision, ragged in an instant from a single act of survival? Could her beauty forever hide the deep dark secret she was choosing to commit?

Eleanor asked, "Would a doctor have pennyroyal extract?"

Leticia held Eleanor's gaze as her lips pursed, "I'm sure they would if my midwife did. Now…" she propped herself up on her elbow and languidly smiled, "…let's rouse this gaggle of girls. There's a good possibility the men will sleep at the hunting lodge tonight, but you never know." She rolled over onto all fours, stretched her back like a cat's, and swatted the girls awake. "Come on, you lazy bags of bones, we've got to clean up a little so the men won't know we've been here."

Despite their sloppy movements and minimal efforts, the beds the girls had used were still rumpled, and some of the men's personal belongings had been shoved underneath. Eleanor was the last to exit.

Chapter 6

Mid-September 1943

Flashes of the word "pennyroyal," glass shards slicing up the tender flesh of her porcelain fingers, the smell of decay—Eleanor woke with a start the next morning because of the vivid and heart palpitating flashes she had dreamed. An unknown full-body ache overwhelmed her as she hunched over to breathe in through her nose. She clenched the thin mattress; another small spring sprang loose. Her breath whooshed out.

She needed to get some pennyroyal so that her life could return to normal, so that she could cast these earth shattering burdens to the wind, unshackle herself from the fate of another's, and be beautiful and gay. Already she could feel this baby sap away her beauty. Her body shape, the part of herself she liked best, would soon change and would forever be marred.

Pimples were breaking out on her face. This baby would continue to grow and take more away from her.

Every day, she productively worked through her piles of papers without having to suffer under Mr. Brooks's thoughtful gazes. Recently, his work had taken him out of the office. Though her fingers were busy typing, her mind was diligently working out how she could take her destiny into her own hands. What would she say to Dr. Barnes so that she could steal some right from under his nose? Would he notice right away that one of his vials was missing? Surely he wouldn't report his suspicions to Mr. Brooks, patient confidentiality and all? She hoped it was a vial not in use very much, perhaps one he stored in the back.

She finished work, and caught Frank making his aviation checks before taking off.

"Please take me with you." She waved to get his attention.

"Do you have Mr. Brooks's permission?"

"I need to see Dr. Barnes. It's urgent. Please." She gave him the sweetest smile she could though she wasn't sure if it would work.

"All right, miss."

Dread, like a suffocating coat, settled upon her shoulders. She breathed it in, and it wound around the sinews of her muscles, making her steps heavy as she walked through town closer to Dr. Barnes's office.

Eleanor knocked on Dr. Barnes's door. No one answered. She squinted through the glass to see if there was any movement within. She could see none. She took a step backwards and looked out toward Charlotte's domain. She couldn't see the old biddy's nosy gaze though it was hard to tell when the windows hadn't been washed in years. The grime was caked on by seasons of sun baking.

She looked all around to see if anyone was looking in her direction. No one else was to be seen. The rest of the townspeople kept to their own business or that of their neighbour's. She was nobody's neighbour here.

Eleanor slinked along the side of the house and spied the back door of his home. She peered one more time at Charlotte's house. Nothing made a stir. She sprinted to the door and opened it easily. Not even the hinges squeaked.

Even though Dr. Barnes was out, she walked on her tippy toes and dared not breathe too loudly. She was breaking and entering, a crime she would never have committed before now. Then again, since she moved north, there had been many sins and more to come that she would never have thought to commit a year ago. She shook her head and said loudly to herself, "Stop the dawdling, Eleanor. He's not here. Let's get that vial."

She rounded into the patient room and zoned onto the amber vials, gleaming like diamonds begging to be touched.

Come find me, the pennyroyal enticed.

Her trembling fingers twirled each vial gingerly to look at each label. She was careful to place them back exactly as she had found them. The letter "p" caught her attention. Her fumbling fingers reached for the vial, tipping another over in the process. The vial shattered into three large pieces and a myriad of pieces too small to pick up.

Eleanor uttered a string of curses. She bent to pick up the large shards. The smallest of the large ones cut her. She hissed, and perspiration began to bead upon her upper lip. The blood welled in the centre of her palm. She grabbed a bandage from the medicine cabinet, wrapped it around the wound, and tied it with the help of her teeth. A garbage can was beside the door. She swept her mess, and the room looked tidy enough.

She took the pennyroyal vial and left out the back door.

When Frank returned to the plane, he asked, "What happened to your hand?"

"Oh, well, when I went to Dr. Barnes's office, I knocked over one of his vials. I tried to help pick up the glass, but then I cut myself."

His eyes screwed in suspicion. "I heard he went on a walk."

"He did, but he returned after I waited around a little."

He hesitantly nodded, "Good, glad you were able to see him."

She hoped he wouldn't try to find a second source to back up her story.

Eleanor stayed up late helping Blade wash dishes after the odd medley of lilting and off-tune female voices sang their final song for the poker-playing men in the mess hall. Usually, the men were eager to play the fools and flirt with the girls late into the night. However, a little bird lamented that it had been a particularly trying day for the men stationed at Raider Island, an island twenty km north of Norman Wells on the bordering Mackenzie River. They weren't sure whether the oil drill would drill quickly enough before the colder weather set in freezing the ground. The first frost had appeared the night before. It seemed as if their daily toils would grind to an earlier than hoped for halt on that particular site.

These days any small anxiety could grow into a tidal wave of fear that buffeted against her weak walls. She wasn't made of stone. If she didn't do something soon, she would be swept away into the storm and drown. Tonight was the night for action.

After all the kitchen volunteers had left, she filled the kettle in the sink. The sound of the water tinkling against the copper sides hurt her ears. She lit the stovetop with her lighter and put the kettle on. It was eerily quiet.

She wrestled with suppressing the guilt of being a thief. She would never have become one if polite society hadn't told her what she couldn't do with her body, what life she couldn't choose for herself.

The whistle screeched. She only placed the black tea bag into the boiling water once she had poured it so that she didn't scald the leaves and ruin the taste. Eleanor peeked around to make sure no one saw the vial she produced from her pocket. She hadn't dared to look at the pennyroyal until now. She frowned. There were barely a few drops left, less than an ounce. She shook her shoulders and hoped it was enough to do the job.

She blew across the tea and sipped. The amber tea tasted like acrid peppermint after she poured what little pennyroyal was left into her teacup.

After drinking every last drop and washing her cup, she looked at the piano. His eyes flashed before her face. She could remember—the rough grasp of his hand upon her arm, the bruises blooming from his digging fingers, as he dragged her from the bench and brought her to his room where the heavy brocade curtains had already been drawn for his next play with his victim. She tried to bite the hand that securely covered her mouth, but it was too big. His salty sweat made her retch. He was too heavy to shove off. The stink of his breath flooded her burning nostrils. Air—air was fleeting—was she dying? Did he intend to kill her today? Her innocence or her life? Her ears rang with the snap of his belt buckle. The skin on her thigh was rubbed red from his frantic grinding.

She could see the piano bench from the corner of her eye. She grasped for purchase, attempting to reach it, to strike some discordant tones that would summon help. Oh, it felt so far away. She couldn't walk to it.

Eleanor drew her palm to her forehead as she fell on her knees. She sucked in air—he was choking her again. There was no escaping his attention. She gave up and rolled over allowing the waves of horror to move her body according to the ocean's command. A clanging cacophony invaded her senses before she was fully pulled down into the abyss.

When one door closes, another door opens;
but we often look so long and regretfully upon the closed door,
that we do not see the ones which open for use.
Alexander Graham Bell

Chapter 7

Eleanor's lids cracked open a hair. They were so heavy she couldn't open them all the way. She closed them again and attempted to swallow. Her mouth was so dry. Blood—that's what she tasted on her tongue. It was swollen. She didn't remember accidentally biting it.

A lithe hand devoid of any calluses swept over her brow. "I think she's starting to wake up." A high-pitched nasal voice flooded Eleanor's brain, causing a swift headache to begin.

Eleanor mumbled, "Water."

A cup met her lips moments later.

"Be careful not to give her too much." A low male voice sounded from before her.

Eleanor tried to open her eyes again and saw Dr. Barnes sitting at the foot of the bed. Behind him on a dresser (not hers) was a family photograph that didn't belong to her. Who's room was she in? She drank the water and croaked, "What happened?"

She turned to look at the hand that had given her water and was surprised to see it belonged to Leticia, sitting in a chair next to the bed. Eleanor licked her chapped lips and looked to Dr. Barnes.

He sighed and clasped his hands together. "You suffered a seizure as, we guess, you were leaving the mess hall. You bit your tongue before Mr. Brooks found you. Due to his turning you to the side after your episode, you didn't choke on your own fluid. He sent word to me right away. Miss Valdez and the other girls have been taking shifts looking after you."

Eleanor groaned, "My head hurts. How long have I been out?"

Leticia cut in. "All night! In Mr. Brooks's bed! It's now mid morning. Gosh, you're lucky to still have a job what with—"

Dr. Barnes interrupted, "Miss Valdez, may you please let Mr. Brooks know how Eleanor is now doing?"

"Sure thing." The absence of her annoying voice seemed to bring down the pain in Eleanor's head a few notches.

Dr. Barnes lightly shook his head and asked, "Does your family have any history of seizures?"

Eleanor replied quietly, "No."

His greying brows furrowed. He opened his mouth and then closed it, seeming to choose his words carefully. "It's very strange that you would have suffered a seizure if it doesn't run in your family. Did you, perhaps, eat or drink anything out of the ordinary? Your symptoms align with someone who's swallowed a toxin."

"Not that I remember."

His searching eyes stilled and grew hard as he tried to read hers. When he couldn't elicit the response he was sure of, he said, "Well, it's time for your ipecac again."

"What do you mean again?"

"You don't remember? I gave you some as soon as I arrived. You were somewhat conscious when I did—" he paused his narrative as he spooned some down her throat. "And you—" He was interrupted by a groan escaping Eleanor's clamped lips as she swallowed it.

"What is it, and why did you give that to me?" The spite in her voice stirred Dr. Barnes to frown and speak to her in a tone that only her father had ever used on her.

"It's an emetic, meaning it causes you to vomit. There's a toxin in your body that God knows how it got in so I have to flush it out. If I don't, there's a good chance you'll die. I've seen this before. You don't know what you've done." The firm deportment of his shoulders indicated that he knew what she had attempted. "I'll be observing you closely over the next two to three days. Your liver could very well fail, your kidneys—I can't guarantee your life."

Eleanor's vision began to swim. She desperately wanted her own life, and it was slipping away like life-giving water seeping through her hands.

He turned around and stated, "Within the next few minutes, you'll vomit. Here's the bowl for that. Also, here's a cup of water to rinse out your mouth. Please leave a sample of your urine in here." He lifted a bin. "Would you like me to ask Leticia to come back in and help you?"

His fatherly overbearing stance prodded Eleanor to shimmy her shoulders back and adopt the wayward child crossing of arms. "No, thank you, I can do it by myself."

The lines in his face softened a touch as he replied, "All right. I'll be right outside if you need anything."

She didn't uncross her arms until the door clicked closed. The gross fear of almost having lost her life and the pain of her tender tongue filled her eyes with tears. She scrunched her sleeves and dabbed them. The action only brought them falling faster. She bit her bottom lip to keep her sobs from sounding beyond the door. These were for herself. She couldn't allow Dr. Barnes to be more suspicious than he already was. Where would that leave her and her parents' situation?

Nature was calling. She unrolled the covers off her torso. Her arms could barely support the weight of her upper body as she strained to lift herself an inch off the bed. Muscle tremors began when she attempted it again. She leaned on her right arm as she moved her legs from underneath the sheets, his sheets. She groaned as she shifted, hiking her knees closer to her stomach into a fetal position. Her feet banged to the floor. As she lifted her bum off the bed, her legs bent inward. She felt as if she were a broken doll barely held together by puppet strings, the subject of a cruel master stringing her along toward a fate she hated with every step she took.

A few drops of pee escaped down her legs as she hobbled toward the bathroom. The shame of her lack of bladder control was reprehensible. After barely managing to clean herself, the ipecac took effect. She clumsily banged her knees on the floor, turned around, and wrapped her arms around the toilet bowl and heaved.

When she finished all her necessities and slowly made her way to the bed, she closed her eyes and escaped to the dream world she much preferred over the hell she was living, the hell she had helped shape.

Recovery was a lonely road. Though most of the girls were eager to help (whether they did so because they truly cared for her or whether they wanted time off their regular work, she couldn't be too sure), none of their pretty-sounding condolences could quench the ache inside her soul. She hadn't bled, hadn't shed the life growing inside her. Her incessant need to be rid of it struck blades with the fatigue of plotting its end. Even though her stomach was slowly growing larger, her soul emaciated with each drawn out day.

At the end of the first week, Dr. Barnes allowed her to return to work as long as she attended weekly checkups.

Would she even be allowed to return to work? Mr. Brooks was not a stupid man, she had to give him that. He knew her predicament, and she sensed he knew her desperation. Would he put her desperation and the incident together and guess she had tried to have an abortion? She wouldn't expect any mercy from him.

She entered his office with the bravest face she could fake although she fought the quiver in her lip. If she failed, there would be no stopping the tears.

As she took her seat across from him, he lifted his eyes from his paper and watched her. His eyes which usually exuded calm now were large in apprehension as if he were hesitant, afraid of what would come next. He let go of the paper and exhaled deeply through his nose. His unusual stance stopped the tremble in her body. Perhaps the tables were to turn in her favour?

"Are you sacking me?" she asked.

He pinched the bridge of his nose and squeezed his eyes shut, "That depends."

She scoffed, "Are you serious? I've just been through—I almost died! Don't play games with me. Are you firing me or not? You are, aren't you? I don't see how that can depend."

An electric atmosphere settled between the two as she finished her tirade and he just looked at her.

He asked, "Marry me." He grew unfocused. His grey eyes saw too much, probed too much.   She opened her mouth to retort but no words could come. She must have heard incorrectly. "I—I'm sorry I didn't hear you. What did you say?"

"Marry me."

"How cruel are you? Did one of the girls put you up to this?"

He spread his hands on his desk. "Listen, it's a simple request."

She jolted from her chair and threw her hands in the air. "This is crazy! Why do you want to marry me? I don't even know you."

They both had the feeling that they were no longer the only ones listening to this conversation. They looked out the open window and saw a few heads dart from their view.

Mr. Brooks strode toward the window and shuttered it.

"Mr. Brooks! Open it immediately!"

"It's Seth."

She rolled her head in aggravation. "No! Mr. Brooks! I won't marry you. You don't even know me. I don't know you. What did you expect?!"

He took a step toward her and put his hands on her forearms, attempting to lead her back into her seat.

She shook him off and stood her ground.

He looked up as if asking for some divine intervention. "What happens if I let you go? You know I have to report your pregnancy and—" He bit back the words any self-proclaimed law-abiding citizen should have said concerning her illegal medical decision. "When I do, you'll be forced to go back, but you can't, can you?"

She forced a sob back. "I need this job for my dad. There's nothing back in Edmonton."

"So stay here, marry me, and have the baby."

"I don't want the baby."

"It's here. You can't change that."

"Why not? Why can't I have the power to do that? To choose how I want to live my life? Why can't I have more?"

"Don't you see? You made a choice. This is the result. Every man—woman is given what fate, God, whatever you want to call it has chosen."

"I don't believe that. I can choose my own destiny. You just watch."

He threw his hands up. "I already did. I watched as your body jerked and fluid came pooling out of your mouth." He pointed his finger at her. "Your choices almost got you killed. Luckily, I'm a light sleeper. Or maybe it isn't luck. I heard a bang on the piano and found you on the floor. Dr. Barnes said it's a miracle you're not dead!"

He paced the room. "I know this is strange. I'm offering a way for you to keep earning a living, a way to help your dad, a comfortable life (as much as it can be here), and an opportunity for you to give up the baby once it's born without killing it or yourself in the process. Don't you think it's reasonable?"

His last question and the reasons before it silenced her. She chewed on the inside of her lip as she mulled over everything he was offering, everything she needed to keep. "I have to marry you for all this?"

"It's the only way I can see. If you have a better idea, I'm all ears."

"If I have to marry you, you don't expect you and I to—?"

"No, that's not part of the deal."

"Once I have the baby, who will take it?"

"There's a local Dene tribe—a family is ready to raise the baby."

"And what happens to us after that?"

He slid his hand over his face. His eyes, those grey pools she avoided at all costs, seized her sympathy with their downturned corners, the veiny skin beneath his lower lashes. "I haven't thought that far. I guess I'll leave that up to you. Any way you look at it, you have all the power in this, whatever this is. Just think about it, okay?"

She tore her gaze away from his eyes when he turned to look at her and bit her lip hard. "Is there no other way?" she whispered to herself. She couldn't tell if Mr. Brooks had heard her question. If he did, he allowed it to fall helpless to the floor and shatter into a million pieces that she couldn't piece together alone.

She asked him, "Why are you doing this?"

Her brows scrunched as he bypassed her question and said, "Get some rest. You can give me your answer in the morning."

"No, you can't do that. Offer me marriage and then conveniently dismiss me after that question. That's not how *this* works. I don't need more rest. You haven't fired me yet so I'm working, starting now."

His eyes grew larger with every curt rebuttal she threw at him. He swallowed, his Adam's apple pronounced. Pointing to a large pile of papers, he said, "I didn't mean for it to come across that way. You can start work on those."

She planted herself in her squeaky chair. Her glare softened. She couldn't account for her forcefulness with her boss. Perhaps his offer had inadvertently and irrevocably brought them closer in ways she didn't fully understand.

He grabbed his coat from around the back of his chair and said, "I'll do my rounds and leave you be."

Before he opened the door, she rose from her chair. The squeak stopped him and made him look over his shoulder.

She sighed, "I know you didn't mean it the way I said it. I'm sorry. I'm grasping at straws, trying to make sure I don't get the short end."

He nodded, a strained smile appeared. "There's not much difference, is there, between those who grasp for power to be free and those who keep power on a tight leash? It looks the same, and people get hurt on both sides." He left.

Two other men entered immediately.

Her fingers flexed over her typewriter before she pounded away at the letters becoming words and the words becoming language. The letters blurred into the scenes of her life, scattered like the seeds of a dandelion from a fierce gale or a gentle blow guiding each piece to a strange new homeland that made them aliens wherever they went and to each other. It was impossible to gather them in and reattach them to their original home, the place of their birth. It was impossible to turn back time and feel whole again.

Whole, unbroken, what did that feel like? She wrapped her arms around her chest, hissing in pain from the pressure on her breast where, long ago, his hand had clamped to make her stay down like a dog while his ferocious grin grew larger. The corners of his mouth inched upward with each rocking motion. He seemed as a demon coming to destroy and to raze. She could no longer look at his triumph. The piano was her only solace, its music her only way to block out his hungry sounds.

She lay still even as he rinsed his hands and combed his fingers through his hair. His hair, which she used to think was so well combed and cut—oh, she wished she could pull it out with a single jerk.

He tutted as he approached her and cupped her chin, forcing her to look into his eyes of desolation. "You're so beautiful," he hissed.

The acid coating his full lips brought a roaring in her mind. She jolted from the bed and swatted at him as she attempted to run away. He caught her by the arms. His fingers dug in, giving her a matching bruise. "Where do you think you're going?"

The rush of adrenaline faded fast. She slumped.

"You don't tell anyone about this. You hear me? If you do, everyone will think your family is crazy. No one's going to believe you or your father. I'll ruin him. Your home won't be home anymore."

The storm in his eyes grew in intensity, its power freezing her will to fight.

"Let's get back to the lesson. I look forward to hearing your Chopin."

She looked at her paper to see she had typed "Chopin" instead of what she was supposed to be typing. She cradled her head in her palm. If her parents only knew the whole truth of her new life in the North and the past.

Julia entered the office at the end of her shift and sat on the corner of Eleanor's desk. "Ellie, is it true?"

"I haven't made up my mind yet." Her eyes were red and puffy, rimmed with tears.

"I didn't realise you and Mr. Brooks were even going steady. I thought you could hardly stand him."

Sure, Eleanor could allow Julia to create her own narrative, one that was a tad scandalous but without indelible blemish.

Julia continued. "I guess it could be a *Pride and Prejudice* situation. I love that book, you know. Funny how my good friend's love life turned out to be—"

"No, Julia, it's not what you think."

"Oh," Julia contemplated. "What is it then?"

"I'm afraid if I tell you won't look at me the same way. I'm not as free and independent as I've made you believe."

"I thought we were better friends than that."

Eleanor nodded. "Okay, I'll tell you."

Pressure buzzed in between Eleanor's eyes as she placed the last sheet of typed paper for the day on the done pile. Julia had been more than sympathetic toward her situation, shedding tears over the fact that Eleanor may have to marry for reasons other than love. It felt good having someone cry over her. Sharing with Julia helped ease the burden of keeping another secret.

She placed another sheet of paper into the typewriter. Her fingers hovered over the keys. She didn't know why Mr. Brooks was offering such an outrageous proposal. Was it out of quiet compassion? Or a warped overextended sense of duty? The more she thought about it the less averse it appeared. Jail, pain, and very possible death were spectres that no longer held sway in her outcome with the help of his offer. She would still have to sacrifice her body on the altar of ugly necessity and come out on the other side forever changed. The marks would show the baby's true intentions, how the baby came to leech off her beauty, to feed its own insatiable hunger, and to be served by all those in its sphere.

Let it use her as an incubator. As soon as she pushed it out, she'd cut off all ties and release it to another who would be willing to love it. She would be free to return to the road ahead of her, to find a place where she truly belonged.

What would her parents say? Would she be a part of the salacious gossip dancing along the twittering tongues of those nosy, hog-chasing, children-spanking, loud-mouthing women from her old home? Edmonton was no longer her home. It hadn't been for a long time. Norman Wells was the place, perhaps, not to set roots but to discover a feeling of belonging, belonging to the wild, belonging to the unknown.

She typed, each key pressed in grim determination.

I accept.

She left her note on Mr. Brooks's desk and slipped out past the mess hall where the usual banter and raucous laughter could be heard. Her voice used to blend in with the cacophony. It had joined the dissonant sounds of bad flirting and over-dramatic squealing. In the thick of it, she had been in a colony of bees all dancing to communicate the all important message of survival, of mating. Looking in from the outside, they all sounded like a herd of pigs tumbling over each other, snorting at the other for attention. Even her love for a fun evening had blackened from the hard reality of her circumstances. She'd rather be a pig than think so much.

The next morning, Eleanor worked at her pile of papers. Heavy, tentative footfalls crossed the threshold behind her. Mr.

Brooks sat across from her at his desk and cleared his throat. "You do good work."

She snapped, "Was that ever in question? I'm the head secretary for a reason."

"No, it's just a compliment."

"Thank you." She sneered.

"I got your note. It's for the best."

"If you think so." She huffed. "You don't know me."

"No, I don't. That's going to change a little, probably."

She halted her work and tented her fingers. "This is a marriage of convenience for me. I'm not looking to get to know you or hold hands and sing kumbayah. I want to go back to not liking you."

A small smile lifted his neat beard. "You're saying you don't mind me anymore."

"I don't know what I'm saying or what I think of you. I hardly think of you except when you irritate me or ruin my life."

He allowed her terseness to pass before saying, "We're going to get married in four days, Friday. You'll need a witness to sign."

"Ah, and here I thought we could get away with a fake certificate."

"Isn't it your plan to divorce me in the end?"

"Yes, it is."

"We'll go to Father Beau's St. Theresa's chapel where he'll —"

"No, no church." There were two reasons why she would refuse such a plan. One was that whenever she did marry for love, only then would she marry in a church as her parents had. Second was that after all the sin she had committed, she didn't want to accrue any extra righteous anger against her. "Why can't we get married here?"

"You want to get married in the office?" he said in a disbelieving tone.

"Yes, in private. I'd prefer no fuss."

"All right, we'll do it the way you want."

"Where will we be living after—"

"There's a cabin on the outskirts of the camp."

"Why aren't we staying where you are now?"

"It's nice for a bachelor. Not a lot of room for someone else, let alone a coming baby. I'll be giving it to Pete, my second."

The gnawing thought of not having any distractions, whether they were female friendship or flirtatious attraction for a good looking bloke, produced a grimace she wished she could snap away.

Even though she was lucky to keep her job, she would walk the lonely way from the office to her soon to be home, which would be equally lonely since her husband wanted nothing to do with her except save her. No mistake, she wanted nothing to do with him either.

"What about your parents?" Seth asked.

She cleared her throat. "Not happening."

Feeling his eyes linger on her downturned face, she said, "That's everything, right?"

"Right. Have a good day."

Chapter 8

Early October 1943

Norman Wells effused a riotous spirit in the wake of another party where lonely hearts and bodies could find reprieve in the touches of ghostly lips, there one day and gone the next or until the conditions were just right for visitation. Five warm bodies were absent from the moonshine's hold.

A single lightbulb shone above the couple whose fates were tied by desperation and, unbeknownst to Eleanor, honour. She faced Seth, noticing the stubble he had allowed to grow on his fresh-shaven face of last week. He had made an effort with his wardrobe. He wore a pair of beige slacks that, Lord forbid, he would wear outside the office. It wouldn't last ten minutes before dirt, water, or tree sap would adulterate its newness as he headed up the construction of more oil tanks and the Canol Road which would run parallel to the pipe they were laying ahead. Earlier in the day, she had heard the girls gossip that he had taken a special trip into town to pick up his outfit.

How could he have had the time to go to the tailor's in town, get his measurements taken, and had his slacks and suspenders made all between his proposal and their marriage? He couldn't have. Somehow he had planned for this and was almost sure that she would accept. The whole scenario was inconceivable. Why would he spend good money on clothing for a wedding that was a sham, a marriage of convenience?

Every facet of his marriage plan was shrouded in fog. She didn't trust him. There was no way he could gain advantage. She didn't come from money anymore. Her past circumstances had made sure of that.

She had also heard that Father Beau had needed to get special permission to marry them since neither of them were Catholic.

That morning, she had sifted through her clothing and found a forest green skirt and paired it with a cable-knit cream sweater. It was the closest she had to white. White—she couldn't wear the virgin's colour. Her innocence was stolen years ago. She grabbed her brush and tamed the tangles of her wheat coloured hair. She reached the bottom of her luggage and grabbed the cream beret, encircled with pearls, her grandmother had left her when she died thirteen years ago. Her grandmother had worn it on her wedding day.

She clipped it in, smoothed down her outfit, and touched the beret with her kissed fingertips.

Instead of walking to the office on the main gravel pathways between camp buildings which the partygoers used this evening, she skirted behind them, careful to stay within the shadows, a bride feared to be seen.

When she walked in and saw Seth, Peter, Julia, and whom she assumed was Father Beau (for he was wearing his priestly garments), the pit of her stomach throbbed and the source of her air shrivelled.

If Seth hadn't caught on that she was losing her grip on the moment, she would have toppled over. He didn't take her hand, nor did he thread his arm around hers. A light touch at the middle of her back was enough to convey that he was there to bring her to the front to make sure that their plans, no, his plans would come to fruition.

Father Beau had a young looking, fair face. The tips of his ears poked a little above the rim of his biretta. He was the shortest man in the room, only a few inches taller than Eleanor. His face was pinched as he read, "God, our Father, whose nature it is to seek the welfare of Thy children, sanction the vows and strengthen the promises about to be made…"

Eleanor drowned out the words and stared at a section of the wall between Seth and Father Beau. What would it be like if she could winnow herself away to the blandness of the wall, a world far away from here where there were no expectations to be a certain someone, a world where hurt and consequences never existed? She pondered the impossibility of her fantasy until two words jarred her back to reality. *I do.*

She looked at Seth with glazed over eyes. What would she be saying yes to?

He angled his head toward Father Beau.

Father Beau led her through the vows she didn't believe in, the vows she intended on breaking, the vows which unwillingly bound her to a sacred bond. "Do you, Eleanor MacKenzie, take Seth Brooks to be your wedded husband? And do you solemnly promise, before God and these witnesses, that you will love, honour and cherish him; and that, forsaking all others for him alone, you will perform unto him all the duties that a wife owes her husband, from this day forward?"

She struggled to voice "I do" because what if God found out and made her pay for her sacrilege? Oh, but He did know. Her "I do" was said in nakedness before a Being she couldn't hide from.

Father Beau told Seth to take her right hand and repeat after him. "I, Seth Brooks, take thee, Eleanor MacKenzie, to be my wedded wife, to have and to hold, from this day forward, for better for worse, for richer for poorer, in sickness and in health, to love and to cherish, till death do us part, and thereto I pledge thee my vow." Seth's voice never faltered.

It was her turn to take his right hand willingly. She couldn't bring herself to do it. Saying "I do" had taken enough from her.

A rough warmth, calloused yet tender, embraced her right hand. Seth gave her hand a light squeeze. She repeated, "I,

Eleanor Mackenzie, take thee, Seth Brooks, to be my wedded husband, to have and to hold, from this day forward, for better for worse, for richer for poorer, in sickness and in health, to love and to cherish, till death do us part, and thereto I pledge thee my vow." Each word she pushed between her lips was like a death knell, ringing ever closer to her fate.

Father Beau asked Seth, "What token of your promise do you bring?"

Seth produced a simple gold band with a tiny diamond nestled in the centre.

Father Beau said, "Do you, Seth Brooks, give this ring in a sincere pledge that you will keep your promise and perform your vows?"

Eleanor looked from the ring in his hand into his eyes and barely breathed when he said, "I do."

He took the ring and slipped it over and settled it in between her long fingers. It was a tad loose. She smiled at the thought that she could easily slip it off and place it in a drawer to be forgotten amongst whatever loose baubles she owned. It wasn't a sign, no matter how inconspicuous, she wanted to flash wherever she went. Her belly would be enough of a neon sign to deal with.

Father Beau intoned, "Bless, O Lord, this ring. May its unbroken circle be the symbol of perfect union of two hearts, two minds, and two lives. Amen."

He continued, "With this ring, I wed thee, in the name of the Father, and the Son and the Holy Spirit. Join your right hands. Inasmuch as you have chosen to marry, and have witnessed your several promises before God and this company, I now pronounce you to be husband and wife together, in the name of the Father and of the Son and of the Holy Spirit."

Father Beau's words dinged in her ears as if a child had taken a musical triangle and twirled the stick around and around right next to her ear, each word tumbling one over the other, clashing, clanging—"…the Lord lift up His countenance upon you…" The echoing slowly subsided.

Seth took a step toward her. She drew in her breath sharply. She focused her gaze on his navy blue tie and dared not look into his eyes, his eyes which looked so similar to her attacker's eyes, which sometimes haunted her before she fell asleep at night. He tilted his head down and paused, asking permission, giving her moments to take a step back.

She didn't; for she was frozen in uncertainty. Would he truly kiss her lips when he didn't , couldn't, surely, care for her in any way? It was all for show. This was her life now. She would allow him this guise, but she wouldn't go quietly into the prison of marriage.

When she made no move, he guided his lips to her forehead and gently brushed them across.

Her breath flowed out from her shaking lips and mingled with Seth's as he eased back.

Peter held out the marriage licence to Seth and Eleanor so they could sign their names. The document made its way amongst all the hands and was folded neatly at the end.

Seth said, "Thank you, Father Beau, for performing the service. Peter and Julia, thank you for being our witnesses."

Peter nodded and clapped Seth on the back as they shook hands. Julia perched her arm around Eleanor's shoulders and squeezed. "There, that wasn't so bad, was it?"

Eleanor's shoulders were hunched as if she could not be warm and comfortable. She managed a feeble smile as she looked at her friend.

Seth touched her on the shoulder. She was startled from her friend's embrace. He leaned toward her and said, "Ready?"

Ready for what? Eleanor stewed over his choice of phrase. She wasn't strong enough to do him bodily harm if he tried to force any lovemaking. The pressure from his hand on her mid back led her to the chair where she had left her sweater. He picked it up and draped it over her shoulders before they left the office building.

Jeering and pleasure-filled laughter floated from the mess hall. There were a few people who whittled out of the doors like drunken clowns attempting to remember what act they should play next.

Seth led her into the woods away from her sacred grove, where the life she resigned to keep was conceived. A five minute walk away from the centre of Norman Wells life, windows shone a warm yellow glow from what was little more than a shack. The outside needed a coat of paint to brighten it up. The paint on the wood was drab and peeling. The outside aesthetic discouraged her from any desire to decorate any part of her new home.

The crickets were in full chorus as he opened the door for her. Although the walls were bare of any personality except for the massive logs stacked horizontally and connected by the mortar, the cabin held simple but comfortable furnishings. She expected it to be all one room, but Seth had already partitioned off a corner of the house with a curtain hung on hooks every couple of feet. She assumed it was for her benefit. There was a wood stove glowing with firewood off the north wall. The east wall between the wood stove and the door was furnished with a sofa. The frame was made out of birch sapling trunks. She walked toward it and sat upon the cushy surface. There were also blankets made from beaver and mink pelts. Eleanor covered her body in them, letting the fur nuzzle her cold face. Her eyelids fluttered closed as she sought shelter.

"Where did these come from?" Eleanor asked.

Seth stood before her with his hands on his hips. His lips drew together before answering. "Nasnana made them for us."

"Who's Nasnana?"

"She's the matriarch of the Dene tribe just north of here."

"How do you know her? Why did she give these to us?"

He exhaled. "I know her because she and her people are my friends. She knew we were getting married and got the men to build some of these pieces. I also helped when I had time."

"You're friends with them?" Eleanor said in a faraway voice. She had never met a Native before.

"That couch you're sitting on, they made it. Your bed, my bed, the chairs, the table…. " He gestured around them.

"Oh, how did you make friends so quickly and easily since you've arrived?"

He chuckled as he stoked the fire in the stove. "You give me too much credit. This area is home. I was away for a little bit. Had to come back when…. " He slowly faced her and gave her a small smile. "You're probably tired."

As difficult as it was to admit it, she nodded and curled into the blankets even more.

"You probably don't want to sleep on the couch. The bed's just as nice, and you can bring those pelts with you although you probably won't need to."

She got up, pulled her partition aside, and ached to crawl into bed. Upon it lay a voluminous bear blanket. She turned back toward him and gave him the smaller pelts.

"I had Julia and Leticia bring over all your clothes and belongings. They put them down neatly in a corner there. See?"

Eleanor was speechless at all the thought he had put into the living space and how she would want her things with her. She whispered, "Thank you, goodnight."

He nodded as she pulled the curtain closed.

She had anticipated the wedding night to be awkward since custom dictated certain activities were expected; yet his lack of insistence of any action on her part resulted in her feeling safe and comfortable.

The smell of frying bacon and the accompanying sizzles woke Eleanor. The last time this ever happened was the morning she had left home to brave the North. Normally, her mouth would be watering and she would eagerly throw on her clothes and saunter into the kitchen. Now the smell accosted her and caused her to throw her blanket over her nose to settle the nausea. The musky smell of the pelts settled her a little. She peeped over the blankets and basked in the little sunlight diffused through the cotton cream sheets hanging around her nest, protecting her from the reality that stood outside its flimsy walls. Moving her head to the side to get air was the wrong move. She vaulted out of bed and swiped her sheets to the side, gunning for the door and the crisp air. She just made it out the door before her stomach somersaulted and heaved the bile. She rested her right forearm across her right thigh and managed to move most of her hair away from the onslaught. When the tremors settled a little, she breathed in through her nose and out through her mouth, spittle dripping away from her lips.

She shifted her hips forward to lift herself from staring at the mess in front of her and wiped her mouth. A chipmunk inched forward to gather a nut before scampering back when it heard the crunch of pine needles.

"Here, take this." Seth held out a washcloth and basin of water. "Was it the bacon?"

She nodded glumly as she accepted his help. Her shaking hand dipped the cloth into the water. She patted her face and neck. She caught a flicker in his eyes as she moved her hair to one side, exposing the curvature from her ear to her shoulder.

He looked away and said, "I'm sorry. I should have known better. I won't make bacon again unless you're out of the house. Wait here." He ducked back inside.

She was able to wipe her face another time before he returned. A quilt hung over his arm. He double pleated it and laid it on the ground. "Why don't you sit here while I air out the house?" He didn't wait for her to sit before he went back in.

She stared in confusion at the burgundy navy blue quilt laying so prettily on the forest floor. She ambled toward the door and heard the shutters and windows clacking open. Who was this man that he should be so mindful?

She wandered back to the quilt and sat cross legged, pondering his character. So lost was she in her thoughts that she didn't notice when a plate of cheese and bread appeared at her side.

Prejudices, it is well known, are most difficult
to eradicate from the heart whose soil has never been
loosened or fertilized by education; they grow there
firm as weeds among stones.
Charlotte Bronte

Chapter 9

Mid-October, 1943

True to his word, Seth never fried bacon, at least not when she was around. Every morning she awoke, he was gone. She wondered if it was because he couldn't take the hassle of her morning sickness.

Whenever she was sick, there was no need to make it outside. The first morning after the bacon incident, a large bowl appeared beside her bed. Next to it was a box with a lid. She swung her legs from beneath the covers and lifted the box to her lap. Inside lay a block of cheese and bread. She was thankful he had the insight to put it in a closed container. She could very well wake up to the squeaks of mice or even worse, the sight of a rat.

Eleanor enjoyed having the place to herself. It more clearly aligned with what she hoped this marriage would be, convenient with total autonomy. Once she dressed for the day and exited her makeshift room, there was a bowl filled with water and a washcloth and a glass of water. It was the greatest service she could hope for in the wild north.

Along the way to the office, Leticia stopped her and joshed, "So, let me see the ring!"

Eleanor answered, "There's nothing to see." She had forgotten to take it off.

Leticia grabbed her hand to take a looksie. "Well, it ain't no Tiffany's, but it's got some sparkle. I guess that's the best you can hope for from a grizzly husband. At least he used to be. That shave gave him some va va voom!"

Eleanor gave a smarmy smile. "Maybe you'll get one like this one day."

Leticia shuffled off and murmured, "Just you wait. I'll get a fat diamond one day."

Eleanor entered the empty office save for Julia. Julia hitched herself to Eleanor's hip and asked, "How was it?"

Eleanor quipped, "Different."

Julia replied, "No! You didn't. Did you?"

"'Course I didn't."

"Good! Or else I would have taken him for a cad."

"You would see the bruise from the socking."

"Mmm, remind me not to get on your bad side." Julia spied Seth entering. She whispered, "Have a good day with hubby! I'll be back."

Eleanor fumed at the intimate nickname and frowned at Julia's retreating. Seth grabbed a few papers off his organised desk and began to head out. The next few words tumbled out of her mouth before she could stop them. "Where are you going?"

He baulked, back rigid from the quick move. He turned on his heel and asked, "You want to know where I'm going?" His soft tone conveyed confusion instead of the irritation she feared would manifest after her words escaped.

She grasped, "I mean, uh, I don't know why I asked that question. It's, uh, never mind. As you were." She raised her shoulder slightly as she cringed walking back to her desk. What kind of farewell was "As you were"?

A moment later she heard the door firmly close.

This routine was standard day in and day out, even the weekends. Not only did she have the cabin to herself in the mornings but also in the evenings. The first night she had declined to spend time with the girls after supper because she was exhausted. Tromping through her doorway, she was eager for a cup of tea. Did they even have tea and sugar? The old wood stove was the only means by which she could boil water. She crossed the room to the stove and spied a kettle beside it. She filled it with water from the basin and placed it on top of the stove.

Now there was the matter of starting the fire. She could adequately start one, however it was one of the chores she disliked the most back home. She was afraid of heat, of a spark jumping upon her skin, of a flame reaching out to burn her. She huffed and wondered if she should just scurry back down to the mess hall and grab ready-made tea. Not willing to be outwitted by fear and a little toil, she set to work on building the tinder into a tepee shape and lighting the match. Little tendrils of smoke, the smell curling sweetly toward her nose, appeared, growing larger with her encouraging breaths. Once a sufficient fire burned, she added a few larger pieces and then a couple logs. She surveyed the fire until the water in the kettle began to murmur against its metal cage. When it sang, she snatched it off the stove and poured the water into a mug with a ready tea bag. She was pleased to find sugar in the cabinet near the stove.

She curled up on the couch with the fur blankets draped around her and tucked her ankles beneath her bum. She sipped chamomile tea and relished the silence. By ten o'clock, she couldn't stay awake any longer. She thought Seth would be back by then. He wasn't.

Each night, her gaze slipped toward the door less and less. It was her time to stretch out her legs on the couch without a care, to sip her tea and to read the only book she had brought with her to the North, her favourite novel *Pride and Prejudice*. Occasionally, Julia would join her in her home, and they would talk about the gossip.

"You know, your situation's proven to work out really well in your favour. You get the house to yourself, there isn't a man to pester you, you're still working the same job and able to provide for your parents—"

"Sure, but my body is changing—I swear I'm losing my figure already, my breasts are getting larger—I never asked for it. I'm always tired. I can hardly keep any food down most of the time. I'm scared."

Julia reached over to hold Eleanor's hand. "You got me. I know I've never given birth, but whatever you need, I'm your girl."

Eleanor hummed. "You know what I need? Another piece of that cheesecake. You think Blade's hiding more of those pieces in one of her refrigerators?"

"Want to go see?"

"Yes," a devilish glint appeared in Eleanor's eyes as she pulled on her shoes and put on a coat.

Julia held out her hand for Eleanor. Eleanor took it and threaded her arm through her friend's. If she ever stumbled on a root, her friend could break her fall. As they crossed behind buildings toward the mess hall, they attempted to stifle their giggles. All the lights were off. One by one they turned them on as they slinked toward the kitchen. Sure enough, a few slices of cheesecake were wrapped up.

Eleanor opened the refrigerator. "Ha! Look! There's three pieces left."

"Poor Blade. Her waist will have to do without the other pieces."

After smuggling the cake into their waiting mouths, they turned off the lights and walked out. They passed the office buildings.

Eleanor asked, "Have you seen Seth recently?"

"I see him every day at work. So do you."

"No, I mean, do you know what he does every night? I don't think he comes to the cabin."

"How would I know? He's not my husband!"

Eleanor threw her a look of mock reproach. "I *don't* know! Have you seen him around?"

"Sometimes I see him at Peter's place. The office light was just on now. Are you worried about him?"

"No! I'm just curious."

"You missing him?" Julia batted her eyelashes.

"Don't be ridiculous! I just find it strange that he has a home, and he's not in it."

"Uh, uh, correction! He has a house, but he doesn't have a home. Would you call it home if the person who lived there made it very clear with their behaviour that they hate you?"

"I don't hate him."

"Okay, you're right, hate is a strong word. You don't want him."

"Now you've got it. I do see what you're saying though."

"Why don't you visit us girls at the Women's Quarters more often? For someone who doesn't want to be married, you sure act like a married woman, no time for your single friends."

She wrapped her arms around her chest. "You're right. Would they still want my company? Even though I'm married, stuck with a boring man?"

"Yes! They always ask about you. I think they're very curious about you and Seth."

"That's the last thing I want to talk about! I want to hear all the gossip and maybe have my own fun on the side."

Julia grinned, "Well, now you'll join us. Welcome back!"

They clasped each other and giggled.

Eleanor moved an arm's length away and groaned, "How did all my plans for the future change forever with a single stroke of bad luck? I was trying to escape my past and all the expectations that came with it. I wanted to hang up the get married and settle down apron for good and never wear it in the first place. You and I, all of us women, we're part of an independence movement. It matters more than anything that we have the chance to be happy this way."

Eleanor gave a small smile. "At least Seth's giving me the chance to be an independent woman again despite all this. Whatever his reasons are, it doesn't matter."

Julia said, "I'm just thankful that you don't have to leave. I wouldn't want this adventure without you, Ellie."

"Oh, Julia, I wouldn't have as much fun without you. Say, has anyone caught your eye? I've been so engrossed with my own problems that I haven't asked about you."

Julia blushed and looked toward a certain hut. "I'm falling in love with Peter."

Eleanor's brow crinkled as she was trying to place the name with a face.

Julia added. "He's Mr. Brooks's second."

"The one with the glasses?"

"Yes. It all happened so fast and—"

"Isn't he kind of quiet?"

"Maybe, but he's also quite cultured. He can recite Shakespeare!"

"That is an accomplishment. I only knew one person who could, some stuck up girl in my class when I was ten."

"He's so romantic. We take strolls under the moonlight, and when we kiss, it's as if I'm soaring like the eagles we see here." She sighed.

Pushing aside her jealousy, Eleanor forced a smile and squeezed Julia's fingers. "I'm so happy for you and can't wait to hear even more. Tomorrow night I'll join you girls. I'm curious to see where Seth is and what he's up to."

Eleanor walked toward the office with Julia following behind. Eleanor said behind her shoulder. "I'll see you tomorrow, goodnight."

"All right, see you tomorrow."

Eleanor entered the office and examined the empty chairs and desks sitting in darkness except for the single light at Seth's desk. His sudden loud snore made her jump. She stifled a laugh and smiled. Seeing his face smashed against a stack of papers made her giggle. His shaggy black hair stuck out at various angles. His large hands lay flat against the dark grain of the desk. She stepped closer toward his face. A drop of drool was pooling on the desk. His full lips were parted. His beard already boasted a few grey hairs. His eyebrows were slightly furrowed.

She felt strange looking at him as if he were some exhibit in a museum. The caption would read, "Seth Brooks, a man who chose a wife who didn't love him, who enriched her life in strangely specific ways."

She tilted onto her toes so her small heels wouldn't clack upon the floor. One step—a board squeaked, and he woke up.

He groaned and slowly pushed himself up with his forearms.

Freezing for the first few seconds, she turned back toward him and smiled, hoping to take charge of the situation by showing that this was her intent all along. "Hi."

He squeezed his eyes shut and then opened them. His right fist came up to dry whatever dribble had collected at the corner of his mouth. "Is it morning already?" He took stock of his surroundings and said, "What are you doing out of bed?"

Her hands folded together at the front. "I'm not some child that needs to be put to bed."

He squeezed his eyes again and shook his head, "I'm sorry. I mean usually when I get to the cabin, you're asleep."

"So I've noticed. I'm plenty happy with the situation."

He gave a small sincere smile. "Probably a good part of the situation is me taking care of my own laundry."

She bit back a smile. "Yes."

"Good. Is everything okay?"

She didn't answer. Her mouth was open in question. "Uh, yes?"

"Okay, well, I'm done here. I'll walk you back."

"I can go back on my own."

"I'm heading the same way."

"All right, then."

It was near midnight and the outdoors was clear of its resident rabble-rousers. It was free to orchestrate its song of crickets, to move with the howl of a wolf cry, to breathe with the wind laced with mountain fragrance. It wasn't interrupted by idle chatter. Only their footsteps and the occasional moan from a lover's tryst somewhere behind a building or near the woods broke nature's symphony. Oh, how it was less for it.

When they reached the cabin, Eleanor moved straight into her room without saying a goodnight to Seth. He gave her about ten minutes to change into her nightgown and settle under her blankets before he walked around the room and blew out the lights.

In the dark, she heard him shuffle to his bed and pull down his suspender straps, unzip his pants, and let his buckle drop to the floor. The sounds seemed so familiar as she imagined it was Paul beside her doing the same things he used to before he left her, before he took away her greatest source of joy, himself. She heard Seth's bed creak as he crawled underneath his covers and finally loosed a breath. Oh, how she wished for the heat of Paul's body.

She had been debating writing him a letter these last couple of weeks, mostly alone with only her work to occupy her mind and her bodily changes to become accustomed to. She hadn't written any letters because she vowed she wouldn't be reduced to a simpering lovesick girl. Was that why she was tempted to write to him? Because she loved him? Or was it because her body was craving what he had readily given her? There was no other man in camp whose essence beckoned to her own. Major Paul Burns was gone. Why did she feel that she needed him when she could take care of herself tomorrow when, in the quiet, she could strum her own tune?

At ten weeks, she still didn't have much to show. Dr. Barnes had sent word to Seth to bring Eleanor for a checkup. Sunday was the only day Seth was available to bring her, being it his only official day off.

Saturday evening he told Eleanor to meet him at Father Beau's chapel once mass was finished the next morning. After eating the small helping of crackers and cheese (which he never failed to put out for her every morning), she noticed the bleeding that had started two days ago was still present. It wasn't a lot, but the small amount she had gave her hope that, perhaps, the baby would pass after all.

Tired of wearing clothing appropriate for roughing it in the woods, she slipped on her favourite buttercup yellow long sleeve tea dress and wrapped the accompanying bow around her waist. Wondering how cold it was outside, she opened her front door.

The air was crisp as the touch of an icicle. The sky was a mottled grey as if it were amassing its storehouses of snow to fall at any given moment.

She ducked back inside and pulled on her white woollen stockings and slipped her feet into her leather lace up fur lined boots. After buttoning up her navy reefer coat, she headed toward the chapel.

Seth struck Eleanor as the dependable goody-two shoes Sunday school boy who had never strayed from his upbringing. Finding out he wasn't Catholic was a little shocking. Perhaps, he was Anglican.

If her parents only knew she had married someone like him, their endless praises for her decision and remarks of "what a good man he is!" would make her smile and be content because they were so happy, but only for a time because she didn't love him. Yet that day would never come. Because once this war and her time in the North was over, she and Seth would be but a hazy memory.

She arrived two minutes before mass ended. As people filtered out, she looked for Seth. He wasn't there. She was surprised to see Leticia walk out with a spring in her step accompanied by Andy Jackson. She had seen them sneak off several times after a late night party. Father Beau stepped out and closed the door behind him.

Eleanor asked, "Father Beau, is Seth here?"

"Your husband? No, he doesn't come to mass, ever. You didn't know that?"

She shrugged her shoulders. "I heard he's not Catholic."

Father Beau's brows quirked.

She explained, "We're still getting to know each other."

He tapped his nose with his finger. "Ah, smart you two are. Better to marry than burn with lust for each other."

She almost laughed in his face at how far his insinuations were opposite from the truth. She pressed her lips tightly together to suppress a giggle. "Precisely. Anyway, he told me to meet him here."

"Well, you'll find him over by the dock, where they load off all the equipment."

"'Kay, thanks."

She made her way over and found Seth standing with his hands in his brown coat pockets at the edge of the dock gazing out toward the other side of the Mackenzie River where Camp Canol was. Beyond, the mountains were snow-capped. An eagle soared over the water and caught a trout. It alighted on a nearby jack spruce. Its talons ripped the scales apart, sank into the pink iridescent meat and sawed the meat from the fish's flimsy bones to swallow it.

When he heard her footsteps, he turned and gave her a small smile. He said, "I'm sorry. I didn't realise how much time had passed."

She joined him at his side and said, "I really took you for a good Christian man."

"What makes you think I'm not?"

"You're not in mass, and I heard you're not Catholic. Are you Anglican?"

"No, what does being Christian mean to you?"

"You go to church, follow the Ten Commandments to the best you can, believe there's a God, and one day when you die, you go to Heaven."

"Seems to depend a lot on what you do, doesn't it?"

"That's the kicker, I like that I'm in charge of my own destiny." Who was she kidding? All the choices she had made until now seemed insufficient for making her happy. She sighed, "It just seems that no matter how hard I've tried, it hasn't been good enough, for my parents, even for me. Just seems kind of empty, you know?"

Seth shared, "Maybe there's something more to it than what they preach every Sunday, some piece that completes the puzzle. I don't know much myself except from what I remember in my younger years."

"Didn't your parents make you go to church your entire life? Mine sure did. Right up until I left to come here."

He didn't answer for a few minutes. She wondered if he'd been offended by what she'd asked about his parents. She stood in uncomfortable silence, rigid in preparation for a comeback.

His voice broke on the first word. "My pa did all those religious things. Of course, my ma, sisters, and I followed along. But that's all it was, a set of cold, hard rules. We did follow them. My pa was a quiet man but when he used the leather strap, he whipped us hard. I flinched every time, not from the pain but from his humming. He found genuine pleasure in making our backsides red. I even asked my friends if their fathers whipped them the way mine did. I understand why I needed a spank sometimes, but how he did it was godless. He died when I was nine from pneumonia. My ma followed soon after. She wouldn't eat or sleep."

"I'm sorry, that's terrible."

He nodded and gave a small smile. "That's when our lives took a turn for the better. See, my pa and ma followed all the right rules, but there was no joy in their lives. Our home was absent of smiles, laughter. My sisters and I would run wild in the woods because our parents would look at us sternly if we let out a single whoop of excitement in the house. Our noise sometimes led to no supper. So we moved our play time outside. We came across an Athabaskan Dene settlement. There we met Nasnana, the matriarch who furnished the cabin we're living in now. Instead of shooing us away, she taught us everything we needed to know about the earth. When my parents died, there was no other family to take us in. The families of our town decided it would be all right if she cared for us as long as she brought us to church every Sunday. Would you believe it that she sat through every service with us?" He cracked a wide smile. "Everyone in church thought they were making strides in reforming her and keeping us in line. Little did they know that our lives were just fine without them. For all their fruitless faith, or so much as I could tell, we found joy in the discovering of ours."

"Where are your sisters now? How many do you have?"

"Three, two married, the other not. Shaina's on the Atlantic Coast, and Christina is in Edmonton. Those are the two that are married. Rowena is at the front right now as a nurse."

"What about Nasnana? I've never seen her."

"No, you wouldn't have."

"What does that mean?" An edge crept into Eleanor's voice.

He bit his lip and hesitated before saying, "You've turned a blind eye to all those who don't look like you or who are different: Charlotte and the coloured troops who have done most of the back breaking work on this project. Why wouldn't you do the same to those whose customs and history are so different from yours?" He turned to fully face her and gave her a gentle smile. "It takes intention to widen our horizons to include all who walk beside us."

Although she had a great urge to look away, to ignore the truth, his compassion grounded her gaze to his. She lay bare before him, expecting barbs in words and action; for she had received them too often more than not from everyone except her immediate family.

Before he could say anything, she looked away and said, "Um, you know, I'm really happy you're not a goody-two shoes Christian. I swore to myself I wouldn't ever marry someone who my parents would approve of, even if—well, you know." She gestured between the two of them. She almost said *even if it was a sham marriage*.

His grinned. "One more good reason you married me."

She lightly chuckled as they walked toward the airstrip for the checkup.

As soon as they arrived in Fort Norman, Seth walked her to Dr. Barnes's home. Then he left to get some supplies for their home from the general store.

Dr. Barnes asked Eleanor, "So how are you feeling? Any concerns?"

"I've got terrible heartburn, throwing up everyday, and some blood, I think that covers it all."

"How much blood?" His voice was tight.

"The last few days, it's been light."

"What colour? Pink, dark brown?"

"Light pink."

"That's quite all right. Please keep an eye on it. You're getting sufficient rest?"

"My job requires a lot of sitting. So, yes, most of the day I'm resting."

"Good, good. The baby is too young for me to hear a heartbeat. That will come later. I'll see you in about a month's time unless your bleeding becomes heavier and changes to a deep red. Have a good day."

Just as he was showing her out after she paid him, a rattle came from his back door. He excused himself to see what the commotion was. Instead of letting herself out, she inched toward the back to see why Dr. Barnes was furtively whispering.

There was Charlotte, her hand raised and covered in raw egg.

She shrieked, "I thought you said it was going to stop!"

"I'm sorry, my dear, I've been speaking to the parents—"

"It's not working! Those rats still threw eggs all over my rocks."

Charlotte's outburst made Eleanor cover her ears and wince. Eleanor stepped on a groaning floorboard. Dr. Barnes's and Charlotte's heads swivelled toward her interruption.

"Charlotte, why don't you go back home? I'll come over and help you clean up," Dr. Barnes said in a soothing voice.

Charlotte frowned at Eleanor before she opened the door with her slimy hand and hobbled over to her home.

Without a sigh or frustrated hiss, Dr. Barnes grabbed a cloth, wet it, and wiped down his door and handle.

"How do you handle her?" Eleanor asked.

He sighed, "Some days are easier than others. The mistreatment from others doesn't help. Would you like a glass of water?"

She nodded.

"Let me ask you this," he said as he filled her glass and passed it to her, "if the whole world were against you, wouldn't you want someone in your corner, someone you could call a friend?"

"Sure, who wouldn't?"

"That's what Charlotte needs. It's not about handling but about serving those less fortunate."

"Haven't the less fortunate made choices, chosen certain paths that brought them to where they are now?" Revulsion curdled in Eleanor's stomach.

Dr. Barnes's bushy eyebrows were drawn in slight surprise. "And you haven't?"

She deflated. Not only did he wound her pride but also hedged dangerously close to detangling the threads of her past she wanted to keep knotted and tucked away.

SETH

PART II

The Shave

Mankind is divisible into two great classes:
hosts and guests.
Max Beerbohm
Hosts and Guests

Chapter 10

"Hold up!" Seth ran toward the coloured engineer corps with a raised hand. "This the new shipment of pipe we've been expecting?"

"Yes, sir!" Private Cyril answered.

"Here, let me help." Seth bent down and wrapped his already dirt-dusted hands around the four inch pipe and lifted. A small groan escaped. Private Cyril lifted the other end of the twenty-two foot long pipe. They walked over in unison to where each incoming nine thousand tons of pipe shipment was to be placed, by the entry to the docks, and gently laid down the pipe.

Seth and Private Cyril continued in this way along with the other coloured men until they had made a significant dent in the pile that had arrived by barge.

Just as Seth picked up the end of another pipe, Private Cyril pointed beyond Seth's shoulder. "You expecting news?"

Seth looked behind him and saw Tadzea walking toward him. "Sorry, mind finding someone to take my place?"

"Course. Looks important. He from one of the Dene settlements nearby?"

Seth answered, "Yes." He turned on his heel and approached Tadzea, placing a hand on his shoulder. "Found him?"

Tadzea grinned, the snake tattoo climbing up his neck and curling under his chin widening. "Almost dead. Not even his wife and child knew when he'd return. It's good I found him. Your surveyor shouldn't go on his own. Next time it could be worse."

"Nick can be stubborn. He's not pulling that stunt again. Almost froze his butt in a snowstorm last winter, I heard. He was warned that without a proper guide he could have almost been killed. Yakecen needs to show him the way. I'm grateful for your help and Yakecen's. You both will be well compensated."

"Thank you. Yakecen and his family have invited you to supper. Oh, and your new wife, of course, she's welcome."

Seth blew through his mouth as he pinched the bridge of his nose. He had hoped he could go to sleep early. Once Peter had found out that Seth was falling asleep at his desk every night, he offered him his bed from six to ten that night while Peter spent time with Julia. Staying up late these last few nights, correction, barely sleeping at all, wasn't doing him any good. Yet he felt he couldn't say no to Yakecen's invitation since they had grown up together.

"I accept. I'll be there when the sun touches the little mount's nose."

Tadzea nodded and clasped Seth's shoulder. "I'll be there too." He ran off toward the Dene settlement.

What would Eleanor's response be to the invitation? Would she laugh at his face and decline in a way that would belittle his friendship with the local tribe?

Once Seth arrived at his office, he set his papers in order for the next day's order of importance. Strange enough, Eleanor wasn't at her desk typing out his forms or notes. It was Monday, a full work day and she wasn't there.

His chest constricted with an urgency to make sure Eleanor was all right. He cleared torn roots and hopped over some boulders to reach the cabin. The door was slightly ajar. He peeked in and almost collided with Eleanor who was just about to round the door with a full load of laundry. The laundry smelt like fresh water and pine. He avoided the crash by gripping her forearms and slowly easing her out at arm's length. "I'm so sorry, uh, I didn't mean—you weren't at work. So are you okay?"

Her startled features slid into a cool facade. A beat later, she sighed. "I know I was supposed to work this morning, but the morning sickness was just too much." She looked down at his hands still gripping her forearms.

He dropped them immediately.

She continued, "Julia came over this morning to check in on me. I asked her to get a message to Leticia asking if she could take over for me until noon. She wasn't there?"

"No, she wasn't."

"Figures," Eleanor muttered. "As you can see, I've been busy with the laundry and heaving into the shrubs. I think my stomach is finally settling. Do you need me right away?"

He rubbed his hands together. "No, not about work. Yakecen, the local Dene guide our surveyor uses, invited me to dinner with his family."

She shrugged her shoulders. "Sure, you don't need my permission."

"Well, he's also invited you."

"Oh." Her forehead creased as her lips thinned.

"You know I don't expect anything from you, even if others do. This is not what we're about. It's only if you want to."

She asked, "They're real Dene Indians?"

Those were the words he least expected. He answered, "Yes."

"All right, I'll go."

He opened his mouth to ask if she was sure. Her eyes suggested she'd cut his words short before he could say anything. He nodded. "We leave around four o'clock. We'll take a jeep down some of the road and walk a trail from there."

"I'll finish hanging these pieces, and then I'll be at work." She nudged him out of the way.

Seth watched her bring her basket to the line he had put up to dry their clothes. He had made it clear that he would wash and dry his own. Thinking of his wash, he realised he needed to get on it tonight; he was down to his last two pairs of socks and his last pair of long johns.

The decision to do his own laundry wasn't because he enjoyed the chore. He wanted to ensure that Eleanor wasn't feeling any compulsion from him to fit into the traditional mould of a wife. His decision to marry her wasn't for any romantic link. It stemmed from his loyalty to Paul and his family, and how he owed them so much. They had paid for his schooling, paid to sweep his dirt under the rug during school, and had highly recommended him to receive this position at Canol.

He remembered when they had arrived at the Rensselaer Polytechnic Institute in New York how they stood before the ancient brick baking in the sweltering heat of a fading summer. The tides of seasonal change would soon sweep through; there the war between seasons was more dramatic than it was up north. He looked forward to experiencing its effects.

Paul and he had been dreaming of attending since they had been fourteen.

Since it was Seth's first time leaving Canada and family, he was a little unsure whether he could succeed at the oldest technological university in the Western world.

Confident as always, Paul snorted. "We'll do just fine although I'll come out on top of our classes like I always do."

A quiet smirk appeared on Seth's face. He murmured, "That's what you think."

"Oh, you're going to pull that meek Jesus act you think makes me stop in my tracks. Get ready to turn the other cheek. You aren't getting any mercy from me."

"That's what you say every time."

One semester in, Seth committed a reprehensible blow to another student under the influence of drink that led to his imminent expulsion. Only Paul begging his father to sway the university with an enormous monetary gift saved Seth. So he owed Paul and his family his future.

He hadn't had a drop of alcohol since then.

He had made a marriage vow he intended to keep. His whole life was built on the pillar of keeping his word because his adopted family and Paul's family had ingrained the importance of doing so. Except for one, their lives were compelling testaments. His blood parents were discredited when their actions hadn't aligned with their words.

Peter, his second, said he was daft to not break his oath only this once.

He returned to his office and scanned the day's missives he had jotted down the night before and the project outcomes pinned to the corkboard on the wall behind his desk. The little trouble they had come across on Raider Island had put them behind in their production of the intended number of barrels of oil.

He had to admit that Paul had run a beautiful operation and had seamlessly transferred it into his care. Some days he had to intentionally banish the thought that he would mess it up. There was much to live up to and not just on the work front.

A pair of footsteps interrupted his thoughts. A young man stated, "The shipment of pipes is all done being laid out. We're sending the barge back out."

Seth concentrated his focus on the man in front of him and nodded. "Could you make sure one of the jeeps is ready for my personal use in about four hours? Please." Despite the fact that he was head of the operation and his orders were to be obeyed, Nasnana had so ingrained within him the necessity of thankfulness and service that he always said his please's and thank you's.

The young man nodded and stepped out. Seth sat down at his desk to finish his paperwork for the day.

At four o' clock, Seth piled his papers neatly upon his desk, grabbed his fur coat off his hook, put it on, strode out to get Eleanor from the cabin. She had come into work a little before noon and left a half hour before four to take down the laundry.

Blue jays hawked in the branches as his feet crunched upon the frozen soil, the scent of pine and sap still tinging the air. He wondered how Eleanor would handle Nasnana and her people. Eleanor's disdain for anything or anyone different grated on his nerves every time her mouth opened to spite. He knew it wasn't his job to change her. She would retreat even further and turn harder against those she believed deserved it. All he could do was be who he knew he needed to be, an aid in her time of need.

Just as he arrived at the house, she was stepping out wearing her coat, a grey Dutch bonnet, and her leather boots. Despite being fully dressed for the weather, she shivered. "Oh, you're here. I thought I was meeting you at the office."

He shook his head and waited for her to join him. They walked in comfortable silence toward the centre of camp life. He led her to the Quonset where a stationed jeep was ready to use. He nodded to the grease spotted young man who rolled out from underneath another vehicle checking who was taking out the jeep.

Seth walked Eleanor to the passenger side. He stood by and watched as she gave a calculating smile before opening her own door, getting in, and shutting it. He jogged to the driver's side, got in, and turned the engine on. He rolled it out on the road toward the local Dene encampment.

They didn't meet another vehicle on the road as they rumbled past a vast panorama of evergreens, birch, mountains, hills, hawks, and bushes that grew almost to the state of trees. A couple miles down the road, he parked the jeep on the road's shoulder and unbuckled. Eleanor followed suit. He grabbed a sack with gifts for the Dene children and pointed out the trail they would follow to the camp.

A minute in, Seth racked his brain trying to come up with a conversation piece that would help her open up. "It must have taken a lot of bravery to leave everything and everyone you knew to come here and make a life for yourself."

She gave him a sidelong glance as she pursed her lips. "It did. However, my whole life before this has been burdensome. When does muddling through life end? Will it ever become clear like a streak-free window?"

"I haven't lived long enough to answer that question with a clear conscience. All I know is that a clean window doesn't stay clean very long. In no time, it's dirty all over again. One way I see it is I'm locked into a room with all the pleasures I could ever want. You play and play with the same old, same old, and that's what it stays, same old. There's a window that gives you a view of a beautiful world on the other side. You put your back into cleaning it so that you can see the world you want to taste clearly. When the window gets dirty again, you keep striving to see beyond. The sad thing is, I don't think we'll ever leave that room, ever open that window until we pass through death to the other side. The greatest gift we can ever receive is a glimpse of that heaven beyond."

"So we're just supposed to die and then we'll get there. Do you believe there's something we have to do? Like be good?"

"Well, it seems that even the best of us aren't perfectly good. Can our good ever outweigh our bad? What if that door is locked from the outside and can only be opened by someone other than ourselves."

The mellow tones of the Dene language wrapped around Seth's ears as they walked into a clearing where log cabins sunk two to five feet into the ground dotted the mountainous landscape. A pair of Dene men were skinning a caribou kill, hung upside down by its hooves. Despite the blood on their hands and the gory muscular tissue glinting in the fading sun, they were smiling and nodding at some joke one of them had made. One caught Seth's eye and whooped and shouted out Nasnana's name.

Nasnana stepped out from her home seconds later, arms wide open, eager to greet her son.

He peeked at Eleanor before sprinting toward Nasnana to give her a long bear hug. Her hair smelled like earth and fresh wind. He nuzzled his nose past her cheek which bore the beginnings of wrinkles. Breathing the same air and feeling her laughter reverberate through their embrace—Seth was comforted that he was back home.

Nasnana broke their reunion first and playfully tapped Seth on the cheek. "This must be Eleanor. She looks just like you described her."

He placed his arm around his mother's shoulders and led her to Eleanor. "Nana, meet Eleanor. Eleanor, meet Nana."

Eleanor quickly glanced between the two of them. Her eyes widened like a hare trapped between two foxes. They stayed that way as Nasnana gathered her in her soft, large arms.

The apprehension faded from Eleanor's eyes. Seth wondered if, maybe, she was ready to embrace company she didn't normally keep.

His mother whispered lovingly, "It's so good to meet you. How do you like your pelts?"

Eleanor visibly slackened and smiled without abandon. "It's heaven on earth every single night."

"Seth hunted the bear himself. He brought it back here, and Tadzea skinned it and prepared the pelt."

Seth shrugged his shoulders and said, "Many of the men took it upon themselves to teach me how to hunt, skin, and prepare pelts so that I could provide for my own family one day."

Nasnana raised a single hand and dipped her head. "We know you live life differently, but I appreciate knowing that you know our ways and can share these ways with your children one day."

Seth asked, "Mother, how can I help prepare for dinner?"

She replied, "No, everything is done. Come inside. There's a nice fire roaring. I've placed some blankets around it where we can sit. I'll join you in a minute."

Seth led Eleanor through the storm shed passageway and into the main room. Her shivering stopped in as she dropped to her knees and comfortably settled on the blankets. He shrugged off his coat, and she followed suit. He sat opposite her.

Eleanor inspected her surroundings. In the main room was the fireplace on one side and the kitchen on the other. On either side of the fireplace hung some moosehide ornaments in the shape of a pair of moccasins hung by beaded leather ties. Beside her kitchen work table was a pile of handwoven baskets made from birch bark.

She cleared her throat and asked, "She knows this baby isn't yours, right?"

He wasn't too sure why her rebuttal of his possible claim over the baby bothered him this time when it had never affected him before. Was his ego bruised because Eleanor couldn't fathom he could ever be her lover? Yet he didn't expect her to feel anything about him except her well-vocalised contempt of his intrusion into her life. He assuaged his turbulent thoughts about Eleanor's baby. Tonight would be instrumental in bringing about a solution for its life.

He answered, "She knows."

Nasnana returned with Yakecen, his wife Peni, and Tadzea in tow. Peni's hair was braided elaborately. Her dress was lightly tanned and full of beaded designs in floral patterns. The sleeves were tasselled and swept down to her wrists.

Standing a foot taller than Peni, Yakecen's straight raven hair was tied back revealing a strong jawline. His broad, muscular chest was the opposite of his wife's petite build.

Nana spooned the steaming venison stew into some bowls. Peni placed platters of warm bread before the intimate dinner party. Once they sat in a circle, Eleanor and Peni on either side of Seth, Yakecen beside Peni, Tadzea beside Eleanor and then Nasnana across from Seth, Nasnana lifted her eyes and murmured something in the Dene tongue. She smiled and said, "Let's eat."

Nasnana made introductions. "Eleanor, this is Peni and Yakecen, her husband and local guide for the road surveyors in the area. Peni doesn't speak English." Nasnana turned to the woman and spoke in her native tongue. The woman smiled and held onto Nasnana's arm as she spoke fervently to her.

Nasnana turned to Eleanor and said, "She says she is grateful you are carrying the child so that she has the chance to have one. You have changed her life for the better."

Eleanor replied, "Please tell her I'm grateful she's taking the baby."

Nasnana turned to Peni and repeated Eleanor's words. Peni then turned from her matron and thrust out her wrist toward Eleanor and fingered one of her beaded bracelets. She slipped it off her wrist and displayed it before Eleanor.

Nasnana said, "She's giving it to you as a gift."

Eleanor smiled and said, "Thank you." She reached over and received it.

Peni looked at Seth. Her cheeks coloured slightly, and she looked up at him through her lashes. Seth returned her smile and nodded his thanks.

Eleanor didn't say much during the meal. Seth translated whenever Peni spoke. He, Nasnana, Yakecen, and Tadzea kept up most of the conversation, speaking in both languages so everyone could understand.

Eleanor took a bite of the stew. "Why did your people decide to settle here?"

Nasnana's eyes' twinkled as she munched on her stew. "Our people don't stay in one place. We move around and follow the animals. We hunt when they seek new hunting grounds. We follow their call."

Eleanor said, "Oh, I thought when I saw your homes—"

"We return every year to these homes when the season is right. Thank you for coming to my home. I wanted to meet you when Seth told me of your arrangement."

Seth regarded Evelyn's features and swallowed.

Evelyn responded. "Yes, Seth mentioned Yakecen and Peni would be willing to take the baby. I'm not in a position to care for it."

Nasnana said, "The spirits sometimes give us gifts larger than what we believe we can accept. They do this to teach us a valuable lesson about ourselves and those we've been called to serve."

After their meal, on the way back to the jeep, Seth asked Eleanor, "What do you think of my mother?"

She replied, "Is Peni, the woman you've chosen to take care of the baby, like your mother?"

He tented his fingers and swallowed. "I don't want to choose for you. This is your, uh, your decision, no one else's. As for whether she's like my mother, she's wise for her years, or so Nana tells me. She holds to my people's values. She and Yakecen have prayed to the spirits for a baby, but they haven't been able to conceive for many years."

"I'm glad she's like your mom," Eleanor smiled.

"Really?" He gave a huge smile of relief.

"I can see how much your mother means to you. You know, when I was younger, my mom—well, your mom reminds me a little of how my mom used to be."

Eleanor gritted her teeth. "After a certain while, she was different and was never the same again. Thank you for bringing me this evening. It's brought me some peace."

Seth smiled to himself, "Even though our marriage isn't going to last and you and I probably won't be in each other's lives once the baby is born, my mom and I want you to know that you will always be welcome to call our people family."

Eleanor blurted, "Speaking of family, Peni has feelings for you."

He threw back his head and laughed. "Why would you think that?"

She gave him a disbelieving look and shook her head. "You're blind."

He blew through his mouth. "When I was growing up, her brother Tadzea and the other boys my age, including Yakecen, were playmates. She's five years our junior. Her brother told me that she had feelings, but nothing ever happened because I went off to school in New York. When I came back, she was married to Yakecen. I didn't realise—naw, that's not it."

Eleanor offered, "She can have you anytime."

Seth put out his arm gently to stop her movement. He turned her shoulders toward him. How could she be so cavalier about his promise to keep her and only her at the centre of his duty and his service at home? "I'm not going to jeopardise my promise to you by bringing Peni or any other woman into the mix. If my focus shifts, I can't be the help that I can be."

Eleanor chewed on her lip. She screwed her eyes and glared at him.

He could feel the heat rising in her small body soon to be expelled. He readied himself for lashing words that would spell out how much she didn't need him. Instead, she turned fast on her heel and stomped the rest of the way back to the jeep.

Walking several steps behind, he wrestled with why she loosely kept him to his word. Would she feel less guilty if he deserted her because she was planning on breaking her marriage vows?

The new knowledge that Peni could care for him began to unravel his thinking. To be sure, she was beautifully made.

Though her forehead was prominent, her dark eyes arrested whoever watched her. Her lithe form, properly hidden behind her masterfully beaded clothing which she made herself, could entice many men. He remembered all the smiles she used to give him, even the smile she gave him tonight.

He thought he saw movement in the trees to his left. It was only a squirrel climbing the bark of a birch tree. He imagined pressing Peni against it, having his way with such a willing partner. He exhaled gruffly and squeezed his forehead.

The slamming of the jeep door alerted him that they were back where they had parked it. He looked through the windshield and saw a fuming wife. He looked at the trees one more time. The image he had entertained blew away like smoke on the wind. Why couldn't he stay in his dream world longer (for that was what it could only be; Peni was taken, and there was no way he would separate two people who had made some form of promise to stay true), and why did he end up with a wife who hated the fact he was around?

The last temptation is the greatest treason:
to do the right deed for the wrong reason.
T. S. Eliot

Chapter 11

Late October 1943

Peter walked into the office laid a hand on his shoulder. "You doing okay? I mean I heard the slam of a jeep door as I was walking by the garage. I saw you both. Trouble in paradise?"

"I didn't think keeping this promise was going to be *this* difficult or complicated."

Peter's shoulders shook as he snickered. "I told ya, when women are in the mix, especially ones who've decided to work up here in the middle of nowhere, you aren't going to get simple. Take Julia. When we started canoodling, I was certain she was only wanting what I'm willing to give, a good time. Agh, now I'm thinking she wants more. Naw, I know she wants more. She's a good girl, but I'm not wanting to settle down anytime soon, you know?"

"Why is that?" Seth asked.

"I still want to travel, see more, h—ll, okay, I want to see more women, be with more women. Anything wrong with that?"

"How long before you realise you're not satisfied with your lifestyle? I mean why can't you travel, do the things you want to do, and be the person you want to be with someone who's willing to stick by your side no matter what, who loves you? There's a sense of home with that kind of scenario."

"It's a shame you got shacked up with a woman who doesn't give you any of that."

Seth shook his head, "It's not about me."

"From whatever you've told me, your whole life has been about helping other people. It's good, but don't you want to live for yourself for a change?"

Seth tapped his pen on his desk and bit his lip. Last evening's image in the trees flashed in his mind. He put down the pen and said, "I don't know what good can come from it."

After dealing with a leakage on one of the oil storage tanks, he checked in on Eleanor, who seemed determined not to acknowledge his quick visit to their cabin. She barely gave him a quick nod when he poked his head in to ask if everything was all right.

Seth decided to visit his mother and, perhaps, see a certain other woman.

A quick glance around the Dene camp told him most of the men were still gone on their moose hunt. The shorter days and cold weather bringing goosebumps and runny noses reminded him that these were the last few times they could hunt moose and bring it to their families for resources before the harsh winter set in.

His people wore snowshoes during the winter when they hunted for smaller game. Moose were too large and heavy to carry back to camp over several feet of snow. Also, they were prone to losing their fat, even their lives by starvation.

Seth's mother exited her home. He always forgot how big it really was; for though the outside of the cabin looked small, most of the house was underground with packed layers of earth insulating the home. There were several rooms within, large enough for a few families of one clan to call home.

Nasnana gave him a squeeze. "I always love it when you visit me," she said.

He kissed the top of her head. "I wanted to know what you thought about the situation between Eleanor and me."

She pinched his cheek. "I know why you married her. You're a good man. It isn't easy to put aside what you want to help someone who can't even see how much help they need."

He took her hands in his. "On the way back to the jeep, she mentioned, no, stated that Peni has feelings for me. I laughed because…. " His next words died down. He felt foolish when his mother shook her head.

"For all the wisdom you've learned over the years, you cannot see the trappings of a woman's heart. Eleanor can."

"She gave me permission to do what I wanted with whoever I wanted, but it's not what I want."

"Isn't it?"

He sighed, "I do and I don't."

"It doesn't help to build a dam to all that you feel just like it doesn't help the fish when we build dams to manipulate what is so mighty in its own right. You must let the flow stay course, but it doesn't mean you can't wield its power."

"You're saying I need to accept what I'm feeling and thinking so that I can decide honestly."

"Mmm, hmm, then you can find the reasons you need to support your decision."

He glanced around hesitatingly. "Is she around?"

His mother held his hands and patted them. "I think she's near the water where you used to go fishing."

"Thank you for your wisdom."

"Thank you for receiving it."

He kissed her temple. "Of course."

He exited Nana's home and stood still, one boot pointing toward the trail back to camp and the other pointing to the water.

Though he knew which way was the wisest, the way that was most helpful in keeping his promise with proper focus, he strayed toward the water, feeling an exciting pull to the unknown, or, what his body deeply longed for.

Peni crouched as she dipped a bowl into the water. She called out in her tongue, "You think you can sneak up on me, but you should know better."

Seth chuckled. "I should know better. All those times your brothers and I tried to scare you, you calmly turned and dared us to do better."

"Yes, I'm glad you've come back. We all missed you."

He took a step closer. "How much?"

She shook her head. "You always tried to make those around you say more nice things about you than they should."

He put up his hands in mock surrender. "You're right. May I help you carry your bowl?"

"Yes, thank you." Before turning her eyes toward her abode, she stared at him through her thick black lashes.

Their steps toward her house grew quicker than the last. He opened the door with eager hands. He placed her bowl upon the kitchen table. He took a step closer to her, his hands itching to touch her. She rounded the table one step at a time, slow like a panther sizing up her prey.

Long ago, Peni had given him his first kiss. It had been cut short by Tadzea's and Yakecen's arrival. He told himself he and she could never work because he was leaving for school. Here she was now. Tadzea and Yakecen were so far away.

"Do you want—?" His breath came out ragged as if the excitement coursing through his body was as if he were opening a gift.

She opened her thin lips to answer and wedged herself between the table and him. The light brush of her body against his propelled his lips to crash into hers. Her already open mouth beckoned his tongue to twirl with hers. She moulded the planes of her body against his. A primal call to release snaked itself around his actions like a vice grip desperate to be satiated. His lips broke from hers as he fumbled with his belt, shucking it to the side like a fetter that had kept him prisoner too long. She shifted closer.

He unzipped his pants, completely focused on the pleasure to come and stopped cold.

She pulled back a little and asked, "What is it?"

He slowly zipped up his pants, training his eyes away from hers. He bent his head and gripped the table as he said, "I don't love you."

Her hands caressed his chin and moved it up so she could look into his eyes. "I've loved you since I was a little girl."

He cradled her hands. "I can't. I haven't been with a woman in so long. I'm desperate. I'm not even seeing you. All I see is your body, and right now that's the only thing that matters to me. You don't deserve that. Do you love Yakecen?"

"In a way, but it's not the same."

"Then focus on that way. Make that way what's most important. I have someone that needs me even though she doesn't know it."

She touched her swollen lips with her fingertips. "You're right. I wish it had turned out differently." She smoothed down her tunic and stepped away from him. "Thank you for helping me bring in the bowl."

Seth ran his hand through his hair. "You're welcome." He grinned. "I would love to hear some stories from the years that I've been gone, but I don't think this is the time. When Yakecen returns, I'll visit."

She replied with a smile, "Until then."

He yanked her door open and speed walked back to the camp.

When he entered his cabin, Eleanor was lying on her side and reading her book.

Her eyes did a quick sweep to him. "There you are." She returned her attention to her book. "We're going to be needing some more firewood soon. Are you going to chop some up?"

He rolled his eyes and stomped outside. The block on which he chopped the wood had the axe wedged in its surface. He rolled up his sleeves and puffed as he yanked the blade out of its hold. He went to the pile, grabbed a log, and laid it on the chopping block. Placing his feet squarely and his shoulders following, he swung down the axe. All that existed was the wood needing to be chopped and the tools to do it. Minutes blurred into what seemed like hours. Sweat streamed down his face; his shirt was soaked. He swung and roared until a pair of boots entered his field of vision. He suddenly stopped and kept his axe above his shoulder ready to swing. He barked, "What?"

"What's got you all hot and bothered?" She crossed her arms, her lips in a pout.

"Why do you care?"

"Well, I was looking forward to a nice quiet evening, but instead I'm forced to listen to a disgruntled bear outside my home. Can't you do it quietly?"

He scoffed. "See, this is what drives me crazy about you! You don't give me peace. It's always about you. You don't care about the needs of others until it affects you. You want wood, you don't want wood. I do all I can to care for you! What else do you want?"

"I want—" she hollered then faltered. Her lower lip trembled. She swirled her back to him, her shoulders hunched forward.

His knuckles gripped the handle of the axe—his knuckles white as hard packed snow—their colour returned as he carefully moved it away from his shoulder and dropped it to the ground. His breath which had been stolen in anger returned to its regular rhythm.

He saw her begin to shake her head and slowly turn back to him. She whispered, "I just want Paul." Her hand flew to her mouth. She inhaled and then shrieked like a dying animal begging release from pain. Her legs crumpled. She was going to fall to the ground, but Seth closed the distance and upheld her in his arms. Her shudders and wailing eventually slowed. His shirt was not only wet with sweat but also drenched from her tears. It stuck to his chest. He stroked her shoulder with his palm to give a measure of comfort.

She vehemently shook her head and said, "No, no, no, no, no, you doing that doesn't help, doesn't change the situation. Don't touch me."

He raised his hands. "I know it doesn't do a thing. I'm sorry. You have to move on. He's not coming back."

"How do you know? Maybe he'll come back. Maybe—"

His fingers slid down the sides of his jaw. "I just know."

Her lips stilled in an instant. Her neck whipped into position as if she were a cobra ready to attack. "You know something that I don't know. Tell me."

"I don't think it will help."

"Who are you to make that judgement call? I don't want your protection. I just want an answer!"

"Major Burns, Paul, is marrying my youngest sister Rowena."

Her fire didn't burn out. Instead it burned hotter. "You knew this whole time, and you didn't say anything!"

She marched off toward a tree, grabbed a light branch, and ripped it off the tree's trunk.

Seth jumped to the side as he attempted to escape her swing.

She snapped her heaving body to attention. "I need to write him a letter to let him know what's happened. I'm sure he'll choose me over her."

"I've already written to him and told him about your pregnancy."

She cried fresh tears. "That wasn't for you to do."

"I did it because I wanted him to do the right thing by you."

"You're lying!" she yelled. "I bet you didn't tell him. Or if you did, you asked him to stay with your sister."

Seth understood that logic and reason were the furthest things away from her mind right this second, but the incredulity of her statement was ridiculous. He chuckled mirthlessly. "What?"

"You heard me."

"Why would I ask the man who cheated on my sister to stay with her when he's proven he's not trustworthy in that area of his life? I wrote a letter to my sister asking her to end the engagement. Although Paul is my best friend, I don't approve of everything he does."

"Is your sister still going to marry him?"

He hung his head and nodded. "Yup, she's completely in love with him, and he's a real charmer."

She glanced up at him, her hands on her hips. He steeled himself for the fact that she would now make his life a living hell. She asked, "Why did you marry me?"

"You needed help." What good would it do if he confessed to marrying her because Paul asked him to take care of her no matter what? It would only prolong her moving on.

"Wow, you only married me to satisfy some hero complex you have. You're just a simpering man wanting to save a damsel in distress. Is it for your vanity? You're too stubborn or dumb to give up."

He gave a self-deprecating smile. "No matter how many names you call me or how far you pull me down, you can't get rid of me."

"The show's over. You don't need to put this much effort into being a dutiful husband."

"You're wrong."

She taunted, "Am I? Why is that?"

"I seriously considered leaving you to fend for yourself. I didn't need this. Then I found you in the kitchen convulsing. When you woke up, I decided I'd marry you, for you and the baby. So you could have a chance at a life, a life that, frankly, Paul helped steal away from you by putting you in this position. Nana, the Denes, Paul, and his family gave me opportunities for a good life. I thought I could do the same for someone else."

She proceeded to sit on the chopping block and hung her head between her legs.

Seth squatted low in front of her and looked into her face. He put his hand on her knee and gently shook it. "Do you need water? Are you okay?"

"It wasn't him that got me into this mess. I pushed for it because I was desperate. I deserve this."

Seth turned his face away, his ears turning pink. "He knew better. Listen, that moment is in the past. You can't change it. Now you have the opportunity to have respect and a good life. I'm doing the best I can to give you your best shot at both."

Grimly smiling, she said, " You DO have a hero complex."

A cool touch on his trimmed beard shocked him. He looked into her eyes as she cupped his chin. Could he safely anchor there?

A tear slipped down her cheek as she whispered, "You've been a rock from the start and you were conveniently the obvious person for me to lash out on. I don't think I'm worthy of the life you're fighting to give me because I've fought against it and fought you on everything. I'm sorry. "

Her apology struck him. It was the first time he had ever seen her humble herself. He said, "I forgive you."

Chapter 12

Eleanor's light snoring kept him from falling asleep, not because it was a sound that could keep him up (he could sleep through any noise) but because the sound piqued his awareness of her presence, a presence that, perhaps, didn't hate him at this very moment, one that might even be a tad grateful. Could it be that he had finally broken through her spiky exterior to touch a thawing heart?

Her head was cradled by her arm on one side of the couch while he sat at the opposite end. Her stockinged feet were a hair's breadth from his thigh. She gave a short cough and moved to get comfortable. Her feet were now fully planted on his thigh. He drew breath in and hardly dared to breathe for fear she would wake and complain he had facilitated her touch.

His arm rested on the back of the couch. He spied her novel *Pride and Prejudice* lying on her stomach. He had never read the novel but knew that every woman swooned over the ever-adored Mr. Darcy. He shimmied it out from under her fingers and opened it to where it lay open.

A whole passage was underlined which read the following: "Vanity and pride are different things, though the words are often used synonymously. A person may be proud without being vain. Pride relates more to our opinion of ourselves, vanity to what we would have others think of us."

Therein lay the synchronicity of their tumultuous relationship. Pride versus vanity. He lay the book back down on his lap and wondered how his pride had played such a part in the momentary yet momentous breakdowns since they had met.

As he pondered, Eleanor croaked, "Were you—"

"Hmm?"

"Were you the one who heard me play the piano that night?

If he admitted it, would it be taking two steps backward? Storing the wins he had gained so far would keep this situation in fragile peace. "I was."

"Why did you leave?"

"When I heard the music drift from the mess hall, I was curious. I grew to love music after Rowena went into musical theatre. When I opened the door and heard it unfiltered—what you were playing was so personal. It was like some memory you needed to relive so you could reach some peace. I left because I wasn't invited to be the witness. No one was." Deflated, he turned to look at her.

"Thank you for leaving." Her throat constricted.

He got up and felt her feet slide down his thigh as he did. He grabbed the pitcher of water and filled a cup and handed it to her. She took it gratefully and gulped it down.

He refilled it when she was done and placed it on the floor beside her. He took his place, and her feet slid back toward her end.

He handed *Pride and Prejudice* back to Eleanor. "Interesting passage you highlighted."

She read it. "Which one do you think I am?"

"I feel like this is a trap."

She rolled her eyes. "Scared I'm going to shave your beard in your sleep?"

Well! It was clear which one she thought he was. He spluttered trying to rein in his guffaw. "I can do without my beard. I already have."

"I don't believe you can do it again."

"Up to you, whatever you want to believe."

"Fine, let's make a bet."

"Ugh, all right. What's the bet?"

"You have a good time with a woman, and I'll leave you alone. You don't, and the beard is off."

Was this woman trying to live vicariously through him? What was her fascination with shoving him in another direction when he wasn't trying to lay a hand on her?

He hung his head in shame. "I already did or almost."

She whipped her head in his direction. "What happened?"

"I went back to my mother's and saw Peni. I was flooded with—it's hard to describe. We went back to her cabin, but I stopped."

"Why?" Her eyes were wary, her voice pitched low with hesitancy.

He listed the reasons on his fingers. "I don't love her. She's married. There's so many reasons why I stopped, but I didn't want to treat her in that way when it wouldn't mean anything other than satisfying myself in the moment. The repercussions of going through with it—I'm not a reckless man. I want to be with the person I love. Whenever I find that love."

"Hmm, you almost had me gushing over a good story, but, tsk, disappointing. I win. Beard is coming off. You could have lied and said nothing."

"It's not how I conduct my relationships, I mean, any relationship no matter how estranged or how close. I'm an honest man." Not telling her the whole truth about why he married her jabbed his conscience.

"It's true. You are even when no one wants you to be."

"You mean you'd rather not hear what I have to say." Tension clung to the air, a gloved hand wrapped around a brittle shard of glass squeezing until…. "Anyway, you won, that's fair. I'll shave it in the morning."

She laughed villainously. "Nu, uh, I'll be doing the job."

"Okay, I trust you." He smiled, amused by her raised brows and open mouth.

"You do?" Disbelief coated her tone.

"Yes, because it seems we've come to a truce. At least we don't hate each other. Maybe we can even say we don't mind being in each other's company?"

She hesitated. "Maybe."

He got up to make her dinner. He fried the drumsticks on high and then stuck them in the oven to allow the juices to sit inside and cook. Then he boiled some carrots, fried them in lard with onions and tossed them into the oven with the chicken. The flitter of pages flipping was his companion as he hummed a tune, a dish towel slung over his shoulder.

Eleanor noted, "'All I Do Is Dream of You' from *Sadie McKee*, the Joan Crawford film."

Seth smiled. "That's right, did you see it?"

"I did. It gave me hope that I could do the same, work my way out of poverty. My family and I had just lost everything due to the Depression but especially from some unfortunate circumstances that I would never have seen coming. All our so-called higher-up friends turned their backs on us."

He paused his cleanup and faced her. "I'm really sorry you and your family suffered. Thank you for sharing with me."

She smiled at him and then returned to her reading.

Not much was said during dinner. He looked over at Eleanor a few times and noted that she regarded him with a look he couldn't peg.

Once they had both finished eating, he got up to clear the plates and wash them, but Eleanor put out her hand to stop him. "I'll do it."

"I don't mind. Why don't you rest while I clear up?"

"I've rested enough today. I need to stretch my legs anyway. Why don't you finish up that small wood pile you've got going outside?" She winked. "That's something I can't do."

"Fair enough, though for the record, you can do it. When that baby is out and you've recovered, I'll show you how. You're strong enough." He exited the house and went to work on his chore.

He hewed enough logs to work up a good sweat. He lifted his gloved hand to wipe the perspiration off his brow and looked into the house through the window. While Eleanor was washing the dishes, she looked up and caught Seth's gaze. Seth gave her a small smile before cutting more logs in half.

When he was done, he went down to the frigid MacKenzie River to wash his face, neck, and behind his ears. He didn't want to soil the water she used in the wash basin.

When he entered the cabin, there was a kitchen chair set in the middle of the floor. Eleanor approached him with a dish towel and his shaving blade.

He asked, "What's this?"

"Did you already forget our little bet?"

He tipped his head back in surrender. "All right. Let's get this over with."

She bit her lip. "Who said it'll be quick? I'm going to make this as painfully long as possible." She held up her hand. "I promise not to cut you."

He settled on the chair. The brush of her warm hands as she wrapped the dish towel around his neck sent shivers down his core.

Wanting a distraction from her touch, he asked, "Have you ever done this?"

"Hush now. You'll make me cut you." She slid the blunt end of the blade down his throat. Then she opened the canister of shaving cream and dabbed the cream with a fat brush all over his beard.

He eyed the sharp edge as it crept closer to his exposed neck. With a clean swoop, she shaved off a portion and wiped the blade on a fresh towel. He exhaled shakily.

"Are you nervous?" she purred.

He was determined to remain stoic and keep his wits about him.

Glide after glide, his eyes strayed from the point on the wall he had chosen to her delicate jawline and slightly parted lips, her pearly white teeth peeping out to entice his gaze. What did she taste like?

Her murmur shattered the spell he was under. "I used to do this for my father. He's been very ill these past few years, hardly ever leaves his bed. My mother is able to, but he sometimes ended up with a small surface nick. I always looked forward to that ritual with him every Sunday."

Looking out at the corner of his eyes, he could see her cheek graced by a single tear.

She caught his surreptitious gaze and quickly averted her eyes.

After a few more glides of the shaving blade, she announced, "Done." She unwrapped the towel around his neck and dipped it in the nearby basin of water and wiped away the remaining cream and straggling beard hairs.

She put out a finger to flick away a single hair. She slid her finger along his smooth jawline.

Instinctively, his hand cupped her fingers to his cheek. The inside of her wrist was a breath away from his lips. He halted any further contact, worried she would bolt and the magic would dissolve.

She slipped her hand from his and turned toward the water basin. "Here," she held it toward him. "Mind filling this up?"

"Sure," he grabbed it, his gravelly voice was foreign to his ears. She didn't step away as he rose from the chair. There was only a few inches between them. Her eyes couldn't settle on his for more than a second. Her gaze dipped to his lips.

The air crackled.

Suddenly, she turned on her heel and walked away. Her fleeing stole all the warmth from where he stood.

He looked numbly at the basin in his hands. Clean water, right.

Once he stepped outside, he dumped the filmy water onto the dirt. He tread toward the river, his mind replaying the previous confusing scene. He reached the river, filled the basin, and splashed his face. He needed to be sharp for what could come next when he returned to the cabin.

When he opened their front door, he spotted Eleanor sitting on one end of the couch. He shucked off his boots and placed them neatly beside the door. He sat on the other end of the couch and grabbed his journal. Just as he was about to write, she asked, "You don't have any work tonight?"

"No, well, yes, some, but I thought I'd take a break and get to it in the morning. Would you like me to leave? I know I'm usually—actually I'm never here so I understand if you'd like the place to yourself."

She shook her head and smiled. "No, just as you said, it's out of the ordinary."

He returned to his thoughts. The breakthrough in their relationship, the laying down of arms and stilling of gnashing teeth, shook some of his mind's gears loose a bit. He needed to write down his thoughts whether they made sense or not so he could turn whatever wires of tension into intentional movement toward a better future with her. Whatever that looked like, however long it lasted, he knew that he had come to take Paul's place at the time he did for a reason.

His mind wandered to Rowena. He had hoped that she, in her own time and way, would see some sign that Paul wasn't worthy of her affection. However, Seth hadn't received word from her after sending her a letter to reconsider her decision, not even word on when the wedding was to take place.

He was at peace having voiced his concerns about Paul's infidelity to Rowena. Though Paul was his closest friend, his treatment of Rowena was a carte blanche Seth couldn't ignore. He wished Paul the best and hoped he would understand why he couldn't in good conscience give his blessing.

If Paul were to give up Rowena and claim Eleanor for his own, how would he react to such a return? In truth, the baby was Paul's not his. But the baby should be his, shouldn't it? He'd done so much more for the baby than his friend ever cared to do. This thought snaked its way down to his quickly beating heart and squeezed it with fear. He must tread carefully and not plant a stake where others wouldn't wish it.

In most cases, Seth would opt for a family's chance to be happy. In this case, Seth wasn't naive. Eleanor was the crux of Paul's obsession when Rowena had been the object of his obsession before. How long would he be content with Eleanor until another woman presented herself, one who could be more beautiful and very willing to give herself just as Eleanor had? What of Eleanor and the baby then? He couldn't trust Paul with a woman, let alone his wife whom he had vowed to protect.

The best scenario for Paul would be to stay far away and never come back.

Eleanor gently snored. Her head lay at an angle upon her crooked arm, the book's pages fanned open.

He placed his pen within his journal and laid it to the side. He stood before her and wiggled her book from beneath her fingers. He gently lifted her head, looped his arms underneath her, and carried her to her bed.

Once he had put her to bed, he slipped into his own and drifted to sleep easily. Pouring some of his thoughts onto paper was just what he needed to clear his head.

Before the sun was up, Peter quietly knocked on his cabin door to alert Seth that there was a hiccup with the next section of land where they were to lay the road. He and Peter took the ferry across the Mackenzie River to Camp Canol, hopped into a designated jeep for their use, and drove to where the civilian contractors were building the road following the pipe laying personnel.

Seth was sure that he would be back before sundown. In case he had to stay overnight, he wrote a letter to Eleanor and passed by Father Beau's chapel asking him to help Eleanor if she ever reached out. As he lay the paper on the dining room table, his hand shook with the momentous observation that she might appreciate such a notice.

Chapter 13

Early November 1943

As the climate shifted to a cooler base and there was more rain to contend with, pits of glue-like icky mud pooled, trapping trucks and heavier equipment up to the hub caps. No matter how hard the workers would rock the trucks back and forth, the mud sucked on its prey like an octopus using its suckers to keep the wriggling fish in place.

Laying the pipe and welding had been simple enough because the Norman Wells crude oil could flow through four inch wide pipes even in temperatures below forty to fifty Celsius.

Building the road over muskeg territory in the Mackenzie Valley was proving to be contentious. The muskeg was a swamp, a mixture of soil, dead organic material, and rich plants of berries and mushrooms and water all covered by moss. It ensnared valuable equipment which would then have to be lifted out by rigs and cranes.

Seth and Peter parked the jeep behind where the excavators were digging three foot trenches on either side of the road until they hit the permafrost. On the section of road ahead, the felled trees and bushes from either side were being dragged onto the road. Whatever substance they were digging off the permafrost would go on top of the felled forestry. Then the gravel would fill in the rest of the space.

Though this method of making the road that followed the pipeline proved overall efficient, another truck had been taken captive by the unforgiving terrain. Yakecen had mentioned that the land wouldn't make the finishing of this project easy. It had a way of protecting its own when man failed to protect what was given him.

Many in the U. S. Army had naively dreamed of malls, theatres, and boulevards dotting this landscape. Seth found it difficult to catch the vision. He believed this territory would always be home to wild hearts and tameless spirits.

The American dream of stamping its handprint upon this area of the world was fading fast just as quick as its gumption and aggressiveness had pressed into the beginning of the work a year ago. The U. S. Army units had shipped out to other fronts of the war. Civilian contracting companies were coming in to finish the work of the pipeline, the road, and to run the oil production at Norman Wells, which included drilling new wells and erecting tank farms.

A worker walked up the slight incline toward them and put out his hand to shake theirs. "Mr. Brooks." He gave a quick nod to Peter. "Come to see the job out here? Norman Wells doesn't have enough work for you?" He elbowed Seth and shared an easy grin.

"I've been hearing some good reports on the job. Of course, there's always the difficulties."

Not only was the project of overseeing the work in such an unforgiving place difficult, but so was the wrestling of the work's purpose. Seth and Peter ambled closer to the work underway.

Peter wondered, "All this work—you think this is going to last?"

Seth shook his head. "I'm not sure. I found out a special Senate committee, the Truman Committee, is investigating the work at Canol."

"Why's that?"

"They're questioning the importance of the project. Already the threat in the Aleutian Islands is lower than it's ever been since they started Canol. One day, this war will be over. Once it is, this project won't mean much even though I hear Imperial Oil has plans to generate more oil."

"What's your next move when this is over?"

"I don't know. I really wish I did. It's frustrating knowing all the joint efforts of the army and us might be for nothing. They've been calling this construction project the greatest one of the 20th century after the Panama Canal. Only difference is this one may fade into history as the least important one."

Doubt chewed at his self confidence. Was he running this operation as well as he could, as well as Paul had? He knew he had the knowledge, the training, the experience, but this project at times seemed daunting.

The building of roads behind the pipe laying and the tank farms; the drilling of thirty new wells to reach an output of 20,000 barrels of crude oil a day—the responsibility weighed heavy on his shoulders. He believed it would be easier to handle if his home life was free of strife. His and Eleanor's last contact was encouragingly civil, even intimate. If it could continue, it would help ease his burdens.

He could ask for her help in keeping the peace and make his expectations clear. However, that move could undermine the natural positive progression of their relationship, dare he hope for friendship. Fear held him back. Fear that whatever progress had been made would dwindle. Fear that he would fail in his marriage. What was his marriage? What was the design he was aiming for? He wasn't aiming for much, for anything if he were truthful with himself.

Marriage thoughts would have to wait because he needed to give his full attention to the men, to the job he was brought in to do. Perhaps, if he were awake enough at the end of the day, he would ponder what his goals were in his fragile marriage after slumping to the caboose the crew had prepared for him and Peter to sleep in.

He took a few seconds to envision a productive, successful day.

ELEANOR

PART III

The Collision

Chapter 14

He just left. Sure, he wrote a note. That was easy, but leaving? Easier, disappointingly easier.

I've got to leave for a couple of days to check the work on the Canol road. If you need anything, reach out to Father Beau.

She had dared to hope that he would remain once she had let down her guard. Was he scared that she had changed her tune, that she, to her own surprise, decided to play lighter notes so that life would be a little less miserable and a whole lot more peaceful? Isn't that what he wanted?

Her head pounded as her stomach vented its own aggravations. She breathed in deeply and exhaled. She rushed to the door, about to heave its contents, when the unsettling feeling faded away.

She slipped on her jeans and groaned at the straining waistline. Casting her eyes about for a shirt that wouldn't emphasise any belly swelling, they landed on one of Seth's folded white collared button up shirts.

She fingered it, hesitating to act on her desire. Looking behind her shoulder to make sure no one could see, she picked it up and pulled it over her head. She bunched the fabric to her nose and inhaled deeply. His smell—sunrise over a rain-refreshed woodland—invaded her senses. Memories of shaving his beard replayed in her mind. She tucked them close as she rolled up the sleeves and tucked in the shirt's bottom.

She put on her winter gear and walked to the office where she sat at her typewriter and typed at an alarming speed.

The feel of someone's hand on her shoulder made her jump and press the wrong key on the typewriter. She would have to redo a page she was almost done typing. "Gosh! Can't a girl just finish her—Oh," she turned her head and saw Julia's teasing grin.

Julia pouted. "Don't get mad at me, please. I didn't realise you weren't in a good mood. I came here to celebrate your hubby being gone, but you're mad?"

Eleanor gritted out, "No, I'm not."

Julia lifted her shoulder and rolled her eyes. "I don't believe you. Guess that baby is kicking around in there too much."

Eleanor's hand naturally floated above her small pronouncement of a baby bump. She was still quite a bit smaller than what she thought she should be at four months. When she and her mother had gone to church and chatted with the pregnant ladies, she always thought they were huge such a short way in. She supposed it was because most of them had already had multiple children, and she was having her first. "Other than the occasional throwing up, the baby has been good. Even the nausea and throwing up is dying down, and I'm starting to feel more awake, like I have more energy."

Julia smiled, "Well, I'm glad you feel that way." She stilled. "Is that your shirt?"

Eleanor's pride withered. "Yes, of course it is!"

"It isn't, is it?"

Why did she give into her strange fancy this morning?

"Fine, it's his! I needed a shirt, and it was just lying there."

Julia whispered, "What does it smell like?"

Eleanor rolled her eyes and changed the subject. "What are you here for?"

Julia chuckled. "All right, all right! I was thinking, why don't we take the ferry over to Camp Canol and visit everyone there when you're done? They invited me and several of the other girls to a party. Even Sworn Off Men Jen is planning on going if you can believe it. It's not like you have a husband that's missing you or expecting supper on the table, right?"

Eleanor shook her head to dispel her previous confusing irritation and smiled wide. "That's right! Thanks, Julia, for coming around to cheer me up."

Once she typed up all the memos for the day, she stepped out of the office and found Julia near the mess hall smoking a cigarette while chatting up a couple of men. Julia peeked around one man that was all brawn and called her name.

"Here take one. Light 'er up." Julia stuffed a cigarette into Eleanor's waiting hand.

The squat man, beside Eleanor, lighted it for her.

After expelling a flirtatious plume of smoke, Julia winked at both men, "Fellas, meet my friend Ellie. Ellie, this stud is Bart, and this is Dick. You have some time to walk us down to the ferry?"

Both men bobbed their heads eagerly. Each man took the arm of either girl and walked down the main road toward the dock. Julia wrapped her arm around the man of muscle. Eleanor lightly placed her hand upon her shorter partner's arm. Her partner, Dick, talked about his love of cars.

She knew a little from listening to Mike's daily monologues (during his childhood) when he scanned whatever car magazines he could get his hands on. Mike would always grab her hand as she was passing through the room, make her drop her load of whatever she was cleaning and show her his passion. She always made a point to sit cross-legged on the floor for even just five minutes so that he knew she loved him, so much so that she would put aside her own interests for his own. She would then pat him on the head, place a kiss, and sweep out of the room. Mike would continue to be engrossed.

Inclining her head and nodding at all the right places without really listening was natural to Eleanor. It wasn't because she was trying to be rude. Her mind kept sneaking down the trail to why Seth would leave the note he had after their–what could she call it? Breakthrough? Their truce, laying down of arms?

Their synchronised walking halted unexpectedly, and her hand was lightly shaken. Dick asked, "Ellie, you okay?"

"I'm sorry, it's just been a long day. What did you ask me?"

"I asked if you could drive a stick."

"No, it's something I wanted to learn but never did."

"Maybe after work sometime, I could pick you up and teach you."

Eleanor swallowed bile and flashed her flirtatious smile, "Sure, that would be great. I'll be waiting."

Dick grinned and continued talking. His words were now a stream of muck as she wondered why he had asked her in the first place. Goodness, she was married and pregnant! Perhaps the pregnancy aspect wasn't too much of a deterrent yet since her figure still looked somewhat the same. As for her being married, well, she guessed that word had spread that she and Seth were not together for any romantic purpose.

The conversation jarred her because it was the first full interaction she had with another man since she'd married Seth.

Once they arrived at the ferry, the men helped the ladies into the tug and headed back to work.

Eleanor grabbed her friend's arm and asked, "Julia, why are you flirting with Bart while you're in love with Peter?"

Julia's eyebrows narrowed.

Eleanor said, "You told me so yourself!"

She picked at her fingernail. "It hurts too much."

"I don't understand."

"I do love him, but he hasn't said anything to me, hasn't even hinted that he feels anything close to it."

Eleanor laughed. "When has that stopped you? You're not shy. Just tell him how you feel. Maybe he needs more encouragement—"

"I've given him more than enough, and he still doesn't get it!"

"Just be yourself. That means telling him how you feel. Life's too short to wait for a man to act. Look what happened with Paul! I should have made him stay, should have fought harder, should have—" Eleanor's voice hitched higher and higher with every word.

Julia's eyes widened. She placed her hands on either side of Eleanor's shoulders. "No, Paul knew what he was leaving. Paul knew you were special, thought you were special. He said so to me himself. He's the one that left."

"But I never said that I loved him. Maybe if I had—"

"Did you love him? Do you?"

Eleanor looked into Julia's eyes as if she were looking into a crystal ball and the answer would magically appear. Within her own depths, she couldn't see. The longer he wasn't around the more she realised that she didn't miss him, she only missed the idea of him. The idea that someone wanted to dance with her at every dance, wanted to touch her, wanted to whisper sweet nothings in her ear and wanted to dream of a future together— those memories faded away a little more every day, crumbling into dust ready to be picked up by the next brisk wind. She was so desperate in retaining the shape of the sand castle they had built together, yet with each ravaging wave of time, a little sank away at a time.

Julia sighed and hugged herself. "Truth is, I put up a good front, you know. I make it look like Peter doesn't mean more than he actually does. Nothing could be further from the truth. The whole time Bart was talking, my heart was sick for Peter. Still is. I kept it up because I thought it would kick in and work. How did you get a man to settle down and provide for you?" Julia laughed shallowly.

"I thought you and I were interested in making our own way in this world, be with whomever we chose, and be who we wanted to be when we wanted to be."

Julia shrugged her shoulders and looked out toward the river travelling north. "I've changed. Don't get me wrong. It's fun, a lot of fun for a time. At the end of the day, I think it would be nice to go back home to someone who I can count on to stay. Kind of what you and Seth have except I'd want Peter. I'd love a man, no, not just a man, Peter to hold me close every night."

She continued, "Just look at Leticia. That girl has slept with more than half of the men here, I'd bet! At first, she looks like the life of the party. She is, but when the razzle dazzle fades, she looks like a husk. I've been bunking long enough with her to see the damage it's done. She even cries herself to sleep sometimes. It's absolutely pathetic. I don't want to be pathetic. I want to be happy, not for one day but for a lifetime. Doesn't that mean finding someone who wants me for a lifetime?"

"I'm looking to get out of my lifetime deal as soon as I can."

"How are you going to do that when Seth would have to prove to the courts that you've committed adultery to get a divorce?"

"He said I'm free to leave as soon as I have the baby. That means leaving all my vows behind. I'll be free to be with whom I choose. Then he can file for divorce, and I'll be free to be remarried or not. See, I've got it all figured out."

"Don't you feel bad about leaving them behind?"

"Seth doesn't care about me in that way, only as a damsel in distress to be saved. The baby won't even know what's going on."

"Seth cares. Why do you think he gave you this opportunity in the first place? He's not getting anything out of it. He may not love you romantically, but he's a good man."

"How do you know he is?"

"You tell me. He bends over backward to make sure you're comfortable and gets everything you need. He doesn't force himself on you. There may not be any passion, but I can see how he loves in the ways that matter more than passion and a one night stand or passion for a time only to be passed over for someone new."

Julia continued. "My parents had an arranged marriage. My mom always said that she grew to love my dad after a couple of years. Their passion is deep rooted. I've always been amazed by their love story."

"Julia, I feel like I'm in a cage. I've beat my hands on the bars, and they don't splinter. I've yelled for someone to let me out. Instead, he came along, opened the door, and barred himself in with me. You don't know what that feels like, to not have a choice."

"Oh, Ellie." She gathered Eleanor in her arms and rested her cheek on Eleanor's head. "In five more months, that door will be wide open for you to walk through."

Eleanor closed her eyes and imagined the prison bars swinging open. Her body tingled as hope filled her. "Yes, it will be."

The tugboat docked at Camp Canol. The ferry captain helped the girls out of his vessel, and they headed toward the music pouring from the mess hall's single open door. The heat from inside hit them strong as they walked in. Every foot of the dance floor was taken up by shimmying, jiving couples twisting around each other.

Julia pointed out. "Look, there's Leticia. Ooo! Even Jen is dancing. Ha! Isn't this grand? We haven't had a party like this since the GI's shipped out."

Julia's face fell as she searched for Eleanor's reaction. "I'm sorry for bringing it up. Come on. Let's go have some fun." She grabbed Eleanor's hand and led her to the dance floor.

Julia was snapped up in seconds. Even Eleanor was asked by several men to dance.

One partner complimented her. "You've got a natural rhythm and great footwork. You're an excellent partner."

She blushed though he couldn't see it since her cheeks were pink from working up a sweat.

Once the dance was done, her partner left her side and returned with some moonshine.

"Oh, um, thank you so much."

He tapped his cup against hers and said, "Cheers!"

"Cheers," she said quietly and sipped her drink.

Guilt nibbled at her conscience. Where she used to feel so at ease, her body shaking to entice, her smiles given to flirt, her touches placed to arouse—she now felt out of place. The handsome men's smiles no longer glinted charm. The din of conversation, plucked guitar strings, banged piano keys, and over-inflated laughter were vapid and shallow.

She excused herself and exited the hall, her coat unbuttoned to cool off. She leaned her folded arms against a wooden railing and watched the show of the Northern Lights. Fluttering ribbons of neon green, blazing white, royal purple, and lavender purple streaked across the sky. It was the first time she basked in its spectacle. Though it was a common occurrence in the North, she had always been so caught up in the chasing of fleeting things. Was Seth appreciating it as she was?

Quiet, unhurried steps broke her focus. About twenty feet away, a man was holding a woman from behind as they also watched the lights.

Eleanor returned her attention to the lights, her hands rubbing up and down her arms, wondering what it would be like if Seth placed his scruffy chin on her shoulder and trailed his hands along her waist to hold her tight.

The body says what words cannot.
Martha Graham

Chapter 15

When Eleanor returned home, the door creaked open. She would have to remember to ask Seth to oil the hinges once he got back. Perhaps, she should write it on paper because, she assumed, the list of house tending would grow quickly. She turned on her flashlight to start a fire in the fireplace. She grabbed the bear skin and bundled it up around her. *Pride and Prejudice* was her companion though it lacked her full attention. She would read a few lines, put it down, and stare into the fire. Seth's face would surface in her mind's view. He was like a stubborn mule that wouldn't stop tormenting her no matter how hard she tried to shoo him away.

Eventually she fell into her bed. She wondered how her pleasure of listening to a quiet house had been short lived. It was subpar to the sound of him sleeping in his bed.

The next day, Eleanor came across a group of girls chittering away outside the mess hall during their break hour as light snow landed upon them. Leticia, the leader that the rest of the girls had formed a semicircle around, was animated. Miss

Dansk stood on the outskirts of the group. Julia was completely engulfed in the middle.

Eleanor stood next to Miss Dansk and asked, "What's got the girls so hyped?"

Miss Dansk gave her a strange look over and shrugged her shoulders. "They've got it in their heads to put on a big Christmas party, as if we didn't have enough parties already."

"I would think you'd enjoy a chance to let loose Miss Dansk."

"How can I when these girls need someone to watch out for them, to protect them?"

"Do you really think you're fulfilling that role of protector when they've travelled a world away from family and everything they've ever known to experience life in the wild and give in to their secret pleasures?"

Miss Dansk shuddered, "Someone's gotta do it."

"Your position only means something on paper. All these girls have tasted what they've wanted to taste and will continue to chase after what's willingly in front of them."

"Just like you."

Eleanor acquiesced. "Just like me."

"Except there's not men lined up to marry them and take care of them should they fall like you have."

Eleanor stepped away from her and moved beside Julia. She whispered, "What's going on?"

"Ah, Eleanor, so glad you've joined us. You're not too old and married to have a little fun, are you now?"

She pasted on a huge smile. "Never."

Leticia smiled coyly as she approached Eleanor, "Good, because in a month's time, Norman Wells will witness the greatest party it's ever seen, and it'll be because of us ladies and gents. It'll be bigger and livelier than the one Camp Canol just had."

Julia giggled, "Sounds like an orgy."

Leticia cut back. "Who said it can't be?" She wiggled her brows high.

Eleanor intervened, "We won't have anything if we don't delegate the tasks. I guess food is the biggest point now."

Leticia snorted. "Food?! What happened to the moonshine? That's what's most important for this party. I guess that baby of yours turned your head to your tummy."

Eleanor said, "Well, I guess we know who wants to go to Handsy Ricky at Camp Canol to ask him for a good supply of it. Or are you willing to share with us all your measly ration of the month of staple alcohol"

"Ricky? Why him? Isn't Dylan still here?"

No, remember? Dylan's shipped out."

"Fine. You take care of the food. You'll have to talk to Blade, the old coon. Have fun with that."

"I'll take care of the decorations!" One girl chimed in.

Julia promised to put the music together and fish around for some local musicians in order to drum up a band. Jen offered to invite the group at Camp Canol to join. Constance said she would oversee transportation of all the supplies and guests.

Eleanor observed Miss Dansk. No man or woman stopped to talk to her while she watched over her charges. Her fingers clenched and unclenched. She sighed at intervals and kept her gaze on some uninteresting object. Eleanor wondered if Miss Dansk had ever been part of a whole.

All throughout the day, Eleanor's focus was erratic. Anytime someone entered the office, she thought, perhaps, Seth would send some sort of word asking if she were okay, letting her know that he was on his way back. Each person that walked in never walked all the way to her desk. Her fingers, usually adept at typing, were sluggish. At the end of the day, she sagged over her typewriter and ground her fist into her forehead wondering why she felt the way she did, so defeated.

Pressing the collar of his shirt to her nose, she inhaled deeply and closed her eyes, trying to picture him in the room with her.

She roughly flattened some papers, slammed her palm down upon the work that should have been completed for the day, and drudged toward the kitchen. She believed she could convince Blade to cater a bigger party than usual. It helped that Blade liked her well enough. Since day one, Eleanor knew to give Blade the honour she expected for the difficult task of running the kitchen at Norman Wells. Respecting the cook who worked tirelessly in the kitchen was a lesson well instilled into her since she was very young.

Eleanor slunk into the kitchen behind Blade as she and others were cooking up a storm for supper. Heavy chilli spice clung to the air.

"Eleanor, you know you can't sneak up behind me when I'm cooking. Just because I'm banging my pots and bowls all over the place doesn't mean I don't know what goes on in my kitchen."

Eleanor leaned against a sideboard table where some mixing bowls were placed and folded her arms. "Would you be willing to put together a nice spread in a month for a large Christmas party?"

Blade huffed, her burly frame buzzing with sheer determination to cook as her passion led. Her biceps, though small in size, were toned by years of picking up large pots and stirring concoctions together. "Why should I? I'm just paid to serve three meals a day. Why would I go through all the hassle of preparing a nice meal, no, even a decent meal to a bunch of men and girls who don't usually appreciate the regular fare? What's in it for me?"

"Now that you put it that way, there's really not that much in it for you, but how about you make the meal and enjoy your own food, the drinking, the dancing, the singing, and a few rounds of poker? Your helpers can do the same. I'll take care of the dishes."

Her eyes crinkled, and she grinned. "I do like a good stiff drink. You mean you're going to do all the dishes? I don't want to come back to a mess the next morning. It can't be half done. Mind you, grab some help." Blade mimed a belly bump.

"I promise."

Blade stuck out her damp hand waiting for Eleanor to shake it. "I get to party with everyone else. I'm looking forward to blindsiding those boys in poker."

Eleanor winked. "I can't wait to see you try."

On her way back to the cabin, Miss Dansk ran to Eleanor and held out a note. "Your husband sent you a message."

"He's not…. " Eleanor was flustered, for it was the first time that someone other than Julia or Leticia referred to Seth as her husband. She caught herself before uttering the deeply held belief that he wasn't her husband in spirit but only by the harsh shackles of the law. Then why did she bite back her words? They surely weren't for Miss Dansk's approval. "Thank you."

Miss Dansk walked off.

She unfolded and read the note. Her fingers curled its edges into a ball and stuffed the note into her pocket.

For the next three evenings, Eleanor met with Julia, Leticia, and a few other girls at the mess hall after their shifts to discuss their plans for the grand party. Their usual evening routine would consist of ogling some of the men, sending flirtatious glances across the room, and sometimes walking toward what their bodies led them to. Eleanor had engaged in the first two of these activities until tonight. She looked around the room at the men around her. Her focus wavered, and she no longer cared. Her gaze travelled less around the room and more toward her water in hand.

Julia nudged her rib gently. "What's wrong, Ellie?"

"Seth sent me a note three days ago saying he's going to be gone until the end of this week. It's good I'm keeping busy with this party."

"No one's catching your eye for a good time?"

"They're all the same, no one new. They're all dull like brass that's been rubbed too often to produce a shine." Eleanor took a sip of her listless water, a mirror image of herself.

"Oh, girl," Julia murmured under her breath.

"What now?"

Julia's smile was exactly like the smile her mother would share when Eleanor was clueless.

A couple of days later, Eleanor decided to take drastic action against her melancholy after supper in the mess hall. She jutted out of her chair, flounced up, strode over to a group of men, and flashed a flirtatious smile. She pulled over little Ben, as his comrades called him. He was short in stature and rampant rumours persisted that he was short in the way that mattered between a man and a woman. She grabbed him by his tie and kissed him resoundingly on the cheek, leaving a mark of red lipstick.

All of little Ben's friends whooped as she pulled him onto the dance floor and ground herself close to his body. Ben needed only a little encouragement to take the lead and spin her around with great ease. Dancing was one of little Ben's secret accomplishments.

It had been secret up until this point because he had always been turned down. Now everyone knew he was the best dancer, and women were lining up to be his partner. His short stature was of little importance after that. As to the rumour of his shortness in other areas, many of the girls were willing to go far enough to test it out.

Like a drum beat drilling into Eleanor's head buzzing out the sound of her own misery and confusion, she moved her body in a way she never had. Her limbs followed Ben's cues. Her body, now having the strength it hadn't possessed earlier in her pregnancy, granted her the abilities she displayed fully that night. As the music crested to a finale, little Ben hiked her leg to his thigh and bent her low, swooping her back to his chest. The entire crowd roared while one man chewed on his lip in thoughtful consideration of the performance before him.

Eleanor beamed at the resounding applause of their dance. Little Ben did the same and gave her a kiss on the cheek.

Julia approached her friend with girlish fervour. "You have moves! So does little Ben! Who would have thought?"

"I just needed a little fun, you know, to get my mind off everything."

"Well, Everything is here."

Eleanor laughed, "What do you mean?"

Julia pointed to Seth.

He was leaning against the table watching his wife's face go from surprise to outrage. She turned her back on him and walked away from him. She grabbed Julia by the elbow and bade her to be her spy. "Is he gone yet?"

"Who? Little Ben?"

"No, Seth."

"Why would you want to walk away? Weren't you upset that he left in the first place?"

"Yes! And now I'm upset again!"

Julia gently placed her hand on Eleanor's arm. "Stop running away and go talk to him now."

"Why don't you follow your own advice and do the same with Peter?" Eleanor spat, leaving Julia behind.

Eleanor slammed her hat upon her head and rapidly stuffed her arms into her coat as she sidled out the side door of the mess hall. She tramped through the woods until she got to her cabin. She dead bolted it. She swiped the blanket off the couch and sat unflinching as her mind waged war against her once again.

A couple of minutes later, she heard a knock upon the door.

"Eleanor." Seth called.

She gripped the edge of the sofa and attempted to use her voice.

"Eleanor!"

Her heart clenched. "Go away!"

"I'm not going to do that."

"You already did."

"Eleanor, I'm not leaving you."

She huffed. "Why not? I want you to."

"I don't think you do."

"You think you know me better than I know myself?" She raised her voice in indignation.

"Can we please have this conversation without a door in between? I promise to leave after a few minutes if that's what you want."

She knew she should open the door, stop acting like a child, but her will made her feet leaden.

"Eleanor, please, let me explain why I was gone so long. Let me in."

She blew out a breath and rose to open the door. The smell of pine and coffee was strong as he stepped past her to walk inside. His borrowed shirt had been a poor vestige of his scent. A small pull she couldn't understand drew her closer to his turned backside. She struggled to fold her arms over her chest. "As you can see, I'm perfectly fine."

He shook his head and sighed. "Okay, you're fine, but you're not good. Why are you upset that I left?"

She pouted. "I didn't care."

"Then why are you upset now?" He indicated her performance with his hand.

She stewed, hoping that if she didn't say a word he would just leave.

He stepped closer. "Tell me what you're feeling." Another step. Her eyes skittered side to side. "Do you want me to be here now? Is your guard down?"

She whispered, "Yes, it is, but it shouldn't be because everyone leaves."

He stilled his advance.

She fought back renegade tears. "Everyone leaves." She struggled to swallow. "So I leave first. When I let my guard down, it happens again, over and over again."

He ran his hand over his beard which had grown over the week he had been gone. He closed the gap and reached out his open palms to hold her hands.

She relented and laid them in his.

He said, "I didn't want to leave you. Peter and I had to inspect the work on the new road. Once I got there, I started getting in my own head. I was afraid of what *this* meant. What's happening to us?"

His nearness was heady. The gentle caress of his fingers burned the cold tips of hers. She slid her fingers away and dared to look in his eyes.

His eyes were deep grey froths of the ocean tossed and bid her to anchor her heart within. She glanced around in fear for the shark which always guarded these waters, with his large smile, pieces of meat stuck in his teeth. Her predator was nowhere near. She breathed, "I don't know."

He raised his hand inch by inch and slid it along her neck, grazing her collarbone. His fingertips wrapped themselves around the base of her head. His bearded cheek slid along her smooth one and he whispered in her ear, "I know you don't trust me. How can I begin to earn your trust?"

He moved his head back to look into her eyes and brushed her lips with his thumb. "I'll keep working to earn it every day until I do. If I ever do, I'll keep working so that you know beyond a shadow of a doubt that there's one person who won't leave you. I know you're planning to leave me once the baby comes. I won't stop you. But I hope you know that I'll be there for you even if we're worlds apart." His breath ghosted the tip of her ear.

Her body leaned toward his, her hips brushing against his.

He inhaled and exhaled heavily and touched his temple to hers. Rearing his head back, he asked, "Do you want me to make you a cup of tea?"

His eyes, once the reminder of her nightmares, now was the source of her curiosity. She nodded, rendered speechless by his intoxication, and walked behind her curtain to change into her nightgown. She wrapped herself in her favourite blanket and sat upon the couch watching Seth squat to stoke the fire in the oven. A calm stole over her and a knowing that he could be trusted. He was here. He was hers until she could release him to someone who could fully appreciate the man he was.

The next morning she woke up to the honking of a Canada Goose. She stayed in bed for a few minutes afraid to move beyond her curtain because Seth was always gone before she woke or was never there to begin with. She peeped out to see his still form underneath his blanket.

She walked around and sat on the floor in front of him watching him sleep. The first three buttons of his shirt were undone. Strands of brown chest hair peeked out, and she wondered what he looked like shirtless compared to Paul. She reached out a finger and stroked his bare skin once, twice, and stopped cold. What was she doing? She was only missing Paul. That was the only reason she could account for the action.

As she pulled away her hand, his hand moved to cover hers and return it close to his chest. Her lashes fluttered, and she held her breath. Was he awake? Or did he only capture her hand as a reflex? She kept her hand in his for another minute before sliding out from his grasp.

Chapter 16

Although Eleanor had opened up to Seth in ways she never
had before, her courage didn't last beyond twenty-four hours.
She retreated to a comfortable defence of dodging one on one
time with him. After work every day, he would follow her home
and help with the washing chores. Once chores were done, she
would constantly make excuses of needing to go to the mess hall
to finalise plans for the party. After party planning, she would
sequester herself with the girls in their quarters and join their
banter.

One night, Julia pulled Eleanor aside and asked, "Why are
you here, Ellie? You know I love spending time with you, but I
need to kick you out for your own good."

Eleanor laughed nervously. "For my own good?"

Julia heaved her off the bed. "Yes, go home to Seth. You
miss him."

"I miss him? Why?"

"Because you love him," Julia said in exasperation.

172

Eleanor groaned, "I don't, I can't."

"Why? 'Cause you told yourself so? That's not how love works."

"It doesn't feel the same way it did with Paul. Paul was simple and fun."

Julia grabbed Eleanor's hands. "You fell in love with Paul. With Seth, you've grown to love him. When Seth was gone, you were simmering. When he's here, you're doing all you can to avoid him because you feel something strong. Why would you go through all this trouble of avoiding him? You definitely don't hate him anymore." She listed the evidence on her fingers. "You're not scowling or rolling your eyes at him. You missed him while he was gone."

Eleanor surrendered. "You're right. I don't hate him, far from it." She pulled at a stray thread on her shirt. "I haven't figured out what I feel for him."

Julia said, "Once you give in, the world will be so much brighter, so much more joyful than you could ever imagine. You need to let go of what you think should be."

"I'm scared."

"Oh, honey, that's the honest to goodness truth. What are you going to do the rest of your life? Hold on to the dark in fear? Or step into the light in love?"

Eleanor shared, "You know, he's made me reconsider how I treat others, others who I've treated with disdain all because of the way he's treated me. Even though I've been, you could almost say, cruel, he's shown me genuine kindness. Do you think he finds me cruel?"

"I don't think he sees you that way. He sees your pain. When you're in pain, you lash out just like you did after your dance with Ben."

Eleanor ducked her head, "I'm so sorry about that. I just snapped, and the words came out."

"I forgive you. I knew you didn't mean it. So are you going to talk to him?"

Eleanor replied, "I have to do something else first."

Julia opened her mouth to argue.

Before Julia could say her peace, Eleanor added, "But I promise to talk to Seth right after."

"You better. I expect a full report." Julia gave her cheeky grin.

After her shift the next day, she headed to the airstrip and came upon Frank whose back was turned to her, she drew her shoulders back and proceeded to clear her throat rousing a commanding air. She doubted he would give her a ride without Seth to approve it. She called out, "Frank! Wait up."

He looked behind his shoulder and gave her a friendly smile. "Hi, Eleanor, how are you coming along with the baby?"

"Everything is fine," she flashed a thin smile. "Well, I think so. Though I do need to see Dr. Barnes for, well, I just don't want to worry Seth. I'm sure it's nothing, but I'd like to know for sure. You understand?"

"I don't know. I think Seth should.... "

She gave him her most imploring look.

He sighed and said, "All right. Let's go. I've got to drop a few packages at Fort Norman anyway."

The true reason for her flight was delaying the inevitable of being around Seth and the necessity to gather her courage and strike down her already wounded pride by asking forgiveness from the last person in the world she wanted to ask. Eleanor went to the general store and browsed the limited clothing.

Suddenly, she heard a woman squawking at the counter.

"Don't touch me!"

Eleanor peeked into the next aisle to see the commotion and recognized Charlotte.

"Dr. Barnes told me to come in and grab his sack of sugar for him. He said he'd settle his account with you later!"

"He didn't tell me anything," the storeowner mildly sneered and winked at Eleanor. "I'm not giving you a sack of sugar. You'll eat too much, and your teeth will rot. Look there, there's one tooth that's had too much, I reckon."

"Fine," Charlotte lifted her wiry arm and fisted it. "Doc, will give you a talk. They never believe me, never." She pushed the door open and went down a step as she held onto the banister. As she went down another, she slipped and barely caught herself before bumping her bottom.

Eleanor kept drawing closer to the door as she witnessed Charlotte's tumble.

The storekeeper chuckled and said quietly as if they shared an inside joke, "That woman entertains me every time she comes in."

Eleanor looked at him blankly and wondered how he could be so unfeeling, so callous, so like the person she used to be. She hurried out, her mouth open searching for words to help alleviate the shame found in Charlotte's hardened eyes.

Charlotte looked back at Eleanor and frowned. She said, "What are you looking at? Had enough laughs?" She hobbled down the road toward her home.

Eleanor ran after Charlotte and put her hand on her shoulder.

Charlotte hissed, "What do you want with me?"

"Let me walk you home."

She screwed her eyes and frowned, "Why?"

"Because I have something important to say and it's not anything at your expense."

"Fine, but any disrespect, and I'll go hollerin' to doc." Charlotte muttered to herself, "I'll take no disrespect in my own home, or she's got another thing coming."

Eleanor accompanied the odd woman home and tip-toed up the front stairs, careful not to tussle any of the tiny faerie rainbow monuments Charlotte had constructed with care.

Charlotte waved her into a living room that was surprisingly clean and organised, simple. The shelves were dusted, the floors had been swept, and the walls were bare, painted a bright yellow. Eleanor sat on the single chair. Charlotte sat across from her on the settee.

Eleanor began, "I didn't expect—never mind, I came here to say that I'm sorry."

Charlotte squeezed her eyes shut and folded her arm against her stomach.

"I'm sorry I didn't help you up at the store. See I—I think I'm better than you. Or I used to think that. Now, I'm kind of seeing that we all have troubles, and that I'm not untouchable as I used to and wanted to believe. It made me feel good making you feel small, but only for a short time. The more I did it, I could feel my heart getting hard, kind of like a lump of clay that sits baking in the sun. Once it's cooked hard, that lump of clay can shatter. I don't want to shatter."

"Ah, so you're just apologising for selfish reasons so you don't hit hard when you fall."

Eleanor pressed her knuckles against her mouth. "Maybe? Isn't it better than no apology at all?"

"What's better is if you back it up. See, I get apologies all the time. Doc makes everyone do it. At the end of the day, they treat me the same. It doesn't change." She pointed at Eleanor. "Change. I don't want no apologies. If you change, I'll believe you."

"I'm not sure how to change."

"Well, whatever it is you're doing, it's working. What I failed to mention is that you're the only one who has come to me apologising without doc sending you. Or did he?"

"No, he didn't."

"See, already there's change. Even at the store when I fell, sure, you didn't help me up, but you didn't join in making fun of me neither. I reckon it's a small step in the right direction. What's got you changed so much all of a sudden anyway?"

Eleanor's eyes widened.

Charlotte went on. "Well, usually, it's someone who loves ya, and you love them. That's how it was with me and my man."

"What was he like?"

"Oh, I'm a personal kind of woman so I won't say much; but he taught me the meaning of true love more than anybody else. My parents hated me. So did everyone else. You got a man?"

Eleanor shrugged her shoulders. "It's complicated."

Charlotte shook her head. "We women say that because we make it out to be and not because it is."

"Maybe you're right. It is a man. Nothing in my life has changed except for that and the baby. Even the baby, I used to hate it, hate that it ruined my life, that it's limiting me and my choices, that it'll scar my body in a way that I can't ever fix, and hating it because I couldn't eat, or barely, the first three months." Her fingers lightly played over the small bump. "I'm still scared crazy, even still hoping it might pass naturally, but I no longer hate it. If it's born, I give Yakecen and Peni the chance to have a child. If it passes, well, heaven is so much better than earth is, or isn't it supposed to be?"

Charlotte's eyes grew unfocused. "I hope it is. I've got to believe it is." She returned her attention to Eleanor. "Just think of it, to hold something so tiny, a little pinched pink face staring up at ya with their wide eyes. Do you ever think of that?"

"I make sure I don't."

"Want a piece of toast with butter before you go?"

Eleanor wrinkled her nose. "No, thank you. I'm pretty full from lunch."

"Ah, I guess not. Now go home to your man."

Eleanor rolled her eyes. "Ugh, why does everyone keep telling me to do that? The more people do, the less I want to go home."

"You can only run for so long from what you know is true. Now shoo! I've got to build another faerie house. I promised them I would make another one today, and the light is dying."

Eleanor stood up and moved toward the door. "Again, I'm sorry."

Charlotte patted her hand, "I forgive ya."

As Eleanor walked down the steps, she turned to look at Doc's porch. He stood at his front door and cocked his head to the side.

Eleanor said, "I came to apologise."

He placed his hand on his heart; his eyes were soft and bright.

When she returned to Norman Wells with Frank, Eleanor went to her home and found it empty. She breathed a sigh of relief. Even the bed that Seth had slept on was completely made up as if he had never slept in it at all.

She sat upon his bed and remembered how peacefully he slept. She didn't know how he could sleep at his desk, but it couldn't be as comfortable as his bed.

Did he stay away because he believed she would be more comfortable, because it was his way of showing care? The way he approached her a couple nights ago was indicative of care, perhaps, even affection. She hadn't pulled away. She couldn't figure out if she truly cared for him or she enjoyed him because he cared for her. Taking whatever he could give her now to later throw it away was excessively cruel and selfish.

He could have cared just enough to provide for her, care for her medical needs while indulging himself with someone who wanted him. He had stopped himself from personal pleasure. He wasn't only committed to her needs but to her.

At the end of his bed, she spied a pair of pants. She unfurled them and found a spot that needed to be stitched. She grabbed her small sewing kit she had brought with her from Edmonton. She pulled the thread through the needle and began sewing.

Sewing was the one activity she had enjoyed doing with her mother. They would take out their baskets holding items needing to be mended and sit together in front of the fireplace.

For Eleanor, it was a time when she could safely unpack what she was feeling. She asked her mother once why their neighbours and friends blamed her for her innocence being stolen.

Her mother reached out to squeeze her hand tight. "Mr. Benson has many connections with the people that matter in this city because of his father, connections that extend to deep friendships with some. You must know that in this world, a woman's word is not always taken seriously, especially when it is up against a man's, a man who will stop at nothing to keep his reputation intact so that he can continue to hunt his prey while wrapped in sheep's wool.

Eleanor's mother lifted her head and gave a small, tired smile. "It must have taken a great amount of courage for you to share the atrocity. Your father and I couldn't help but extend that courage to the world. It was a gamble. Sometimes the world is ready for such courage, and sometimes it isn't. Only time will tell if the truth will be accepted. Until then, we keep our chin up and live the best we know how."

Eleanor finished stitching up Seth's pants and folded them the way she had found them. She passed by the office, wary of coming across Seth. He wasn't there. Instead a great big pile of notes on Raider Island's operations were laid on her desk. She sat down to type some of them out.

It was an unusually quiet night when she left her desk. She enjoyed it while she could because when the big party was thrown, there would be frolicking until the early morning hours. She opened the door to her home and found Seth sitting on the couch with the pants on his lap.

He stood up and fingered the pants, a satisfied smile gracing his face. "You fixed them for me."

She smiled shyly. "I saw them this evening, wondering why you had left them there. I picked them up and found the hole."

"Thank you."

"You're welcome."

"You all right? You're home late."

She shrugged. "I swung by the office and found that big pile of papers I had to type out. Some of them were late. How come you didn't remind me about the work? I'm finding it difficult to keep track of everything these days, almost as if my brain is muddled at times."

"It's common, your muddled brain. My sisters Christina and Shaina went through the same thing when they had their babies. I do apologise for some of those notes with earlier dates. I found a few I had misplaced. I knew you'd get to it in the morning. There's no need for me to hound you."

"It's okay. You can tell me when I'm running behind on work. It's the professional thing to do, isn't it?"

He ran his hand through his brown waves. "Right, professional. yup."

Eleanor added, "I won't hold it against you for asking me to do my job, or even small things that aren't related to our professional relationship, like mending your pants." She took a step closer. "Is there something I can do for you now?"

He swallowed and gently smiled, "No, thanks. Wanna cup of tea?"

"No, thank you, I'm going to get ready for bed. Are you doing the same?"

He stilled and held his breath a beat longer than usual. "Hmm, mmm, it's okay that I'm sleeping here, right?"

"Sure, of course, it's not only my home."

The air shifted, a current poised for activation. There was so much that had been said and so much more to be said. The in-between was a maze, and she wasn't sure what the end goal was, let alone how to reach it.

As if there wasn't enough air in her lungs to abate the lightheadedness descending, she attempted to take a deep breath. She took a second glance at him before shutting her curtain and quietly sitting on the edge of her bed, reaching underneath for her nightgown. She shifted out of her day clothes and put them in a basket she had designated as her dirty laundry. Her basket was full in time for tomorrow's washing day. She would grab Seth's at the same time.

Doing his laundry would be a way she could bridge the gap between them, a way she could intimately assert herself into his life. Would he appreciate such a move without them discussing it?

She sighed and lay down under the covers and rubbed her tummy. It was now large enough for her to cradle it. As her fingers glided across it, she wondered how her skin would be affected, if it would be marred by the life growing inside or if her skin were blessed with the ability to bounce back untainted.

A flutter met her skimming fingertips. She stilled at the contact. Her breath hitched as she flexed her palm over the spot where she had felt the baby stir. A ripple reached out and faded inside itself once more. She yanked her hand away as if the contact had burned an imprint and cradled it close to her chest. The baby had moved. It was no longer some abstract idea she could dismiss. It was big enough, strong enough to reach out and declare its existence.

A whimper escaped her lips, and Eleanor began to cry. She was suddenly horrified that she could have been the cause of this baby's death. It had been her life against its life; a stalemate.

Seth moved the curtain aside. He padded in, lamp first and illuminated a trapped woman. He sat on the side of her bed, making sure he wasn't touching from her prone form, and asked, "Are you okay?"

Eleanor's hand peeped from underneath the covers and grabbed his. She lay aside the top blankets and laid his hand on her tummy. His eyes never wavered from hers as she guided his hand. It only took a couple of minutes for his eyes to go from training on hers intensely to widening in wonder.

He whispered, "That's…. " He smiled big. "That's the baby. It's incredible." He looked away from her tummy to her face, and his joy melted to sorrow as he took in her reddened eyes, bitten lip, and shallow breath. With his other hand, he cupped her cheek and said, "You're a brave woman. In the face of what you fear most, you're still here with a measure of compassion for someone you've never met."

Eleanor nodded. "It's the first time I've ever felt the baby move."

"How do you feel?"

"I don't know. I'm feeling things I've never felt before. I don't know what to do with them, the feelings. It feel like an insurmountable wave that will crash into me and drown me. I'm not sure how I'll turn out on the other side, and then there's the chance I might not turn out at all."

He rubbed his thumb across her wet cheek and said with authority. "No, don't say that you're going to—"

She cut in. "You're not in control of whether I die or not. There's always a possibility."

"There's always a possibility of dying a thousand different ways every day. You're healthy. Dr. Barnes said so. You don't have any complications so far as he can see. You and the baby are going to make it through."

"Wouldn't it be easier for you if I didn't? You didn't ask for any of this. Why did you do this?"

He looked away for a moment and returned to focus on her. "I married you and took on this responsibility because I saw you in need of help. I felt compelled to go down this path. You not making it through wouldn't make my life any easier. It would change me forever."

Eleanor grabbed the corner of the sheet and dabbed her wet eyes.

With the pressure of her hand gone, he lifted his hand and began to stand.

Eleanor snatched his hand and said, "I don't know if I can be alone with it tonight. Would you—please stay tonight."

His breath hitched as he walked around the other side of the bed and sat down. After the bed creaked, he paused. She wondered if he would lie by her side as she had asked. She heard him lay his head down on the pillow, but didn't feel his heat.

A moment later, she twined her fingers with his and draped his arm over her body. She nudged her shoulders backward into his. He gave her a little squeeze before staying completely still. A few minutes later her breathing deepened and her body stilled its restlessness. As she drifted off to sleep, the thought that she was safe and anchored flit into her mind and nestled there as a cat pads the space it has found as refuge.

When morning came and her eyes slowly opened, she faced Seth's chest as he held her in his arms. Her head was buried near his collarbone. His scent filled her senses like cinnamon sticks filling the air on a cold Christmas night. A few of his beard hairs scratched the uppermost tip of her forehead. His lips were embedded in her messy hair.

How could she disentangle herself without his realising she had nestled herself within his refuge? There could be no more crossing of lines with unsaid words, engaging looks, or stolen skin touches. The future was never a subject they talked about. Her past was off limits like a padlocked chest sunk beneath the waves. Only a foolish diver would brave the dangers to unlock the hurt.

Only, she was certain that she couldn't use him for her own gain, pleasure, or retribution. Yes, he was only too willing to give, and give, and give. She felt from now that anything beyond this moment could only attach itself with a promise, a promise she didn't know she could keep.

She reached over her hip and lifted his wrist. She released it on his side and sidled out of his grasp. He lay there, fully clothed yet naked to her assessing eye. She shifted a shock of hair from his temple.

Suddenly, she felt the baby tumble in her belly, an invitation to respond.

After looking over her shoulder at Seth and making sure he was sound asleep, she whispered, "Hello, there." She gently massaged where she had felt the baby move.

"I don't know why, but I have a feeling you're a girl. What do you think of the name Melody?" There was no answer for a moment, but then her baby answered with a flip.

"All right, then. Melody it is. It'll be our little secret for now." She paused. "Only I'm not sure if you'll be able to keep that name. I…. " How to explain that she was leaving her child to be raised by strangers? No, Seth was no stranger. Surely, he would be around to watch over and make sure she was loved and cared for.

"You see, there's a wonderful couple, Yakecen and Peni, who wants to adopt you and make you theirs. I've met them, and I think they can give you all the love you deserve and teach you so much. Seth will be here for you also. I'm leaving you…" her voice broke, "...in good hands."

Tears pricked her eyes. She blinked them away and swiped a stray one before grabbing her clothes for the day. After dressing, she lifted her laundry basket and Seth's and brought it to the laundry station. Next, she walked to the office, sat down at her typewriter, and continued to work on the shrinking pile. She was determined to have everything in order before he reached the office.

Leticia popped in and took a seat on one of the men's desks. Her lean legs were crossed and dangled beside the man like a bait on the end of the line. He laughed flirtatiously, and she patted him on the chest.

Determined to save the married man from shame and potential infidelity, Eleanor made a beeline toward her. She tugged at Leticia's arm and took her to the side. "I forgot to tell you I've got Blade for the party. She'll take care of everything so long as she gets to enjoy it."

Leticia pouted, "Pooh, we don't want any old people being a drag."

"Fifty is not that old. Afraid she'll steal your thunder?"

"Oh please, what kind of life does she have aside from chopping all those horrid vegetables and making passable food?"

"Who knows what kind of life she lived before coming here. Did Julia get all the music and musicians in order?"

"Yes! We even have a new pianist coming in to provide us with some real talent on the keys for a month. Morale for our work in a frozen wasteland. Won't that be dandy?"

"Sure, will. Where's he coming from?"

"Edmonton, maybe you'll know him."

"Do you know how big it is, how the population has grown? It's a city, not like here where everyone knows everybody else. I remember you said your mother was from Mexico and your father from Montreal. Where were you born? Where did you grow up?"

Leticia averted her eyes and puffed out some air between her thin lips. "No one has ever asked me that question before. I guess most people come north to start new so it almost doesn't matter where you've come from—"

Eleanor added. "Or what you're running from."

"Yeah, that's—that's it, isn't it? We're all trying to hide from each other, from ourselves. I'm from Sault Sainte Marie, a mining town. Guess I thought I'd be a good fit here cause I'm used to rough living (though I don't look it) but far enough and different enough from home. You?"

"I thought I was running toward a bright future, but the future is a cruel dream that will always seem iridescent so long as you're not close enough to touch it. Right before you do, it disappears and reappears a long way down from what you thought was the end so that you're off chasing it again. It's tiring chasing a dream that will always be just that, a dream."

"Ain't that the truth, sister!"

If they had met under different circumstances, she wouldn't have considered Leticia a friend, let alone a sister. However, sharing close quarters, eyeing the same men, trading laughs at work, and staying by each other's side when calamity descended banded them all into a mismatched sisterhood she wouldn't trade for a higher salary. "Sister."

*No passion so effectually robs the mind
of all its powers of acting and reasoning as fear.*
Edmund Burke

Chapter 17

Early December 1943

It's a strange sensation, an eclipse of horror and familiar dread when a past spectre haunts and taunts the soul.

In the merry cacophony filling the packed mess hall, in the explosion of popping corks and bubbles flowing down long necks, in the pounding drumbeat of shaking bodies and suave connections, in the stark scent of booze and sweat mixing together, in the grip of sheer terror, Eleanor was frozen in place desperate for air, imperceptible tremors coursing through her body. All faded in the emptiness of his eyes, the eyes that had held her prisoner to his cold, raking pleasure.

The voice speaking to her sharpened into focus. "Eleanor! Earth to Eleanor! Grab the man's hand, girl."

"Of course, sorry." What else could she say? Reveal her shame to a waiting audience? Who would believe her?

It had seemed like the whole city of Edmonton had shunned her and her family after she had been taken advantage of when she was twelve. She wouldn't give people here the same opportunity. She inhaled sharply and stuck out her hand as if it were a sword she could use to impale the man in front of her. She made sure her grip wasn't too strong; for she was tempted to squeeze his hand until it turned the same violent shades he had inflicted upon her. "Nice to meet you."

Did he know? She didn't look away; she needed to know if he knew. His grey eyes twinkled in the merriment of the evening, the sheen on his brow from his energetic playing made her want to heave all over him. Bile began to rise. There was no guaranteed clue that he remembered. She would always remember. "I've got to go. Enjoy your evening!"

Should she let him run loose? Loose like a panther stalking around for delicious unsuspecting prey. She looked around for little girls and was slightly comforted there were none. Of course, there were none here at this drink-filled party. But the few she had seen belonging to local families, who would protect them from this monster? Somehow, she had to.

What of the girls partying? She hated admitting he was good looking enough to have a good time with more than one girl. The years had only amplified his chiselled cheekbones. His salt and pepper hair paired well with his aristocratic air. Would he push himself on anyone who didn't want him? Looking around, so many girls wanted a willing partner, heck, even Blade might not even pass the slime up.

She patted Blade on the shoulder as she passed her and walked into the empty kitchen. Julia swept in and wrapped her arm around her shoulders. "You okay? Leticia said you completely blanked out on Mr. Benson when she introduced the two of you."

Flustered, she breathed, "Yeah, just all the noise is getting to me is all. Are you going home with Peter tonight?"

Julia smacked her red lips playfully. "Yes, he's my man. I love him. I told him tonight while we were dancing. I just couldn't hold it in anymore."

Eleanor smiled wide. "You did? What did he say?"

Julia's happy expression dimmed. "He didn't say it back. He said I was his girl. That's fine, but I want more than that now."

"Maybe that's his way of saying it. Why don't you go back out and have some fun? I promised Blade I'd have her place spick and span clean."

"First, I'm going to help you."

Eleanor objected. "NO! I mean, no, thank you. Please, go out there and have fun." She couldn't have another soul see how rattled she was, her focus unravelling with every minute.

"What about you and Seth? Are you going home with him?"

Eleanor spluttered and said, "What a silly question to ask! I'm going home with him, just not *with* him. More like we're going to the same home—"

"Something has changed between the two of you. I saw it in that dance."

They danced before she had been *introduced* to Mr Benson.

Earlier that evening, the keys which had been playing a lindy hop had slowed down.

One of the best female singers in camp went up to the microphone and sang "I'll Be With You in Apple Blossom Time" in a sultry rich soprano that winded down all the dancing couples. Eleanor stopped her shaking to the upbeat rhythm and moved to the side of the dance floor near the ten foot pine fully decorated tree the men had chopped down to use as the camp's Christmas tree.

A hand touched her elbow. She turned to find Seth's outstretched hand. She placed her hand in his, and he led her to the dance floor, his eyes never leaving hers. Her titillated fingers found a mooring on his broad shoulder. Her hand that was wrapped in his found safety.

Though their bodies started off a solid foot apart, they drew nearer inch by inch until his groomed stubble pricked the flushed skin of her temple and ear.

He covered her hand on his shoulder with his and brushed his thumb across the ridges of her knuckles.

She nuzzled his neck and even felt so brave as to graze her lips across his pulse point.

He inhaled sharply and moulded the planes of their bodies so that one couldn't see between them.

When the song finished, and they reluctantly parted enough so they could look at each other, Leticia interrupted and insisted on introducing her to Mr. Benson. In one fell swoop, Leticia had knifed Eleanor in the gut all without knowing it.

In the kitchen, Julia put the back of her hand to Eleanor's forehead. "You are really off tonight. Well, you're not sick."

"No, I promise I'm not. I was just thinking about the dance. It was the best part, beautiful and—"

"You've got to tell him." Julia pressed her point.

"What good would that do?"

Julia's eyes sparked. "It would encourage him!"

"But I don't want to do that!"

"Why not?" Julia asked incredulously.

Eleanor admitted. "I don't want him thinking I need fixing."

"Ellie, don't you know we're all broken in some way? If you choose, it doesn't feel so bad being fixed up, especially by someone who truly loves you." She hugged Eleanor and walked out.

Reliving her dance with Seth couldn't deter her panicked thoughts from tormenting her for long. How would she be able to live with Mr. Benson here at camp? She had to find a way to make him leave. If he recognized her, what was his consequent nefarious design?

She just needed to get through tonight. Her futile plans for the next few days were erratic and unfocused.

Leticia entered with more dishes. "Just because I prepared for this party everyone thinks I'm the one taking care of dishes.

Can you believe it? I was surrounded by dishes on all sides. I'm not taking another dish from anyone."

Eleanor asked, "Could you find Seth and ask him to come here please?"

Leticia quirked an eyebrow. "I'm really confused about the two of you. I heard you married him because of some arrangement you had, but that dance you shared—it almost looked like you could just eat him."

"Could you just?" Eleanor raised her eyebrows.

"Fine, fine. Don't get into a hissy fit!"

As Eleanor laid the dirty dishes into the warm bubble-filled water, Seth walked in, combing his hand through his hair. "I've been looking for you! I got waylaid by a few of the men." He drummed his fingers on a counter. "What are you doing here?"

She scrubbed a plate with her sponge. "I promised Blade I would clean up here. I just wanted to ask, I mean, you don't have to—"

He moved to her side, placing a hand on her shoulder. "What is it?"

Eleanor's eyes began to well up and a sob escaped.

Before he could envelop her in his arms, she held up her wet palm, stopping him from drawing closer. "No, please, I'll tell you later. Could you stay until everyone else leaves please?"

"Of course, but—"

"Later, okay?" She blew out a shaky breath.

He rubbed her back and then said, "All right. I'm just going to finish talking with Lawrence, and then I'll come back to help out. It's a big load."

Eleanor admitted, "I'm used to carrying big loads."

"I know, doesn't mean it isn't nice to have help along the way." He winked at her and walked out.

She couldn't hold back the sobs anymore. Her sudsy hands attempted to wipe away her tears. Instead of a small part of her face being wet, it was all wet, and her eyes burned from her soapy touch.

A little after midnight, the party strains died down. A couple had bashed through the kitchen doors attempting to fondle each other, hands desperately lifting the other's clothing. When they realised where they had wandered, they apologised.

"Is almost everyone gone?" Eleanor asked.

The man's words slurred as his partner literally hung off his shirt, her nails scraping down his exposed chest. "Yup, we're going to get going ourselves. Have a fine evening."

When she had finished cleaning up the dishes and began wiping the counters, Seth strolled in and smiled, "I'm sorry I took longer than I expected. I was done talking to Lawrence and then struck up a conversation with the new pianist, Eric Benson. Because he's here for the month, I thought it would be friendly to show him around and—"

"You can't." She bunched and unbunched the cleaning cloth.

His brows furrowed. "Oh, can I ask why? Do you know him? He's from Edmonton just like you."

She whispered, "Yeah, I know him." She inhaled deeply and said flatly, "When I was a little girl, he raped me."

As soon as she voiced the truth she could not run from in Edmonton, the truth she wouldn't dare cry out in the North except to him in a brash moment of desperation, she made a dash toward the door. Seth caught her elbow and gently swivelled her to face him.

Seth stilled momentarily, then squeezed his eyes shut. They flashed open and blinked rapidly as he pressed his fist to his mouth. He touched his forehead to hers, saying, "I'm going to take care of it. I'm going to take care of him."

Life is the flower for which love is the honey.
Victor Hugo

Chapter 18

All the way back to the cabin, each snap and creak the woodland animals executed made Eleanor jump and clasp Seth's hand even tighter. The increasing snowfall and howling wind made her shiver and draw her reefer coat close. Her nerves made her lose her footing on the snow-encrusted ground. Her grasp of what little control she had was loosening, unravelling into helplessness.

As soon as they returned to their cabin, she sat down on the couch and draped her fur blanket around herself. Only her face peeked out. Seth went straight over to the stove and stoked the fire to boil a kettle of water. As she cowered, his angry grunts soothed her ringing ears. He paced back and forth, back and forth until his task to feel useful had finished. He put a teaspoon of sugar with a squeeze of lemon and put the teacup and saucer on the table in front of her. He sat beside her and tented his hands, letting them rest on his stubble. "I believe you."

She whispered, "I'm scared the same thing will happen here, that all of Norman Wells will believe him over me. That's what happened in Edmonton. He was never even charged. He comes from an influential family. I believe he's the youngest son. His father was my father's textile business competitor. It was startlingly too easy for the senior Mr. Benson to spread pernicious lies against my father and me. The lies were splashed on the front page of the Edmonton Journal. One by one, my father's business allies withdrew their support, the banks and creditors called in their loans, the money was tied up, and we went bankrupt. My father was forced to sell his factory for peanuts. We barely managed to pull through the Depression. My father weathered us through with his undying faith and infectious optimism. Because of what *he* did." Her voice hitched. "He ruined us. He hurt me. That's why I'm not saying a thing, and I don't want you to say a thing."

He exhaled sharply. "You don't feel safe."

She shook her head. "I'll never feel safe knowing he's around, lurking. There's nothing I can do."

He angled his body toward her. "Don't ever believe your family suffered because of you. Something unspeakable happened to you. You were brave to tell the truth all those years ago to your family."

Elearnor teared up. "That girl died a long time ago. I'm not as brave as she was."

"That's not true. I won't force you to say a thing. I can get him to leave. I'll do this for you."

She placed her head on his shoulder. "Why do you care so much?"

He sighed and wrapped his arm around her. "Do I really need to answer that? You're my wife. I thought after all we've been through, you would know I care."

"I know."

He squeezed her closer. "I'll look into who employed him, talk to them, and send him packing."

Her arms emerged from their hiding place and reached for the tea. "Thanks. It's calming."

"Let me get my own. Hang on a minute." He looked out the window. "Wow, there's a storm whipping up out there."

She took a sip of the tea and smiled. It tasted just as she loved it. "How did you know how to make my tea? You didn't ask."

He smiled to himself. "I've probably seen you make that tea more than a dozen times. How could I not notice?"

She giggled. "But it's just tea."

"Maybe to you it is. To me, it's part of who you are."

She blew across her teacup and sipped tentatively. "When I look at myself in the mirror, I see I'm not whole. My reflection is cracked into a tiny million pieces. I can't put together a clear picture. But you—do you know who I am?"

He touched his knee to hers and said, "The fur blanket that keeps you comforted and warm—the needle that you used to patch my pants—the stacks of typed notes I see on my desk—the waters of the river where you've splash your feet—all these pieces of you paint a brilliant masterpiece." His curled fingers brushed along her jawline. Warmth radiated from his exquisite touch. "You're a hard worker despite finding yourself in a situation you didn't think you'd be in right now. Your strength is inspirational. You don't need fixing. I know you think I believe otherwise. What you need is a safe and encouraging space to bloom."

She reached for his fingers with hers and closed her eyes. "You're wrong. I need some help, a little fixing. Julia and you, especially you, have helped me see that bearing it all on my own doesn't need to be the way. I would be missing out on your kindness which has caused me to grow in such important ways. I needed a good dose of fixing. I'm sorry I've been hard on you and sabotaging our marriage. Even though it's temporary, it could have been a nicer experience from the beginning if I hadn't been so pigheaded."

He cupped her face in his hands. "What matters is that, I think, you've learned to open your heart up to a little kindness and accept it. You're changing who you are, no one else. You've taken who you are and opened up a whole new world of potential that you can fill with more of who you're meant to be."

"I never wanted to change, just to make a man appreciate me more. You never asked me to. Thank you." She broke from the cradle of his hands and looked down at her tummy. "And thank you for looking out for me and the baby. You'll keep looking out for her once I leave, right?"

He nodded vehemently, "I promise."

"You'll never let what happened to me happen to her?"

His grey blue eyes shined like steel as he said, "As much as it is in my power, yes." They softened. "How do you know it's a her?"

Rubbing her tummy, she replied, "I don't know. It's a gut feeling. I'm starting to, ugh, never mind."

"Please tell me," he said, placing his hand on her bump.

She smiled at him. "I'm talking to her, trying to explain that she won't be seeing me that much, maybe even never. She'll understand, won't she?"

"I can't say. All I know is she'll be raised well and healthy just as I was."

Eleanor grabbed the edges of her blanket and wrapped them around her once again. "What are your plans when the pipeline is completed?"

"I haven't thought much about what happens after this. This was the plan. I could continue to work on contract for the American army, go anywhere in Canada where they would need a civilian engineer, but what I really want is to stay. This is my forever home. I'd want to discuss it with.... " He went silent.

"With whom?"

He grinned. "Uh, with my wife. It's important to me that we'd be on the same page."

"Unlike us." She rolled her eyes.

He playfully bumped her shoulder with his. "We've hit a lot of bumps in the road, but we're doing okay."

She straightened and smiled smugly. "I'll concede to that."

"What about you? What's next?"

She brought her knees to her chest. "I keep trying to envision my future. When I left Edmonton, I was all about here, living my own life on my own terms. Didn't last long, did it? My mum is looking out for my dad with my brother, Mike's help. He and I aren't too close, and don't get me started on his wife. I don't know for how much longer I'll have my dad. After everything that happened all those years ago, things weren't ever the same. I don't know how to stop chasing happiness. I'm scared all the time because if I don't chase it, where will I end up? At the same time, it's exhausting. You want it to be easy, but it never is."

"How old are you?"

Eleanor gave him a smug questioning curve of her lips. "I'm trying to figure out if I should be offended. I'm twenty-one."

He exhaled. "I wish I could tell you you'll figure it out years later. I haven't yet. Sometimes I think that I've reached the point where I've got it. But you're right, the balances upend and I'm climbing against all odds just to have a taste of happiness again." He rose to his feet and held out his hand.

She took it and stared at their intertwined hands. He placed her right hand on his shoulder achingly slow and gauged her reaction.

She asked, "Didn't we already dance tonight?"

"I thought I'd set your mind at ease before you go to bed and give you a taste of happiness."

"You think you did that when we danced before?" Her past sharp instinct to hook a barb into his soft flesh and pull to tear had faded. Instead, she wanted to place soothing kisses on the scars on his heart.

He gathered her closer and whispered in her ear, his breath sending shivers down her spine. "I saw it in your eyes. Tell me I'm wrong."

She leaned in closer and pressed her lips to his ear. "You're not."

He gave her hand in his a little pressure and stepped toward her. She stepped back. He quietly sang,

> "A cigarette that bears a lipsticks' traces
> An airline tickets to romantic places
> And still my heart has wings
> These foolish things remind me of you
> A tinkling piano in the next apartment
> Those stumbling words that told you what my heart meant
> A fairgrounds' painted swing
> These foolish things remind me of you
> You came, you saw, you conquered me
> When you did that to me
> I knew somehow it had to be"

She couldn't note how long they moved across the worn floor. After the second line, their bodies ceased to waltz. She snaked her arms around his neck and pressed herself against him as she lay her head on his chest. Desperate for more contact, his hands pressed on her lower back.

Once the song was done, she placed her palm on his stubbled cheek and kissed it. "Thank you for giving me a taste of happiness."

He gingerly held her fingers and kissed their tips one by one. She tipped her head back and angled her lips so that they could naturally fit in the embrace of his. He inched toward her, his nose brushing against hers as he closed the distance.

Suddenly, she turned her head slightly so that his lips landed on the corner of her mouth.

She bit her bottom lip as she disentangled herself.

Seth asked, "Wait, please, I have something for you. I was going to wait to give this to you on Christmas, but this is the perfect moment." He covered her eyes with his hand and said, "Promise you'll keep your eyes closed."

"I promise," Eleanor said. She heard him rummaging underneath his bed. Suddenly, he slipped one of her arms into a coat and then the other. Only this was no ordinary coat. It was fur. She looked down at the vibrant caramel colour fur and hugged it. She breathed, "It's beautiful!"

"I want you to be the warmest you can be. Unfortunately, your reefer coat doesn't suit a Norman Wells winter.

Eleanor turned to face him and said, "But I didn't get you anything." Before he could respond, she wrapped her arms around him, finding her utmost comfort in being close to him.

His voice rumbled over her hair. "This is the best present you could give me."

Drinking in his scent, her eyes fluttered closed in satisfaction and fatigue. "Thank you. I'm—I'm about to fall asleep on you. I should go to bed, goodnight, Seth." She entered her partitioned room and lay in bed, placing a hand over her racing heart.

SETH

PART IV

The Perdition

Violence is the last refuge of the incompetent.
Isaac Asimov

Chapter 19

Every abrupt rustle of Eleanor's sheets, every minuscule whimper she uttered urged Seth to keep watch over the curtains circling her bed. Every crackle of a twig moved by the quickening wind outdoors, the animal noises that speckled the night—all these sounds which had never before caused him to lose sleep did so that night. He told Eleanor that she was safe in this house and by every fibre of might in his being he'd make sure his word was true.

He couldn't say whether Mr. Benson was the type to prey upon his past conquests or whether he was a man who enjoyed the screams of young girls and breaking the beauty of naivety. He wouldn't leave Eleanor's safety in question just to take the time to find out.

The twilight gleam of early dawn around nine o' clock filtered through his windows. He rubbed his bleary eyes and knew he wasn't a pretty sight. He rolled his legs off his bed and sat hunched, running his hands over his face and down through his hair. He quietly tiptoed toward Eleanor's curtain. He peeked and was immediately relieved to find her alone and safe.

He walked to the window peering into the quiet forest for anything other than the wildlife roaming its domain. What was he to do? He couldn't be by her side every hour of the day. There were obligations he had to fulfil that required him to be out of office and out in the field. He would have to enlist the help of the girls. He didn't trust Mr. Benson to not recognize her from so long ago or to keep his distance. He had to find a way to get rid of him so he could go back to the rathole he had come from.

Seth waited for Eleanor to wake up and dress before they walked down to the office together. He gathered the notes to be typed and placed them on her desk.

He kissed her blonde locks and said, "I have to go. I promise you'll be safe."

She smiled. "I trust you."

As he was exiting the office, he spied Private Cyril walking by. "Private Cyril?"

"Yes, sir?"

"Please make sure the new pianist doesn't enter this office."

"Yes, sir."

"You may leave once Julia arrives. She's got red hair and freckles."

"Yes, sir."

He jogged to the Women's Quarters and knocked on the door. Miss Dansk opened the gateway to her wards. Her jutting chin reached around the door. "Yes, Mr. Brooks, what can I do for you?"

"Is Julia here?"

"That girl came in very late after having spent the night with your friend Peter. You have some influence. You should talk to him about how spoiling a girl isn't decent."

"Miss Dansk, I'm not here to interfere—"

She wagged a finger in his face. "I won't take no for an answer. You want this operation to move along well enough, don't you? Then we need to take care of the moral character of our young people on this base so that we can work with purpose and focus."

"You—Fine, I'll look into it. Now Julia?"

Miss Dansk glanced behind. "Here she is. Don't forget what I said. I feel as if I'm the mighty Sisyphus pushing the rock up the mountain. I'm strong, but these past two years have been wearing me down. Young people don't listen these days. They've got some tomfool notions about carving lines into tradition, of burning the bridge behind them. You're not one of those, are you?"

Julia poked her head above the Gorgon's head and said, "I'm here!"

Her timely entry saved him from stumbling on his answer. He had no time to have a philosophical debate when he was sure that only a full surrender to Miss Dansk's side would ingratiate him into her good graces.

He led Julia by her elbow away from the hut. "I was hoping you could shadow Eleanor today."

Her eyes went wide. "I'm not going to be your spy."

He scrunched his brows. "No, no, nothing like that. I want you to make sure she's safe. I can't say why but there's someone here at camp that she doesn't feel safe around. Until I sort this out, I was hoping you, Leticia, and the other girls could watch her when I'm not around. It's probably going to be more than just one day."

"Well, I'm sure you're not the problem."

His brows shot up and his mouth hung open.

"What I mean is when you two were first married, all she talked about was getting away from you. She really didn't like you. Now that time has passed, and I've seen you two together, she's at peace when she's around you. I know you help her feel safe. It's a good thing. So this other person…?"

"It's not my story to tell. It's a private matter. If Eleanor wants to bring it up with you, then she will."

Julia nodded. "Of course, I promise to look after her."

He went to Lester, the man in charge of hiring on base and inquired as to how he could request a leave of an employee without offering any personal details.

Lester asked, "Well, what has he done?"

"As I said, I can't divulge any details, but there's a lady on base who's afraid of him for good reason."

Lester's pen was primed to write. "Does he have a record? Was he ever charged with anything?"

"I don't know if he has a record, and no, he was never charged."

The pen was put away. "Look, I can't fire him on those grounds."

Seth's shoulders sagged. "You're doubting her word, aren't you?"

Lester shrugged.

Seth asked, "Is there no way to get rid of him?"

"Catch him doing something he shouldn't. In the meantime, keep the lady safe."

He should have known that, having no hard evidence against Mr. Benson, he couldn't have him fired by the proper channels. So full of desperation was he to keep her safe, to ensure she wouldn't suffer the same harm she had incurred in her tender years. He would do anything even if he knew it to be futile.

He returned to his desk to read some reports and marvelled at how often his eyes strained from the words on his page to her exposed neck and her straw blonde hair falling across her opposite shoulder. Her straight back revealed her excellent posture which he admired greatly, especially since she was five and a half months pregnant and now showing much more than the first half of her pregnancy. She'd already had many of her clothes altered by a woman on base.

Her eyes flicked to his and caught him staring. He expected her to duck her head. Instead, she gave him a gentle smile before slowly re-engaging with her work. By the power of her gaze, that tiny flame that had been desperate for her oxygen, turned into a searing heat. Not like the cold heat that he had felt when he had almost cheated on his wife but a heat that filled in all the dry cracks of his wilderness, a heat that made any tender shoots of green spring into a blossoming desert garden.

He would do anything for this woman. He would die for his woman. Although in the deepest, most vulnerable place in his heart he knew these things as truth, he worried if she would even care that he wanted to. His doubt dampened the blaze as a bucket of ice water would. She would leave.

She could never feel the same about him because of why he married her. He could forgo telling her Paul had asked him to look after her, giving their relationship a chance to mean what he desired it to mean. If she ever found out, she would abandon him without a backward glance and curse his memory forever.

That evening while Eleanor stayed behind to catch up on some work, Julia with her, Seth went to the mess hall where Mr. Benson enigmatically played some jazz tunes. All the men and women present danced to the Pied Piper. After working up a sweat, Mr. Benson slowed down his playing to some soft ambient music.

Seth sidled up to the piano and asked, "You've got quite the gift, Mr. Benson. How did you come about learning to play like that?"

Mr. Benson nodded and continued to play as he answered, "Please. It's Eric. I grew up in a pretty well to do family with many brothers who were all interested in the same things my father subscribed to such as fishing, boxing, hunting. I tried my hand at all of them and failed miserably. Got pushed around for it quite a bit. Made me develop a thick hide. Anyway, I finally got around to picking up the instrument and took to it really well as you can see."

"How do you come to make a living out of it? Are there really enough entertainment contracts like this one to make it a feasible trade?"

Eric's eyes screwed tightly as he broadened his greasy grin. "Are you thinking of taking up my profession? Got some musical talent yourself?"

Seth replied, "Me? No! It's something I've always wondered when I've seen any kind of musician. Just curious."

"I used to give lessons. For a long time, I enjoyed teaching the little ones how to play. At some point, it got tedious."

Seth leaned in. "Mmm, tedious—too much for you to handle."

Eric frowned. "Something like that. Now if you'll excuse me, I'm going to strike up a jig, and I can't talk when I'm doing that." Eric swung his head to the opposite direction and banged on the keys.

Seth walked around and chatted with a few of the other men so it didn't seem as if he had singled Eric out. He left, determined to smoke out the evil from camp.

He wondered why Eric had come in the first place. If he had wanted fresh prey, he could have gone to a brand new city where no one could guess what dark deeds he dabbled in. The fact that he was in the same camp as Eleanor—it couldn't be coincidence. It felt personal, it felt like revenge.

Seth had never had someone to fight for. If it came right down to it, he would.

The next night, everyone was down at the mess hall, including Eleanor and him. The girls had done an excellent job of keeping Eleanor company when he had to leave her behind for work.

Peter came to sit at his table. He pushed his glasses higher up on his nose. "Isn't she just beautiful?"

"You're talking about Julia? She sure is."

Peter blurted. "I want you to be my best man."

"I thought you had different intentions. What changed?"

Peter said, "What you said got me thinking—it's not about what I can get now but what I can do to secure future love."

"That's one piece of the puzzle. My marriage to Eleanor has made me realise that my service to her and her needs and her acceptance of them has made me happy. Living for myself, by myself isn't much of a life."

Peter asked, "How's it going now compared to what it was before?"

"It was a rough go at first. The way she treated me—I never went home to sleep. I couldn't be at peace with someone who clearly didn't want me around. Then something happened. She's changed slowly and is still changing. I'm changing too."

"I don't think I could be that patient with someone who I don't think deserves it." Peter acknowledged.

"Do any of us really deserve it? Having a measure of patience in your future marriage will serve you well."

Peter chuckled. "I'll try to remember that."

"So, you already asked?"

"Not yet, but I will. Just working out the details of how I'm going to ask her."

"Good, Miss Dansk tasked me with telling you how you've got to stop spoiling her and make an honest woman out of her."

"Sure, we fool around, but we haven't done the deed."

"Oh?" Seth raised his brows in question.

"I've done it with so many girls before, but she's not like those other girls. She's the one. So I wanted to do things differently. Be different for her."

"That's very noble."

Peter asked, "Are you getting any?"

"No, I'm not, not that I need it," Seth admitted.

"I thought after the dance at the Christmas party, the way you two were looking at each other—"

"I don't think it's ever going to be that way. She's still planning on leaving."

Peter shook his head. "Not if you tell her."

Seth searched the room for Eleanor.

Eric stood in front of her, his smile dripping with venomous charm as he squeezed her forearm.

Seth got up to haul Eric out, but Leticia arrived first and threaded her arm through Eric's to lead him away.

Eleanor snatched back her arm and rubbed it. Seth pushed past bodies until he reached her side. Her eyes were lined with tears, and she bit her lip.

As soon as she saw Seth, she shook her head, mouthed, "Not now," and headed over to Julia.

How could he have been so caught up in a single conversation that he had failed in his duty to protect her? He was thankful that Leticia could be trusted to do the right thing for a friend.

His nostrils flared, and he flexed his fingers. He employed every ounce of self-control to not stalk across the room and punch the living daylights out of Eric. He would get what was coming to him, but not in a crowded room where he would draw any kind of attention to Eric's connection with Eleanor.

She sat on the side as the others danced. Seth kept no more than ten feet away. Eric abstained from nearing Eleanor the rest of the evening.

On the way home, Seth gingerly touched Eleanor's arm. She handed it to him without a word. As he inspected the finger shaped bruises, she viewed the river.

Seth said, "You know why he's here, don't you?"

Eleanor replied, "He's not here to destroy my body. He's here to destroy my soul. I could tell by the way he was looking at me that he doesn't intend to do what he did all those years ago. The thrill of the chase wasn't in his eyes, but he's scheming to do something to me. He wants to hurt me just not in the same way. I just don't understand how he knew I was here."

Seth reiterated. "However he got here, I'm going to find a way to get rid of him after—listen, I have to go up to first pumping station along the Canol road to assess some damages the it received from the storm."

"But—"

"I'm not leaving you behind. You're coming with me."

He could see the sheen of Eleanor's eyes glisten in the moonlight. "Really?"

"When we married, I promised to protect you."

"Is that all?"

His breath caught in his throat. He looked deeply into her eyes through their mingling puffs of breath and wondered if he could open himself up so fully in complete vulnerability and trust. He wanted to believe she wouldn't laugh in his face, that this hadn't been a cruel joke to string him along just to kick him down. He took both of her gloved hands in his and brushed her knuckles with his thumbs. He longed to take courage and place a longing kiss upon them, to share a small window into how he felt about her. He stared at them for so long that he kept expecting her to remove them from his grasp.

She stood there waiting.

Slowly, he curled her fingers around his palm and raised them to kiss them. The searing touch branded his lips. Oh, to root his hands in her hair and devour her mouth with his, to run his hands down the curves of her body against a tree. Instead, he lowered their clasped hands. "Come, let's go."

That was all he could give tonight because no matter how much more he wanted to give, he couldn't handle the fallout of rejection or losing her when she decided to leave. Not when he had ever loved this passionately or quietly.

The following day, Peter, Eleanor, and he met some dog-sledding teams of native men at the docks waiting to bring them across. Seth tucked Eleanor into the bed of one of the dog sleds. Peter hopped into the bed of another while Seth stepped onto the step boards of Eleanor's sled and held onto the handle.

She leaned her head back and asked, "You know how to mush?"

"Of course, I do," Seth winked and then shouted, "Mush!"

The other teams followed as they travelled across the ice to Canol Camp. As they approached the Canol's shore the teams shouted, "Easy!" followed by a "Whoa!" soon after.
Then the three hopped into a jeep and drove down the Canol road as they followed a snow plow. Eleanor was wrapped up in furs in the back.

As Peter was driving, he asked Seth, "How bad do you think it is?"

"It wasn't a huge snowstorm. There might only be minor damages to repair."

Peter shared, "I've been thinking a lot lately about the grand vision for this project. Do you think it's everything it's cracked up to be?"

Seth answered, "Time will tell if this project turns out to be the glorious salvation of the North that the Americans keep trumpeting. The way things are going on the different fronts, there may not be a Japanese invasion after all. If that's the case, this pipeline, well, it might have been for very little."

Peter's lips were set in a grim line. "It's hard to think of the value of our work here for these last couple of years in the scope of all you've just told me. How do you go about living life in the moment when you're sure that it might not amount to anything at all six months from now?"

Seth looked out the window for many minutes toward the Mackenzie River. "Maybe it's like the river. In the rush of the current circumstances, the river is forced into a current with only one way to go. In that current there's room to move and to swell. Yet all the while, she moves to her destination. Whatever ocean she must meet, she's moved in ways that make her ready for the beast she must contend with."

Seth continued, "Even if this project ends and the work we've done in this short amount of time is soon over, I believe we'll come out on the other side stronger because of all we've lost: lives, hopes, time and because of all we've gained: dreams, love, and character. That's nothing to shirk."

Peter shrugged, "Maybe."

Once they arrived at the first pumping station along the road, Seth deposited Eleanor inside a warm cabin where there was a roaring fire and some coffee and biscuits available to eat. He said, "I need to make a thorough inspection. As soon as I'm done, I'll be back." He quickly cradled her cheek in his hand before marching off to work.

The men running the pumping station gave him a tour of the critical equipment such as the pumps, motors, valves, and control systems. Next they moved onto the pipelines to identify any leaks or cracks and to ensure the oil flow hadn't been compromised. They discovered two cracked pipelines. Seth jotted down notes as Peter took pictures with their De Vry camera. He then asked the men running the pumping station to provide him with its inspection history and data.

He sneaked a peek through the cabin's window where Eleanor waited for him. He saw her clapping her hands with gusto and smiling widely at a one man show.

He smiled to himself and walked over to the office where he gathered all the documentation and his notes on the inspection and put together a repair plan which included the services of a welder.

Seth, Peter, and Eleanor stayed until the sun set at three in the afternoon after the welders had repaired the cracked pipelines.

On the way back to Norman Wells, Seth and Eleanor sat side by side in the back of the jeep lost in their own thoughts.

Eleanor said, "You've been asking the girls to keep tabs on me, haven't you?"

Seth smiled. "I thought it wasn't that obvious."

"It's not, but I'm never alone at the office anymore. I used to be sometimes."

He bristled in anticipation that she would be offended by his care, by his desire to protect her.

"Thank you." She placed her hand on the arm of his wool jacket and gave a little squeeze. "Usually I wouldn't appreciate it, but I find I'm barely capable of thinking a full thought when

I'm in the same room as him. I'm scared that he's coming after me. I know I can barely defend myself like this." She moved her hand over to her belly and stared off toward the river.

"May I?" Seth asked.

"Here," she took his hand and placed it near her ribs.

He waited for a movement, any movement to take his breath away. Just when he thought Eleanor might be feeling awkward having his hand on her body for so long, the baby gave a flutter kick, and he belted out laughing. "That's incredible!" He lowered his head so that his mouth was near where the baby had kicked and said, "Whoever you are, I hope you know you have a wonderful mother who's strength over these last couple of months has inspired me. You always remember it now."

Eleanor's lips curled down. "I don't think the baby will remember me."

"She may not have memories of you, but you can be sure that Peni and Yakecen will tell her all about you if that's what you want."

"I don't know if that would be fair. What if she asks what happened to me, why I left her behind?"

He sighed. "If it were up to me, I would tell her the truth. Any little white lies you concoct will bring her a world of pain because not only will she have to go through the pain brought on by the lies but also whatever pain lies in the truth."

"I don't want to think about that right now." She rested her head on his shoulder. "I just want to love her right now by keeping her warm on a chilly night, touching her as she somersaults in my belly, and having you talk to her just like you did. Everything after tonight can wait."

Seth wrapped his arm around her and leaned his head on hers. "You're right. You're giving her all she needs right now."

Chapter 20

The next day Seth decided to gamble for the first time in his life. He was always the safe one. He never made speculative investments, never skirted or took the shortcut to protect those he was charged with, and he always factored in the pros and cons of every decision except for marrying Eleanor and except for the decision he was making now.

He was stepping beyond a door he always made sure stayed closed tight, and he was afraid that this idea would blow in his face and hurt Eleanor in the process. He decided to proceed because he couldn't see another way out.

He left his desk and gave Eleanor a small smile which she returned before he got up to do what needed to be done.

He didn't have to look far for the snake that had nested comfortably in their territory. He was curled up on the piano bench practising some tunes for tonight's entertainment.

Seth's mind was sheathed in red as he remembered the bruising on Eleanor's arm. He grabbed a chair and planted it right next to Eric's bench.

Eric didn't skip a beat, pretending as though Seth hadn't changed the atmosphere. His long, limber fingers flowed up and down the octaves.

Seth cleared his throat and waited for him to slow down, to stop his song.

He didn't. He kept on playing, hitting the crescendo with gusto. Swiftly, Seth slammed the piano cover down narrowly missing Eric's fingers except for his fourth finger which was caught for a second before Eric hissed and shot it out to suck on it like a little baby.

Seth growled, "Stop playing games."

Keeping his facade in place, Eric replied, "I don't know what you're talking about."

Seth's hand shot out like a viper and squeezed Eric's wounded finger. "Your simpering attitude isn't going to save you from this. Instead, it's making me more upset, and you don't want that."

"I'm not afraid of you." The tendons in Eric's neck were strained as he attempted to pull away his finger.

"Why are you here all the way up in Norman Wells? This base isn't full of little girls."

Eric's eyes narrowed and his wet lips trembled.

Seth stretched Eric's finger backward close to its accompanying knuckle and continued, "Look at you, you're not man enough for a woman. You have to go after the ones that are too young to defend themselves, the ones that don't know how to voice their hurts. That was my wife when you raped her!" His voice was a shout. "You prey on the weak. That makes you weak and pathetic." He caught his breath. "That's why you're here, isn't it? You're here to torment her."

Squirming, Eric licked his lips and stayed silent.

Seth pushed the finger further. "I'm going to break your finger if you don't talk right now. How will you be able to play then?"

Eric whimpered. "Fine! She ruined my career. Had to blab her mouth to her parents. Then they made a fuss. A couple of other girls thought they would add wood to the fire, and they all smoked me out from my home. She started it, and now she'll pay for it. When my nephew showed me her picture, I knew it was her."

Seth strained the finger a hair more. "Who's your nephew?"

Eric sneered. "Wouldn't you like to know."

Seth grabbed him by his blood red tie and began to choke him. "Who is it?"

Eric's hands scrambled to find an opening for his breath to flow.

Seth let up an inch.

Greedily gulping some air and choking on his life force, he wheezed, "Corporal Tranter."

When Corporal Tranter had left without ever having gotten back at Eleanor, he surmised Tranter wasn't as malicious as he thought. To think that maliciousness had come back in the form of his uncle who had enough determination to grind Eleanor into the dust was staggering.

Seth leaned in closely barely able to stand the smell of his cheap cologne. "You're going to leave Norman Wells and never come back."

Eric laughed maniacally. "I'm not. What are you going to do? Kill me?"

"It's tempting to say the least."

Eric held his chin up. "If you do anything, I'll make sure everyone knows she's damaged goods."

Seth bared his teeth. "If you do anything other than leave, I'll make sure everyone knows you're a predator with a taste for young girls. No one's going to want you here in the North. So crawl away to a hole."

Eric balled his fists and attempted a swing. Seth caught it in his palm and executed a swift left hook. Eric's head hit the top of the piano.

He spluttered as he cradled his cheek, "You just hit me! I'm going to tell your superior."

"You tried to hit me first. Who do you think they're going to side with? The top civil engineer or the musician who's a rapist?"

Eric scrambled away and tumbled toward the door. Just as he put his hand on the knob, the door was opened by Eleanor. She froze on the spot.

Livid and red to the roots of his salt and pepper hair, Eric's eyes flashed with madness. Then…

Seth launched toward him when Eric wrapped his hands around Eleanor's neck and banged her against the door. It seemed as if no matter how quickly Seth sprinted he was wading through a bog. He closed the distance and pried Eric's hands off her neck. Seth took him by the shoulders and slammed him down to the ground. By that time, the commotion had caused a couple of other men walking by to aid Seth in restraining him.

Seth yelled, "Get him out of here! Now! Make sure he leaves Norman Wells."

Both men hauled him up and brought him to his quarters so he could collect his belongings.

Seth pivoted immediately and bent down to where Eleanor, eyes vacant and breathing shallow, had fallen against the wall. "Eleanor, you okay? Stay with me—hey."

She nodded absently, and her hand searched for him although she didn't look at him. Her lips moved without a sound, and tears silently rolled down her cheeks. He wiped them with his thumbs.

Why did she come through this door? If only he had reached her sooner—if only….

"Forgive me." He gulped back his tears. He placed his head against hers and held her close. "I was just trying to help." He sat back and saw she was in shock. He didn't know what to do or how to help her. Should he keep her comfortable here and call for Dr. Barnes? Or bring her to him so she could be treated as soon as possible? Would Dr. Barnes even be in?

He ordered Peter to phone ahead to ensure Dr. Barnes was waiting for them and to fetch a medic to meet him at the airstrip.

Heart pounding loud in his ears, he lifted Eleanor and waved down a running jeep. He got in and commanded it to take him to the plane.

He and the medic lifted her into her seat and Seth gingerly draped his arm around her shoulders. With his other hand, he cupped her head.

Though she showed no outward physical injuries other than the blooming bruises on her neck, she was unseeing and unmoving. Was it too late to reverse the damage?

Seth rested his head in his hands as he waited outside the patient room. It seemed like hours being separated from her, not knowing if she was going to be okay. Dr. Barnes finally slipped out quietly and said, "She's suffering from shock. Her symptoms are similar to Combat Fatigue, something soldiers at the war front are experiencing a lot these days. Tell me what happened."

Seth related her past, and how it had all come to a culmination when he ordered Mr. Benson to leave.

Dr. Barnes said, "The encounter she had today was a mirror of the original. It brought on past memories that can be quite debilitating when reliving them in the mind. I've given her tea to calm her. She has some bruises around her neck. He didn't squeeze for very long, but there's quite a bit of damage to her vocal chords. I'll have to monitor her specifically for the fall she took. The road to recovery is going to be a long one."

Seth asked, "The baby?"

"The baby is fine. I found the heartbeat, felt it kicking around. For now, it is unharmed."

"What if he had punched her in the gut?"

Dr. Barnes's brows rose. "Did he?"

"No, not that I could see. But what if—?"

"Seth, it didn't happen. Count your lucky stars. They're watching over her and the baby. Why don't you go next door to Charlotte? I popped out and told her what happened. She made some coffee for you and has something for the baby."

Seth shuffled next door. His legs were numb. The thought of losing Eleanor was like a jagged-edged knife ripping his heart. His usual reasoning and level-headedness couldn't staunch his panic's blood flow.

He ground his palm into his eye. The baby—God, he wanted her to live so he could cherish her even if Eleanor left.

Charlotte opened her front door, her features downcast. "I saw you brought Eleanor to doc's. I'm so sorry. Let me get you some coffee. You can do with a drink."

He sat down at her small round kitchen table on one of the two chairs. So deep was he in his sorrow that he didn't see Charlotte give him his coffee at first. She gently pushed it into his hand. "Drink."

He said, "Thank you. You're right. This is what I needed."

She sat across from him and drank from her own cup. They sat in comfortable silence.

He said, "I'm sorry I'm not great company now."

She waved him off. "No need to be. I don't need to have a fancy conversation."

Seth said, "Dr. Barnes said you had something for the baby?"

She patted his hand before making her way out of the kitchen. She returned with a knitted green hat and a yellow knitted sleeper for the baby. "You tell your girl that I'll be making an outfit for that babe of hers every year."

"That's very kind of you." He downed the last of his lemonade and thanked Charlotte again.

Eleanor was sleeping peacefully when Seth quietly entered the patient room. He pulled up a chair beside her and took her hand between his. The gentle slope of her nose rose and fell to the rhythm of her soundless breathing. Her bow-shaped lips were closed. The purple bruises ringed around her neck threatened bile to rise in his throat. He peppered her hand with kisses and then whispered, "I love you." He felt like a coward for not telling her when she was conscious.

He spoke as he pressed her fingers against his lips. "I really didn't mean to come to love you. All of this was for Paul. He asked me to take care of you by any means possible. This was the only way I could think of. I wrote to him to let him know. We'd do anything to keep our promises to each other. He knew he couldn't have you because he's set on marrying Rowena."

He swept a lock of hair from her brow. "You really made it difficult to get to this point. You put up the best fight, but instead of making me walk away, you bewitched me. I want you. I've never felt this way about anyone. For how long do I have you? It seems like you'll slip out of my grasp at any moment. Is my love powerful enough to keep you? I'm desperate for an answer; I'm just too scared to ask for it."

He wondered if she could hear his words or if she was sleeping so deeply that no sound could penetrate her barrier of unconsciousness.

When he and Eleanor arrived home, Eric Benson had been long gone. The two men that had carried him away said he was sent packing on the next plane out. They politely inquired about Eleanor and the baby and went back to work.

Seth placed Eleanor in bed and said, "I promise you he's gone. You'll never have to see him again. You're safe."

She squeezed his hand to communicate that she understood and rolled over. He pulled the curtains closed and went to chop some wood.

Over the next few days, Eleanor attempted to speak more and more. At first, her voice was grating but smoothed out with a little more practice every day. By the end of the week, she could speak quietly without straining too hard.

After lunch one day, Seth entered the office, and Eleanor stood up to hand him the typing she had done at his request. Then she bent over, her hand rubbing her lower back. His eyes were drawn to a dark red streak down her leg. "El, you're bleeding." Despair squeezed his heart. He shook his head to dispel the constrictive hurt so it wouldn't hinder his ability to take action.

Her trembling lips were the only moving parts on her ashen face. "The baby," she managed to whisper.

"Don't move. Let me bring you home. Sit here for a moment." He helped her back to her chair.

He popped his head out the door and called to Peter, "Get Julia and the medics and bring them to my cabin. Tell Frank to get Dr. Barnes. It's an emergency!"

He proceeded to pick up Eleanor and carry her home.

He laid her on his bed; for it was overall more accessible than hers in the corner. Like a whirlwind, he grabbed the basin of water, clean cloths, extra sheets and put the kettle on to boil water. He pulled down her stockings and dipped a cloth into the water.

Julia came in, her dampened eyes honed on the blood Seth was wiping from Eleanor's legs. The medics followed right behind.

Seth handed Julia a cloth, "We need to stop the bleeding."

She bit her bottom lip and nodded. "Okay."

As she pressed cloth after cloth to staunch the flow, one medic checked her vitals and attempted to find the baby's heartbeat while the other medic worked alongside Julia.

Oh, the wait for Dr. Barnes' arrival seemed like a lifetime. Never had Seth been so poised to spring at a moment's notice, to abandon any physical comfort of his to bring comfort and life to another.

After Dr. Barnes fully examined her in her bed (Seth had moved her there after they had stopped the blood flow), he led Seth outside and said quietly, "I can't find the baby's heartbeat."

Seth asked, "You're sure? Is there no way…? What happened?"

"The bleeding has stopped which is very good. I'll stay overnight and check again tomorrow. With the amount of blood she lost, it's not looking good. This is probably due to the fall last week. I believe she's had a partial placental abruption."

Seth asked, "What is that?"

"The placenta has partially detached from the uterine wall."

Seth pulled his hair. "How? Why now? Last week, everything was fine. I don't understand."

"Sometimes only time tells. It's good one day and the tables change the next. It doesn't look good."

Seth's voice hitched. "Is there no hope?"

Dr. Barnes sighed. "It's a small possibility, not likely."

Covering his mouth with his hand as he stabilised his arm, he murmured, "Thank you for everything."

Dr. Barnes squeezed his shoulder. "I'm sorry Seth."

Seth put his hand on Julia's slumped shoulder and thanked her for her care and attention in crisis.

Julia took her leave. Her sorrowful expression was paired with tremors that she attempted to still and failed miserably.

When he entered Eleanor's room, she was turned away from him. He sat on the side of her bed and reached for her hand that was resting on her hip. He squeezed her fingers lightly and asked, "Are you awake?"

Her head shifted downward ever so softly.

He said in a gravelly voice, "Dr. Barnes said you're very likely going through a miscarriage. Have you—have you felt the baby move at all?"

She didn't answer for a long time. He wondered if she had fallen asleep or perhaps she wasn't ready to share such an intimate detail. Finally her voice broke, "Sometimes I think I feel a flutter, but with the amount of blood—it must be all in my head. I'm scared of myself for having thought this would be a relief."

Seth looked at her without judgement.

She went on. "Now that it's happened. I wonder if I've made a terrible mistake for wanting this in the first place. What if God made this happen as a punishment for wanting it? Do you think He can be that cruel?"

"I believe everything happens for a purpose. I don't really have anything to back me up, but I want to believe—I do believe God isn't cruel. I'm just as lost as you are in all of this."

"Even though I didn't want this baby, I didn't want to lose it this way."

"No, only you were okay with losing it the way you chose." As soon as the words slipped out, he knew they came from a deep crevice in his heart that was still clinging to spite, bitterness. He believed that all life, whether plant, animal, or human, was a gift not to be spurned. Her reiteration that she had never wanted the baby triggered what he really felt about her decisions. His retort was callous and vengeful for the life he had fought so hard for.

Eleanor burst out bawling and scrabbled to grab her sheets to dab her eyes continually.

He groaned in contrition. "I'm sorry I said that. That was ugly and mean."

"No, you're right. I won't deny that I wanted it gone before I got attached. I told myself that I wouldn't get attached. Over the months, I've let myself feel things I didn't want to feel. I know beyond a shadow of a doubt this baby deserved a life. I just didn't want it impeding mine."

They didn't speak for a long time. Their intertwined fingers stroked a language of comfort that both clung to. The frail light of the end of day painted the sky with its last brush strokes before hanging up its brushes to get out of the way for a few stars to scintillate on their stage. Eleanor tugged for him to spoon her and to place his hand on her belly. In perfect unison, her palm with his on top moved from spot to spot on her belly. At each spot they waited with bated breath for any sign of a miracle. Over and over in their grief, their hands wandered to touch life.

Seth dreamed that he was standing outside an enormous bubble. Its iridescent film shimmered in the soft moonlight glow. He tentatively walked toward the sheen and placed his palm on its surface. It didn't break as he thought it would. He gently pressed against it, and it yielded. It was transparent, nothing and no one to interact with. He turned around and faced a black landscape. He turned back to it and pressed again harder. The inner wall of the bubble fogged from within and a ghostly baby's hand appeared and lightly pressed against his.

His eyes shot open, and he gulped air. His lips touched Eleanor's neck; she curved against him. There! A movement against his hand. Another one, stronger, as if the baby demanded to live. He kissed her pale skin and smiled. "El."

She grunted and drew the covers higher.

"Wake up. I feel the baby."

Her hand shot down under the covers and searched for his. He guided her fingers to the site of the miracle and held her close.

She gave a strangled cry of elated joy and bottled fear. She took a long moment to feel the joy before shoving Seth out of the bed and demanded, "Get Dr. Barnes now!"

He didn't take offence, only looked back at her and saw that her reaction was just as genuinely happy as his was. He ran to the base and found Dr. Barnes getting ready for the day.

"You've got to come now. The baby moved."

Dr. Barnes's expression was jaded with suspicion. Seth was sure Dr. Barnes thought he was blinded by optimism.

He pressed on. "Really! It wasn't even movement. She kicked against my hand."

Dr. Barnes grabbed his bag and ran out the door with Seth following on his heels. When they got to the cabin, Eleanor was still in bed holding her belly and beaming down. "The baby is all right. Thank God!"

Dr. Barnes immediately took out his stethoscope and lifted her shirt to listen to the baby's heartbeat. He made a cutting motion through the air to relay he needed quiet to listen. He moved it around shaking his head. He went back to the original spot again. His brows lowered, and his tongue stuck out between his two front teeth.

Then he lowered the sheets past her knees. "I have to take a look down there."

Seth caught Eleanor vehemently nodding before he looked away.

After he rolled the sheets back to her belly, Dr. Barnes announced, "The bleeding has stopped. No fresh blood, a strong heartbeat—it looks as if you two will be parents after all."

Seth grabbed Dr. Barnes's hand between his and said, "The baby is going to be okay?"

Dr. Barnes harrumphed. "Well, I'll still need to keep an eye on things. Eleanor will have to keep her activities to a minimum. No work, and no, umm, bedroom affairs."

Seth glanced at Eleanor and saw that her cheeks had reddened more than he had ever seen them. To save her the embarrassment he quickly said, "That's not an issue at all."

Eleanor piped, "I can't miss a week of work. My parents depend on every penny I send."

Dr. Barnes furrowed his brows. "What do you do?"

She answered, "I'm a typist."

"Ah, well, you can type in your home." Dr. Barnes answered.

Seth agreed. "You won't have to miss work. I'll set something up for you right here."

Eleanor asked, "How?"

He knelt beside her. "I'm going to get one of the carpenters to rig a quick writing table where you can put your files and typewriter."

"How will I get the files that need to be typed and get the ones that have been typed back to you?"

"I'll come visit at least once." He kissed her on the head. "And I'll see if Julia would like to work here with you."

Seth winked at Eleanor. As long as she could continue to work to send money to her family, he had a chance at a life with her, one where she was in charge of her own destiny and able to depend on herself.

Dr. Barnes chimed in. "Good, that's settled. The next two weeks I'll come to check on the baby twice a week. After that, I'll come once a week." He gathered his bag, shook both their hands to congratulate them, and chuckled as he walked out the door.

With glittering eyes, she asked Seth, "You'd do all that for me?"

"I'd do anything for you." As he knelt in front of her, he caressed her hands. His breath ghosted across her knuckles before he gave them the faintest of kisses. He murmured, "I'd die for you." He beheld her and, for the first time, believed she could truly love him back. Maybe his fantasy wasn't all in his head.

Her trembling hand slid across the short scratchy hairs of his beard. Her fingertips reached all the way to the back of his neck. She said, "You love me, don't you?"

He wondered if this was the perfect time to mould his lips to hers, to taste her as he had been dreaming of, hoping for. He didn't have the chance to wonder long because Eleanor pressed her hand upon his open, vulnerable heart and leaned in to kiss him. He closed the gap and captured her lips with his. Their lips moved in unison, parting and closing in time to the melody they could only hear.

As their kiss deepened he covered her hand on his chest with his. She tugged on his shirt and nipped his lower lip. His lips continued their dance of adoration as he smiled, his desire to explore every inch of her unquenchable.

Eventually, she stilled her bruised lips.

A roar in his ears begged to insist more, but he pushed it down and quieted.

She smiled brightly and gave him another chaste kiss on his lips.

"I...."

Dare he tell the whole truth now?

He tucked her in and said, "You rest, and I'll go talk to the carpenter to build your new workstation."

"All right."

Within a day, the carpenter cobbled together a suitable station for Eleanor and Julia.

Julia fluttered in and said, "I'm so honoured you want me to stay here with you. I'll run to the office and back to bring your work. I'll fetch your tea, your food. Will you need help going to the outhouse?"

Eleanor threw back her head in laughter. "No, silly goose, I don't need you to do all that. I just want your precious company."

The next day as Seth was carrying a folder of papers for Eleanor to type, he neared the cabin and heard the two women laughing through an open window, the cool air of late fall filling the home.

Just as he got to the corner of the cabin, he heard Eleanor blurt, "I kissed Seth."

Julia giggled.

He decided to eavesdrop, all the while cursing himself for it.

Julia said, "I was wondering when—"

"I don't know why I did it."

His brows furrowed.

Julia asked, "Did he kiss you back?"

"He did," Eleanor said breathlessly.

"Girl, that man is head over heels in love with you!"

"How can you say for sure?"

After a pause, Julia said, "He looks at you the way Peter looks at me and the way I look at Peter."

Eleanor asked, "How do I look at him?"

There was a long moment before she replied, "Your look is complicated. You love him, but I'm not sure you're letting yourself love him fully."

"I asked him if he loved me, but he didn't answer. He just kissed me back."

I should have said it. It was on the tip of my tongue.

Julia playfully chided. "Well, you started the kiss. If a girl offers her lips to a man, chances are he won't be talking, he'll be kissing."

"But he didn't say anything after!" Eleanor's frustration was palpable.

"He's probably scared," Julia said placatingly.

"Of what?"

"Look at your short history. It's just gotten better, maybe that's why."

Eleanor's voice rose. "But he doesn't get scared! Not like I do, not like I am."

"Every man decent enough to love is scared to love, I think."

"That's hard to believe. Paul said it the first time we had sex."

Julia's voice was tinged with exasperation. "Paul isn't here! He's gone to marry someone else. How's that love working out for you? You've got a good man fully committed to you and that baby. You're going to think about Paul the rest of your life when you've got him?"

"I guess not."

"I'm telling you as a friend who loves you that you've got to grab hold of the good you've got in your life. God knows you need it after all you've been through."

There was no answer from Eleanor. The sound of Eleanor's typing commenced, followed by Julia's. He waited a few minutes mulling over the women's conversation and how he felt about Paul's ghost. He opened the door and gave Eleanor the folder.

"You came," she said.

"I told you I would."

Happy families are all alike;
every unhappy family is unhappy in their own way.
Leo Tolstoy

Chapter 21

Mid-January 1944

The following month was the happiest time of Seth's life. He hoped it was the same for Eleanor. He didn't want to be straight and ask her outright for fear she would bolt. Then he realised he didn't need to.

Every morning she greeted him with a smile and a kiss on the cheek. When he brought files or picked up her typed ones, her fingers would firmly slide over his as the documents changed owners. Evenings were spent together. They engaged in tender caresses which demanded his utmost self control in going no further than what had already come to pass. Those nights they shared their thoughts, their past, but never their dreams. It was an understood safe not to be opened at all costs for fear their happy present times would crumble into their shaky foundation.

A niggling thought haunted him; the longer they steered clear of the inevitable the harder it would be to overcome. Something had to give and soon.

With each week that passed, Dr. Barnes declared Eleanor could be less reliant on the initial bed rest prescribed. By the end of the month, she resumed her regular comings and goings.

One morning, as Seth entered the office, Eleanor pointed out, "Seth, there's a letter from your sister, Christina. I saw it on your desk when I came in this morning."

"Thank you." He kissed her shoulder as he passed by her.

Christina's beautiful penmanship was something that Seth had always envied. Although his writing was legible, it was hardly fit to be read by the king.

He broke it open and noticed the water stains scattered over the page, slightly rippling the paper where they had landed. He read:

Dear Seth,

There's never a good way to say what I'm about to say. You've always been better with your words than I have been and stronger to bear bad news. I wish you were the one writing this letter so that it could give you the best chance of, I don't know, a better feeling? But how could any good feeling come from this?

Rowena is dead. She was driving an ambulance on the front when a mine blew up killing her, the paramedics, and patients.

Gosh, you think that when you're young you've got all the time in the world, but this war has been enough to show us that we're not immortal no matter how much we believe it. I don't want to believe this. I can't accept this.

The funeral is here in Edmonton on the 30th. Please say you'll be able to fly out and make it. I know you're doing important work up there. I hope you get this in time. I can't call now. I don't think I'd be able to speak. If I don't hear from you in a week's time, I'll call you.

Your loving sister,

Christina

He placed his hands together in a praying stance and touched his forehead to his fingertips, squeezing his eyes shut. Rowena had been a devout Catholic. If she had been right about what happens after death, he could be at peace that she was in a better place, in bliss far away from the cares and dangers of this world. He also had peace that she had dodged a bullet by not marrying a man who wouldn't stay faithful to her for very long.

Eleanor gathered some papers, her brows knit in confusion. "What's wrong?"

Seth leaned against her desk and faced the window. "My sister died. Rowena, the one who was an ambulance driver. She, uh, got blown up by a mine." He let out a large breath and hissed. "I have to go, but after what's happened with you and the baby—"

"I'll go with you."

"You can't. Can you?"

She planted herself in front of him and slid her hands down his shoulders. "Don't tell me what I can't do. Ask Dr. Barnes to come out and examine me, give me a clean bill of health."

He retorted, "It's a rough journey."

She clucked, "I've done it before."

"Yeah, but not like this." He cradled her belly.

She wrapped her hands around his neck. "If Dr. Barnes lets me go, I promise I won't push myself. I'll sit most of the time. I'll behave. I want to go with you."

"Why?"

She didn't meet his eyes as she replied, "I want to be there for you if you want me there? Do you?"

He nodded and grasped one of her hands. "I do. I just want what's best for you."

"Well, ask Dr. Barnes to come over."

Because Eleanor had convalesced per all his instructions, Dr. Barnes stated she could go on condition that she heeded his guidance on her travels. He also lifted her ban on *all* activities.

The day before they left, Seth suggested, "Why don't you call your mom? Let her know you'll be returning. You can use the office phone."

"Okay," she said reluctantly.

"What's wrong?" he asked.

She fiddled with her fingers. "I've been faithfully sending money every month, but it isn't the same as a letter. I haven't written to her since I found out about my pregnancy."

"Ah, and you're not sure what to say."

She blew through her lips. "It's time I rip off the bandaid, isn't it?"

He nodded.

"All right."

He watched her clench her hand before she swooped up the receiver and dialled the operator.

After a moment, she said, "23821"

As she waited, she tapped her fingers on the desk. It looked as if she would hang up if she waited another second.

She exhaled a shaky breath. "Mike, how are you?"

Seth barely registered a male voice answer.

"Yes—"

Mike said something that etched guilt on Eleanor's face.

"About that, I'm sorry, it's just been—"

Her lips quirked up in a small smile.

"You are?" She shrunk as if her guilt were squashing her. "Yes, I do. I called because I'm coming home, just for a short visit."

A pause.

"We're leaving tomorrow."

Eleanor's eyes met his as she said, "Yes, mum, I'm married."

After listening to her mother, she added, "He's a very good man. You'll meet him soon. I can't speak for long. We have to pack, and there's plans to finalise—"

Her mother interrupted.

"I can't wait to see you, too, Mum, and Dad. Even Mike and Lily—oh! And my niece or nephew?" Her mouth opened in an *O*. "Luke is a strong name. Please give them my congratulations."

Another pause.

"I will, mum. Bye."

The next day they packed lightly and set foot on the Army transport plane that would bring her back to the staleness of her past life. After setting down and lifting off ten airfields from Norman Wells to Blatchford Field, Edmonton, they boarded a streetcar of the Edmonton Radial Railway (ERR) and bought their tickets from the woman conductor. All the seats were taken. A young boy of about fifteen offered his seat to Eleanor. Seth stood beside her.

Eleanor gazed out the window watching the rush of bodies hurrying, carrying bags of groceries and other goods, bumping into strangers as they hurried to reach their goals at the expense of others.

After they stepped off, Seth carried their bags as Eleanor led the way to her parent's home a block away.

Eleanor rapped her knuckles on the front door of her parent's home.

He heard someone inside hurrying to the front door.

A thin yet vibrant face crowned with white hair peeked around the door first before opening it all the way. Eleanor's mother's frail arms wrapped tightly around her daughter. Although her mother looked frail, the strength of her love was made manifest in her embrace.

Her mother whispered, "I couldn't think that you would be more beautiful than when I last saw you." Her mother's tears flowed freely.

Eleanor let out a sobbing laugh and squeezed back hard. "I missed you, Mum."

"How long can you stay?" her mother asked as she smushed Eleanor's cheeks.

"Uh, three days, we're here for his sister's funeral," Eleanor said.

Eleanor's mother's hand covered her gasp."Oh, I'm so terribly sorry. Please accept my condolences on your sister's death."

Seth replied, "Thank you. I appreciate that."

"Can't you two stay more than three days?" her mother asked.

Eleanor pulled away and slipped her hand around Seth's arm. "Mom, this is Seth, my husband. We'd love to stay longer, but we both have to get back to work. And I can't have the baby here."

Her mother's brows lifted in surprise. "A baby—I felt your belly when we hugged! Why didn't you ever say anything?"

Eleanor shrugged her shoulders. "I didn't know how to tell you."

"You say it like it's bad news. Why, it's the opposite! A beautiful thing to celebrate! Your father is going to be so pleased. He's really looking forward to meeting you, Seth."

Seth nodded and gave a huge smile. "I'm looking forward to meeting the whole family. It'll be nice to celebrate a family reunion before the funeral tomorrow."

"Come inside," Eleanor's mother ushered them in.

As soon as Seth and Eleanor settled their bags after her mother showed them their room upstairs, they returned downstairs and followed her mother into the room immediately to the left of the entrance.

Eleanor's mother rounded her father's bedside to check if he was awake from his nap.

Her mother whispered, "He's asleep. Perhaps later."

A feeble voice uttered, "Eleanor."

Her back stiffened as she squeezed Seth's fingers. She walked toward the bed and sat gingerly by his side, bending her ear to hear his quiet words. She spoke with him and nodded after some time. She returned to Seth with tears in her eyes. "He wants to speak to you if that's all right?"

Seth replied, "Of course."

Eleanor and her mother closed the door and left him with his father-in-law.

"Sir," Seth extended his hand. "It's an honour to meet you. I'm sorry that we never—I never asked for your blessing. Our marriage was born from unforeseen circumstances."

Her father smiled knowingly. "You mean the baby."

"Yes."

"It's not yours, is it?"

Seth opened his mouth to speak, but how could he do so without betraying Eleanor in some way, without letting her tell her own story to her father? He couldn't take that from her.

Her father spoke up, "I know my daughter. Marriage and a baby were the furthest things from her mind before she left. She wouldn't have given up her independence for any man, at least not willingly. I appreciate you not wanting to say anything. I assume the man she slept with isn't in the picture. How did you come to marry her? Why?"

"The man she slept with is my best friend who's set—I mean who was set to marry my youngest sister Rowena. She's the one who just passed. Before he left, he made me swear to look after Eleanor. I wrote to him about the baby, but he was bent on going through with marrying my sister. The only way I could spare the baby's life and help El keep her job was to marry her and provide a family to look after the baby once it's born."

"The baby is going to a good family? If I still had my money, I would—" a violent cough wracked his lungs. "I would help support Eleanor's baby, my grandchild."

"I'm sure you would if you could. Please know that I'll also be around to help the baby."

"You respect her, and I couldn't ask for any better than a man who respects her. Do you love her?"

"I do, sir. I hope it's enough for her."

Her father made a guttural noise. "Whatever happens, whatever decision she makes, I'm grateful that you've protected her and enabled her to do what she desperately wanted to do, that is have her own life. However, I urge you to tell her if you love her. She'll hold it against you. She doesn't do well with things kept in the dark."

Seth pondered the meaning behind her father's last words. "Thank you, sir."

"Please call me Edward."

"All right, Edward."

"May you please ask Eleanor to come inside? I'd like to catch up with my daughter."

Seth nodded. "I'll get her."

When Eleanor brushed his arm with hers on the threshold of her father's door, he could think of little else than to kiss her right then and there, to explore her mouth with his.

Her mother, with red-rimmed eyes caught his attention, and he followed her down to the kitchen where a whistle from the teapot sang.

He offered, "Ma'am, can I help with anything?"

"No, no, you sit on down. Please don't call me ma'am. If you're not comfortable calling me momma, then call me Sandra. Tea okay? Or do you need a cup of coffee?"

"Tea is my preference, Sandra." He really wanted to call her momma. However, he felt he couldn't call Eleanor's mom by momma when they weren't meant to last. He had never referred to Nasnana as momma. All his life he had called her Nana.

"You've got it." Sandra poured his tea.

"I hear Eleanor has a brother who's married, and he and his wife have a son."

"Yes, his wife's name is Lily. My grandson is Luke. They just went out for the afternoon shopping and other outings. They thought it would be nice to give you two some space to be with us."

Seth smiled. "That's really thoughtful of them. I'm very thankful for how welcoming you've been."

Sandra placed her hand on his arm. "You've been taking care of our girl. She's our gem and been through so much. I can see she's eating well. She doesn't look pale."

Seth divulged the scare they had with the baby back at Norman Wells but didn't go on to say why that baby almost passed.

"Oh my Lord, He is good. To think that she's feeling well enough to come down. It's a funny thing how you were the one to marry her."

"How's that?"

"I don't know how she got past your eyes. I don't mean it as a compliment. You do have nice eyes, but they look too much like—"

"I know about him," Seth acknowledged.

"Hmm, as I said, you must have a way about you if she can be near you, let alone squeeze your hand. It's a wonder."

He added milk and sugar to his tea and sipped it. "How are you doing with Edward?"

"Edward is it? That's good. Means he likes you. I thought that when Eleanor left I would feel desolate, but instead I've risen to the task. I see Edward and I were holding her back from finding a life of her own for too long. My son and his wife are a good enough help, not so much with Edward specifically but with the general running of the house. Lily's really good at cooking so I never have to do that anymore. My son runs the overall affairs."

She sipped her tea. "It has given me the time to completely devote myself to Edward. I'm falling in love with him all over again. I know it doesn't look like much because I'm having to care for all of his physical needs which can be strenuous. But I've become stronger. This is what real, unconditional love is, loving the person through thick and thin and showing that you'd never let them go no matter how easy it would be to do it."

Seth tipped an invisible hat. "You're the golden standard."

"Ah, don't underestimate how much of that you're already doing yourself."

"You can tell?" he asked.

"I can sniff out a selfless person."

He admitted, "She's the one who's brought me out of a place I never thought I could come out of."

"What place is that?"

"A place of self and the mundane."

She nodded, "That's exactly what love does, no doubt about it."

Eleanor's brother Mike returned with his wife Lily and their son Luke. As soon as Mike unwrapped his scarf and hung it, he wordlessly hugged Eleanor. Mike's round face was an echo of his father's.

Lily, an able-bodied brunette of medium build, gave a friendly wave.

Eleanor hesitated before giving her a short hug. Then she asked, "May I?" holding out her arms to hold Luke.

Lily passed Luke to Eleanor. He gave her a big toothless smile.

Eleanor laughed and gave him a big kiss on his cheek. She held him a little longer before passing him back to Mike.

Sandra announced, "Supper is ready. Let's eat. Mike? Seth? Would you be willing to help Edward to the table? He's feeling well enough for this momentous occasion."

The two men slipped each of Edward's arms around their necks and slowly walked him to the dining room.

As they ate, laughed, and talked, Seth glimpsed how Eleanor would have been as a child surrounded by a loving family, unscathed and whole.

After supper, while Mike and Seth washed the dishes, Sandra asked Eleanor to sit at the table while she fetched something. When she returned, Sandra said, "Here. I've written out notes and instructions on what bodily changes you can expect after giving birth, what routines you could put in place for the baby, that is until the Dene family can take her. I thought I'd give it to you before I forget. I hope it's not too much."

Looking over his shoulder, Seth saw Eleanor scrape her chair back so she could hug her mother. "Thank you, Mum. It's very helpful."

Once the dishes were done, Seth and Eleanor retired to their room. As she began to open the door, she giggled, "This is the first time I've ever brought a man home. It's just strange."

He wrapped his arms around her from behind. "I'm not just a man. I'm your husband."

Her already flushed cheeks grew rosier. "So you are."

Her old room had been turned into Luke's nursery. For the two nights that Seth and Eleanor were staying, Mike had set up her bed in the corner with a handmade quilt draped at the end of the bed. Seth went over and fingered the quilt. "Did you make this?"

Eleanor smiled as if reliving a distant memory. "I did. My mom taught me how to sew and quilt, training me to be the perfect little housewife. I was supposed to marry my childhood friend Anthony, but I didn't love him. Because my plans were too different from his, he wouldn't have wanted me anyway. Not like you do—I mean not that you want me—but you care for me despite everything and—"

She couldn't get another word in because Seth's lips ghosted over hers and stilled her words. He lifted his hands achingly, slowly over the curves of her waist and brushing against the sides of her breasts to cup her face. His lips, flat against hers, opened slightly, asking her to accept his invitation. She angled her head to allow him deeper access. Without interruption from the outside and without interruption from their own frenetic minds, they allowed their tongues to explore the unknown territory they had previously been afraid of. His breath ragged, his hands aching to move down to other parts to touch, he said, "I want you. I never thought I would or could. Every play of this game has been dead set against us. I've allowed the walls to keep my growing love for you from you too long. I want to tear down these walls with my bare hands and throw myself at your feet begging you to think of me the way I hope you can."

She gave his bottom lip a playful yet gentle bite, "Then tear down those walls."

He tugged her shirt sleeve down so that her shoulder peeked out. He kissed it softly over and over as her fingers roamed his hair. Her cardigan was thrown to the corner, her skirt slid to the ground. He reigned back his fervour and trailed featherlight kisses down her collarbone, sternum, the tops of her breasts, and down to her bulging belly.

He stepped back and unbuttoned his shirt all the time watching her reaction to see if he needed to stop or if her desire beckoned him to continue.

They moved to the bed. She slid under the sheet, and he moved in tight beside her. As he kissed her, his hand trailed to an unexplored heaven.

When her breathing had lulled to a gentle rhythm, he kissed her shoulder and smiled. They had finally breached the walls, and the destiny he dreamed of was now at hand.

Then a cold, rude awakening was planted in his mind. He had kept the most important thing from her. After such a tender, vulnerable step, he feared she wouldn't forgive him. He couldn't put it off any longer. After the funeral, he had to tell her.

Seth woke when Eleanor shifted to be more comfortable. Now that she was more advanced in the pregnancy, her nights were characterised by several different movements throughout the night. It was a miracle he had slept through them all. He drew her closer to his core and kissed her shoulder.

"Seth," she said clearly, "I love you."

Would she love him still after the revelation? He slapped his fear away and inhaled the scent of her hair as he said, "I love you too."

They slowly got up and dressed in silence, eyeing each other with coy smiles and flirtatious glances. Before they opened the door, Seth gently wrapped his arms around her and peppered her neck and jawline with sensual slow kisses. She responded by reaching behind and running her hands through his hair and thrumming happily. When his arm reached beyond her to open the door, she halted his movement, turned, and kissed his lips.

She whispered, "Now we can go."

As they sat down to breakfast with the family, her mother asked, "How was your sleep?

Mike chortled, "Not sure how much sleep they got."

Seth proudly smiled as he glimpsed Eleanor's frustrated response.

She asked, "How old are you again?" She trailed her finger along Seth's leg underneath the table. Her magnetic touch sent shivers to every nerve, a switch that caused adoration to blossom.

Mike raised his hands in mock defence. "We're all married here, aren't we?"

Eleanor smiled, "Yes, we are."

Seth and Eleanor quickly finished the remainder of their meal and left for the funeral.

They arrived at the cemetery just as Seth's other two sisters did, Christina and Shaina. Seth introduced Eleanor to them. Eleanor shook their hands and gave her condolences. Seth realised that it was an awkward time to mourn while also sharing news of their celebration of the upcoming baby's birth. His sisters took notice and gave small smiles and their congratulations. He hadn't had a time when he had to navigate both death and life.

They made their way to the graveside where the extravagant white coffin lay next to the hole that had been dug in the earth.

It was surreal that his brave, younger sister, the one who had always encouraged him in his endeavours as he had always encouraged her in hers, was now gone. His heavy heart cracked open, pain rushing out from the depths to drown him. His lower lip trembled as he attempted to hold back his tears. He scrunched his nose to force his tears back from where they came.

Eleanor's fingers held his, and he acknowledged her kindness with a little squeeze.

The priest made his way to the front with another man, head turned away and bent down low beneath a fedora hat.

Suddenly, the warmth of Eleanor's fingers slipped away.

Seth shifted his gaze from Rowena's grave to peer down at Eleanor's face. What had caused her to flinch? He followed her gaze to the man beside the priest. The man ever so slightly turned his head. It was Paul.

ELEANOR

PART V

The Fantasy

Chapter 22

January 30th, 1944

Of course, Paul would be here because his fiancé was now dead. The woman he had loved more than Eleanor was gone, and now she could—she paused and reached for Seth's fingers again to reassure herself of the torn down walls that had led to green pastures. She couldn't turn away now.

Though she tried with all her might, Paul's presence was magnetic, bringing back all the scintillating memories of her first exciting months at Norman Wells. Yet Seth's presence was essential. She felt pulled between two poles. The more the feelings grew, the more she became dizzy. Her tentative fingers on Seth's arm moved to wrap tightly around the crook of his elbow.

Seth knew, oh, he knew. How could she hide her surprise, her dismay, her increasing anxiety as to how she would figure this out?

She prayed that Paul would take one look at her, a look of disgust, turn on his heel, and walk away. That would make it easy, and she needed easy.

The family began to take turns passing the shovel and throwing in some dirt. She prayed Seth would go on without her to take part so that Paul wouldn't notice her presence. Instead Seth took her hand and drew close to the grave. He scooped some dirt and threw it in. Then he handed it to Eleanor. She hoped she wouldn't faint and fall into the opening. As she took the handle from Seth, she could feel Paul's eyes on her. There was always an intense heat that radiated from them, and she could feel it now as if time hadn't passed.

Those who weren't family began to leave the grounds. The family would welcome them soon enough into Seth's sister Christina's home. Paul was the last who wasn't in the immediate family to leave. He gave Seth a bear hug and whispered his condolences.

Fear planted Eleanor to the spot. Should she approach? Let him approach? What was right in this situation of past and present colliding?

Paul stood before her, looked down at her belly, and kissed her forehead as he braced his hands on her shoulders. "It's good to see you, Eleanor." Then he walked away.

She jumped when Seth wrapped his arms around her shoulders and led her away from the grave. Though Eleanor had long given up blaming someone else for her circumstances, a disgusting thought, a dishonour to the dead, rose into her mind unbidden. Rowena deserved her grave after putting Eleanor in hers.

Horrified at her own indecency, she furtively looked around, a little afraid someone could overhear her thoughts. How could she desecrate and condemn Rowena for her own problems!

They all made their way to Christina's home which was just barely able to fit the amount of people who had shown up to pay their condolences. There were all sorts of people streaming through the door though they were no more than fifty. Some were ladies in their fifties who had cooked casseroles and baked goods so that Christina and her family wouldn't have to buy their own groceries for two weeks. There was an odd family member or two who was constantly swiping wine from the liquor cabinet or sitting morosely in their chair not deigning to converse with anyone.

From the front of the room, Christina began the remembrance service with listing Rowena's accomplishments and kindnesses and reading from some of her letters. Other family members joined in, and Eleanor forgot her dramatic troubles as she mourned with the family. She could almost say that she knew Rowena just from listening to every letter read and everything others said about her. She was beginning to understand why Paul had chosen Rowena over her.

Seth remained eerily quiet beside her and never once offered a story or a memory of the sister she knew he was closest to. He held a dram of whisky, occasionally sipping and swirling it in his mouth. She had never seen him drink. Perhaps, it was a tonic he allowed himself when comfort was far from hand.

When a few of the family members got up to get some refreshment, Seth sat up in his chair and said to her, "I'm going outside to get some fresh air. Is that okay?"

"Of course, I'll make myself useful and wash some dishes." She put her hand upon his forearm and bent to kiss his cheek. She hated that, during her loving display, she wondered if Paul watched her. He hovered on the other side of the room with Seth's other sister Shaina. She felt dirty, and it wasn't because of anything he was doing. It was because she allowed herself to lust after him just as she had when they had first met.

She moved to the kitchen where she told the old woman washing dishes that she would take her place so that the old woman could mingle with the company. The window overlooked the backyard, one half dedicated to growing some plants. The other half was filled with sand and sand toys for little kids to play in. Seth started a bonfire in the outdoor fire pit and sat upon one of the two chairs overlooking the garden facing the kitchen window. He didn't see her standing there watching him. Already she could feel the distance growing between them—a chasm she wasn't sure she could cross again. How had they moved so far away in the space of six hours?

Paul entered the backyard and sat in the chair next to Seth. He held a bottle of whisky and a shot glass in the other hand. He filled their glasses and clinked them. Eleanor felt as if she were invading a space that was never meant for her even though she couldn't hear a word they said. They didn't even speak. They just sat in silence staring at the garden in front of them.

Christina sidled up to Eleanor and murmured, "Those two helped Rowena build that little garden two springs before the war."

Curiosity piqued Eleanor. "How long did Paul know Rowena?"

"We've all known each other since we were young. Paul's father was employed by Imperial Oil for a time long ago."

"Yes, Seth told me. Sorry I meant, how long were they together?"

"Ah, well, while Paul's father was stationed up North, they couldn't stand each other. Then Paul's father found work in Edmonton and moved the family there. I moved to Edmonton several years later with Rowena. We rang up Paul to reconnect. It only took one night of drinks and dancing for them to fall in love hard, deeply. It was a fairytale story."

Eleanor gulped. Did Christina know that she was the wrench in the story, that this baby had changed all their lives forever? Christina didn't intimate that she knew anything beyond what Eleanor and Seth had already told her.

Afternoon passed into evening, and the evening passed into night. Everyone had left. Eleanor napped in the armchair situated near the fireplace in the living room. Muffled shouting woke her up. She had forgotten where she was.

Christina and her family were nowhere to be seen. It made sense that they would have retired to the quiet of their rooms after being in company most of the day.

The shouting started again. Eleanor rose up from her seat and followed it to its source in the backyard. It was Seth gritting his teeth and pointing a finger in Paul's face. She moved to the side door and opened it a bit so that some of the words floated to her anxious ears.

Paul's voice was calm and steady as he said, "I didn't think she needed to know."

A loud, cutting laughter ripped out of Seth. "Didn't need to know that the man she had been in love with for years, the man she was waiting to marry after this d—m war, had sex with another woman and got her pregnant. What did you think would happen? That I wouldn't say a word to her?"

"Well, that was troublesome. It almost ruined everything. Anyway, I got you to take care of it."

Seth swung his finger toward the house and seethed, "It was my duty as her older brother to warn her against you. What you did was a breach of trust against her and, as a consequence, against me. I did the right thing."

He rose up swiftly from his chair and continued, "Eleanor and the baby are not a mess to take care of. You didn't deserve Rowena and sure as h—l don't deserve Eleanor and this baby!"

Paul vaulted from his own chair, took a step forward, and punched him straight in the nose.

Seth reeled back, cupped his hands over his nose, and howled. Blood spilled. Dead calm laced Seth's voice as he replied, "You sure you want to go that way? You know there's no way you'll leave this place intact."

Paul shook his hands at his sides and fisted them. "I want her, and I still love her."

The air rushed out from Eleanor's lungs at Paul's declaration of love. For so long, she had longed to hear the words as evidence that what they had been more than just a fling. She had longed for it. Did she still now?

"You don't know what love is. You never have. You know why? Because it's all about you, your needs, your life. Everyone next to you is just along for the ride. Oh, and it's a fun one for a while! Except she's going to pay for all of it. I can't let you do that."

Paul smirked. He ran his hand through his hair as if he now had the upper hand in this conversation. "Do you really think she'd pick you over me?"

Seth sucked in a breath and kept his gaze down as if he were a dog that had been kicked down.

Bolstered by Seth's reaction, Paul crept closer, squatted, and peered into Seth's face with a sneer. "You're a man used to getting his buddy's scraps. What would she say if she knew that you married her just because I asked you to? She'll hate you for it."

She could finally insert the missing piece into the puzzle she had pieced together these last few months. Why did she ever believe a random stranger would marry her just to save her, as if she was a princess needing saving from a locked tower? Instead there was an outside force all along, Paul who had loved her enough to make sure she was taken care of. The man who really wanted her from the very beginning was standing right there, and now he was available. How could she not go back to the father of her child? They could live together as one family

Would Seth have done it if Paul hadn't asked? Unlikely— very, very doubtful. Never.

The glimmer that had broken her resistance down into a malleable love for a man who was the opposite of who she had dreamed of loving had been based on the premise that he had chosen her simply to show her love without prodding. It was a lie.

No matter how much she wanted Seth to emerge as the victor, especially these last few weeks, he had been doomed to pick the short straw. She pitied him. Pity was a dangerous feeling for her to engage in because it usually led to her disgust. She wanted to turn away before that could take place. She wanted to preserve whatever regard for him she had left. She couldn't bring herself to hate him, not after everything they had been through.

Paul slapped him on the back and said, "You'll learn to love again."

Seth swatted his hand away and yelled, "You have no respect for the dead. Rowena isn't even cold in the grave, and you're going to take my wife. You're a piece of sh—."

Paul exited through the side gate. A rattle from behind Eleanor made her swivel. There was Christina with her mouth wide open, just staring at her. Eleanor couldn't face her surprise, her questions. How could she when Christina was already devastated at the loss of her sister? Eleanor felt as if her very presence stained the home. She swept past Christina and grabbed her fur coat, hat, and leather gloves while she waited for Seth to meet her at the door.

A moment later, the screen door leading to the backyard slammed shut. Eleanor waited quietly with her hands folded over each other. With the whiskey bottle still in his hand, he lumbered bleary-eyed into the entrance. The state he was in—he was in no condition to be walking her home back to her parent's house.

She cleared her throat and said, "I'm going to my parents' now. You can stay here tonight. I'll see you in the morning."

He squeezed his eyes shut and wiped a hand across his beaded brow. He said, "I can take you home."

Her voice wavered, "No, you can't, not anymore."

His pain-clouded eyes elicited her deepest sympathy. Torn in her decision to leave him, she held onto the hope that her original plan was now tangible and in sight. Perhaps that's what this whole time with Seth was for, to grow in ways she never could have, for this very moment of receiving what she always desired.

He took a slow step toward her and another. His strong arms cradled her as he kissed her forehead and whispered, "I love you."

Just then the front door opened, breaking them apart from each other. Paul stood there and held out his arm for her. "I came back for you. Can I take you home?"

Eleanor looked from one man to the next ready to make her choice. She slid her hand over to Paul's arm and said to Seth, "Thank you for everything, but this is the end of our story."

She walked out of Christina's home ready to embrace her new future.

Chapter 23

Early February 1944

Paul drew her close to his chest as soon as Christina shut the door in their faces. Eleanor leaned into his touch remembering how all these long months she had ached for it. Now that she had it, she wondered if it somehow felt different, something less thrilling, less blazing. Yet wouldn't it feel different? So much had changed these many months apart.

Paul murmured against her hair. "Eleanor, I want us to be a family. I'm free to do that now, and I was hoping that you'd say yes. We fit so well together in all the right ways. I want you and the baby. I've got a house set up already on West Jasper Avenue, a good job. I can also help take care of your parents. They won't need or want for anything. You and me, we're a dream come true."

These were words that Eleanor had been dreaming of hearing for such a long time. Finally she heard them from his lips and not just the ghost of his voice. "I missed you," she said.

"Ah, baby, come here." He led her to the side of Christina's house and pressed his lips hard all over. The intensity of his kiss made her feel woozy. She moaned in response, and he deepened it. His hand slid up her thigh making her press herself hard against him. It was just like old times, the appeal of his physicality driving her crazy all over again. She relished it.

As they walked to her parent's home, Eleanor eagerly told him all about the baby though she did leave out how she attempted an abortion and how there was a pregnancy scare a few weeks ago. She was also very careful to leave out Seth completely.

Paul didn't do or say too much except rub his hand all over her back and down to places that left Eleanor completely heated. When they arrived, Paul kissed her goodbye.

She opened the door quietly, for she assumed everyone was sound asleep. Eleanor ascended the stairs and entered her old room.

She changed slowly and remembered a set of eyes watching her earlier that morning. She hunkered into bed and wrapped the blankets all around her. Sudden tears pricked her eyes and she stifled a cry. The sheets smelled like him. Snapshots of their first night together as husband and wife shuffled past, taunting her decision to officially close that door.

She cared for him more than she had ever been willing to admit. Could it not be that he had served his purpose for the time they had together? Wasn't it always the plan? She had been willing to change the plan after he and she had found an oasis in the desert when they thought there was none.

It would be easy for Seth to believe she was still fickle. After all, it was the pattern she had lived up to until a couple months ago, before she was open to change for love. She could let him believe it one last time, couldn't she? If it gave him a clean break with the least emotional damage, she would let him believe she was a monster.

Eleanor got up at six in the morning and went to the kitchen to scrounge for breakfast.

Her mother entered a few minutes later. She asked, "How did you and Seth sleep? How did it go yesterday?"

Eleanor looked at the floor before answering, "Mom, marrying Seth isn't the whole truth. There's a lot more I haven't told you." She shared how the baby was really Paul's, but still left out why Paul had deserted her in the first place.

Her mother listened and kept silent, asking questions with concern, but never berated her, never expressed disappointment. Then she voiced, "Your father should know the truth."

Eleanor nodded mutely.

"Would it help if I told him what you just told me?" her mother asked.

"I couldn't bear to be a disappointment to him!" Eleanor whispered, tears threatening to fall. "I know I already am, and —"

Her mother interrupted, "No, that's not true. You've made decisions we haven't always viewed as wise, but we pray that you will learn from them and gain wisdom as you do. That doesn't make you a disappointment. It makes you human."

Her mother kissed her brow. "I'll come get you after I've talked to him."

When her father woke around eight in the morning, her mother went in and relayed their daughter's history of the past several months.

An hour of waiting was torture to Eleanor. What would her father say about this turn of events?

When she was summoned to his room, he feebly lifted his hand and waved the tips of his fingers, beckoning her advance. She did and held his fingertips in her hands. "Dad?"

He wheezed, "Why are you giving him up?"

She gently rubbed his hands as she said, "The man I really love, Paul, he's available again. The baby is really his as mum told you. My arrangement with Seth was just that, an arrangement that Paul himself put together to protect me. That's how much he loves me, Dad. He cares for me and this baby. He wants us to be a family."

"Why was he unavailable after you got pregnant?"

That was the crux of the whole matter. He had left her for a woman he was supposedly in love with for so many years. He had been honourable in keeping his promise to Rowena, right? So what did that make him when he had left Eleanor with child? Was Paul honourable? What was honour? What did it look like in a man?

She didn't have the answers to those questions yet, questions she was sure her father would ask because he was the kind of father who challenged her to think about the factors of the whole situation and how it would affect any decision she made. So she decided to keep the truth to herself. "He was called away to the front, and he was afraid that we'd be left alone and not provided for. So he asked Seth to marry me. I didn't know it at the time. I only found out last night."

Her father lightly squeezed her hand and said, "I saw you standing next to Seth, saw you feel protected, respected, even loved, and I knew I could leave you in his care. How can I know the same of Paul?"

"Oh, Daddy, we've got to leave at noon because of Paul's work so there's not much time to meet and spend time with him, but rest assured we'll be back to spend some time with you and Mum."

He asked, "Are you sure about this?"

She couldn't find the resolve to answer him with a "Yes" so she nodded.

"You know I just want what's best for you, baby girl. A man who's going to put you first above everyone else."

Her voice broke as she answered, "I'm sure, Daddy." She pressed her forehead to his, and he kissed her cheeks. He mentioned he was tired and needed to close his eyes.

Eleanor left his room and gathered her belongings. She lugged her bag down the stairs to the front door. Paul would arrive any minute. She fished an envelope out of one of her pockets and handed it to her mother. "If Seth comes around looking for me, can you please give this to him?"

Her mother sighed, not one of exasperation but one of pain. "Are you sure this is right?"

Eleanor put on a happy face. "It's what feels right, Mum. You'll see. I'll live much closer, and you'll be provided for without my working a job and braving the North. I'll be able to spend more time with you and Dad. He said he'll take good care of all of us. He's a good man."

Her mother cupped her face and gave each of her cheeks a kiss.

A knock on the door rattled their attention.

A large bouquet of flowers preceded Paul's entry. Another large bouquet of flowers followed him. He presented both before the two ladies.

Her flabbergasted mother sputtered, "Thank you very much. I haven't had a bouquet like this grace my table in a long time. You must be Paul."

He bowed and kissed the top of Sandra's free hand.

Eleanor buried her nose in the fresh garden roses. "It's a perfect start."

"Isn't it?" He beamed. "Right off, let's get going. I'll bring you to our home and then make an appearance at work."

"Will you take my bag for me?"

"No need, my man here is going to take that." He fished out a bill for the taxi driver.

The greasy haired man swiped the bill out of his hand so quickly and stuffed it into his back pocket.

Paul picked up Eleanor and swooped her out of her parent's threshold. "Oof, you're going to have to lose a lot of weight once the baby's out, won't you?"

"Well, I heard it can take some time—"

"Let's get going, man."

Eleanor asked, "Why are you in such a hurry?"

He huffed, "Because—because—oh for God's sake—that's why." He spun her toward his source of irritation.

Seth was approaching her parents' house. He put up his hands as if he were startling two skittish deer. "I just want to speak to Eleanor before she leaves."

Paul barked, "We have to go."

Eleanor patted Paul's breast pocket as a signal to put her down.

"Fine," Paul growled.

Eleanor met Seth halfway. She noticed her fingertips stretching out toward him before he took her hands in his.

Seth begged, "Please, El, stay. You know that I'll take care of you and your baby, love you and your baby."

She bit her lip as her resolve wavered. "This feels like the right thing to do."

"You know just as well as I do how feelings can't be trusted," he reminded her.

"Paul is this baby's real father. He wants her. Shouldn't we be a family if we can?"

Seth bit his lip and placed his hands on her belly one last time. "I hope he's deserving of you and this baby."

She wound her hands behind his neck and embraced him for a final goodbye.

In the hollow of her ear, he whispered, "I'll always be yours, that was my vow."

"I'm releasing you from your vow."

He shook his head adamantly.

"Goodbye, Seth." She left in the taxi with Paul.

As they pulled away, Paul said, "I'm sorry he put you through that."

What could she say to him? That she was happy she saw him one last time even though her heart strings were tugged and bruised? That she bristled at Paul's words because he viewed Seth as an annoyance and she never could?

Paul muttered, "Growing up, my family and I gave him so much, opportunities, money, and work. Deep down, I think he's always wanted what I have. I wonder if he was ever satisfied with our generosity. Him trying to stop you from going with me is the last straw. If he ever comes crawling back, he'll get nothing."

She wondered for a second if she had made the right decision after all; for he sounded like a spoiled child.

Suddenly, Paul drew her attention to a bay window of a pretty house on the corner of the street. "Our house has a bay window just like this one overlooking a small park. Overall the house looks similar, maybe a little bigger, just as clean and beautiful. We'll have lots of space all to ourselves unlike these people who choose to board the soldiers."

She looked at the house and marvelled that she could live in such a beautiful home after so many years of scraping by in a hovel after she and her family lost their well groomed and spacious childhood home. Her soul was light and finally felt it could rest and cover itself with a cosy blanket. Striving in life would be a thing of the past. She sighed happily. "Do you think I can decorate it the way I want? Are we renting it?"

He squeezed her close. "You can do whatever you want. We—I mean it was a wedding gift to, um, well now it's ours."

"Sure," Eleanor replied. Was she now filling in Rowena's shoes? Who loved and doted on Rowena so much that they had gifted her a house? It couldn't be Rowena's family, for the only family Seth and his sisters had was Nasnana back in the North. It must have been gifted by Paul's.

Did Paul view her as a fill in for Rowena? Could she make this life her own and not be haunted by Rowena's ghost?

Her eyes lit up and she "awed" audibly when they arrived, her Colonial style home dressed in white to match its environment. The blue-painted front door was decorated with a simple spruce wreath, its fragrance meeting her as they walked up the porch steps.

"I can't believe this is…. " She was about to say mine. However, this had never been intended for her. She settled for "ours."

Once they freshened up, they had afternoon tea in their new home. Their housekeeper had it all laid out on a small round breakfast table which was tucked in the corner next to a bay window. The walls were bare white, a perfect canvas for her to paint and decorate the way she envisioned. Although she wanted to tackle the decorating right away, there were too many days she couldn't do as she hoped. Her belly was swelling, and her body demanded more sleep during the day.

She had asked Paul a few days after they arrived if he could find her a doctor that could follow up with her pregnancy. Each day she asked if he had found someone. He would shake his head and smile saying that there had been many obligations at work and that he had forgotten. He believed there was no hurry because he was always ready and more than able to care for all her physical needs. Only he didn't know how necessary it was for her to have regular checkups due to the placental abruption she had already suffered.

She allowed his excuses to slide for a week. When he had failed to do the bare minimum, she decided she would find her own doctor. It was a small exercise in independence that she was eager to challenge herself with. Conveniently, there was a new practice that had opened up a few blocks down from where she lived.

She was a beautiful picture in her new navy wrap coat. The frigid tinged air sparked an extra deep pink in her cheeks. As she turned to lock her front door, she felt a presence, *his* presence. Her eyes snapped up and took in her surroundings. The street was quiet with only a few people walking out. None of them were he. Could he be here? In her and Paul's haste to leave, she hadn't left an address. It was hardly likely he knew her location. One more purview showed he was nowhere near. Perhaps, she had not shaken off her thoughts of him as much as she would have liked.

She walked into the doctor's office and registered as a new patient.

The doctor checked her vitals. Then he took out a sphygmomanometer, a rubber cuff attached to a mercury level next to a graduated scale that he applied to her arm to diagnose her blood pressure. Noting it was on the low end, he cautioned her not to rise too quickly from a sitting or lying position.

After sharing the entire history of her pregnancy, including the placental abruption and how she and the baby had regained full health, the doctor declared that she was a miracle.

He cautioned, "I wouldn't engage in any bedroom activities if I were you since I can't be sure if they could cause or aggravate a relapse."

Eleanor responded, "Oh, my doctor at Fort Norman said I was cleared for *all* activities."

The doctor scoffed, "I don't know what kind of doctor would be so careless having such a different view. Please stick to my recommendation."

Eleanor believed it would be impossible to sway Paul in following the doctor's advice.

April 20th, 1944

When Paul returned home from work, he told Eleanor there was a special gala dinner that he had to attend and that she would be expected to go with him. The idea was a cheerful and exciting prospect. She enjoyed going out into the city at night as they had many times the past two months. They would drink from champagne towers, dance until Eleanor's ligaments ached, and then make love until the early morning hours. Being back in civility held a certain sway over Eleanor's material soul, over her satisfaction in pleasing others and garnering attention.

The glamour of her new life was one of the tempters leading her away from making contact with her family, yet her shameful actions in leaving were the real reason she couldn't stir up the courage to reach out.

When the night came to prepare for the party, she felt overly fatigued. Pressure in her abdomen swelled and ebbed. She couldn't rouse herself in time. He came home and strode into their room to change. As soon as he saw her laying in bed, seeming pummelled without having been in a fight, his jaw dropped. "Why aren't you dressed? I told you to be ready at five thirty. It's nearly five forty-five!"

Eleanor moaned, "I really want to go, but my body is just not feeling up to it. I'm sorry."

He hurried over, moved his hand up her thigh, and said firmly, "Maybe I can get it to where it needs to be before we go." He smiled seductively.

"No, I really can't." She pushed his hand away.

He begged, "Listen, I need you there. You're expected. I need you to throw a dress on, put on some makeup or whatever you girls do to look glamorous, and come with me."

"I'm not an ornament you can command at will."

"You know that's not what I mean, baby."

She raised her voice, "Then what do you mean? Because I'm telling you that I was really excited to go, but my body is just not cooperating right now when I want it to."

He stroked her flush cheek, "What I mean is that I won't be able to get through the night without you. You're the one person I look for in a room. When I'm with you, all I see is you."

She remembered all those times up north when he had told her those very things. She had believed he meant every word. Did he now or was it a script he had planned?

She crawled over the edge of the bed and wondered how she could get into ship shape for him. She breathed, "Okay, give me ten minutes?"

He spritzed himself with cologne and gave her a peck. "Be quick. The taxi should be here any minute."

She found herself almost falling asleep as she drank from her glass of water at the party. The music was just a tad too loud. She cradled her head and her stomach at the same time because it felt a little too stretched, and it was itchy. For all her attempts at looking smart and sophisticated, her condition didn't help at all.

Paul's declarations of needing her were unsubstantiated. He had checked in on her twice throughout the long hours of the party. Since she wasn't able to keep up with him for longer than an hour, he had dropped her off at a cushy corner of the bar with water to keep her hydrated.

She had an unsettling feeling that she had met all the people he thought she needed to meet to make the impressions he aimed to make. After her use, she was discarded. When a few of the older women passed by her, they asked if she was all right. She nodded with a tired smile, not in the mood to speak of the growing sickness inside her. They patted her hand and took her at her word even though her word at this moment was a hollow note she could barely play.

Blearily she made out the time to be nine thirty. Bed was calling to her. She didn't think she could last any longer. Heavy with exhaustion, she heaved her body out of her chair and wobbled down the hallway, the sea of faces making her nauseated and dizzy. The live music became muted as if she were under water. She stumbled, and an older gentleman was deft enough to grab her hand and help steady her.

"You all right, miss?"

"Yes—uh!" She caught the edge of a nearby table. She was vaguely aware that there was yelling and hands grabbing at her arms, pushing down on her forearms, her thighs, and her shoulders. She tried to swat at their hands. Everything was too hot, sticky, ringing, flailing, and then—dark.

Something in her body was growing, enlarging, bringing pressure to her side. Her fingers trailed to her side and to the other in order to help ease the pain. A greater shock of pain shot through her abdomen causing her leg to crank up. Finally, she opened her eyes and was flooded with white, bright lights. She looked around her and saw a stranger.

His lips moved, and she only recovered her hearing when he said, "You're eight centimetres dilated. This baby is coming soon. Your water hasn't broken yet. You'll feel gushing close to when you have to push." He continued, "I'll let you know when it's time. If you start to feel like you need to use the toilet, that means you have to push."

Pain spasmed through her body. She fisted the sheets and squeezed her eyes shut attempting to breathe in deep through the agony tearing her body in two. Uncomfortable cramping led to an internal earthquake. She yelled in response.

The doctor spread her legs and ducked under the sheet to check her cervix again. "Okay, it's coming. Are you ready?"

She growled in response—then whimpered. "No, I'm not ready. I don't think I'll ever be ready."

Then she felt it. A blinding pressure which was fuelled by an inconceivable force.

The doctor said encouragingly, "All right, now push!"

She shook her head and bit her lip. She searched for Paul's hand, but he was nowhere to be seen. She gripped the side railing.

She inhaled quickly three times, and exhaled as she pushed. The beads of sweat ran down her temples, her baby hairs sticking to the frame of her face. She was suddenly struck by how her body was primed to do the work that lay before her. Never had she felt so empowered and powerless at the same time.

After many pushes and trembling at the ring of fire when the baby's head crowned and stretched her cervix to the apex, her baby was delivered into the waiting arms of a nurse and whisked away.

She breathed, "My baby, please."

The doctor and nurses ignored her pleas to see her baby.

One sympathetic nurse bent close to her ear and murmured, "We'll return your baby once we've cleaned her up and done a whole checkup. Don't try to get out of your bed or move too much without a nurse to help you. Soon we'll bring you to the Deluxe Private Room your husband paid for. Until then stay put."

After an infernal amount of time, another nurse helped her sit up and move to the proffered wheelchair. She could feel a gush of blood empty onto the pad she held between her legs. Shakily, she maneuvered into the wheelchair and was brought to her room.

Paul was waiting at the entrance of her room with a bouquet of flowers and a box of chocolates. "Darling, well done! What is it? A boy?"

Eleanor reached for her gifts. "Thank you. She's a girl."

Paul muttered, "I was hoping for a boy, but I'm happy as long as she'll look like you."

Eleanor asked sincerely, "And what if she doesn't?"

Paul laughed lightly and said, "Ah, why wouldn't she? You're the mother after all." He stood up quickly and said, "I'm going to go looking for something to eat, a glass of water. You want some?"

"Yes, please, water would be perfect."

After the nurse helped her into bed, another came in with her baby. The first nurse brough her a bowl of water and soap. "Wash your hands before you feed your baby."

As Eleanor washed up, the nurse holding her baby said, "Now don't go unwrapping her. She's wrapped up for her health and safety. If you want to see her unwrapped, ask one of us to do so. After you feed her, don't smoke or use the telephone until after we've collected your baby to bring to the nursery."

"All right. Thank you." Eleanor eagerly reached for her baby, cradling her close once she was deposited into her arms.

With the nurses gone and Paul hunting for a snack, Eleanor took the opportunity to marvel without distraction. Her daughter's lips parted and sought for food and comfort. Eleanor shook off her sleeve and brought her baby's lips to her nipple. The baby sucked without hesitation.

As she looked at her daughter's round cheeks pulsing as she nursed, Eleanor whispered, "Do you remember what name I gave you?"

Her daughter's eyes opened a sliver in response.

"Melody."

Eleanor's fingers traced the lines of Melody's face, committing to memory the wonder of the moment, the miracle of life in her arms. She couldn't fathom how she had ever wanted to take Melody's life away just so she could fulfil a piece of hers. Instead, her life was fulfilled by the very person Eleanor thought would rob her.

SETH

PART VI

The Cost

Chapter 24

Early February 1944

El turned away. It happened the way he always knew it would happen. Oh, he had hoped that somehow she would stay, that she would choose him. Her gentleness in leaving had cleaved him in two. How was he to go on? What was he to do?

He chided himself. His work was waiting for him when he returned. His home, Nasnana, and his adopted family wanted him near.

Before leaving, he was determined to say goodbye to El's family.

He trudged toward her parent's home and knocked on the door.

Sandra opened the door on the first knock. Her red-rimmed eyes were forlorn. A bouquet of flowers lay on the floor behind her. She quivered, "I think she's making a terrible mistake, and I couldn't stop her. I don't even know where he's taken her. Please, Seth, forgive her."

Could he after they had broken down every wall between them, and still she had left?

He closed the front door not wanting any more cold air to enter their home and hugged Sandra.

After a few beats, Sandra patted his chest and said, "You must stay the night. Catch the first streetcar out in the morning. Please, it would be our pleasure to get to know you better."

He smiled, "One night, thank you for your hospitality."

Her lips trembled. "You're family now. You'll always be after what you've done for my girl."

That afternoon, Sandra, Seth, and Lily, along with baby Luke, took their tea in the drawing room. Mike was at work, and Edward was taking an afternoon nap. Lily set Luke on his tummy on the wooden floor with a couple toys around him and sat beside him.

Sandra asked, "How was the funeral? And your family, how are they coping?"

Seth answered, "It was a beautiful service. Even though Rowena left at the beginning of the war, all her old friends came to pay their respects. She was well loved." He blinked back tears as he gulped his too hot tea, scalding his tongue. "Ah! Hot! Uh, the reception at Christina's was also very lovely until…."

Sandra placed her hand on his arm in sympathy. "I'm so sorry. If this is too painful—"

"No, I need to confess. It's my fault El is gone." He put his saucer and teacup on the coffee table.

Lily's head jerked in surprise. "That can't be. I'm sure—"

He ground his fist into his forehead. "It is. I didn't tell her the whole truth about why I married her. Then yesterday Paul and I were talking, and she overheard us. I've never seen her disappointed in me. Annoyed, frustrated, confused—but never that. I couldn't even bring her home because I was so drunk."

Sandra rose from her seat and said, "Chin up, Seth. Just because you allowed your fear to hold you back, to convince you to lie doesn't mean you're not a good man. Your testimony of how you've treated my child these past many months is a testament to your good heart." She took his hand and patted it.

She turned to Lily. "Would you mind starting the supper? I'll come help you once I've checked on Edward, and then I'm sure he'd like to see you, Seth."

Sandra left the room. Seth followed Lily into the kitchen and asked how he could help.

She gave him an onion to cut.

Sandra yelled, "Lily, Seth, help!"

They both rushed to Edward's room.

Sandra cried, "He's cold and clammy. He looks awfully pale."

Seth gently moved her aside by her shoulders, picked up Edward's wrist and found his pulse. It was languid. Edward's fight was waning. "We need to bring him to the hospital right away. Sandra, call the ambulance."

Edward uttered a barely whispered "No."

Seth bent his head closer to Edward's. "What was that?"

Edward wheezed, "No hospital. I want—I want to be at peace in my own home."

"Please, Ed, you must go." Sandra's voice quavered.

Edward lifted his hand an inch toward her face. "No, let my last night be here tonight with you."

With a genteel fortitude, Sandra nodded, tears streaming freely down her cheeks. She grasped Edward's hands in hers and kissed them fervently.

Seth led Lily back to the kitchen, and they cooked in silence.

Once Mike returned home, Lily embraced him and said, "Your father is in a really bad way, and Eleanor left."

Mike spied Seth and asked, "If Eleanor's gone, what are you still doing here?"

"She left me for Paul."

"Who's Paul?"

"The baby's father."

His eyes crinkled in confusion as he tried to form a coherent sentence. "But why? How?" He cradled his head in his hands and asked, "Did you send her a message?"

Lily shared, "She didn't leave an address. We have no way of reaching her."

Mike stared at the floor.

Seth filled a bowl of soup for him and laid it on the table. "Eat up. You'll need your strength."

After supper, Seth checked on Edward and Sandra. He padded over to the bed. Sandra sat on a chair beside the bed and stirred when Seth walked in.

She whispered, "This time I'm going to lose him. It's been a long time coming with many close calls, but I feel like my time with him has run out."

Seth took her hand and kissed it sweetly. "I'm about to head to bed. We've left some soup for you. Would you like me to watch over him while you eat?"

She exhaled a shuddering breath. "I can't leave him when all my moments are being counted and will soon be taken away."

"I understand. The soup will be on the—"

Edward whispered, "Sandra."

She bent forward. "Oh, Edward, I'm here. What is it?"

"Go eat for a few minutes. I want to talk to Seth."

Seth switched places with Sandra and leaned toward Edward. "Sir, is there anything I can do for you?"

Edward didn't answer right away. Seth thought perhaps it wasn't as apt a question as he had thought.

Edward said, "Eleanor has left you despite all you've done for her. I thank you from the bottom of my heart. You are the man that is good for her. Please, please forgive her. All I ask is that while she's your wife you love her. I don't necessarily mean a romantic love but a love that comes from God."

Seth admitted, "I don't know if my love is from God. He's never been an important part of my life, but I think I understand your meaning. You're asking me to love her unconditionally."

Edward gave a small smile. "That's right."

Seth said, "That's all I've ever tried to do, and while she's my wife, I'll continue to do so. Whatever protection she asks for, I'll give it to her."

Edward shook Seth's hand weakly and asked for Sandra once again.

The next few days Sandra, Mike, Lily, and Seth took turns sitting with Edward so everyone could take the necessary time to sleep in a bed, eat, and take a bath.

Seth made some inquiries into acquiring Paul's number. As soon as he received it, he dialled the operator.

"Number please."

"23874."

"Hold please."

A woman's firm voice answered, "This is the Burns' residence. May I ask who is speaking?"

"This is Seth. Is Eleanor in?"

"I'm afraid she's indisposed at the moment."

"It's urgent. I really need to speak to her."

The woman's voice became hard as stone. "I'll take a message, sir."

He rolled his eyes and said, "Please tell her that her father is dying. She needs to see him right away. We don't know how much time he has left."

"I'll relay the message, good day."

Click. Ding, ding.

He clenched the receiver. A phone number wasn't good enough. He'd have to dig for an address.

Every time he inquired for an address, the person he was speaking with would ask who he was. After sharing his name, they refused to share an address. Door after door closed in his face.

On his way back to Edward and Sandra's home, he passed by a private investigator's office. He slowed his steps, chewing on the idea of hiring one to discover Paul's address. He entered the building to seek out the investigator and pay for his services.

One afternoon, while Mike was sitting with Sandra and Seth in the dining room and taking tea together, Lily and Luke were out at the grocers.

Though it was a humble dining room—worn, scratched hardwood floors, dents in the table, chipped teacups—Seth admitted that Eleanor's family made it feel like home. He had never had that feeling with any other family except Nasnana's. Not even Paul's family had ever made him feel as if he belonged.

Sandra sighed and began to cry, "I don't know what I'm going to do for Edward's body when he dies. Heavens! I've put off thinking of this for so long, and time is running out."

"What do you mean?" asked Seth.

"Our plots in the cemetery—we had to sell them when hard times came. We thought we'd have time for plan B."

"Which cemetery were you planning on?"

"We had ours at the Edmonton Municipal. Now we'll have to cremate him." She muttered under her breath, "It was never his wish."

Helping Eleanor's family through the despair was a healing balm. He would've thought that being close to her loved ones would be painful. Instead, serving them in their time of need gave him a purpose other than running back to work and finding fulfilment in it alone.

The next day Seth left their home after breakfast and headed to the Edmonton Municipal Cemetery.

He returned that evening in time for supper. Sandra greeted him at the door and asked, "Seth, where have you been? I've been worried about you."

To most, her last words could be construed as an inconvenience, an annoyance to be handled. To Seth, they were precious, for in their timber resonated love and care that he had not known from his own mother, or at least not what he could remember of her.

Nasnana had never uttered those words. Although she was a very loving woman, she kept her deepest feelings close to herself.

A mother's worry was a rite of passage he never would've thought he'd walk. He gave her a dear smile and handed over a paper and said, "I've got some very good news."

Chapter 25

Seth woke up early, near four in the morning with the feeling that something was amiss. He tiptoed out of his room afraid to wake Sandra from what little precious sleep she had received these past few nights. There was also Mike and Lily's sleep to think of. Luke was still waking up at least once during the night.

At least El's baby had a nearby cousin to play with whenever she decided to contact her family.

One step then two down the stairs—a sniffle from Edward's room snagged his attention. He placed his ear against the door and heard Sandra attempt to quiet herself. He opened the door and saw her hunched over Edward's still form. Not a movement of breath could he see from Edward.

Seth asked, "Sandra?"

She wiped her nose. "He's gone, really gone. He passed away in his sleep sometime in the night."

Seth put his arm around her quivering shoulders and prayed for the first time in his life.

The day of Edward's death, life stopped for the four mourning souls in their humble abode. The day was spent crying, sleeping from emotional exhaustion, sharing memories of Edward, making tea, and drinking a few sips and letting the rest cool, not to be touched again. No substantial meal passed their lips. There was no joy to be had in their house of mourning.

Although Seth was poised to do something, anything to alleviate their suffering, there was no comfort he could give other than mourning with the family, being a stable presence during their grieving and a sounding board for their stories.

All the while his imminent return to work vied for his thoughts. He wanted to make sure they couldn't want for anything before he left. That left him a couple days to organise everything for the funeral.

He came to sit at the table with Sandra. "Sandra, I have to leave in two days. I can't prolong my trip any longer even though I wish I could. Please tell me everything you want for Edward's funeral, and I'll make it happen."

She held his hand. "Oh, Seth, what a Godsend you are! What will we ever do when you leave?"

"You've got a strong man in Mike. He's worked hard for you all, and he'll keep on working to provide for you, Lily, and Luke. Trust that you've raised him well."

Over the next hour, intermixed with crying bouts, Sandra expressed Edward's desires of what kind of coffin they should acquire, what songs were to be sung during the funeral, which church and reverend were to preside over the service, and who could be put in charge of handling the reception afterward.

Seth went from meeting to meeting to put in stone all of Edward's wishes. When he returned to the house, Sandra informed him that a private investigator had called for him. Seth promised to return and left to receive some news on the investigation.

The investigator didn't have too much trouble finding the address after posing as a lawyer needing to serve Paul a phoney court summons. Paul had given strict commands for no one to breathe a word of his home address, West Jasper Street, where her childhood home could be found. El's fortune had lifted after all.

He grabbed a sheet of paper and pen and began to write a letter to El.

Dearest El,

I'm so sorry to tell you that your father died on the 7th of February. Please accept my condolences. Having spent these last few days with him has been a great honour. He loved you more than he could ever say. It was always evident when he said your name or whenever you came up in conversation.

Please call your mum. She'll let you know all the details for the funeral. Your family needs you.

I tried getting a hold of you sooner and even left a phone message with your housekeeper. When we didn't hear from you, I hired a private investigator to find your address.

I have to leave tomorrow because I can't put off work any longer. I wish you all the best, all the love your heart can receive and carry, and all the joys of this world.

If ever you need anything...

Yours always,

Seth

Holding the letter in his hand, Seth searched for Sandra. He found her sitting on Edward's bed. "Sandra, I finally found Eleanor's address. I'll write it down for you. I wrote her a letter explaining everything. Before I go back north, I'll pass by their home and leave this in her mailbox. I'd give it to her personally, but I don't think she'll want to see me. I'll take a look in on her from afar to make sure she's okay."

Sandra reached for him. He walked over and placed his hand in hers. "Thank you for taking such good care of Eleanor and us. You'll always be a part of this family. Say you'll visit?"

"I will next time I have off."

Sandra, Lily, and even Luke hugged Seth. Mike had asked the women to give Seth his regards since he had left very early for his shift at the factory.

As Seth rode the streetcar bound for Paul's home, he wondered how he should approach the home. Should he walk straight up the steps to their mailbox and chance being discovered by Eleanor or Paul? Should he stakeout any movement before making sure it was clear? The most important question was how he would feel if he saw Eleanor? Already his heart was beating a little harder, a little louder so that it seemed as if all could hear its erratic rhythm.

His fingers kept folding the corners of the envelope over and over until the creases began to rip.

At his stop, he hopped off and walked toward Paul's home. The walk over was a much more calming mode of transportation because whatever nerves he had could fizzle through his moving members. Just as he was about to round the corner, he spied a head of blonde hair on a porch. After freezing for a second, he backtracked behind a tree trunk and watched.

He held his breath watching her radiant smile, her eyes closing against the sun's kiss. She was a pretty picture of colour against the white backdrop of her and Paul's house. Her air of ease and happiness settled whatever questions he had of whom she truly belonged with.

Her belly was more pronounced. She wore it with contentment and resolution to build this new life with the actual father of her child. Undeniably, she was looking at home with the man she loved, in the city where she could dazzle and visit regularly with her family.

She opened her eyes and began to look at her surroundings in earnest. Had he made a sound when he admired her from afar, a sound she could hear? The neighbourhood was quiet, yet there was still the faint hum of city sounds blending in the background. She couldn't have heard him. Did she somehow know she was being watched?

Cowardice didn't become him. He was always a straightforward man. Go in and get the job done. Taking his usual approach wouldn't suit this time not because he feared rejection but because he didn't want to cause her any kind of hurt.

The letter weighed like a brick in the pocket of his coat. His missive contained the information that would cause a great hurt he couldn't help mend. There was no protecting her from the inevitable passage of Time. He hoped she would be able to find comfort in being with her family, Paul, and the new life growing inside her once she read the news.

He watched her go down the steps while holding the railing. She was careful not to slip on any residue ice from the night before. She walked in the opposite direction of where he stood, giving him an opening to slip to her porch unnoticed and drop the letter inside her mailbox.

Then he left for good.

Chapter 26

Mid-February 1944

Seeing El for the last time was the fiery brand he needed to cauterise the terrible aching in his heart to a permanent scar. His journey back north was filled with lift offs, pit stops, change of aircraft; the impermanence aided him in focusing on the task at hand when he returned to Norman Wells.

Peter was on the airfield with a large flashlight to welcome him back. His eyes were wide when he asked, "Where's Eleanor?"

Seth's lips were set in a grim line. "She's not coming back."

Peter nodded and bowed his head in recognition that there was to be no discussion of Eleanor's nonappearance for the time being.

The wind blasted snow onto their faces until both their beards were covered with frost in less than a couple of minutes.

Seth said, "Let's move inside. It's strange to be back in near constant darkness." The memory of El's face soaking up the sun haunted him. "What did I miss these last couple of weeks?"

"I have a full report waiting for you on your desk. There's been replacement of pipe due to several different reasons, primarily equipment damage. Tank farms are holding. The road is near completion." Peter grinned.

"I had full confidence that you could run the operation while I was gone. Thank you. Uh, first thing I'll need is a new typist. Could you look into that?"

Peter eyed him sideways. "Sure thing."

"How's Julia?"

"I took your advice and thought about what my future could be like with one woman to love, to love me back, to build a life with. She's easy to love." Peter admitted.

Seth put his hand on Peter's shoulder and shook it lightly. "You've got a good woman. Don't let her go."

When Seth entered the office the next morning, Leticia was sitting at El's old spot.

"Good morning, Mr. Brooks."

"Good morning, Leticia, how are you doing?"

"Good, thank you. I'm sorry to hear about Eleanor."

He gave a tight-lipped smile and waved her concern away. "It's all right." He rummaged around his desk, the setting feeling slightly foreign to him without his wife's presence. He grabbed a pile of papers. "Here, can you have these done by the end of the day? I'll be out most of the day, taking stock of Norman Wells."

"Yes, sir."

"Good, you have a good day."

He made his rounds by rote habit. It was like a well-worn glove that slipped back on with ease. The operation was running smoothly; his last couple of weeks had been anything but smooth. The late afternoon shrouding of darkness over the land clung to the scraps of sadness in his soul.

It was tempting to trudge to his desolate cabin that night, but he veered to the mess hall and grabbed his dinner with Peter and Julia.

As soon as he sat down, Julia's hand shot out to give his hand a squeeze. She didn't say a word, only smiled sympathetically.

He didn't want to be the low spirit that brought others down so he forced himself to converse.

"If you'd like, Julia, I can give you El's new address so you can write to her." Seth offered.

"Oh, would you? I'd like that very much. She's my best friend. I'm going to miss her." She twirled her fork in her spaghetti.

Peter cleared his throat. "Seth, I'm sorry to bring this up, but I can't go on with you being the only one who doesn't know. Julia and I are engaged."

Seth's eyes wandered to Julia's ring finger resting on Peter's arm and the little glimmer of a gold band on her finger. "Don't be sorry. I'm so happy for the two of you. There's always time to celebrate something important like this." He chewed on his next bite and said, "You two will be needing your own place."

"That's true," Julia said. "Do you know a place we could use as a home?"

Seth nodded, "You're going to take the cabin."

Julia's eyes widened in horror. "We can't. That's yours and —well, that's your place."

Seth shook his head. "I don't need the room anymore." He lifted his spoon and pointed it at the two of them. "You both will be needing it. Consider it my wedding present. Please, it's yours."

"Thank you, Seth," Peter exhaled. "Will you be my best man?"

"I'd be honoured."

The next morning, Seth was at his desk when the office door was wrenched open by Peter. "Leakage at the north tank."

Seth nodded. He grabbed his coat, hat, and gloves and ran after Peter. "Where's the leakage coming from?"

"Bottom of the tank."

It was common knowledge that unfavourable conditions such as severe temperature fluctuations, tension increase from the flow of incoming oil with some frost shock to the material could result in the formation of cracks on the oil tank that could hold as much as 80,000 barrels of oil. If the crack was formed in the higher level shells, then the shells could be readily tightened to stop the leak.

Bottom leakages required much more work.

The men arrived to see a steady stream flow from the crack to the surrounding ground until the oil hit the firewall surrounding the tank. The workers were already pumping out the oil from the tank to empty it completely. Seth and Peter oversaw the work of removing the bottom plates completely. Once they had been removed, Seth gave them the call to thoroughly clean the existing gasket material instead of replacing it completely. They bolted the plates back into place and covered the seams with Prestite, a foam sealant that would expand and contract to accommodate any movement due to whatever stressors presented themselves.

Seth inspected each step carefully, standing alongside the men who worked on repairing the oil tank.

The considerable amount of oil that had leaked was mostly recoverable. The ground couldn't soak up the pollutant easily because of its frozen state. The one hazard they would have to be wary of was the high flammability of the site.

Although the work was arduous, Seth was grateful that being good at his job and handling a problem kept his mind off the one problem he would never be able to fix.

At the end of the day, he snowshoed his way to the dark yawning cabin. He had no energy to light a fire, to find comfort in his home. He moved straight to her bed and buried himself under the pile of blankets that would keep him warm whatever cold weather raged outside. Her smell floated over his senses like the calming effect of lavender, and he fell asleep.

The next day, he checked on the retainment of the fixed oil tank. Satisfied it was holding and all the testing was being done, he snowshoed to Nasnana's encampment not knowing if she still lived there or if the tribe had moved on to other grounds.

He was thankful the weather was calm with barely a wind to move the Jack pine branches, but, oh, it was freezing. He piled on his layers, carried one of the pelts from his home, and hiked.

A faint light from one of the homes warmed his heart to almost leaping with happiness. His mother was here. He knocked on her door.

She opened it and smiled from ear to ear. "Seth, you're back. It has been too long. Come in." She touched his cheek with the back of her hand. "Sit by the fire. It is healing."

As he did, she ladled black spruce tea into a cup and handed it to him.

She said, "Your favourite tea to fight a cold."

He chuckled, "I'm not sick."

"But I am." She coughed hoarsely. "You drink it, and you won't get sick because—"

"Because the sickness is afraid of it," he finished her saying.

"It always works, hasn't it?"

"You have always taken good care of me." He stared into the fire.

"How's Eleanor? And the baby?"

He sighed, "She stayed behind in Edmonton."

"With her family?"

"No, with Paul. I mean, yes, she'll see her family more often, but she chose Paul."

"She will see the foolishness of her ways in time. I sensed a devouring nature within him, an instinct to take everything he wants," Nasnana clucked.

"I went to see her before I left. She didn't see me. She looked happy, and she got the ending she always hoped for."

"This is not an ending. It's a beginning. Time will tell if she can walk the road she's chosen. If she decides to return, will you take her back?"

He squeezed his eyes shut. "I promised her father I would care for her always while I'm her husband. I don't believe she'll come back when she has all she wants in Edmonton. There's nothing for her here."

By the light and healing of the fire, he shared how he had grown to love Eleanor's family in the short time he had stayed with them in Edmonton. Nasnana asked how Christina and Shaina were managing after Rowena's death.

His heart was lightened a little by sharing its load with his mother's heart.

ELEANOR

PART VII

The Absolution

Having a sweet baby's face close to your own,
for so long a time as it takes to nurse 'em,
is a great tonic for the sad soul.
Erica Eisdorfer

Chapter 27

Mid-April,1944

Even though Eleanor was allowed visitors for the sum total of one hour a day in increments of thirty minutes, Paul could hardly be bothered to visit for a little less than thirty. She couldn't help wondering if Seth would move the Mackenzie Mountains to visit for every single minute he could be given had she chosen him over Paul.

She wouldn't feel so lonely if Melody were allowed to be her constant companion. Whether she cried or slept, Eleanor would be honoured to drink in every second with her and care for her needs. It was not to be. Melody was kept in the nursery with the rest of the newborns at all times unless it was time to nurse her. The nurse would come in and deposit her into Eleanor's restless arms. As soon as she slipped her nipple into Melody's eager wide open mouth, the room was silent, all except for the excited little breaths that made music more sweet than the twitters of the birds that had floated through her open cabin windows in the North during the fall.

Eleanor was surprised by how engorged she was. She reread the instructions her mother had written and had managed to give her before the funeral. It would have been sweeter and more helpful if they had talked about it in person, but Eleanor had swept in with her husband and swept out with another man.

The second day of being in the hospital, Paul kissed Eleanor on the head and said, "It's high time I go home and let Mom and Dad know about how everything went. I've also got to get the nursery ready, you know?" His intonation was similar to that of a salesman pitching his idea.

Eleanor asked, "You didn't tell them yesterday?"

"God, no! I crashed hard when I returned home yesterday." He ran his hand through his hair. "Today was a long day at work. That's why I can't stay long today."

She sighed, "You'll come visit every day until they let me out, won't you?"

"I sure will."

Anytime she wasn't nursing, Eleanor would sleep. She wasn't always tired, but she thought it would be prudent to take advantage of any time to sleep because of the pressing notion that she was alone. The solitude began to prey on her insecurities of whether she would be a good mother, or if she couldn't give up the selfishness she knew stood at her heart's door. It had been a daily pattern for so long. Could she shake it off and sacrifice for the sake of her daughter?

Paul didn't come on the third day nor the fourth. He came the fifth day, the day she was to be let out of the hospital. She was glad that the war had changed the hospitals' policies to keep new mothers in the hospitals for a lesser time than it had been pre-war. She couldn't imagine being cooped up for another five to six days.

Wearing the scents of cigar smoke and gin and tonic, Paul fell into the chair beside her bed and said, "I'm sorry I didn't come visit you and the girl yesterday. I got caught up with some friends who wouldn't let me leave the bar. They were determined for me to celebrate the baby's arrival."

"It wasn't just yesterday. It was the last two days."

"You sure? I swore to myself it was only one day."

"Did the same thing happen two days in a row?"

"Mmm, what? Oh, no, it was my parents' turn to treat me out the day after."

Her lips screwed together as she wondered if he would truly be this inebriated in front of his parents. "Are your parents going to visit us tomorrow?"

"No! I mean, they hate hospitals, stench of illness, death and such. Can't blame them, can you?"

"But I'm leaving today, no more hospital."

"Yes, well, they like to give some time before they see someone who's just been out of the hospital, germs and all."

She rolled her eyes and wondered what they would do if one of his parents ever had to be in a hospital. She schooled her features and embarked on a different tangent. "Everything has been going really well. Melody is feeding perfectly and—"

"That's great! As soon as you're out, we'll go out just the two of us to the Danceland Ballroom, a hit nightclub. Here I brought you this. Put it on." He held up a cleavage-revealing slinky black dress.

"You mean the two of us and Melody."

"Why would Melody be there? It's a nightclub."

She offered, "Why don't we go somewhere else, a low key restaurant, maybe? Or we could just go home."

He looked at her as if she had just declared the moon is made of cheese. "Low key restaurant? Go home? Nonsense! The Danceland Ballroom it is. We'll hand her off to the nanny I just hired."

His words inundated her like a tidal wave. They rose higher and higher, and the word "nanny" drowned her whole.

She frowned, "What nanny?"

"I put out a job posting while you were in the hospital, and some nice young girl snapped it up. She's got a good head on her shoulders, seems capable."

How would he know if a woman knew the in's and out's of raising children, specifically babies? Perhaps, references were all one needed.

Eleanor strove to remain calm. "When did we ever talk about hiring a nanny?"

He laid his arm around her shoulders and nipped at her earlobe. "Did we need to talk about it? Lots of people have one."

Instead of growing warm with desire, she grew cold with disappointment. "That doesn't mean *we* need one, at least not now. I'm going to be spending most of my time feeding Melody, holding her, teaching her about the world. Maybe when she's a little older, we can hire one, and I can go back to work."

He licked behind her ear. "Of course, you won't work right away, but think of all the women you're going to want to spend time with, all the time you're going to want to be out of the house. I know you, you're going to go stir crazy."

She held her tongue and was struck. True, before Melody, she would have broken the walls down just to get out and live, work, flirt, sleep, do it all over again for the thrill of it. Since Seth had entered her life, her past lifestyle barely shimmered like unpolished silver. She had all the treasure she needed right in front of her.

"I've changed," she declared.

He huffed and pulled back. "What do you mean?"

She looked him in the eyes. "Now that Melody is here, I don't want all that."

"You changed in an instant?" he asked incredulously, mockingly.

She bit her lip and wondered how much she should share. "No, I think over the past several months my life and priorities have been different. They've shifted, slowly to this."

He put his fist under his chin. "He's got something to do with it, hasn't he?"

Why did she speak? She closed her eyes for a brief moment and then laid her hand gently on his. "I chose you."

"You're not answering the question." His monotone sliced the tension.

"I think he may have been part of it, but mostly, I think this is what happens to a woman who's growing a life inside her."

Paul looked at Melody as if she had ruined his birthday plans. "I'll keep the nanny for a bit. Maybe you won't be so different at all."

Why didn't he listen? "Did you check her references?"

He bristled. "'Course I did. I wouldn't just hire any pretty face."

"I really don't think we'll need her for a little while."

He cut the air in a slicing motion. "Just test her out a little, will you?" He stood up and ran his hand through his hair. "I'll call the nurse and sort out your leave."

She planted both of her feet on the floor before getting out of the hospital bed. Moving slowly, she collected her things and placed them in the suitcase Paul had brought over. Once she was finished, she sat, patiently waiting for the nurse to bring Melody and for Paul to walk them out.

The nurse brought in Melody. Paul returned with another nurse who held out a pamphlet to Eleanor. She took it, and the nurse said, "Be sure you follow all these instructions."

Eleanor said, "Thank you."

As the nurse holding Melody was handing her off to Eleanor, Eleanor asked Paul, "Don't you want to hold her?"

"Sure, pass her over." He held out his hands as if he were going to grab a ball.

Eleanor directed, "You've got to form a cradle with your arms. See? There." She made sure Melody's neck was supported by his arm. Even though he held her in the proper position, he looked uncomfortable and held her too far away from his heart.Would he always be like this? Surely, there must be fathers who didn't fit into their roles naturally from the start. How long would it take him to become what she hoped he would become, meet her at the place where she was at?

As they stepped out of the hospital, Eleanor expressed, "Ah! I'm free to breathe the fresh air once again." They entered a taxi and drove away. As soon as they reached their house, Paul held his arm out to cradle Melody. At least, he held her a little closer than he had the last time. After a minute, he opened the car door and stepped out with her.

Eleanor asked, "What are you doing?"

"I'm taking her to the nanny so we can go out and celebrate."

She said firmly, "I told you I don't want to go without her."

Paul reasoned, "Come on, we won't have much time together once we settle in with her. I've already taken the trouble of making reservations. Do you know how hard it is to get one? Won't you let me treat you after you've done such a magnificent job of bringing her into the world?"

Watching Melody be transported over the threshold of the front door was almost more than she could bear at the moment, and yet he was trying to show her love, wasn't he? She forced herself to turn her body away and waited for him to return. "All right, we can go, just not for too long. Missing one feeding might be feasible. I'll need some cloths." She gently cupped her breasts.

Paul's eyes flashed dark, then faded as he recognized her meaning. He cleared his throat and looked away. "Right, I'll get the housekeeper to hand me some."

He returned to the car with the cloths and handed them to her. She unbuttoned her shirt and lifted it away from her skin. As she pressed the cloths into her bra, Paul looked away and tapped his fingers on his knees in a nervous fashion.

As soon as they arrived at Danceland Ballroom, he eagerly pulled her out. She slipped her hand from his grasp to make sure her sanitary pads were in place. The last thing she wanted was to leave blood stains on the chairs. The dazzle of the clinking of champagne glasses that used to be Eleanor's favourite tunes sounded dull and flat. Food that once would have shimmered in her gaze as if it had been made by the gods seemed muted. She could barely eat half her plate.

Paul smiled at her occasionally and ate his food with sophistication. He matched this world perfectly, whereas she no longer did. She had always aspired to reach this pinnacle of fashionability. She held it within her grasp, but her soul couldn't align.

They both made small talk about his parents and the house party his parents had hosted last night, about who had drunk too much and made a fool of themselves. Eleanor inquired into his work with the army. He didn't offer any details but made vague declarations of how everything was going well and how he felt satisfied.

After a pause, he said, "There's an opportunity for advancement coming up. Remember when I went to Washington after I left Canol?"

She nodded quietly as she took a small bite.

"Well, there's a good chance they want me to move there for good. That's what the position would require."

She kept her breath steady even though her heart began to beat hard. "That's wonderful. Do you really need to move there?"

"We would move there. We're looking at the next few months."

She pushed her food around. "I really don't want to move."

He scoffed and smiled sardonically, "Coming from the girl who left everything and everyone behind to find freedom and adventure in the North."

"That was then. I've been trying to tell you I'm different now. I've got a baby now."

"Yes!" His voice raised a notch, enough for several people from the neighbouring tables to look at them. "Sorry, yes, the baby, is this how it's going to be? About the baby all the time?"

"Well, for a little while, I think. I don't know! I've never done this before. I don't know how it's supposed to be. That's why I'd rather stay here than in Washington. I'm closer to my mum here." Her guilt reared its head. She had to contact her family right away. "She can help me with the baby, with how to be a good wife—"

"You're not my wife, remember?" His voice cut her like a knife.

She acquiesced. "Right, well, that's how our choices led us, isn't it?"

"Get a divorce." He flicked off an imaginary speck from the table.

Those three words were the sickening twist of his knife.

What could she say to that? She supposed that if she had chosen him she should be wholly tied to him. "Are you going to marry me?"

"Pfft! What do you mean?"

"Well, if you want me to get a divorce, I'm expecting you to marry me. Will you ask me?"

He held up his hand, indicating for her to slow down. "I will when the time is right. First, get that divorce."

The waiter brought their desserts.

She imagined it was natural that everything changed when a baby came into the world, but could it change so much between a man and a woman who loved each other? Or did they ever really love each other at all?

Paul throwing a bunch of bills on the table roused her from her pondering. He held out her coat for her and led her out by placing his hand on the small of her back.

Once they arrived home, Paul stated, "Feed Melody and then come to bed."

The fresh-faced blonde nanny placed a tear streaked, red faced Melody into her arms.

Eleanor whooshed into the nursery and opened her buttons as quickly as she could while Melody continued to howl for nourishment. The relief that washed over Eleanor as her baby sucked brought a wave of tears she could no longer hold back. She cried the entire time.

Drunk and blissful, Melody settled in her crib. Eleanor was able to tiptoe out of the room without waking her up. She breathed a sigh of relief and went to her bedroom.

Paul had already stripped off his shirt. He strode toward her like a mountain lion waiting to maul its prey.

Eleanor gave a little smile and said, "Ready for bed?"

He trapped her in his arms. "I'd like to be with you tonight, especially after such a nice dinner."

She could hardly contain a small scoffing noise. "I'd like to, just not tonight."

His hands on her waist tightened. "I want you. I've waited so long."

"Paul, it hasn't even been a week! I'm still sore and bloody. I'd much prefer waiting at least another week. I'm sure I'll be fully ready by then."

"Another week isn't now." One hand of his flicked open her shirt buttons one at a time while his other hand grabbed her bottom possessively.

"I know. Please try to understand, come, you can spoon me." She grabbed his hand and led him to their bed. As soon as they found their mould, his hands roamed all the places that would usually awaken her desire. Now, they were compelling signals that Paul wasn't listening. Instead of stoking the flames, he was blowing them out dead cold. "You can touch, just not—"

He slipped out of his boxers and ignored her. She bit down on her lip so hard until she could taste a slight tang of iron. Her insides were tight as a coil, and every movement of his was grating, jarring. She could barely inhale and exhale for fear that Paul would view it as an encouragement to continue. So she managed, hanging on by the end of a thread until he finished. As Paul cursed in ecstasy and turned over to fall asleep, Eleanor's tears were still wet on her cheeks.

Chapter 28

Late April 1944

The next morning she moved open her legs to sit up and cried out because the soreness had increased doubly. Because of last night, she feared her recovery would take twice as long. She took her time getting out of bed to feed Melody. The nanny had bottle-fed Melody the previous night with one of the few bottles of her own milk she had pumped with the pumping machine at the hospital. Eleanor didn't want to depend on anyone else to wake up in the middle of the night to feed her baby, but after last night—she wouldn't have been able to. The nanny knew about the emergency supply on hand.

To get through the next couple of weeks without sex, she went to sleep after Melody's six o'clock feeding so Paul wouldn't have an opportunity to have his way with her again until she was fully ready.

A month into having their baby and living life together was very different from how she had pictured it would be. Paul was gone all day. Since she was able to move more, she bundled

Melody and placed her in her buggy so they could walk to the nearby park.

Melody's eyes were widening in wonder at the sights and sounds around her. Melody's first stare into Eleanor's eyes, her first toothless smile, her first whimper at a sudden cracking sound, her first coo—all these firsts transformed Eleanor's world one healing at a time.

She would stand at the window with Melody, hold her close, and speak to her of the world around her, mostly of the world she had left behind, the beauty of the North, the wilderness that had first called out to her wild streak. How long ago it seemed! She hoped Melody would one day visit where Eleanor had conceived and carried her daughter for most of the pregnancy.

One day, when Eleanor felt she had exhausted every other topic, she mustered the courage to speak what was heavy on her heart. "I haven't spoken of someone very special yet because I thought I'd save the best for last." She nuzzled her nose against Melody's cheek. "You probably won't remember any of this when you're older. I'll just have to tell you the story again then. When your daddy left mommy, a very special man took care of your mommy. His name is Seth. When mommy was in desperate need of help, he took care of her and you. As he and I got to know each other, he fell in love with you before he ever knew you. He also loved me very much."

Speaking the truth of their love story peeled the scales off her eyes. She blinked rapidly, and a great big grin spread over her face. In response, Melody's lips widened and opened. How Eleanor had been so, so blind! She had to follow not where her heart led her from feeling to feeling but what she knew to be true.

A giggle burst from Melody's bubbly lips.

Relieved the nanny wasn't around, Eleanor walked into Melody's room and grabbed her old suitcase. She placed most of Melody's belongings inside and slid the suitcase beneath the crib. She didn't want Paul to arrive at the house and find two suitcases in the hallway. With all they had been through, she didn't want to be cruel. She put Melody down for a nap and went to her room next door. While she packed her things in the new suitcase Paul had bought her, she could hear Melody's cooing. Even though she wasn't sleeping, she was sure Melody could benefit from some alone time. She packed the essentials because where she was headed, she didn't need the baubles. She marvelled at how many material things she had accrued in such a short time.

When it was time for Paul to arrive at the house, she was gazing at Melody in her arms in the living room and enjoying the heat from the fire burning in the fireplace. He passed through the front door and took a double step when he realised that she was waiting for him.

"I finally see you awake." His cold accusation hung in the air like a guillotine over her head.

"Please sit down. I'd like to talk to you about something."

He shucked off his jacket and hung it up. "Not right now. I'd like to grab a drink. It's been a long day."

She persisted. "It's about us."

"D—mn it! I've been thinking about us this whole time, and you're the one who's never wanting us!" he shouts.

She attempted to keep an even tone in her shaking voice. "I told you I've just had a baby."

"Ugh! The baby again!"

"You don't understand how my body needs to recover. You haven't been thinking of us. You've been thinking of yourself, what you want. Look at her. Won't you hold her?"

His stern gaze softened a twitch when he took two steps closer to look down at Melody while she was in Eleanor's arms. He retreated and said, "No, thank you. I'm going to get my drink, and then I'll be back."

Eleanor chewed on her bottom lip while she waited.

When he returned, he sat opposite Eleanor, looked at her over the rim of his glass, and cocked his eyebrow.

She began, "Remember when you took me out a month ago —"

"I forgive you," he mumbled.

She reeled back, and her eyebrows knit together. "I'm not apologising."

He took a sip of gin. "What are you saying then?"

"Let me finish please. You asked me to divorce Seth."

He straightened in his seat. "Yes, did you do it yet?"

"I'm not going to."

He took another sip and swallowed hard. "I told you to do it."

"Why won't you ask me to marry you?"

A sinister air swept over his brows. "You need to be divorced first."

"You're still not answering my question."

"Why won't you?"

She would get her answer. "Can you promise me that you'll provide Melody and me security?"

He launched out of his chair and started pacing. "What kind of a question is that? Look at everything I've given you. A house, a nanny, clothes, food, what more do you want?"

Eleanor sighed and chose to answer his anger with patience. "I guess I want your whole heart. But you can't give it, can you? You're good at giving things. But if I don't have your heart, how do I know that one day you won't leave me for someone else."

He halted and pointed his finger at her. "I could leave you in marriage or not in marriage."

"That's just it! Marriage is supposed to signify a commitment to the other person, that for richer, for poorer, in sickness, and in health, you'll stand by them. You don't want to make a commitment like that. Your answer just tells me that you've already thought of a way out."

He raked his gaze across hers and didn't relent in his broiling anger.

"Will you let Melody and I go?"

He looked away.

She got up and drew close to him. She laid her hand on his cheek and said, "I really thought I loved you. You made me feel so much, so intensely. We were knit together by sex, not by love. You deserve better, and so do I."

His head remained turned away from her, away from Melody, away from the fictitious and hope-filled future Eleanor had imagined for almost a whole year. He focused on the dancing flames of the living room fire.

Eleanor put Melody down after her final feeding of the night and asked the nanny to wake up with her. She hated depending on the nanny, but she thought this arrangement would help her have the energy she would need to leave Paul for the journey back home in the morning.

How disappointed her father and mother would be. She knew they wouldn't turn her away, but how could they look at her and be proud?

She had wanted to reach out so many times, to speak with her mother. She yearned for wisdom, but she was ashamed. Her parents knew what she had thrown away and probably shook their heads at her choices like she believed they always had. Were they tired of her mistakes and tired of cleaning up after her messes?

Eleanor went to bed alone and didn't wake until she had to use the bathroom in the middle of the night. She padded out her door and across the hallway to the bathroom. Harsh breathing noises came from the opposite end of the hall. She blinked and rubbed her eyes. Two figures were draped over each other slamming against the other. Eleanor opened her mouth and quickly stole into the bathroom. She quietly closed the door and listened to Paul and the nanny. How many seeds had he planted before her? Had Rowena known of his thirst for flesh?

She was surprised by how unaffected she was after the initial twinge of anger and jealousy springing from within her. He didn't love her, and she didn't love him. Let him decide how and who he would satiate himself with, but she would no longer be a slave to his whims. She was free.

Even after conducting her personal business, she stayed in the bathroom until the final moans in the hallway died, and their footsteps faded. Eleanor opened it a hair and peeked out. Once she confirmed the coast was clear, she returned to bed. Relieved to see it empty, she fell into a deep sleep.

The next morning, the house was empty. Eleanor was sure the nanny was sleeping somewhere after the excitement of last night and waking up once with the baby. Eleanor went to

Melody's room and cooed over her daughter. She picked her up
to feed her, change her diaper and clothing. After quickly
packing up the remainder of Melody's things and hers, she
fastened Melody to herself with a wrap and boarded the nearest
streetcar.

Eleanor clutched Melody to her chest even though the wrap
held her taut and comfortable against her body. She nuzzled her
face close to her daughter's hair and smelled its fresh lavender
fragrance from her bath the day before. Melody was fast asleep
unaware of the testing her mother was experiencing for the first
time. Her daughter's peaceful sleep relieved her rattled nerves
and fraying resolve in travelling alone for the first time with a
baby in tow.

Thoughts of her gilded cage of the past months propelled
her to seek the freedom she had truly found in the visions of
white streaked river water with black spruce and Jack pine for its
borders, in labour, order, and dignity of life, in log cabins built
into the earth and intricately beaded garb and moccasins, in the
flecks of grey gracing a beloved beard, in eyes that no longer
reminded her of her childhood monster but of a love so vast that
she felt safe bobbing in its embrace, in breathing his ocean's
oxygen. These images danced in her mind and called to her—
home—home. She hadn't felt a sense of belonging, of deep,
truest knowing in the longest time. Even home with her parents
had lost its soul after her childhood rape. The North had
promised her freedom but not in the way she had expected. Life
was never the way one expected.

As she daydreamed, her thoughts grew in tendrils, always
reaching for him. She would catch them and pull them away to
remember Charlotte, Dr. Barnes, Julia, Leticia and the girls. Then
they would skitter from her grasp and rush toward their cabin,
the large log that held his wood splitting axe, his bed across from
the couch, her bed behind the curtain where they had lain
together holding each other, his hand cradling her belly. She
couldn't hold them back. The tendrils grew into huge vines that
blossomed all over her mind painting the prettiest picture she
never would have been able to paint by herself.

As soon as she made her way to her parents' home, she eagerly knocked to see her beloved parent's faces and show them the miracle they had been waiting for even though she knew there was a possibility that they would be disappointed in her decision to leave in the first place. Her mother opened the door.

Even though Sandra's eyes rekindled a spark when she saw her daughter standing all by herself with the grandchild she was never told had been born, the lines in her face sagged, and her usual alert posture drooped ever so pitifully. Sandra's sincere, deep smile wavered. She put her hand to her opening mouth and wept. "I didn't know! Why didn't you ever tell me? Your father and I—we waited. And now…." her mother shook her head. "Oh Eleanor, he's gone."

A rush of tears sprang from Eleanor's already watery eyes from seeing her mother's degenerated spirit and body. Her knees buckled, and she held onto Melody with one arm and the doorframe with the other. "That can't be."

Her mother nodded, and her mouth crumpled in all different directions trying to hold back a moan.

"When?" Eleanor could barely hold back a strangled cry.

Melody began to whimper.

Sandra barely managed to say, "Soon after you left with Paul, a week at most. It's been almost two and a half months now."

Eleanor wished she could drop her bags, walk away, and find a safe place to cry, or a place where she could wallow in her shame. She was disappointed at how she had left, disconsolate that she hadn't tried harder to reach out, regretful that she had been so close to her father yet so far when he had passed.

Even though her mind raged to find a place to cry on her own, she couldn't. Her mother needed her to remain not flee, not even for shame's sake. Eleanor moved her leaden legs forward, wrapped her free arm around her mother, and hugged her tight. Eleanor kissed her cheek, her temple, her grey hair. Her tears drenched whatever spot of her mother she touched.

Her mother's hands reached toward Melody asking for relief from the dagger that still staked her soul.

"Of course," Eleanor garbled as she unwrapped her daughter from her chest.

The two women sat on the couch together and took turns holding Melody until the day turned to the evening. The door squeaked as Mike and Lily entered.

Mike exclaimed, "You're back! What happened? Oh.... " He saw Melody snuggled close to his mother's chest. The two of them had fallen asleep.

Eleanor's fluttering lids snapped open. She made a quieting motion with her hand as she stood from the couch and followed Mike and Lily into the kitchen. Lily got the tea kettle right away.

They sat at the dining table.

"Please tell me what happened to him?" Eleanor asked.

Lily rubbed Mike's back as he said, "He passed away in his sleep."

Eleanor croaked, "A few days after I left?"

Her brother only nodded.

Her tears began to flow. "You blame me, don't you?"

He placed his hand on hers and looked at his feet for a long moment before he said, "At first I did. I was really angry because Dad was concerned when you left. But I realised, no matter what you did or where you were, he was always concerned. It took me a long time to acknowledge that you've just been trying to find your own way. I could say my piece, mom and dad could do the same, but, in the end, you figured it out. Just like I've had to figure out my own troubles."

"I don't know how to feel. My heart—my head is in a state of constant turmoil. I really do feel as if it's my fault." Eleanor broke down and placed her forehead upon the table for fear of opening so much to her brother. She didn't know him. She hadn't known him for a long, long time. That was her fault. She had shut so many out. Looking back, even her father had been shut out. So much time had been wasted because she was so busy nursing old wounds and defending herself.

Then Seth—he had entered her life and listened with no expectations of reciprocity. Not only had he given her a safe place to flourish but also hadn't allowed her to bury herself in the ground.

Lily made their tea and left the room so they could grieve together.

After they were sipped their tea, Eleanor asked, "Where was he buried?"

"At the family burial site."

"I thought dad and mum had to give up their plots, sell them, after everything."

"Seth bought them back."

Her teacup on the way to her lips stilled. "What do you mean?"

"Of course, you weren't here. Right after you left with Paul, Seth stopped by to check in on dad and mom. Mom told him to stay the night before leaving the next morning. He did, and that afternoon dad took a turn for the worse. Mom and I had a feeling that dad wouldn't recover from this bout of sickness like he had in the past. It was almost as if we could smell death on him."

Mike averted his eyes. "I'm ashamed to say it, but I didn't know what to do, how to act. Seth just took control. He was going to bring dad to the hospital, but dad didn't want that. He helped Lily clean the house, do groceries, just made sure everything was in order. Dad died a few days later. Before he died, mom mentioned she didn't know what she was going to do about where to bury him. She always thought she had more time, but time was catching up and about to close in. Seth asked about it some more. The next morning, he went out without telling any of us where he was going. He came back in the evening saying it was all taken care of, that she and dad had a plot together."

She shook her head. "It's all too much.... "

"He helped mom arrange the funeral, everything. He had to leave a few days later because of work."

"I can't believe it," she breathed.

"You can't? I think you know more than any of us how good of a man he is. You left Paul, didn't you?"

She nodded.

"Seth tracked down Paul's number and left a message with your housekeeper about dad's death. When you didn't call back, he tried to track down your address. It seems Paul was determined to keep it a secret. So Seth hired a private detective to find you. By then Dad had died. Seth wrote you a letter and left it in your mailbox. You never got the message or the letter, did you?"

Eleanor teared up again. "No, are you saying Paul kept me in the dark?"

"I'm not even attempting to imply anything. That's just what happened."

Eleanor covered Mike's hand with hers. "Why didn't any of you visit?"

He sighed. "Mom almost did several times, but then she'd stop herself because she didn't want to butt in. She didn't want to repeat the past, stepping on your toes and then you getting frustrated and retreating further into your own world. Knowing how much you value your space, she tried to do what you've always asked her to do, and that is, letting you make the first move."

So long ago, she had believed with all her heart that she and Paul were a match made in heaven on earth, that twining their bodies and giving herself night after night meant that he cared for her body, soul, and spirit.

The one who loved her wholly, in all the ways she longed to be loved—could he still love her after she had accepted and then returned his free gift and walked away? Her constant fickleness could only be too much for even the best kind of man.

Mike continued, "When dad became really ill, Seth sat with him for many long periods, talking, listening. You should ask mom what dad said. It might be important."

Her lips wobbled. "I don't want to put mum through that. It's too much."

He gently shook her hand. "She's had time to put the worst behind her. It's still bad, but this is important for you to live the life you need to live, the life that will be good for you."

Eleanor nodded. She heard Melody's hungry snuffling and went to take care of her. Her mother gave her up and patted Eleanor's head as she fed Melody. For the first time in a long time, she felt at home, not in Edmonton, but with her family.

Chapter 29

Late May 1944

Eleanor tiptoed around the conversation her brother said was necessary to have with her mother. She put it off by watching her mother hold Melody for hours on end. It was a blessing that Melody was such a peaceful baby considering the pregnancy had been anything but. She put herself to work cleaning the walls, the furniture, the floors, the toilets, cooking the food, finding something to do since she felt completely useless. She was constantly plagued by the single thought that she hadn't done anything for her father as he was passing. She hoped that her father was looking down on her from heaven, smiling to see his daughter helping the wife he had left behind, and saying, "Well done." Eleanor almost felt as if she heard his whispers floating down from above.

A week passed.

She approached her mother and said, "Mike said I needed to ask you something specific. Do you know what Dad told Seth before he died?"

Her mother teared up.

She rushed to hug her mother. "I'm sorry, Mum. Please never mind, I shouldn't have asked. Just you've been looking so happy these past few days. He said I really needed to ask you…."

Her mother placed her hand on hers and smiled. "I'm glad you have. I'm ready. Your father told Seth that he knew he was the right man for you. He thanked him with all his heart that he had taken you in and sheltered you from the loss of your job, from the attention of scoundrels, and from almost losing your baby."

"He told you about everything?"

"Don't be angry. He didn't relay the information to put you down in any way. He—actually, it was an integral piece to your story about how you have changed into a beautiful woman, how you overcame your selfishness and defensiveness and became open to his loving you and open to carrying this child in love. Your father and I were—are so proud of you. We don't judge you. We understand the difficult position you were in."

Eleanor mulled it over, and her growing anger snuffed out. "Did he say anything more to Seth?"

"Your father asked him that as long as you were his wife, even if you weren't with him, that he would look in on you."

Eleanor was puzzled. "I never saw him."

"No, you didn't. Before he went back to work, he tracked you down. He said you looked happy. You were still pregnant. After you left the house, he slipped the letter into your mailbox. Then he had to go back. Seeing you happy, he knew he could let you go."

Eleanor cried, "I'm sorry, Mum, I never knew about the phone call or the letter or else I would have come right away."

"I know you would have. Your father also asked him to forgive you for leaving him even though you loved him."

"I do love him! I've been such a stupid, foolish girl. I had everything right in front of me, but I threw it all away for a scam."

Her mother wrapped her arms around Eleanor until her tears subsided. "What will you do now?"

"There's no question. I'm staying with you."

"Are you sure about that?"

Eleanor hung her head. "I can't go back to him."

"Why not?"

"Our worlds are so far apart now. I feel as if I would be cruel in going back to him. I've been going back and forth for so long. I just need to stand on my own two feet. I need to know that I can love without lust, without constantly needing and not giving in return. Seth would make it too easy because he's like that, you know? He just loves even if I'm a horrid, stupid girl. I'm not saying he's perfect because I've seen everything to know, but he completes me in a way I never thought he could. I need to do this. At least for a little while. I don't know why. I just need to."

"You don't need to explain yourself to me. I—it's not my journey to take."

"Thank you, Mum."

After Edward had died, Sandra had set up her own room in his. She gave Eleanor her room upstairs permanently for her and Melody. Until she found a crib that a neighbour was giving away, she set Melody down in a blanketed drawer. Once she had the crib, Eleanor felt her personal life was settled enough that perhaps she could find some work. She knew she couldn't be a burden on her mother, Mike, and Lily. They were having a hard time making ends meet as it was without an extra mouth to feed.

She pulled her old typewriter out from her closet and blew off the dust. She wiped down all the nooks and crannies, inspected all the metalwork to make sure it was in working order, threaded a paper through and typed.

Dear Seth,

I know I said I never needed saving, but I did. With mercy and grace, you saved me time after time even when I spurned you over and over. You sacrificed your time, your money, your happiness, and your peace to save an ungrateful woman.

Your patience and tender loving made me see how broken I really was. You carried my broken roots to the thriving garden of your love and planted them in soft, fertile soil. I couldn't have grown in any other garden the way I did in yours.

When my soul was knit with yours, my life was complete. There was no greater joy to be had, no greater vulnerability to encounter, and no greater strength to bear.

Please forgive me even though I couldn't deserve your forgiveness a hundred years from now.

Yours and only yours,

Eleanor

She freed the letter from her typewriter, put it in an envelope, and mailed it.

The next few days she walked down the streets and knocked on the doors of any potential leads Mike and her mother could think of. Each of them answered her and shook their heads saying they had needed a typist a week earlier, a month earlier— always earlier—or not at all. She went to the newspaper office and inquired about a job posting. Who was she kidding? They probably wouldn't employ her if she couldn't work in the office.

She approached the receptionist. "Hello, I'm looking for typing work that I could do from home. Would you know if any one in this office would be willing to hire me?"

The receptionist shook her head. "I've never heard of such a thing happening. We can't help you."

"I need to do the work from home because I've got a young baby. I promise I can do the work. I can pick it up everyday and drop it off. My mother is at home to help with the little one. I just want to be home to nurse her."

At the mention of the word "nurse," the receptionist wrinkled her nose as if a dirty diaper smell wafted in the air. She was about to retort when a woman put her hand on Eleanor's arm.

Eleanor turned and was surprised to see the woman behind her smile so genuinely. "Come here. I think I can help you if you can help me."

Eleanor followed the woman into an office. The woman motioned for her to sit. "My name is Doreen. I'm a journalist here at the gazette. I'm d—mn good at my job. Excuse my language. Only thing is I write everything down on paper. I don't do typing. I mean I can, but, oh, it takes me forever. So I've come to the conclusion that I either take time off work to better my ability (I don't have extra time besides work to dedicate to it), or I delegate the task. You can type?"

Eleanor said, "Yes."

"How many words per minute?

"Two hundred."

"Gosh, what's your work experience?"

Eleanor tried to work saliva into her dry mouth. "I worked as a typist for a company here in Edmonton for a couple of years before I went up North to work as typist for the American army."

"You were up North? What was it like?" Doreen's eyes gleamed for a taste of the wild.

Eleanor smiled. "It was unlike anything I could imagine, and yet it's home. I'll never be the same because of it."

"Oh, to be touched in the way you have! You know, most of us only dream of living such an adventure. Who can I contact for a reference up North?"

"Oh…. " Eleanor's voice dropped noticeably.

The woman's eyebrow cocked upward in disappointment or in challenge?

"You can contact the head engineer Seth Brooks at Norman Wells."

"I had a feeling you'd be perfect. I just let go of my last typist. Her work wasn't up to standard. You'll start today. I need this piece done and…" She pulled out a few sheaves of paper. "...this done by tonight. Can you do that?"

Eleanor fingered her saving grace and smiled big. "Of course!"

"I'll still run the reference just to make sure everything is in order. You prove you're good on your word, and you'll have permanent work. Is seventy-five dollars a month good?"

It wasn't at the bottom end of what she could make, but it wasn't what she had hoped she could get given her experience. "Let's make it eighty a month."

The woman's mouth screwed together. "You surprise me. We can definitely work together." She put out her hand to shake Eleanor's hand.

Eleanor grabbed the papers and promised to hand them in by the evening. As she traipsed out the front door of the office, she looked back on the receptionist, who eyed her warily. She smiled in return and almost ran home.

She fed Melody, and then her mother played with her and held onto her while Eleanor worked. The woman's handwriting was difficult to read. However, Eleanor wasn't about to be turned away by a crucial part of the job. She worked through it and, eventually, after a little less than an hour, she was able to read it with ease. It felt good to have her fingers work at their craft. She had to deal with cramping since it had been too long. At the end of the day, she grabbed the typed pages and flew out the door. She ran to the office. Doreen was just leaving.

Eleanor yelled, "Wait! I have them!"

Doreen turned around with a knowing smile. "I just knew I could count on you though you did give me pause these last few minutes. I'm still going to run the reference, but consider yourself hired."

Eleanor was beyond happy that she had regular work. Even some of the other journalists passed on their notes for her to transcribe when their typists were overloaded and couldn't get to the material. Eleanor was making enough to cover Melody's expenses and feeding herself.

Doreen had told her Seth had written a glowing reference for her.

Eleanor wondered if he had received her letter. Could she hope that there was enough room in his heart to forgive her? Eleanor couldn't help remembering that her husband had always loved her work ethic.

Early June, Eleanor and her family put up the house for sale. It was much too big for their needs. They sold it to a pair of sisters who were going to open it up as a boarding house for all the influx of soldiers and civilians growing Edmonton's population.

Once the family was settled in a smaller cottage-sized home, Eleanor announced that she and Melody were leaving.

Startled, Mike asked, "What do you mean? Where will you go?"

"I know," her mother answered. "You're going home."

Eleanor nodded.

"Home?" he asked.

"To the North, to Seth," Eleanor said. "I need to see him in person now. I'm ready."

Her mother drew her into her arms and whispered into her neck, "Be brave. Fly back to your nest and build your home."

She held her mother's hands and asked, "What if he doesn't want to see me?"

"That man will always want to see you."

"How do you know?"

"Because of the way he loved you."

Eleanor hesitated. "I hurt him too many times to count. When I left him for Paul—I don't know if he could take me back after that—"

"Would it be worth the risk of your own hurt to find out if he still loves you?"

"I'd like to say yes. I need to tell him I love him. He needs to know about Melody. He's loved her ever since she was inside me. We're a family."

"Then go. Don't you worry about me. Mike, Lily, Luke, and I, we'll stick together."

"I promise to come visit with Melody."

Mike nodded. "I promise to take care of Mom." He pulled her in close and gave her a long hug.

Next she told Doreen that she was leaving to go home.

Doreen begged her to reconsider. "What am I going to do without you?"

Eleanor had the foresight to reach out to an old friendly acquaintance with whom she had attended secretary school. That friend was more than happy to receive more work.

Doreen said, "If you vouch for her, I trust you." She held Eleanor out at arm's length. "Oh, I envy you. You're taking your life into your hands, with a baby no less, and gunning for the man you love."

Eleanor chuckled, "Who said anything about a man?"

Doreen sighed. "I just know. I did the same thing once."

"What happened? Did you get the second chance you were hoping for?"

Doreen touched her cheek gingerly and gave a sad smile. "I didn't learn my lesson the first time or the second. I'm still wondering if the third time's a charm. Don't let the vanities of this world or your own vanity pull you away from what truly matters. I wish you all the best, dear girl."

A week later, Eleanor bought all her tickets. Her family went to Blatchford Field with her and Melody. It was the sweetest goodbye she had ever received and knew that it would one day lead to a sweeter reunion.

Chapter 30

Mid-June 1944

Even though Eleanor believed she had been blessed by the best of babies, there was only so much upheaval and lack of sleep a baby could take, especially as she landed onto and took off from ten different landing fields to reach Norman Wells.

When she reached Fort Norman, she set right off to see Dr. Barnes. Walking down the familiar road to Dr. Barnes—she had used to think it was the road leading to purgatory. For every checkup that she had gone to while pregnant, she had just barely managed to bear the poking and prodding for the sake of someone she never knew had so much value.

As she neared his house, she noticed a "For Sale" sign outside Charlotte's residence. She slowed her steps, searching for Charlotte's weathered face. All the faerie structures and tiny rock monuments had been removed from the porch steps. The house, which had oozed an eccentric charm, now looked hollow and monotone.

She rushed to Dr. Barnes' door and heard him call from inside, "Give me a moment. I'm coming." As he opened the door, his gaze was riveted on Melody. He laughed heartily. "You're back! It's wonderful to see you. She's beautiful and so healthy and strong. I'm almost done with my patient. Why don't you sit with Charlotte while you wait for a few minutes?"

Eleanor gasped, "Charlotte's here?! I saw the sign and—"

"Ah! Yes, she's staying with me now. Here, I'll allow her to explain."

Charlotte came around the corner from the living room and reached to brush Melody's cheek.

Dr. Barnes walked back to his office, clapping his hands gleefully.

"Sit down," Charlotte waved her toward the couch. "You've come back for Seth, haven't ya?"

"I have." As her adrenaline ebbed, the realisation of her momentous decision sank in.

"He's a good man, that one. Just like my—I mean Doctor Barnes."

The "For Sale" sign, her staying in the same home as Dr. Barnes, his attentive care to her every need, his trust in her faithfulness to tell others of his whereabouts—all the evidence pointed to…. "Doctor Barnes is your husband, isn't he?"

"He is."

"Then why have you been separated all these years? Living in different homes? Acting as if you were only good friends? I don't understand."

Charlotte flapped her hands. "Don't go judging him. I'm the one that insisted I live in a different house all this time so that he wouldn't be ridiculed. I'd do anything for my man."

Eleanor grimaced. "He didn't insist you live together?

Charlotte lifted her head high. "He did, many, many times. I wouldn't let him. When Seth returned and told Steven, Dr. Barnes to you, that you stayed behind, Steven marched right over and said to h—ll with being separated. He said it doesn't matter if the town knows he's married to the most eccentric woman they ever laid eyes on. Life is too short to stay apart any longer. He was in such wind I was afraid he'd die from overexcitement on the spot. As soon as I said okay, he packed my things in boxes and brought them over here. He emptied it in one day and put the house up for sale the next."

Dr. Barnes escorted his young patient down the hallway off the room they were sitting in. He joined the two ladies and asked to hold Melody. "Charlotte has filled you in?"

Eleanor smiled brightly. "Yes, she has. I would never have imagined. So, that photograph in your office, that's the two of you, isn't it? And the boy, he's your son, isn't he? Does he live nearby?"

Charlotte began to bite her lip and ruffle her skirt.

Dr. Barnes said in a low voice, "We were living in Victoria at the time. Our son Josiah died soon after that picture was taken. He contracted polio. I did all I could to save him, but it wasn't enough. Charlotte was never the same after his death. I made the decision to move North so we could have a fresh start."

Charlotte cut in, "I knew people would talk about how I was off my rocker. So I came up with the idea of living in different houses, side by side. I lied to you Steven all those years ago of not wanting to share a home with you. I'm sorry."

He reached for Charlotte's hand and squeezed it.

Charlotte continued, "I made my home a safe place for me, the ghost of my son, and his friends, the faeries."

Dr. Barnes said, "Now that the town knows about us, well, people still need my services. I believe claiming you as my own has softened the hearts of the people toward you, Charlotte."

She murmured, "I should never have lied to you, Steven. It kept us apart when it didn't need to."

Eleanor's eyes were wet with tears, "What brought the change of heart Dr. Barnes? Charlotte mentioned it was after Seth returned without me."

Dr. Barnes's eyes moistened. "Seth is an inspiration to me. He would do anything for you. In all my years, I've never seen a love so strong. After he shared the circumstances regarding your separation in Edmonton, I knew I needed to put everything on the line for Charlotte."

She blew her nose with her handkerchief. "I'm sorry about your son. My father passed away a few months ago, and I wasn't even there for him. Does it ever get easier?"

Dr. Barnes sighed, "It takes a long, long time, at least it did for me. Even now, it's not easier, maybe more bearable. It's very fresh for you so take all the time you need to grieve and don't ever be ashamed or frustrated with yourself because you think you're taking too long or, maybe, you're not grieving enough."

Charlotte nodded her agreement.

Eleanor said, "I'll try to remember that." She fiddled with her handkerchief. "How's everyone? Is everyone still around?"

Dr. Barnes replied, "I heard some of the girls have left. The very loud, brash one, Leticia, yes, she's gone. Frank told me she couldn't take the desolation anymore and went through all the pickings pretty quickly. Julia, your good friend, is still here. She's to marry Peter in a few weeks."

Eleanor laughed with joy, "What good news!" She prodded. "And—"

"Yes, Seth is still here," Charlotte cut in.

Eleanor ducked her head. "I know you may think I don't have a right to ask, but how is he?"

Dr. Barnes answered, "He's managing very well at his job. With the rest—he's managing."

Biting her lip, Eleanor asked, "Do you think he'd want to see me?"

"I don't want to presume, but yes, I think he'd like to see you. He had sent a couple of letters."

"He had? When?"

"You never received them? He sent a couple soon after he returned." Dr. Barnes asked.

"No, I never received them. Paul must have hidden them as he hid the first one. I sent Seth a letter a month and a half ago."

Dr. Barnes concluded, "You're here to see him, aren't you?"

Eleanor clasped her hands to her heart. "He's my home if he'll open the door. I'll walk in and never leave even if the world throws everything at my feet. I'll close the door on all of it just to be with him."

"It warms my heart to hear you say that," Dr. Barnes said.

"Don't let us keep you. Go to your man and love him," Charlotte added.

There was no more putting it off. Frank was about to leave Fort Norman to return to Norman Wells when she hailed him at the airstrip. As they flew over the scenery her soul called home, it all seemed to pass in a blur as her heart ached for the one in whom she could solace.

Once they touched down, she strode over to the camp all the while wondering how she would go about seeing him. Should she knock on his office door and jump in? Should she ask someone to be a messenger and ask them to tell him to meet her on the docks? Her fingers twisted and knotted in the woollen fabric of her skirt. She finally settled on being straightforward, to the point. Men appreciated that, didn't they?

First she would check in on Julia.

Eleanor knocked on the door of the Women's Quarters expecting to see Miss Dansk. Instead, Julia popped her head out.

"Ellie!" She shrieked. Her eyes doubled in size as they took in Melody wearing a pink dress. "You're back with your beautiful baby girl! Come in." She grabbed Ellie's sleeve and pulled her in. "Did you tell anyone you were coming back?"

Eleanor merrily laughed. "No, you're the first one here that knows other than Dr. Barnes, Charlotte, and Frank. Came in on Frank's plane."

Julia held out her arms. "Pass me your baby, please. It's been forever since I've had my baby fix. I love holding babies! What's her name?"

"It's Melody. Actually would you mind holding her while I —"

Julia interrupted. "Go see Seth. Of course. Here, pass her to me. I promise to take the best care of her. She looks so much like you." Julia's eyes filled with happy tears.

Ellie's eyes matched hers. "Thank you. I'll be back."

She walked into the head office. As she was knocking, Peter opened the door form inside.

Peter's brows shot up above his glasses as he sputtered, "El —Eleanor? What are you doing here?"

She beamed. "I came back!"

Peter pointed his pen toward the cabin. "He's up at the cabin."

"Thank you!" Eleanor gave him a grateful peck on his stubbled cheek and ran home.

The closer she got to the cabin, the more her heart pounded within, yet never did she experience the need to turn and run. She was done running, especially from him. She would only ever run to him. Now at his mercy, nothing could save her now except him.

The sound of an axe cleaving wood thunked in the air. She finally came into the clearing where she could see his shoulders lift in a stretch. His back muscles rippled through his soaked shirt as he swung the axe high, and it bit into its target.

He didn't hear her approach at the edge of the clearing, nor when she stood ten feet behind him.

He took a short breath from his swing, and she made a rustling noise with her foot over some leaves. He looked over his shoulder and froze the second he saw her. He breathed, "El…" and stopped short. His brows drew together in consideration of her appearance.

She gave a little wave. "Hi."

He flinched and grimaced. "Why are you here?" He shook his head slightly and looked behind her as if he expected someone else to follow in her wake.

Was he expecting Paul? "I came alone, well, not alone. I brought Melody. She's with Julia."

His gaze immediately fell to her belly, taut after several months. He stepped forward and breathed as he smiled ruefully. "She's a girl. You were right all along."

"I… " She was tempted to look somewhere else because the intensity of his gaze made her burn. Never again would she look away. "I've been so stubborn thinking that I knew best for what I needed, for what I wanted, when the best thing, no, the best person was always right in front of me. I didn't want to give in because I didn't choose you at first. I felt weak. I felt chained."

Using that last word was as if she had slapped him across the face. She had to tell the whole truth even if it hurt.

"So I chose him because he was my first choice. I'm ashamed to say that one of the reasons why I left him was because I came to discover he doesn't love me and Melody, not the way a husband and father should. But I'm not coming to you so I can leech off your love. I don't want to linger on how you can love me, but how I can love you. I may not have chosen you at first, but I'm choosing you now. You're my husband."

Seth pressed his lips together, scratching his cheek.

He didn't ask her to stop so she continued, "He asked me to officially divorce you. I knew I couldn't. Before I fully understood, my spirit cried out to be linked to yours, to bridge the gap and come back to you."

He closed his eyes and took a deep breath.

Her fingers twitched as she whispered, "Please say something."

He ran his hand down his chin and blew out his cheeks. "El, I want to believe you. I've dreamed this scene a thousand times, wished you'd be there right beside me, but you weren't."

The power of his presence drew her in. "I know. I've nothing to say in my defence. I take full responsibility for hurting you, for using you, for belittling you, for leaving you when I told you I loved you." She fell to her knees on the ground several feet before him and clasped her hands. "I'm begging for your forgiveness."

She had never felt as vulnerable as she did now. His steps crunched toward her, and the toes of his boots entered her view. She jerked her head up as he knelt in front of her. He gathered her clasped hands in his warm one. He turned her left hand over. The ring he had given her on their wedding day still encircled her finger. He kissed her palms. Her lashes fluttered as she tried to see every hair on his head, every line on his face through her tears. Was this the tenderest of goodbyes or did she have a chance to love him the way he deserved?

In a husky voice, Seth said, "I forgive you." He continued, "I'm not the only one that needs to forgive. Can you forgive me for not telling you the whole truth of our marriage?"

Eleanor vehemently shook her head and sobbed, "Whatever you have done cannot compare to the hurt I caused you."

He cupped her cheek, and she settled into his exhilarating touch. He said, "It's not about comparing your faults to mine or vice versa. We both need to own up to what we did to each other. I forgive you. Do you forgive me?"

With trembling lips, she cried and kissed his hands over and over again. "Oh, thank you, thank you, God! Of course, I forgive you. I love you." When her tears slowed, she added, " I know you don't trust me now. Would you be willing to give me a chance to show you?"

He rested his forehead on hers and looked deep into her eyes. "I reckon that's what forgiveness is all about. Choosing to —what's the saying? Cover a multitude of sins?" His building excitement waned a touch. "What about Paul?"

She wiped her tears. "He won't be a problem. I think he liked the idea of us being a family, but he made it clear he wasn't willing to take us into consideration when it came to his choices. He's what I used to be, or at least I hope I'm no longer that way. I'm changing to be more selfless."

He brushed his calloused thumbs over her cheekbones, his featherlight touch holding a mighty sway over her soul. "You've changed so much. The first time you came here you were running away from your ghosts. This time you ran to the future you want." Pain clouded his eyes. "You're right. I don't know if I can trust you. How about we build this slowly?"

She nodded as he tilted her head back and swept his lips over hers.

Her heartbeat raced. Longing to taste him, she grazed her lips against his in response. As he pulled away, a shudder ran through her weary body.

He offered his hand and helped her up. He turned to look at the cabin. "I don't live here anymore. I was chopping wood for Peter and Julia. They're getting married soon."

"Dr. Barnes and Charlotte told me. Where do you live now?"

"Back in my bachelor bunk, but that won't be suitable for us."

She gasped, "You want to live together?"

He turned to face her. "That's what being husband and wife is about, joining our lives together. This isn't easy, but this is what I vowed to do. I'm taking care of you and Melody. If you still want to work, you can do that. We live together."

Eleanor hesitated. "Does that mean we're also sharing—"

He pulled her close, interlocking fingers around her lower back. "A bed, if that's what you want. We'll take things slow and talk things through."

Eleanor baulked. "Are you sure you want me?" She wrapped her arms around herself. "I gave myself to someone else after I told you I love you. I'm so sorry," she whispered.

He squeezed her tight. "My forgiveness covers all." He placed his palms over the sides of her face and said strongly,

"There's nothing that you can say or do that will take my love away from you. You're mine, and I'm yours."

She repeated as if it were holy liturgy, "You're mine, and I'm yours."

"We don't have to have all the answers. I'm committed to figuring it out together. I'm committed to being one with you."

ACKNOWLEDGMENTS

Jesus, you have loved me fully and unconditionally. "Greater love hath no man than this, that a man lay down his life for his friends." John 15:13 You lay down your life on the cross for those who hated you, for all mankind that is dead in sin. No one and nothing can surpass your great love.

James, I couldn't publish this work without your valuable constructive criticism and insight. Thank you for reminding me to set the scene.

Felicity, you have a big heart full of love for others. Never fail to shine God's love to all around you.

Edward, when you cried because you found out I had named a character after you, my heart was full of wonder that you would consider it an honour. Thank you for that special moment.

Elena, your care and attention to how I'm doing is incredibly touching. Thank you for being a bright light.

Titus, I love your bright eyes and ready kisses.

Selena, no matter how quiet or loud you are, your voice is beautiful.

Serenity, I loved our little dance parties during my breaks.

Willow, you have filled me with indescribable love.

Dad, thank you so much for supporting me in so many ways in this venture and for always encouraging me to keep writing.

Mom, your excitement for this work has kept me going. Thank you for always making me laugh.

Aaron and Joash, I'm so blessed to have such amazing brothers who carve out so much time for my family and me.

Grace, thank you for reading through this work and pointing out when things didn't make sense and when I needed to show rather than tell.

Em, you are my social media cheerleader! Thank you! I appreciate you for being my beta reader.

Alex, you haven been such a wonderful author friend and support over these last couple of years. Thank you for your notes on slowing down the scenes. It encouraged me to write beautiful new scenes a few days before the last proof edit (even during the proof edit).

Alexis, you slay every single time! You gave me so many perfect possible covers. I was blown away. Your dedication and passion for bringing my vision to fruition never ceases to amaze me.

Amy, my Ellie, thank you for gifting me, a stranger before our work together, your time and zest to be Ellie on the cover. Strangers no longer!

Phil, thank you for your prayers.

The Delectable Reads ladies, I love to read books with you! Thank you for your support.

Dear readers, old and new, lovers of history and the stories of people, live your stories with excellence, truth, and grace. One day, your story will be told.

AUTHOR'S NOTE

I was inspired to write about the Canol construction project after reading a book titled *Six Years' War* that my father-in-law had lent me randomly. It's a book that covers real people's stories during WWII. There's a section on accidental deaths, life on the home front and the war front, and many more aspects of the war. One section highlighted the Canol project with only a few stories to be shared. What caught my attention was that it's a piece of American and Canadian history not given much spotlight. *Unborn Melody*'s story was soon born.

Eleanor Mackenzie's name was picked by one of my readers who won the privilege of picking a name for one of my main characters. It's the name of her grandmother.

Not only did I want to write the narrative in Eleanor's point of view but also in that of my male main character who turned out to be Seth. Writing in dual POV has been challenging yet so rewarding.

I spent a lot of time researching the entirety of the Canol project. I printed out a large map and, on its back, wrote so much information of transportation of the materials to build the road, timelines of when certain constructions took place, the Norman Wells oil operation, and of the overall engineering of the project.

One treasure I read in its entirety was a novel called the *Mackenzie Breakup* by Jean Kadmon. Although it's fiction, the story and information within is based on Jean's own experiences of being a typist at Camp Canol during the project. It was an invaluable resource.

The Canol Pipeline Project: A Historical Review by H. T. Ueda, D. E. Garfield, and F. D. Haynes written in October 1977 was key to understanding the intricacies of engineering the project.

A History of Canol Trail, a documentary that was produced by the Signal Corps in collaboration with The Northwest Service Command, was a thorough introduction to many details of the project as a whole.

One of my favourite highlights in the book is the Dene people who were instrumental to the project's success. They were employed as guides and workers in the building of the Canol Road. It was an honour to feature them in this work.

One other historical aspect I realised I needed to brush up on was how pregnancy was viewed in the 40s and how labour was handled in the hospitals. All I can say is how happy I've had my seven babies in the times I live compared to having babies then.

For you book lovers, here's fun piece of trivia I came across researching the Edmonton Radial Railway. One of the ways the railway wanted to lift people's spirits was by setting up a library housing 2,000 books at different locations where they could park it semi-permanently without blocking the tracks. Librarian H. C. Gourlay proposed the idea.

Lastly, I would like give honour to all the men and women who served in the Allied Forces to secure our freedoms. May we never forget.

If you want to take part in exclusive giveaways,

receive books news first,

and have special access to works in progress,

sign up for my newsletter

@

leahlindeman.com

You can also follow my socials

@

linktr.ee/leahtlind